The Protectors

BY

DAVE BROWN

To my partner, **Jim Bannerman**,
the better half of my soul.

THE PROTECTORS

A Golden Feather Press book / March 1999

This is a work of fiction. The characters, incidents, and dialogues are products of the author's imagination and are not to be construed as real. Any resemblance to actual events or persons, living or dead, is entirely coincidental.

March 1999

Published by: Golden Feather Press
                  PO Box 481374
                  Denver, CO 80248

First Edition

Library of Congress Number 98-093975

ISBN 1-878406-20-5

Printed in the United States of America

www.goldenfeatherpress.com

INTRODUCTION

Jim yawned and said, "David, it's three in the morning. You have to stop editing that book."

"I know it's late. But if you think Mo and I are going to put up with 'two-room room house' type errors, you're crazy. Errors break involvement in the story."

"David, nothing is perfect in this life. Get The Protectors out there. Your readers deserve it. You left them hanging."

"You're right. It's Time."

* * *

Sit back, take a few deep breaths and lift yourselves into the sky....

Soaring high overhead and looking down, the raven watched the long trail of dust grow behind the silver truck as it sped along the twisty dirt road. He knew within minutes he would be gorging himself on wondrous tasting goodies brought from somewhere beyond the eastern range of mountains. It was not often the two men in the truck came here, sometimes being away for months at a time, but the treats they brought always made up for the wait.

The raven soared higher and looked out over the land he lived in. He loved it up there, higher than the top of Bristlecone Peak. As he gazed over the immense basin of South Park, surrounded on all sides by high mountains, he remembered the bumpy top crust of the apple pie he had found last week on someone's deck. From this height, the gray-green bunch grass and silver, feather sage gave the treeless hills a soft, dusty look in the bright sunlight. Other hills, dark with forests, wandered in scattered curves and broken lines through the rumpled landscape.

Wings stretched flat, the raven allowed the air current to carry him higher. He spiraled above the men's cabin, then soared over his own home in the rock outcropping on the side of the ridge that pointed south a hundred yards to the west.

He liked the men who lived near his rock. They were quiet, respected the land, loved all the animals and birds, and best of all, gave wonderful handouts. For the treats, he even put up with their big fuzzy dog.

As the silver truck drew closer, the raven swooped down to search the area for any signs of danger just as he had done every day for over a hundred years. But today, he felt edgy and remembered the other two men who had lived here in the distant past. The ruins of their cabin rotted at the bottom of the cliff only twenty yards from the present structure. Those men had suddenly disappeared without a trace one-hundred and seven years ago. Right after that, he'd been chosen to guard this area, and he'd faithfully kept his lonely vigil. After those men were gone, no one had lived anywhere close by until the two men, now maneuvering their truck up the steep, rocky driveway, bought the land and built their cabin on the top of the cliff with a sixty-mile view to the south.

As the truck approached the small frame house, the raven dived to the old dead tree that still clung to the top of the cliff and waited impatiently while the men climbed out of the truck, poured water for the dog, then unloaded boxes and more boxes.

Finally, one of the men brought out the square, red canister containing the goodies. The clang of the lid being popped off was the raven's cue. Today, even though he felt anxious, he decided to add a little soaring and swooping to his begging, overjoyed with the short wait this time. The men had been here twice yesterday.

* * *

"Thank God, we're finally living here!" Jim shouted as he stood at the edge of the cliff. His voice echoed from the high ridge that pointed south like a knobby finger. He spun around, grabbed Dave in a bear hug and whispered softly, "God, I didn't think this day would ever come."

"Neither...did I," Dave said, choking on the words.

Jim patted Dave's back. "The money from my dad's estate should keep us secure for at least five years. By that time, maybe I'll have my counseling practice built up and you'll have found an honest buyer for your gemstones." He squeezed Dave harder. "Five years of bliss!"

The dog's barking became unbearable.

"Why does Winnie always do that when we hug each other?" Dave asked.

"Do you think he's jealous?"

They pulled away from the embrace and laughed at the shaggy, gray dog jumping two feet off the ground. Jim bent down, grabbed Winnie around his middle and picked him up. "This fat ol' dog needs a hug, too."

Winnie's legs stiffened and stuck straight out, his willing-victim expression clearly visible through the long, silver hair hiding his eyes. Dave laughed and kissed the dog's nose. When Winnie turned his head away, Jim relented and put him down. The instant Winnie's feet touched the ground, he ran for his ball.

"No tennis ball," Dave said sternly. "We still have unpacking to do." He followed Jim into the cabin.

One hour later, Jim glanced around after he'd emptied the last box. He loved this cabin. He and Dave had built it from the ground up and, even though it still wasn't finished, it had always been their real home. Living in Denver had been temporary.

Jim glanced at the two walls in the kitchen that still needed paneling, then at the strip of sheet rock missing in the living room ceiling. Lightning had struck the cabin over a year ago and had exploded that section into a million pieces. He watched Dave open a box in the loft that jutted out into the room under the vaulted ceiling. Someday they would have to put a railing along the edge. Jim shook his head, amazed neither of them had ever fallen off.

He sighed. Only able to come here occasionally, there had never been enough time to finish all the smaller projects. Until now. Jim was suddenly anxious to start on anything. But first, he was starving. They hadn't eaten since before they'd left Denver at ten, and now it was three. The two hours they'd spent in the grocery store on the way here had made the trip twice as long.

"Want me to make you a sandwich?" he yelled up to Dave.

"You don't have to," Dave hollered back. "I only have a few more clothes to hang up and I'll be down."

Fifteen minutes later, Dave sat at the kitchen table spreading mustard on a slice of bread. He shoved back the deli bags stuffed with sliced meat and cheese to make room for his sandwich. Winnie sniffed it.

"Winnie, lie down! You're slobbering on my leg." Dave grabbed the bag of ham, tore off a piece of meat and fed it to the dog. "There, now lie down."

Winnie swallowed the snack whole, then slowly dropped to the floor with sassing growls.

As Dave wolfed his sandwich, he watched Jim break down cardboard boxes in the living room and breathed a sigh of relief. Yesterday had been a long day. They'd loaded up the car and the truck at their house in Denver, drove a hundred miles up here, then back again in both vehicles. Twice. Last night, they'd all piled into the truck and returned to Denver for the last load.

"Jim, do you realize for the number of miles we put on both cars yesterday, we could have almost driven to San Francisco."

Jim glanced into the kitchen and shrugged. "I'd rather be here."

Movement caught Dave's eye, and he looked out the window at a dozen chipmunks vying with jays and chickadees for the birdseed and potato-chip crumbs Jim had scattered on the rocks. He smiled and shook his head. Living in South Park with a house in Denver had to be the best of two worlds. Especially since they were financially secure for a few years.

Dave suddenly noticed the raven jumping from branch to branch in the old dead tree, always looking down the cliff in the direction of the ruins. The bird seemed to be scolding something.

Jim walked into the kitchen with a pad, pencil and tape measure. "Will you hold the end of this tape against the wall?"

Dave tore his eyes away from the huge black bird and looked at Jim. "I thought we were unpacking. What are you measuring?"

"We have to finish paneling in here," Jim said. "I want to go to Fairplay tomorrow and get more. We also need sheet rock for the ceiling where the lightning hit."

Dave held the end of the tape measure to the wall. "Can't we spend at least one day relaxing? We just got here."

"You can relax. Now that we're living here, I want to finish the cabin."

Dave shook his head. "It isn't easy to relax while you're balanced on the top of the ladder hammering at a nail farther than you can reach."

Jim grinned, then wrote measurements on a pad. "I wonder if they sell carpet in Fairplay?"

"Carpet! We haven't covered the sub-flooring with plywood yet."

Jim tapped his forehead with the pencil. "Let's see, the kitchen is twelve by twelve, the living room...sixteen by eighteen." He wrote the figures on the pad, then glanced at Dave. "The loft is nine by eighteen, isn't it?"

"Yes, but we decided not to carpet the kitchen," Dave said. "Sparks fly out of the wood cookstove when the top plate's off. Plus, it'll get splattered with grease."

"You're right. I don't know why I mentioned the kitchen." Jim erased a set of measurements.

"Do you need me any more?" Dave asked. "I promised to play b-a-l-l with you-know-who."

Hearing the spelling of ball, Winnie barked and bounded toward the door. The instant Jim shook his head no, Dave and Winnie ran outside.

* * *

"Fifty-two. Winnie, that's the last one. I can barely lift my arm." Seeing Jim carrying two plastic stack-chairs out the door, Dave yelled, "Jim, you can't sit down. The paneling isn't finished yet."

"I decided you were right. I'm not doing anything the rest of the day. Maybe not even tomorrow."

"Thank God," Dave whispered as he headed toward Jim. He looked down at the dog jumping at his side with the slimy, mud-covered ball still in his mouth. "Winnie, don't you ever get tired?"

Jim positioned his chair in full sunlight on a flat rock near the edge of the cliff. He dropped his tube of suntan lotion beside the chair, draped his African-patterned beach towel over the back, then slid into it.

Dave lowered himself onto the edge of his chair beside Jim. He gazed out at the vastness for a moment, then sank back, took a deep breath, glanced at Jim and smiled. He loved it when Jim wore nothing but his brilliant, orange swim trunks and dirty, frayed tennis shoes. At twenty-six, Jim still had the body of a left tackle from his college days. His muscular arms and legs, powerful chest, sparingly fuzzed with light brown hair, and lean, rippling torso, all deeply tanned, made Dave think of a trek across the Australian outback in an open-air Jeep. Jim's blue eyes, short brown hair and beard added to this illusion. All he needed was a beat-up, leather Aussie hat.

It had been five years ago in the Pit Stop bar when his heart had skipped a beat after seeing Jim for the first time. Jim had been wearing a pair of black leather shorts, stretched to the max, and a white tank top pulled taut over his flat stomach and firm pecs. Dave remembered Jim had turned and smiled at him, a wide smile, with perfect white teeth.

Aware of Dave staring at him, Jim sat up straight and shaded his eyes from the sun. "Why are you looking at me like that?"

Dave chuckled. "I was just remembering when I first saw you in the Pit Stop. You were the most gorgeous man in the place." Dave reached over and ran the back of his fingers over Jim's bare leg. "I hope you wear your leather shorts again sometime."

Jim relaxed into the chair and smiled at Dave. "I'll never forget you that night, either. When I saw you sitting on the meat rack, wearing only skimpy Levi cutoffs, with your muscles and crotch bulging, all I wanted to do was..." Jim looked deep into Dave's hazel eyes.

"Was what?" Dave asked. "You're always telling me to spit it out. Now it's your turn."

Jim reached over, slid his hand up Dave's muscular leg, snuck his fingers into the side slit of his red silk, work-out shorts and lightly touched his balls. He resisted the urge to grab Dave in broad daylight knowing the neighbors could be watching from their cabin on the top of the ridge to the west. Jim shot a glance at the A-frame perched high above, then slowly pulled back his hand and rested his elbow on the arm of his chair. "Well...I wanted to take all my clothes off...and rub my entire body against your big hairy chest. I also wanted to lick the hairs of your moustache...clear down to where it stops at your jaw...and run my hands up and down your big arms."

Dave jumped forward in his chair. "Whoa! I've never heard you talk like *that* before!" After a moment, his smiled faded into a frown. "You want help with the paneling, don't you?"

Jim laughed. "Now that you mention it." He reached over and squeezed Dave's leg. "Just kidding. You always help, and I know you hate building things. I'm just glad you still look like you did when I first met you. And I'm glad you still wear your moustache to your jaw. It makes you look like a bronc rider."

A screech from the raven caused them to both shade their eyes and look at the sky. The bird soared in spirals over the ruins of the cabin below. Jim shrugged, then slid his butt forward in the chair, leaned his head on the back and closed his eyes. "I think I'm going to let my hair grow. We're closer to the sun up here, and I'm afraid my head will get sunburn."

Dave settled back and gazed to the south. The white tooth of Crestone Peak thrust skyward sixty miles away. Thirty miles closer, but still on the horizon, Black Mountain, a near-perfect shark fin, sliced a flat cloud with its scythe-curved eastern slope.

Dropping his gaze to the cliff, Dave stared at it a few moments, then stood up and peered over the edge.

Jim opened his eyes and shaded them with his hand. "What are you looking at?"

"It was a wet winter. I was just wondering if the water table rose enough to cause that little spring down below to start flowing again."

"I'm sure that spring hasn't had water in it for a hundred years. Whoever built the cabin down there probably had to move when it dried up."

Dave studied the orderly jumble of moss-covered logs. "I'd love to know who built that cabin. Whoever it was had the smarts to build it against the cliff and channel the water under the floor." He sighed. "Maybe it was a hunky trapper with lots of muscles and a big dick."

"David, you're always thinking of sex. How do you know he channeled the water into the cabin?"

Dave sighed and plopped into his chair. "Men, Jim. I'm thinking of men. Men are God's most beautiful creatures."

"How do you know he channeled the water?"

"Last summer, I discovered a broken cement ditch." Dave scooted forward in his chair and pointed down the cliff. "It starts at the old spring and runs along the base of the cliff to the cabin, then continues down the slope to a cement-lined hole where those huge old aspens are."

"Cement?" Jim asked. "Did they have cement in those days?"

"Of course. Even the Romans built their aqueducts with stone and stuff similar to cement." Dave stood up, looked down at the ruins for a moment, then dropped back to the edge of his chair. "Remember when I went to the 'Alma Gazette' office? In one of their old papers I read an article about two men who'd built a cabin in this area. It caught my interest because it mentioned Bristlecone Peak." He shook his head. "I forget their names, but the article said they had caused a stir in Alma when they became blood brothers in a bar." He turned to Jim. "Do you know, that bar was called the Silver Heels back then, too."

"Too bad the Silver Heels closed. We had good times in there," Dave said. He shoved his clasped hands between his knees. "Remember when we were there on that below-zero Saturday night and that gorgeous drunk guy tried to pick us up, then passed out with his face in his pizza."

"I felt sorry for him, but all I could think of was Winnie freezing to death in the back of the truck."

"He didn't freeze. He'd buried himself in his down comforter. Besides, we were only in there an hour."

"Getting back to that article, what was it about?" Jim asked.

Dave settled back in his chair. "From what I could tell, some men attacked the blood brothers at their cabin. One of the partners got shot and was bleeding a lot, but when the attackers stormed the cabin, the two men were gone. No one could figure out how they'd escaped since their horses were still in the corral. A mountain man named Thunder Joe led a search party."

"Did they ever find them?"

"I don't know. The office was closing, and I didn't get to finish the article. I think the year was eighteen eighty-six. Now that we're living up here, I want to go back and re-read it."

Jim picked up his tube of tanning lotion and unscrewed the cap. "What made you think of that?"

"Just looking at the scenery, I guess." Dave swept his arm to the south. "According to that article, all this used to be called the Castille Ranch. I read up on it at the Denver Public Library."

Jim rubbed lotion on his arms. "Remember when we brought Ken Dancing Bear up here? He said this area gave him pinpricks on his skin. He said he felt it held great power and mystery." Jim squinted at the sky. The raven was gone.

Dave shivered. "Now that you brought that up, I'm getting goose bumps, too." He stood up again, leaned over the edge of the cliff and looked at the rotting cabin. God, would it have been wonderful to have lived back then. Dave sighed and headed toward the cabin. "I'm still hungry. Want me to bring you something?"

"No, I'm going to make another sandwich." Jim wiped his hands on his legs, then spotted the raven in the dead tree at the edge of the cliff. He thought the bird looked nervous the way it ruffled its feathers, jumped from branch to branch and scolded something down the cliff.

Jim sprang out of his chair, glanced down at the rotting logs of the old cabin, then followed after Dave. "I hope you don't mind if I don't cook anything this evening. It's almost four."

"Let's order a pizza."

Jim laughed. "From where? Fairplay? We'd have to tip the driver twenty dollars just for gas."

The raven let out a loud "awk" and flew toward his home in the rocks on the ridge to the west. The two men watched it, then glanced at each other before going inside.

At the kitchen table, Jim chuckled. "Dave, rolling up slices of meat and cheese like that is making Winnie slobber."

"I'm giving him some." Dave smiled at the wiggling dog. "Aren't I, Winnie. You get the end pieces, don't you."

A sudden blast of wind shook the cabin. Stinging sand tore at the structure. Blinded momentarily, Jim fought the gale and managed to slam the kitchen window. Dave ran into the living room and shut the other two. Choking dust filled both rooms.

Outside, pebbles and pine cones pelted the walls. Trees bent and swayed wildly. Pine branches snapped off and sailed through the air. Some slammed into the cabin.

"God! Where'd this wind come from?" Dave yelled as the cabin groaned and shuddered. "If it gets any stronger, the whole place might blow over!"

An instant later, the wind stopped, plunging the area into a dead calm.

Winnie's loud bark made both men jump. The dog snarled, ran to the door and pushed at it with his nose, trying to get out.

Dave rushed to a window. The raven swooped out of sight down the cliff, scolding something unseen. Dave shuddered. "What the hell's going on?"

"I don't know," Jim said. "That wind was enough to scare anyone. But Winnie acted that way when the bear came around last year, remember?"

"Well, if it is a bear," Dave said, "we'd better put the food away. I don't want it pushing the door down like one did in Fairplay."

As Jim helped Dave shove the food into the refrigerator, they were startled when the raven flew from down the hill and landed on the narrow ledge outside the kitchen window. The bird flapped its huge wings and pecked the glass. Winnie barked, lifted his front paws to the sill and whined.

"The raven looks like he's trying to tell us something," Dave said. "This whole thing is freaky."

"I don't care if it is the bear," Jim said. "I'm going out there."

The instant Jim opened the door, Winnie pushed by him, bounded outside and down the slope. His deep, threatening bark warned of an intruder. The raven sailed down the hill after him.

Jim and Dave piled out the door, ran across the flat rocks and looked over the cliff.

"Who's that?" Jim asked, clutching himself.

"God, I don't know," Dave said, breathlessly.

CHAPTER 2

Amid the ruins of the old cabin below, Jim and Dave saw a man lying face down with another man draped over him, as though shielding him. Winnie ran circles around them, baring his teeth and snarling.

The man on top raised up and swung his arm. "Help! Go away, dog!"

Dave gasped as he looked down on the two men. "How did they get there? They weren't there a few minutes ago." He ran across the rock and scrambled down the slope. Jim followed right behind him. "Help! Help! Get away, dog!"

"Winnie, it's okay!" Dave yelled when he reached the cabin ruins. "What happened? Who are you?"

The blond man with a short darker beard raised up and squinted at Dave. "I'm Jake." He glanced down at the man under him. "This here's Wiley." Jake suddenly jerked his head back toward Dave and Jim. "Who the hell're you?"

Hearing the men's names, Dave felt a shock through his body. He'd just been talking about two men who had disappeared in eighteen eighty-six and instantly remembered their names had been Jake and Wiley. "I...I'm Dave Younger," he stammered. "This is my...er, partner, Jim Parnell. What are you doing here?" Dave couldn't believe how gorgeous Jake was. The man's muscles stretched his shirt so tight each ripple showed through. He looked like a professional wrestler.

Dave looked at the man lying face down with his left pant leg cut off about mid-thigh. Wiley appeared just as big as Jake, but Dave couldn't see his face, only his coal-black hair. He shoved from his mind the coincidence of the men's names from the article he'd read in the "Alma Gazette," and forced himself to wonder if they might be construction workers building a cabin somewhere nearby.

Jim edged closer and pointed to the man named Wiley who wasn't moving. "Is he okay?"

Eyeing the strange men for a moment, Jake diverted his attention to the man lying next to him. "Wiley got shot." He looked at Dave pleadingly. "I gotta get him to Doc Colter's. He's lost lots'a blood an' he's gotta bad fever."

Jake tried to stand, got halfway to his feet, became dizzy and sat back down. Where was he? What was happening to him? He felt groggy, like he'd been sleeping off a drunk...for a long, long time.

When Jim saw the two holstered guns flopping at Jake's side, a chill rushed through him. "Wiley's been shot? Did you shoot him?"

Shocked at the thought, Jake said, "Me? Hell, no! Wiley's my partner an' blood brother. I wouldn't never shoot Wiley." Jake reached over and felt Wiley's forehead. It was burning with fever, and it scared him. Jake glanced up at Jim. "You gotta help me get him to the doc's before he dies."

Dave nearly fainted when he heard Jake say they were blood brothers. That article he'd read had mentioned blood brothers.

Jake slowly scanned the area, then frowned. "Where the hell are we? An' what're these old logs doin' scattered around here?" He stared open-mouthed at the cliff, then yelled, "That there rock wall...that's Wiley'n me's wall!" Jake looked around frantically. "What's goin' on? What happened to our cabin?"

Jim realized the breathtaking man was near panic, but so was he. Carefully stepping over the logs, he placed his hand on Jake's shoulder. "Let's get Wiley up the hill to our cabin. Then, we can talk about what happened." He wondered if the two men were criminals and prayed Jake wouldn't shoot them.

Jim's offer calmed Jake. He felt Wiley's forehead again. It seemed warmer, and he panicked. When he tried to stand, Jim grabbed his arm and helped him to his feet. He flinched at Jake's ripe aroma.

"Where we takin' Wiley?" Jake asked. "I gotta get him to the doc's."

Jim pointed up the slope. "For right now, let's carry him to our cabin. It's on top of this cliff."

"There ain't no cabin up there! This here's where Wiley an' me built our cabin!" Jake focused his attention on the two men. "Why're you two pretty well naked? An' where'd you get them funny shoes?"

Dave glanced down at himself, then at Jim. "We have shorts on."

They both looked at their feet.

"These are just tennis shoes," Jim commented.

Dave raised an eyebrow at Jim. "I'll be right back." He scrambled up the hill and quickly returned with a folded yellow tarp tucked under his arm. After climbing over the spongy logs, he spread the tarp out next to Wiley. "Let's get him on here so we can carry him up the hill easier."

Gently, the three men turned Wiley over and lifted him onto the tarp. Jim gasped when he saw the brown patch of dried blood that had soaked into the shirt tied around Wiley's leg. He noticed a small spot of bright red that had oozed out from one side of it. That blood looked fresh.

Jake grabbed the tarp at Wiley's head and Jim took the other end. After gingerly stepping over the ruins, they started up the hill. Dave ran ahead and held back branches, making their climb easier.

As Jim struggled up the hill holding the tarp, he tried to watch where he was going, but kept diverting his eyes to the man he was helping to carry. Wiley's massive body, dressed in Levis and a rawhide shirt that partly exposed his huge, hairy chest, staggered Jim's mind. He wondered where Wiley had gotten that crescent-shaped scar high on his right cheek and couldn't tell if he was more handsome with or without it. Wiley definitely looked like a tough character, especially with his short, black beard. Jim knew, despite any of Dave's objections, he could easily jump into the sack with this man...for a week. It would be an experience of a lifetime.

Nearing the top of the slope, Jake stopped. "Damn! How the hell'd *that* get here?"

"That's our cabin," Jim gasped, straining from Wiley's weight. "Let's get him in there. He's heavy."

With Dave's help, they made it up the steps, through the door and into the cabin. The three men gently lowered Wiley onto the daybed in the living room.

Wiley wondered if he'd really been sitting Indian-style, deep in the forest...with Grandpa Gray Feather. He'd felt someone jostling him, then a fog had closed over him, engulfing Grandpa and the forest. More jostling, then the fog cleared.

Wiley opened his eyes a slit and saw trees and the sky. Opening them wider, he realized the jostling was caused by him being carried in a yellow cloth, held by a handsome, shirtless stranger. He felt intense pain in his leg from the cloth pressing against the bullet wounds, and he closed his eyes against it. The fog returned and spun him around until he felt himself being placed on a bed.

Once again, Wiley opened his eyes. He was inside, but nothing looked familiar. "Jake?" he rasped.

Jake dropped to his knees and put his hand on Wiley's forehead. "I'm here, Wiley. These two men helped me get you up the hill. Wiley, our cabin's all wrecked. Winder must'a done it." Jake jerked his head up and looked at Jim. "Damn! I forgot! We gotta be careful! Winder's still out there!" He jumped to his feet, grabbed one of the guns at his side and ran to the door. "I had 'em pinned down in them rocks over there."

Jim and Dave froze.

Wiley turned his head toward Jake, then saw Dave for the first time. What were two middle-weight wrestlers doing here? Was he back in Philadelphia? Whoever the men were, he could tell they were terrified about something. From somewhere in his head, he heard a voice warning about Jake's gun.

"Jake, put your gun away," Wiley said hoarsely. He raised up slightly and focused his eyes on the two strange men. "I don't know who you are, but I need a doctor." Exhausted, he fell back and closed his eyes.

Jake holstered his gun, rushed over and knelt at Wiley's side, then looked up at Jim. "D'you got a horse an' buggy to get Wiley to the doc's?"

Jim glanced at Jake's two guns, then at his face. "A horse and buggy?" He looked at Dave with wild eyes.

Dave shrugged. "We don't have a horse and buggy. We have a truck."

"How we gonna get Wiley to the doc's if you ain't got no horse an' buggy?" Jake lowered his head to Wiley's chest. "I don't rightly know what's goin' on, Wiley, but I gotta get you help."

Jake raised his head and yelled, "The old Indian!" He grabbed at his shirt and pulled out the rawhide bag. Jake stared at it for a moment, then asked Dave and Jim, "Are you them pertecters?"

"Protectors?" Jim asked. "I don't know what you mean." He shook his head. "Dave, maybe we should get the truck ready. I'll get some blankets for a bed in the back." He took two steps at a time to the loft and quickly returned with a load of heavy quilts and blankets.

Still kneeling on the floor, Jake leaned against the daybed and glanced around the room. Who were these two men, and how did this cabin get here? He remembered a few things Chief Eagle Rising had told him and said, "Chief Eagle Rising said we'd be goin' to a strange place, an' for us to beware." He touched each gun at his side. "That's why I got Wiley an' me's guns on." He looked up at Dave and Jim. "An' he said we'd find pertecters where we was goin'. Are you them?"

Dave took the blankets from Jim and peered over the stack at Jake. "Chief Eagle Rising? I've read about him. He died in the eighteen eighties. You say you've been talking to him?" Dave started toward the door, sneaked a glance at Jim and raised his eyebrows. "You may have found your first client." He turned, rushed outside and nearly stumbled down the steps. Something about all of this reminded him of that article he'd read. Again, he tried forcing the thought out of his mind.

When the screen door slammed, Wiley opened his eyes. He groaned. The pain in his leg was making him queasy. He turned toward Jim. "Do you have any whiskey? I need something to dull the pain."

"Dave does. I'll get you some."

Jake struggled to his feet and followed Jim into the kitchen. "Damn! You sure must be rich! This ain't no cabin. It's nice as Miss Castille's house but not so big. How'd you build this here house when Wiley an' me didn't see you?"

Jim shook his head. "I haven't the foggiest idea, Jake." He wondered why the name Castille sounded familiar.

Jake ran his hand over the cast-iron top of the 1922 Quick Meal brand wood cookstove, then opened the oven door and looked inside. "This here stove's sure somethin'. I ain't never seen a yeller one before. An' it's big, too."

With a shaky hand, Jim filled a juice glass with bourbon and handed the plastic, half-gallon bottle of whiskey to Jake. "Here, help yourself. Glasses are in the cabinet behind you." Jim wondered about Jake's puzzled expression as he squeezed the plastic container and his comment: "I ain't never seen nothin' like this here bottle my whole life."

Jim knelt beside the daybed, lifted Wiley's head and helped him take a few swallows.

After Wiley drank half the glass, a little color came to his gaunt face. He smiled weakly. "Thanks. That's excellent whiskey."

"We're mighty thankful to you," Jake said as he walked into the living room holding a half-filled tumbler of bourbon. "We'll buy you more of this here booze for drinkin' so much. How much is it comin' in that..." He glanced back at the bourbon on the kitchen table and frowned. "That rubbery kind'a bottle."

"I think Dave paid about twelve dollars for it. It's not the highest priced bourbon, but he likes it the best."

"Twelve dollars!" Jake yelled. "Damn, Wiley. We'd better not be drinkin' no more. We ain't got that kind'a money." Jake drained the glass and set it on the cable-spool coffee table.

"What's wrong?" Dave asked as he opened the door and entered the cabin. "I heard yelling."

Jim shrugged. "I gave them some of your bourbon, and Jake said it was too expensive to drink."

"Don't worry about that." Dave looked at Jim. "The bed in the truck is ready. I'll back it up to the door so we won't have to carry Wiley so far. But first, I'm going to get dressed."

As Dave stripped off his silk shorts and pulled on his pants, Jake eyed him up and down. "You two kinda look like Wiley an' me, only not so big."

The two strangers scared Jim. They smelled strongly of stale sweat and horse shit, but he could hardly keep his eyes off them. He knew Dave also struggled with it. Where Jake and Wiley had come from and how they'd gotten down the hill was beyond him, but he knew they both were willing to drive Wiley to the Fairplay clinic, even if the two men were criminals.

Once Dave dressed, he grabbed his wallet and keys and ran out the door. After Jim put on his clothes, he helped Wiley take a few more sips of bourbon while trying to keep an eye on Jake and his guns. The man seemed too curious about everything. Was he casing the house?

Jake pointed out the window and yelled, "Damn! What the hell's that thing?"

Edgy, Jim jumped at Jake's outburst and spilled bourbon on the bed. He got to his feet, looked outside, then squinted at Jake. "Are you talking about the truck?"

When Dave opened the door, Winnie bounded in, went to Wiley and sniffed him. Jake's head jerked around when the dog buried his nose in the crack of his ass.

"Hey, dog! Don't you be smellin' my butt!"

"Winnie, stop it!" Dave scolded. "Let's go. The truck's ready."

Jim bent over Wiley. "Do you feel like traveling?" When Wiley opened his eyes and nodded, Jim said, "The road's real bumpy. Finish the rest of this bourbon, and you won't notice it as much."

Jake still had his nose pressed to the window when Dave approached him. "Jake, I think you'd better leave your guns here. The sheriff will arrest you if you wear them in town."

Jake spun around. "But what if Bingsly an' Winder or the Harrises are there? They'll gun us down before we can blink. I gotta have 'em with me."

Dave wondered if the men were running from the law, but couldn't help liking Jake. He suddenly had an urge to take this big, boyish man, who should be posing for his own Colt calendar, into his arms and calm his fears. There were other things he'd like to do to Jake, but not until he smelled better.

"No one's going to shoot you in Fairplay." Dave hoped.

"Leave the guns here, Jake," Wiley whispered. "We have to trust someone."

Jake frowned. Slowly, he unbuckled both belts and dropped them on the round coffee table.

"Do you mind if I hide your guns?" Dave asked. "If someone looks in the window while we're gone, they might break in and steal them." He knew no one would come around with Winnie guarding, but said that for an excuse to get them out of sight. He carefully placed the two holsters on the floor behind the hide-a-bed couch opposite the daybed, then said, "Let's go!"

Jim and Jake grabbed the tarp and lifted Wiley. After they struggled out the door, Dave leaped into the truck bed and helped them gently position the wounded man inside the shell. Wiley groaned, then relaxed into the soft quilts.

"I'll ride in back with Wiley," Jim said. He noticed Jake started to protest and put his hand on Jake's arm. "You ride up front with Dave. Don't worry, I'll take good care of him."

Jake grabbed Wiley's ankle and squeezed it, then walked to the front of the truck. "Where do you hook up the horses?"

"It doesn't need horses." Dave said. He wrinkled his nose and squinted at Jim as he closed the tailgate and shell window.

"Then, how do you get this thing to go?" Jake asked. "I ain't never seen nothin' like this thing my whole life." He kicked one of the tires. "Damn! These here wheels look like punkins. What's in 'em?"

"Air," Dave said as he approached the front of the truck. He wondered what Jake was trying to pull and decided to ignore it. "Better get in so we can go."

"How the hell do I get in there?" Jake asked, frowning at the front of truck.

Irritated that Jake might be leading him on, Dave grabbed his arm and led him to the passenger side of the truck. When he felt Jake's massive, rock-hard muscles, Dave was thankful the man didn't object.

Jake jumped back and gasped as Dave pulled the latch and opened the door. He felt the edge of the truck door, rapped the side with his knuckles, then ran his hand over the smooth metal. "This here feels like ice, but it ain't cold."

Dave forced a smile. "Get in."

Jake stared inside the cab. Timidly, he slid his butt onto the seat. Both of his boots caught on the door as he brought them inside. He wrapped his arms around his knees.

Dave rolled down the window before he shut the door. "I'll be right back." He ran into the cabin and came back out with Winnie's food and water dishes. "Winnie, you stay and guard the place. We'll be right back."

After he climbed into the truck, Dave noticed Jake had rolled the window up and was unrolling it again.

"Put on your seat belt."

"Put on my what?" Jake watched Dave fasten his belt. He reached around, grabbed the silver buckle hanging beside the seat, pulled it out and stuck his head through. The belt started to retract. "Damn, this here thing's grabbin' me!" Jake yanked on the belt. It locked. "Help! Get me outta this thing!"

Dave grabbed the strap near Jake's shoulder and held it. "Don't fight it. Just relax and it'll release."

Jake yanked the belt once more as hard as he could. His right knee bashed the glove compartment, and the door dropped open. A pair of sun glasses and two blister packs of mustard fell out and landed on his boots.

"Help! Get me outta here!" Jake hit the door with his arm, trying to open it.

Dave grabbed Jake's left arm. "Just relax! The more you struggle, the tighter it gets." He managed to slip the belt over Jake's head, and it snapped back beside the seat.

Jake glared at it.

"Shall we try it again?" Dave asked. "This time don't put your head through."

On the third attempt, Dave succeeded in shoving the buckle into the catch.

Jake looked at the strap and grinned. "I knowed my idea about tyin' yerself to the wagon while racin' was a good one."

"Can we get moving?" Jim yelled from the back. "What's going on up there?"

"We're going!" Dave hollered. He scooped up the sun glasses and mustard and stuffed them back into the glove compartment, then opened the window between the cab and the shell so they wouldn't have to shout.

CHAPTER 3

When Dave turned the key in the ignition and started the engine, Jake leaped off the seat and banged his head on the cab roof. He sat down hard and grabbed his head.

"Are you okay?" Dave asked. "What happened?"

Jake peered out from his hands. "What the hell's that noise and all that shakin'? Is this here thing gonna blow-the-hell up?"

"Of course not. I just started the engine." Dave shifted into first gear and slowly drove the truck down the sloping rocks. He glanced at Jake. "How's your head?"

"I feel like a chicken with its neck wrung." Jake glanced around inside the cab. "This here's pretty tight quarters." He finally noticed they were moving. "Damn! This thing's sure somethin' the way it goes without horses. It's sorta like a li'l train with no tracks." He looked out the window at the ground. "An' it rides smooth, too, not like that ol' wagon I run the race in. That thing about shook my nuts off." He watched Dave turn the steering wheel. "What're you doin' with that wheel?"

Jake's comment about his nuts sent a shock wave through Dave. He glanced at Jake's crotch. Jake's tight Levis accentuated his cock and balls bulging out between his huge legs.

Dave jerked the steering wheel to the right, narrowly missing a current bush. He sighed, knowing it would take extreme concentration to drive while sitting next to Jake. Wondering why Jake had asked about the steering wheel, he said, "I'm steering the truck. You can't tell me you've never seen anyone drive before."

"I ain't never seen nothin' like this thing my whole life. What do you mean steerin' the truck?"

Dave suddenly wondered if this might be one grand joke thought up by two druggies trying to cover up a bad drug deal. He turned the wheel sharply. "See, when I turn it this way, the truck goes this way."

Jake grabbed the side of the door as the truck lurched to the left. "Damn! An' with no horses, neither."

"David, Wiley's being thrown around back here!" Jim hollered.

"Sorry."

Dave carefully maneuvered the vehicle down the steep, rocky driveway that curved through an aspen and pine forest. He loved this short road. He and Jim had worked long hours placing the rocks in it so anyone, not knowing of the rock-free tracks that wove back and forth down its middle, would have a rough time driving it.

When they approached the county road, Dave carefully veered to the left through the field of rocks positioned so the first ten feet of driveway could be lethal to oil pans. He made a sharp right onto the wide gravel road, stopped and shifted out of four-wheel drive.

"What are you doin' now?" Jake asked.

"I put the truck into two-wheel drive."

"Two wheels? We're gonna be goin' with only two wheels? That's like the wagon race I was just in." Jake stuck his head out the window. "Where'd them other punkin wheels go?"

Dave heard a snicker in the back. He glanced in the rear-view mirror and saw Jim grinning at him. Dave looked at Jake hanging out the window. Was he on some drug trip? Everyone in the world knew what a truck was and a steering wheel.

Still leaning out the window, Jake watched the trees go by. What was happening? Where had Jim and Dave come from and how had they built their cabin without he and Wiley knowing about it? Could he trust these two men? Maybe they were working for Billingsly? Where did Billingsly get this truck? He had Wiley to look out for and wished he'd kept his gun with him.

Dave switched on the radio to block out thoughts of the article he'd read in the "Alma Gazette" or that Jake and Wiley might be druggies. Tuned to a talk show, a man's voice blared out of the speakers.

Jake jerked his head back inside, smacking it on the window frame. He squinted and rubbed the spot, then pointed at the dash. "Who's in there?"

Dave glanced at him. "You're going to knock yourself out. No one's in there. That's the radio." He felt like he was talking to a visitor from another planet. "The man's voice is picked up from the outside by that antenna." Dave pointed to the slender rod mounted on the fender. Why had he done that?

Jake stuck his head out the window, again. "I don't hear no talkin' out here."

"You need the antenna to pick up the signals." Dave sighed and switched off the radio. "Enough of that," he muttered.

Jake knew he didn't hear that man's voice outside and figured he was just too dumb to know what Dave was talking about. He listened again, then pulled his head inside. Seeing the knobs and dials on the dashboard, he asked, "What are all these things for?" He grabbed the heater lever. "What's this here thing?"

"That's the heater." Dave switched the fan on high and slid the lever so the air blew on Jake. Why was he doing this?

Jake gasped. "That truck's blowin' on me!"

"It's for heat." Dave turned off the fan. "We don't need it in the summer."

Jake grabbed the long handle sticking out from the steering column and accidentally pushed the windshield washer button on the end. Washer fluid sprayed on the front window.

Jake ducked and covered his face. "Is this here truck peein'?"

Dave didn't want to, but had to laugh. "That cleans the windshield." He turned on the wipers.

"Hell, lookit them arm-things wipin' that pee off." Jake tapped the windshield. "Is this here glass?"

Dave switched off the wipers. "Yes. It keeps the wind out of our faces."

Jake glanced over at Dave, back at the windshield, then shook his head. "This here truck sure is somethin'. It keeps the wind off yer face an' blows it on yer nuts."

Dave snickered. If this was an act, Jake was good at it. "Where are you and Wiley from?" he asked, hoping to catch Jake in his scam.

Jake settled into the seat and looked straight ahead. "Wiley's from Vermont, an' I come from Kentucky. We been partners an' blood brothers for a month." He sighed and lowered his head. "An' ever'body's wantin' to kill us, too."

An icy chill gripped Dave's gut. The men in the newspaper article had been blood brothers, and they had disappeared while being shot at. But he couldn't remember if the story mentioned why they'd been shot at. All at once, Dave wondered if Jake had read the same article and that was how he'd cooked up this story.

"Jake, are you wanted by the law?"

"Hell, no! We ain't wanted by Sheriff Cline, but lots of men're after us. Them Harrises from back home want me..."

Jake gasped and pointed at the hills on the far side of the narrow valley. "Where'd all them houses come from an' all these here roads? When did these roads get made in Miss Castille's ranch?"

Dave shuddered at hearing the name Castille, but was now convinced Jake had read that same article in the old "Alma Gazette." Maybe the article was famous and he'd just never run across it until now. He'd done research on this area of South Park and wanted to know where Jake had learned of the Castilles.

"Who is Miss Castille?"

"Belinda Castille. She owns this here ranch. Wiley an' me work for her. We built us that cabin an' been roundin' up her cows to keep 'em off Bingsly's land." Jake glanced out the side window. The southern slope of Bristlecone Peak slipped by so quickly. Jake remembered a few minutes ago their cabin had been a pile of rotting logs. What had happened to it?

"Jake, do you know when the Castille family sold this ranch?"

Jake gasped. "Sold it? She ain't sold it. Leastways, she ain't sold it before Wiley an' me went to the wagon race. 'Course we been gone three days an' ain't seen her since we been back." Jake turned and looked through the connecting window. "Wiley, Dave said Miss Castille sold this here ranch while we was gone."

Dave squinted at Jake. "She sold it way back in nineteen twenty-eight."

"Nine...? What do you mean *nineteen* twenty-eight? What're you talkin' about? This here's eighteen eighty-six. I ain't smart like Wiley, but I know what year it is."

Trying to keep the truck on the road, Dave said, "Jake, this is nineteen ninety-three."

"Nineteen ninety-three?" Jake shrugged. "I might be dummer'n hog shit, but I ain't never gonna believe that!"

Dave shot him a glance. "You read the same article I did in the 'Alma Gazette,' didn't you?" He was sorry he'd said that and sighed with relief when Jake didn't comment.

Jake peered into the bed of the truck at Wiley, then looked at Dave. "I don't know what's goin' on. I see all these here different things an' know I ain't never seen 'em before. If it's nineteen ninety-three, how'd Wiley an' me get here?" His face brightened. "Chief Eagle Rising! He said we'd be goin' to a strange place! You must be them pertecters he told me about!"

Dave side-glanced Jake but kept his focus on the road. "I've done a little reading about this area. Chief Eagle Rising died in Leadville. I'm pretty sure it was eighteen eighty-four. Even if you are from eighteen eighty-six, how could you have talked to him if he'd been dead for two years even back then?"

Jake felt the familiar pain in his gut that Dave thought he was dumb. It riled him inside. "I know he died then! I heard some men talkin' about it in the Regal Cafe. But Chief Eagle Rising was in Wiley an' me's cabin. Winder was outside wantin' to kill us."

Jake grabbed the cord around his neck, pulled the rawhide bag out from under his shirt and held it toward Dave. "Chief Eagle Rising gived me this here bag. It was full'a sand. Then he gived me a golden feather an' told me to put it in the bag. He said we'd be goin' some place strange-like, an' we'd find pertecters who'd help Wiley get better." Jake stared at the bag. "It don't hardly seem possible anythin' like this could happen."

Jake remembered seeing the feather on the cabin floor. He hadn't been able to pick it up before the wind had started blowing. He dropped the bag and covered his face with his hands. He and Wiley were stranded here forever! Jake squeezed his eyes shut and bit his lip. Wiley would be furious with him. Shoving the bag down his shirt, Jake peered out the window at the fast-moving landscape and tried to get the fearful thoughts out of his mind.

Dave found it increasingly hard to keep the truck on the road. Everything Jake had said seemed to confirm the article about two men named Jake and Wiley who had disappeared while being shot at. These men couldn't be the same ones. This was real life, not the movies. He shivered from the cold chill still gripping his spine. But what if Jake and Wiley really did come from the past? Dave quickly dismissed the thought, but hoped like hell Jake was telling the truth.

The truck sped down the road that twisted and turned as it hugged the western side of forested hills that stretched in a line toward the north from Bristlecone Peak. The range paralleled a similar one a thousand yards to the west, and cabins dotted both sides of the treeless valley nestled between.

Catching a whiff of Jake's strong odor, Dave looked at the big man hunched down in the seat.

"What's the matter, Jake?"

"I ain't never gone so fast my whole life!"

Dave shaded the speedometer with his hand. "We're only going thirty-five, but it's too fast for this road." He slowed to twenty-five.

Jake sighed and sat up straight. "Lookit all them cabins down there. An' all these here roads and fences. There weren't nothin' like this when Wiley an' me'd ride here lookin' for cows."

As the truck topped a ridge, Jake pointed at a snow-capped mountain in the distance. "That there's Mount Silverheels!" He lowered his hand and glanced around inside the truck. "Lots'a things is different, but others ain't." Looking at the road ahead, he saw a cloud of dust approaching. "What's that red thing comin'?"

"It looks like a VW bug."

"A bug! What kinda bug's that big? We'd better get the hell outta here!"

Dave chuckled. "It's a car. It's like this truck only smaller. It's shaped like a beetle and that's why they're called bugs." He caught himself talking like Jake really was from the past.

As the VW approached, Jake grabbed for his gun, then remembered Dave had made him leave it behind.

The red VW sped past.

"There were *people* in that bug!" Jake turned clear around and looked through the back window. "Wiley, there's some kinda big red bugs here that have people in 'em!"

Jim laughed. He'd been listening to Jake while bouncing around in back next to Wiley. He didn't believe Jake's story any more than Dave did, maybe less since he'd counseled some seriously deranged people in the past three years. He loved Jake's comments but had no answers to why the man seemed completely in the dark about modern things. Even if Jake had been in prison for years, he would have seen a truck or a VW bug. Jim wondered if Chief Eagle Rising was Jake's drug dealer who'd sold him some powerful LSD or peyote. But physically Jake didn't act like he was on any hallucinogen.

The man was breathtaking. Wiley's massive chest pushed his rawhide shirt open so the crisscross lacing fenced patches of curly black hair. Wiley's rugged face, with a few weeks' growth of black beard, made Jim think of Hercules or Sampson. He was getting used to his masculine odor. It was becoming a turn-on.

The truck bounced over a cattle guard, and Jim lurched against the side. Who were these men? They were both gorgeous. Colt calendar men should be so lucky. He leaned forward and felt Wiley's forehead.

At Jim's touch, Wiley opened his red, watery eyes and smiled weakly.

Jim's heart skipped a beat. "Uh...we'll be at the doctor's in Fairplay in about fifteen minutes." Hoping for a different explanation than the one Jake had given, he asked, "Where are you and Jake from?"

Wiley studied the lean, muscular body of the man sitting beside him, then raised his eyes to Jim's. "Jake told it right. I...I've ever known Jake to lie. I don't know what's happened."

He remembered hearing a deep, whispery voice talking to Jake in their cabin. Had that been a dream? Had he really sat in the forest with Grandpa Gray Feather? Was riding in this...truck?...a dream? Wiley closed his eyes. He had no idea where he was or what he was riding in. The only thing he did know for sure was Jake's yelling in the front seat was making him confused and edgy. Jim's calmness seemed to ease his wracked mind and body. Wiley opened his eyes and grabbed Jim's knee. He smiled and closed them again when Jim placed his hand over his own.

"Lookit all them fences!" Jake yelled. "Why'd all them fences get put up all over?"

Dave rolled his eyes. "They're to keep cattle off the road so they won't get hit by cars. And ranchers don't want anyone walking or driving on their range." Dave remembered he'd always wanted to be a tour guide in the mountains, but this was like showing the world to a Martian. Or possibly someone from eighteen eighty-six? Another cold shiver swept through him.

When the truck pulled up to US 285, Jake sat forward and looked out at the paved highway. "What's that black strip a'stuff for?"

"That's the road into Fairplay. Now the ride will be a lot smoother for Wiley."

Dave turned the truck north onto the highway. After he got the speed up to sixty, Jake crouched in the seat, eyes shut tight.

"Jake, what's the matter now?"

Jake opened his eyes to thin slits and peered over the dash. "This here's like we're flyin'." He opened his eyes wide, yelled and covered his face as an oncoming semi roared by. Jake turned and looked through the back window. "Damn! What the hell was *that*?"

"That was a truck, like this, only bigger. They're called semis." Convinced Jake was faking, or crazy, Dave felt stupid playing into his comments, but figured it might be safer. It was like acting in a sci-fi movie. He wished he knew what was happening. The thought again crossed his mind that Jake was telling the truth--that they had jumped ahead in time over a hundred years.

Always busy on Sunday evenings, they found Fairplay alive with activity from weekend tourists returning to Denver from Breckenridge and beyond. As Dave drove through the center of town, Jake leaned out the window and yelled about the cars, the clothing people wore, neon signs and the absence of horses and buggies. His big frame filled the opening and his voice sounded far away to Dave, except when he yelled "Damn!"

CHAPTER 4

After Dave parked the truck in front of the Fairplay medical clinic, he slid out, ran to the back and opened the shell window and tailgate. When he looked through the truck and saw Jake still sitting in the front seat, he yelled, "Jake, we'll need your help to get Wiley inside."

"How the hell do I get these straps off'a me!"

Irritated that Jake was carrying his druggie game to the extreme, Dave ran to the passenger side of the cab, flung open the door and shoved himself across Jake's legs to release the seat belt. As he fumbled for the catch, he felt Jake's hand slide across his back. Once the belt snapped back, Dave looked up into Jake's handsome face.

Jake grinned. "Thanks for helpin' Wiley."

Shaken by Jake's touch, his strong, masculine aroma and his sparkling blue eyes, Dave became light-headed and felt a stirring in his crotch. "Uh...don't mention it," he said breathlessly.

"I need help back here," Jim yelled.

The two men smiled at each other. Jake slid out of the cab and followed Dave to the back of the truck.

While Jim ran inside the clinic for a wheelchair, Dave and Jake pulled on the blankets to get Wiley closer to the tailgate. When Jim returned, Jake gently lifted Wiley into the chair, and Dave covered him with a blanket.

Wiley gritted his teeth through the ordeal, but said nothing, barely having the strength to lift his head. For some reason, the whiskey had intensified the pain in his leg and made him slightly queasy.

Dave held open the door, and Jim pushed Wiley into the clinic. A petite woman in her early twenties, with short curly hair, freckles and wearing oversized rimless glasses, sprang out of her chair behind the counter. As she approached the group, the blanket fell away from Wiley's leg, exposing the bloody shirt tied around his thigh.

"Oh my God!" the woman gasped. "Here, let me push him over to the examining room door, then I'll get the doctor." She grabbed the handles of the wheelchair, got a whiff of Wiley and quickly put the back of her hand over her nose and mouth. "Oh my God!"

Forgetting the wheelchair, the woman rushed across the room. "I'll be right back." She glanced back at the four men, opened the door and slipped into the next room, then closed it firmly.

Dave grabbed Jake's arm. "Jim and I will do the talking. Don't say anything."

Jake nodded and looked at the floor. Dave must not trust him. He felt dummer'n hog shit, but as he glanced around the room he noticed everything was so white it almost hurt his eyes. He gasped when he saw the bucket-shaped, plastic chairs lined with bright red cushions.

Jake grabbed Jim's arm and pointed. "Them chairs look like hip tubs."

"What's a hip tub?"

Jake wondered why Jim had never heard of a hip tub. He let go of Jim's arm, shoved his finger through the gap between two buttons of his shirt and touched the rawhide bag. He remembered Chief Eagle Rising telling him he and Wiley would be going to a strange place. That must be why Jim didn't know.

"A hip tub's a half-tub you sit in to wash yer nuts an' shit hole. 'Course you can wash everythin' else, too."

The same door the receptionist had disappeared behind suddenly opened. A tall, black-haired man in his fifties came into the waiting room. His white coat, open full length, softened his stern features. Dave thought of a grouchy Steve Allen. The man frowned when he saw Wiley's leg.

"I'm Doctor Blakely. Wheel him in here, please." The doctor studied the men as Jim pushed Wiley into the examining room.

Doctor Blakely grabbed Wiley's arm, then looked at the others. "Help me lift him onto the examining table."

It took all four men to get Wiley onto the table.

"Don't you men ever bathe?" the doctor snorted as he untied the bloody shirt around the wound and gently removed it.

Everyone gasped when they saw the red, pus-filled wounds. "How did this happen?" the doctor asked. Suspicion and irritation clouded his face.

"We was bein'..." Jake said, then snapped his mouth shut when Dave poked him in the back.

"It was an accident," Dave said. "He was...cleaning his gun, and it went off."

"That ain't right..." Jake saw Dave's frown and stopped.

Doctor Blakely squinted at Dave. "The angle the bullet went through his leg would make that impossible. It went in the back and out the front." He looked sternly at all of them. "Now, what really happened?"

"To tell you the truth, doctor, we don't know how it happened," Jim said.

Doctor Blakely glared at him. "We'll get to that later. Help me pull his pants down. And be careful. I don't want those scabs to break open. He's lucky the bullet didn't hit the bone."

Wiley groaned as the doctor, with Dave and Jim's help, gently pulled his pants down to his knees. The front wound began bleeding as the ragged scab split. Red rays of infection had already started spreading.

Doctor Blakely scowled at Wiley's underwear. "These long johns are filthy. You men need some lessons in cleanliness. There ought to be a law. What century have you been living in?"

Jake screwed up his face. "I don't rightly know anymore, Doc. Wiley an' me washed up yesterday after wrestlin' in horse shit, but we didn't have no soap." He shook his head. "I think it was yesterday. I ain't rightly sure no more."

Ignoring Jake, the doctor said, "Let's gently roll him over. I need to give him a couple shots in his rear."

"Why you gonna put booze in his butt?" Jake asked.

Dave snickered, but stopped when he noticed Doctor Blakely shoot Jake another angry glance while rolling Wiley onto his stomach.

"Oh God!" Wiley groaned.

Jim grabbed Wiley's shoulder. "Hang in there, Wiley. The doctor's going to give you something to fight the infection."

The three men of the twentieth century stared at seat flap of Wiley's underwear.

The frayed material, stretched tightly over Wiley's firm buttocks, was smudged with black soot. Flattened sap blobs with bits of pine bark and broken needles glued to them and several wide brown smears of dirt made the three men realize that Wiley spent much of his time outdoors in just his long johns.

Doctor Blakely started to unbutton the seat flap but stopped and glanced at Jake. "You unbutton them. I'll get a washcloth and prepare the shots."

Jake unbuttoned the flap in Wiley's underwear and pulled it down, exposing his firm white butt. Dave and Jim glanced at each other and sucked in air.

"Doc, you gonna have Wiley an' me arrested fer not washin'?"

Doctor Blakely turned his head to Jake. "Of course not! What's the matter with you? It's upbringing. I'm sure you didn't spend your childhood in a horse corral."

"Not hardly," Jake said. "It was a hog pen. Pa'd toss me in there 'bout every day. Sometimes more."

Thinking it merely a funny comment, Dave snickered, but stopped when Jake appeared hurt.

The doctor washed Wiley's buttocks, dried them and applied alcohol wipes. He went back to the sink and returned with two syringes.

"What're them things for?" Jake asked when he saw the needles.

Jim grinned. "Those are the shots."

Doctor Blakely gave Wiley a hypo in each buttock. Jake cried out in mock pain seeing his blood brother lurch.

"Hold still!" the doctor snapped.

The doctor applied a small plastic bandage over each tiny puncture.

Jake slid his finger across one of them. "Was there booze in them pointy things, Doc?"

Doctor Blakely put his hands on his hips and faced Jake. "Will you stop! This is no time for comedy. If you can't keep your comments to yourself, you can wait in the other room."

Dave grabbed Jake's arm. "Let's go outside. I want a cigarette, and you can tell me about Kentucky. I've never been there." He nodded toward the others. "They'll take good care of Wiley."

"But...!"

Dave looked straight at Jake. "If you get the doctor angry, he might stick one of those pointy things in *your* butt."

Jake glanced back in horror and allowed Dave to lead him outside.

The doctor sighed and shook his head when Jake was gone. He looked at Jim. "Someone is going to have to watch this man for several days. It's a good thing you got him in here when you did. If you'd waited any longer, I'd have to admit him into a hospital."

"Dave and I will watch him," Jim said. "We'll bring both of them to our place. They can stay with us until Wiley's better."

After the doctor gave Wiley a tetanus shot, he cleaned and dressed his wounds, then showed Jim how to change the bandages.

"You have change them every day, especially if they get wet. Now, be sure and get him in here immediately if his fever doesn't break or if he seems worse tomorrow. I also suggest that you report this to Sheriff Daly. You don't have to tell me what happened, but you'd better tell him."

"I will," Jim said, not at all sure he wanted to let the sheriff know about Jake and Wiley. At least not until he and Dave had a chance to talk to them. Even though they had guns back at the cabin, Jim wasn't afraid of them. Not now. If they needed psychiatric help, turning them over to the law would only compound their problems. Yet, if they were wanted, he and Dave could would be guilty of harboring criminals. But after watching Wiley in the back of the truck and listening to Jake's comments, he couldn't bring himself to believe they were dangerous.

"If the sheriff lets them stay with you, make sure they take a bath!" the doctor snapped. "They smell to high heaven. But, from what I know of Sheriff Daly, they won't be going with you."

Drifting in and out of consciousness, Wiley felt his pants being pulled up. Pain wracked his leg as the cloth slid against his wounds. He knew he should endure the pain in silence like Grandpa Gray Feather had taught him, but under the circumstances he found himself in, he didn't want to deal with it. Wiley groaned and opened his eyes. "Doctor, can you give me some laudanum for the pain?"

"Laudanum! What are you, a druggie? Son, I'd suggest you give up opium, and whatever else you take, and learn to take care of yourself. You're a fine looking man. Don't throw your life away on drugs. Were you shot during a drug deal?"

"I don't know what you mean, doctor," Wiley said feebly. "I've only taken laudanum one other time for pain. If you don't have any, I'll get by." Reading a warning on Jim's face, Wiley relaxed back to the table, glad Jim was with him.

Doctor Blakely grumbled something about the younger generation as he sat at a desk in the corner of the room and wrote out two prescriptions, one for penicillin and the other for a pain killer. After handing the prescriptions to Jim, he helped Wiley sit up and gave him a pain pill with a cup of water.

"I shouldn't give you this pain pill since you've been drinking," Doctor Blakely said, "but the two together will help you sleep. I want to see you again next Saturday." He turned to Jim. "If he stays with you, get him back here then. And give him plenty of grape juice and red meat. He's lost a lot of blood."

Jim helped the doctor get Wiley into the wheelchair. As Jim pushed it into the waiting room, he noticed a man and woman sitting across the room reading magazines. A young girl sat at a small table shoving her Barbie's bent-back arms into a red coat. They all stared at Wiley's leg. As Jim approached the front door, the receptionist ran to open it for him.

Halfway to the truck, Jim placed his hand on Wiley's shoulder. "Thank God, we're out of there."

Once they had Wiley nestled into the blanket bed, Jim wheeled the chair back to the clinic. While he paid the bill, Doctor Blakely came to the counter.

"Be sure and tell Sheriff Daly how that man was shot. If there's someone out there loose or if the man with him did it, the sheriff needs to know before anyone else gets hurt. You included."

The couple gasped and looked at each other.

"I will, Doctor," Jim said. "Thanks for everything."

When Jim reached the truck, he found Dave and Jake sitting on the open tailgate.

Jake looked up at him. "I'm thankful for what you done for Wiley. If I lose him, I don't rightly know what I'd do." He stared at the ground. "Me an' Wiley are the best partners there ever was. If he dies, I'd most likely hafta go back to Kentucky an' marry Sara Jean." He shook his head. "Or Seth'll hang me."

"I'm sure Wiley will be all right," Dave said. "But who's Sara Jean and Seth?"

"Can we get out of here, first?" Jim interrupted. "I don't want to stay in town. I'm afraid the doctor will call the sheriff about Wiley being shot, and we have to get his prescriptions filled. Let's use the drug store on the highway so we don't have to stop in the middle of town."

Dave smiled at Jake. "You can tell me about Sara Jean in the truck."

"Sure thing." Jake slid off the tailgate, started toward the front but stopped and spun around. "Maybe I should be with Wiley."

"Wiley and I will be fine back here," Jim said as he climbed into the back. "You ride up front. You can see more up there." He handed Dave the two prescriptions. "Wiley needs to drink a lot of grape juice. Why don't you get six frozen ones."

Dave nodded as he closed the tailgate and shell window. He started toward Jake to open the door for him.

"I did it!" Jake yelled. "I opened 'er up my own self!"

Dave drove the back roads through town and came alongside a green and white gas station that sat back from the highway. He stopped the truck and looked around for the sheriff. Not seeing him or any of his deputies, he drove south for a short distance before turning left into the drug store parking lot. He parked the truck and glanced at Jake. "Do you want to go in with me? We can pick up some beer."

"Sure!" Jake fumbled with the arm rest trying to open the door.

Dave unlatched both seat belts, leaned over Jake's lap, grabbed the handle and pulled it forward to unlatch the door. Jake put his hand on Dave's back and smiled at him. Dave looked up and returned the smile, then shoved Jake's door open, intentionally falling across his legs.

Jake slid his right hand under Dave's chest and gently lifted him. "I reckon I'd a'done the same thing my own self," he whispered.

Not knowing what Jake meant, Dave straightened up, opened his own door and slid out of the truck. The erotic odor of Jake's body clung to his nostrils. He breathed deeply as Jake walked beside him through the parking lot.

Jake stepped through the door, stopped and slowly looked around. "Damn! What *is* all this stuff?"

Dave glanced at him. "Just things people need. Let's go this way." He started down the main aisle.

Jake lagged behind. He stared at brightly colored boxes of nasal spray, sinus pills, laxatives, headache pills, backache pills, plastic bandage strips and shoe odor inserts. On his right, he passed plastic bottles of shampoo, cans of hair spray, deodorant tubes, and hand lotion. Farther on, sun glasses, orange and red plastic bats and balls, multicolored frizbees, bubble packs of Barbie clothes and dozens of other toys all seemed to vie for prominence.

"What's all this stuff for?" Jake yelled.

Dave ignored the question and headed for the pharmacy window. He handed the prescriptions to the man behind the counter, then hurried to the row of coolers.

When Jake caught up, Dave asked, "What kind of beer do you like?"

Jake glanced around. "I see all kinds'a stuff in this here store an' don't know what none of it is. I sure as hell don't see no beer."

Dave pointed to the cooler. "It's right here."

"Canned beer?" Jake shouted. "I ain't never seen no canned beer my whole life!"

Dave noticed several patrons turned and gawked at them. One older man snickered, but the others seemed annoyed.

"I'll pick out some I think you'll like." Dave grabbed two six-packs of a locally made beer and a pack of dark ale. He handed two of the six-packs to Jake.

"Damn!" Jake yelled, nearly dropping them. "This here canned beer's cold as ice! How'd it get that way? This here's summer."

Dave quickly piled the store's last four cans of frozen grape juice on top of the ale, hurried to the liquor section and grabbed a plastic bottle of his favorite bourbon by its neck. He glanced across the store and saw the scowling pharmacist holding up Wiley's pills.

When they neared the pharmacy window, Jake grabbed Dave's arm. "What kind'a chicken laid these here big, shiny eggs?"

"That's panty hose, Jake."

"What the hell's that?"

"Women wear them on their legs."

"Women wear *eggs* on their legs?"

Jake spun around to the woman they'd just passed and stared at her legs. She glared at him.

"This is your prescription," the pharmacist snapped.

Dave rushed over and grabbed the bag. "Thanks." He turned to Jake and whispered, "Let's pay for this and get out of here."

Jake stood beside Dave at the checkout counter and fingered items on the racks filled with candy bars, gum and bags of potato chips. "What's all this here stuff?"

"Those are snacks, Jake. I'll buy you one." Dave grabbed a candy bar and handed it to him. He smiled sheepishly at the older, chicken-faced woman with frizzy red hair standing behind the check-out counter. Her half-glasses were perched on the tip of her long nose, and she peered over them at Jake.

After he ripped off the end of the wrapper, Jake let the candy bar slide into his hand. He looked at it for a moment then wrinkled his nose. "What do I do with it?"

Thumbing through his wallet, hoping he had forty-seven dollars, Dave mumbled, "You eat it."

"Eat it!" Jake yelled. "This here looks like dog shit! I already ate enough shit yesterday when Wiley an' me was wrestlin' in the horse corral." He looked at Dave. "Why's dog shit wrapped up like this?"

The cashier gasped. Her glasses slipped off the end of her nose and were caught by the plastic-jeweled chain around her neck.

"Get that man out of here!" the pharmacist yelled. "And, don't bring him back until he can talk decent. This is a drug store, not a bar!"

Dave waited impatiently while the cashier slowly bagged the items. Her eyes were glued to Jake as he turned the candy bar over and over in his hand. After she finished, Dave hefted the plastic bags, nudged Jake's arm and said, "Let's go."

On the way to the truck, Dave burst out laughing.

Jake frowned. "You laughin' at me? What'd I do?"

"Jake, that's not dog shit. It's chocolate. I think you'll like it."

"Chocolate? I had me some chocolate once in Denver, but it didn't look like this here thing." Jake took a bite, smiled, then stuffed the whole candy bar into his mouth.

Dave chose a rarely used road back to the cabin, taking them beside three small lakes. "These are Bristol Lakes," he said.

Jake pointed to the smallest of the three. Even after the wet winter, it had dried up completely. "That there's the one Wiley an' me scrubbed Thunder Joe in. All that brown stuff comin' off'a him must'a dried it up."

Thunder Joe? Dave remembered that name from the old newspaper article. Not wanting to dwell on that again, Dave said, "Last year, that lake had water in it." He paused. Unable to stand the suspense, he turned to Jake and asked, "Who's Thunder Joe?"

"Smelliest ol' fart in the whole world," Jake said. "He's an ol' mountain man Wiley an' me latched on to. He helped us build our cabin an' talked me into buggy racin' at the Harrington ranch." Jake's face lit up. "The wagon busted all to hell durin' the race, but I won an' got a hunnert an' fifty dollars. Wiley an' me gived Joe fifty of it."

"When and where did you say that race was?" Dave asked, hoping to catch Jake at his story.

"At the Harrington Ranch, Saturday, June fifth, eighteen eighty-six. Leastways, that's what Wiley told me the sign said. What day is this, anyway?"

"Sunday, June sixth," Dave said slowly. Then added, "Nineteen ninety-three." He chuckled. He'd found a way to prove Jake's story wrong. How could the dates match even if Jake and Wiley were from eighteen eighty-six? A perpetual calendar would prove that Jake was making up the whole story.

Deep in thought, Dave sped toward the cabin.

CHAPTER 5

The whiskey and pain pill had knocked Wiley out long before they arrived home, and he slept soundly through the ordeal of getting him out of the truck and onto the daybed in the cabin.

Since Dave had talked Jake into taking a bath, Jim started a fire in the cookstove, knowing it would take awhile for the two large pots of water to boil. Now that they had company, he felt like fixing dinner.

Dave headed for the door. "I'm going to move the truck to the carport."

Jake followed him outside, wanting to look at the other thing with punkin-wheels parked on the north side of the outhouse. He hadn't noticed it until they had approached the cabin from the other direction. Jake climbed into the truck and rode with Dave the short distance to the shelter where both vehicles were kept. As soon as the truck stopped, he jumped out and ran to the gray Honda hatchback.

"Is this another truck?" Jake peered through the windows. "Why do you have two of these here trucks, but no horses?"

Dave smiled as he walked over to Jake. "This one's called a car, not a truck. And to answer your other question, most people don't use horses for traveling."

"Do these here trucks cost lots'a money?"

"Yes, but you can't get places without a car or truck. Places are so spread out it would take forever to get anywhere without one."

"But ever'thing's spread out far where Wiley an' me come from, an' we get places. Takes longer, that's all. Nobody'd believe me if I said we'd gone to Fairplay an' back in three hours."

Dave shrugged. "I guess life was slower...back then." He looked dreamily into space. "It would have been nice to have lived in eighteen eighty-six. I've always felt like I was born a hundred years too late. A slower lifestyle has always appealed to Jim and me.

That's one of the reasons we moved out of Denver. Did you say you were in Denver?"

"Sure did. I was there for a month buildin' houses." Jake lowered his head. "Then the Harrises caught up with me. After that's when I come up here to Alma. That's where Wiley an' me met. Wiley saved me from them Harrises an' bought us a bottle of whiskey in the Silver Heels Bar."

"The Silver Heels Bar? That's been closed for five years."

"Well, it weren't then. Wiley an' me become blood brothers in there that same night. We'd only knowed each other for a few minutes too. Lots'a miners cheered us."

Dave suddenly felt light-headed from believing and not believing what Jake was saying. He leaned against the side of the car and closed his eyes. What in God's name was happening?

Jake put his hand on Dave's shoulder. "You okay?"

Dave sighed. "I just got dizzy from everything you've been telling me." He opened his eyes and stared at the big man in front of him. "Jake, tell the truth. Where are you really from? Why are you saying you're from eighteen eighty-six?"

Jake let go of Dave's shoulder and balled his fists. "You callin' me a liar? You ain't got no right callin' me no liar! If you wasn't littler'n me, I'd bust you in the mouth! Don't you go callin' me no damn liar!"

Dave nearly wet his pants. He had no doubts Jake could easily toss him halfway down the driveway.

Jake reached down his shirt, pulled out the rawhide bag and shoved it into Dave's face. "This here bag's how we got here, an' you gotta believe it! Like I gotta!"

Jim heard Jake shouting and ran outside. "What's the matter?" He ran down the path between the cabin and the rock garden and stopped beside them. "Please don't fight. After all that's happened today, it won't help anything if you two start fighting."

"I don't take kindly to people callin' me no damn liar!" Jake shouted. "I ain't smart like Wiley, but I ain't no liar!"

Dave raised his palms toward Jake and backed up a step. "I'm sorry, Jake. I didn't mean to call you a liar. It's just hard to believe you're really from eighteen eighty-six. Things like that don't happen in real life." He hesitated, then extended his right hand. "I want us to be friends, no matter what's happening."

Jake's angry face softened. He let the leather bag drop to his chest, looked down at it and shook his head. "I ain't never heard of nothin' like this happenin' neither." He grabbed Dave's hand, then Jim's. "Hell, you're both friends after what you done for Wiley." He let go of them, looked at the ground and scraped a depression in the spongy soil with the toe of his boot. "I don't mean gettin' so riled." He glanced around with teary eyes. "Bein' here...an' with Wiley all shot up, I...I feel all mixed up inside."

Jim slid his arm across Jake's back. "Wiley will be fine. I'm sure we'll see an improvement in him tomorrow."

Dave walked to the truck, opened the back window of the shell and pulled out a plastic bag containing two six packs of beer. "Jake, can you help me carry this stuff into the cabin? I promise I'll believe you from now on."

Jake rushed to Dave's side, grabbed the bag and held it up in front of his face. He poked at the soft plastic with his finger, lowered the bag and looked around the wooded area. "Won't Wiley be surprised when he wakes up an' finds out where we's at?"

After Jake clunked the beer on the kitchen table, he returned to the living room, dropped to his knees and felt Wiley's forehead. He kissed Wiley's gaunt face, then rested his head on his chest, grateful to feel him still breathing. Jake buried his face into Wiley's chest and whimpered. Everything seemed so confusing.

Again, Jake remembered he'd seen the feather on the floor of the cabin before all this happened. He raised his head. Chief Eagle Rising had told him, "If bag or feather lost, you stay in distant place forever." Jake shuddered. They couldn't stay here. Chief Eagle Rising said this Time was bad. And Wiley would be furious with him for having to stay here. Jake scrambled to his feet. Jesus would think of something. He'd have to.

Jake felt Wiley's forehead again, then bent down and kissed it. Somehow it didn't seem as hot. "Jim said you'll be gettin' better, Wiley," he whispered. He kissed Wiley's cheek, then ambled into the kitchen and watched Jim feed wood into the cookstove.

Jake pointed at the yellow enameled cookstove with beige trim. "This stove sure is somethin'. Do all stoves look like this one in this here Time?"

Flames flickered out the round hole as Jim gingerly shoved a few more wrist-size branch pieces into the stove and replaced the cast-iron plate. "No, this is nineteen-twenty vintage. We have a modern stove in our house in Denver. It cooks with gas, not wood." He pulled up the lever to heat the oven only because he needed the entire top surface of the stove hot to boil water and cook.

"You got a house in Denver, too? You must be rich." Jake glanced at Dave sitting at the table, then at Jim. "Are you partners an' blood brothers like Wiley an' me?"

"We're lovers. Partners. But not blood brothers. Are you and Wiley really blood brothers?"

"Hell, yes. Wiley cut my hand, an' then cut his. Then we shook. Wiley already knowed about blood brother stuff cuz his grampa was an Indian."

"So that's why he's so strikingly handsome," Jim said as he snuck a peek into the other room.

Dave stood up and opened the refrigerator. "Jake, do you want a beer?"

"Sure thing." For the first time, Jake noticed the refrigerator. "Why do you keep the beer in that yeller cabinet?"

If Jake was acting out a charade, he was perfect at it. The thought that Jake might actually be from the past thrilled Dave, and he couldn't resist pretending it was true. "Come here and put your hand inside."

Jake stuck his hand inside the refrigerator, then jerked it back. "Hell, it's like winter in there."

Dave shut the door and opened the freezer. "It's even colder up here. This is for frozen food."

Jake hesitated, reached in, touched a box and quickly pulled his hand back. "Damn, that's like ice in there. What's in that box?"

"Peas." Dave pulled out several boxes. "See, this is peas, this is corn and this one's spinach." The frosty box slipped out of his hand and hit the floor with a bang.

Jake picked it up. He turned it over and over and tried to squeeze it. "This here's spinach?" He remembered Ben Harrington built his adobe house out of bricks of mud and straw. "You gonna build you another cabin outta this?"

Jim chuckled. "No, but an Eskimo probably could."

"Then, what's it for?"

"We eat it," Dave said, trying not to laugh.

"You *eat* this?" Jake stared at the box and grabbed at his front teeth.

Jim gently pulled the spinach out of Jake's hand. "I may as well fix it for dinner. Dave, could you take out a chicken for tomorrow." He eyed Jake. "Better make it two. And find one of those steaks for Wiley. "

"Sure." Dave put back the peas and corn, then handed Jake a frozen chicken. "Just put it on the table." After handing Jake the second one, he retrieved a frost-covered plastic bag with a single steak and slammed the freezer door.

"Where's them chickens Jim wanted?" Jake asked.

"I just handed them to you."

"Them things is *chickens*? Hell, I thought they was rocks." Jake inspected the frozen chickens closely. "What happened to 'em?"

Dave laughed. "They're stuffed into plastic bags, then frozen. Once they thaw out, they look like chickens." He opened the two beer cans and handed one to Jake.

Jake took a swig, then held up the can and frowned at it. "This beer ain't no good. It tastes like river water from back home."

"You don't have to finish it. I bought some ale. It's stronger." Dave grabbed an avocado from the fruit basket on top of the refrigerator, sat down at the table and cut it in half for the salad.

"What the hell's that thing?" Jake asked. "It looks like a rotten ol' pear."

"It's an avocado. They're grown in Mexico and California and shipped here in those big semi trucks we saw on the highway."

Jake cocked his head and listened intently. He leaned toward the window and looked at the sky. "What's that noise? Sounds like thunder, but there ain't no big clouds up there."   .

Dave and Jim looked at each other as they became aware of a jet overhead. Being right under the flight path from Denver to California, they'd become use to the noise and rarely noticed it. The roar suddenly became an irritant for both of them.

Jim sighed. "That's an airplane."

"A what?" Jake asked.

Dave set the avocado down and headed for the door. "Come on, I'll show you." Pretending Jake came from the past was a kick.

Jake followed Dave outside. Dave pointed to the tiny silver object gliding across the sky far above them. It glistened from the setting sun and left a pink trail far past the ridge to the west.

"What is it?" Jake asked. He gaped.

"It's an airplane. It carries people from one city to another."

"There's *people* up there?" Jake stared. "How'd they get up there?" He pointed to the west. "An' how's it makin' that long, skinny cloud?"

"That's a vapor trail. It's kind of like a cloud."

Jake frowned. "That thunder ain't comin' from that thing. It's comin' from way over there."

"It's hard to explain, Jake. The plane is going faster than sound. When Wiley gets better, we'll take you to the Denver airport. You'll be able to watch the planes take off and land."

Jim appeared at the window. "Jake, the water's hot. Do you want to take your bath in here or out there?"

Tearing his eyes away from the disappearing jet, Jake pointed to the cliff. "I wanna take me a bath out here an' look down on Wiley an' me's cabin."

Dave carried the oval, galvanized tub to the edge of the cliff and clunked it down on the flat rocks. "Is this where you want it?"

"Sure is. Now I can take a bath in the sunset an' think how Wiley, Joe an' me built our cabin." Jake peered at the ruins and shook his head. "Seems so long ago we done it."

Crimson puffball clouds, some connected by the widening vapor trail, caught the last of the sun's rays. Jake gazed at the sky. "This here's Wiley an' me's first night in nine...nineteen ninety-three. I hope like hell Wiley's better tomorrow an' can talk to me." He lowered his eyes to the rotting logs below. "I miss Wiley somethin' terrible." He glanced at Dave with misty eyes, then looked away.

After Jim poured boiling water into the tub and mixed it with cold, Jake stripped off his boots and clothes and dropped them in a heap on the rocks. He gingerly stepped into the tub, held his balls and carefully lowered himself into the steaming water.

Jim and Dave ambled to the cabin. They fumbled at finishing dinner and found each other silently staring out the window at the god-like man sitting in the tub on the edge of the cliff. Between occasional pops and hisses of water droplets exploding into steam on the cast iron stove-top, the only other sound was Wiley's labored breathing in the next room.

Jim whispered softly, "Dave, what's happening? Who are these men?" He reached across the table and grabbed Dave's arm. "People don't travel through time." Forcing himself to remain positive, he added, "Who knows, like you said, I may have found my first client. Did you find out anything else when you were talking to Jake?"

"Nothing other than he believes they were transported here by something in the rawhide bag hanging around his neck." Dave pointed out the window. "Look, he didn't even take it off to take a bath."

They watched as Jake flung the rawhide bag over his shoulder before he washed his chest.

"He's one of the most gorgeous men I've ever seen," Dave whispered. "And Wiley's the other one. They're true men. Not like the overweight, wife-pecked wimps with matching suits that seem to be everywhere nowadays." He sighed. "All men do now is sit in front of the TV watching sports, trying to spark some life into their dried-up masculinity."

Jim raised an eyebrow. "Are you on your soapbox again?"

Dave shrugged and looked out the window at Jake. "If they are from the past, they grew them big and beautiful then." He turned toward Jim, forced a wide grin and squinted his eyes. "It must be because they had to use their bodies to work, not just their swollen brains, like now."

"David, we're not in Denver any more," Jim whispered loudly. "Can't you stop your cynicism? And you're talking like you believe Jake and Wiley really are from eighteen eighty-six."

"It's easier than thinking Jake's crazy, because I know he's not. He's a country boy. I'll bet he only went to school for a few years. He's wonderful. So innocent. I like Wiley too, but I haven't talked to him." He looked back at the naked man outside. "Did Wiley talk to you?"

Jim's eyes followed Dave's. "A little. Wiley was in pain, but from what I could tell, he seems to be a nice guy. Even if he's not a nice guy, he's definitely the most sexy man I've ever seen." He shrugged apologetically to Dave. "Sorry, but I have to be truthful."

Dave chuckled. "Hey, I'm in total agreement. A four-way with them would be the closest thing to heaven I could imagine."

The movement of Jake splashing himself with water seduced their eyes again.

Jim sighed. "I think Jake's yelling in the truck was getting on Wiley's nerves."

"Jake gets so emotional." Dave turned to Jim. "We'll have to watch what we say to him. He gets offended real easy. I thought he was going to beat me to a pulp earlier. I'm glad you came outside when you did. He told me if I'd been bigger, he would have hit me in the mouth."

"Did you call him a liar?"

"Well, not exactly. I asked him to tell the truth where they were really from."

Jim touched Dave's arm when he saw Jake stand up in the tub and reach for the towel. The mountains to the south had become black against the dull, blue-gray sky. The two men stared at Jake's muscular silhouette as he dried himself.

Jake stood for a few moments with his back to the cabin, gazing at the scattered lights in the distance. They made him feel closed in, and he longed for his time when there were no lights anywhere. He shivered when he wondered if he'd ever see his and Wiley's time again, then flung the towel over his shoulder. After he emptied the tub over the cliff and watched the rushing water disappear, he picked up his clothes and boots and headed toward the cabin. When he spotted Dave and Jim watching him, he smiled and waved.

Jake walked into the kitchen stark naked except for the towel over his shoulder and the rawhide bag around his neck. "Where can I put these here smelly clothes?"

Jim snapped out of his stare. "Uh...just put them on the washing machine." He pointed to the wringer washer in the corner.

Jake looked at it, shook his head and plopped his clothes down on the flat lid of the machine. His pants made a heavy thudding sound.

"I ain't got no other clothes. Chief Eagle Rising said what we had on back there, we'd have on here, an' he weren't funnin'."

Dave sighed. "I guess you'll just have to go around naked." Seeing Jake's startled expression, he added, "Just kidding. We may have some sweat pants that will fit you. Jim, remember those extra-large sweats I got for Christmas last year from Aunt Nattie? Where are they?"

"I'll get them." As Jim left the kitchen, he purposely brushed the back of his hand across Jake's smooth, firm butt. Dave heard him mutter, "I'll need a pace-maker before long."

"Can I be arrested fer bein' naked?" Jake asked Dave.

"What gave you that idea?"

"You're lookin' at me like I done somethin' wrong."

"Jim and I aren't use to seeing a big muscular man standing naked only a few feet away. To tell the truth, we like looking at naked men, especially ones like you." He hoped Jake wouldn't get angry about that comment.

"You sound like Wiley an' me. Bill said lots'a partners is like us. He said even Sheriff Cline sometimes likes a man. Most people don't say nothin' about it, 'cept for Reverend Quick, an' nobody listens to him."

When Jim returned to the kitchen, he handed the sweats to Jake. "This part slips over your head, and these are the pants."

After Jake struggled into the dark blue sweats, he stepped under the bright kitchen light and looked down at himself. "These're sort'a like broken long johns." Seeing his privates perfectly outlined, he added, "Bein' it's you an' not Winder, I'll wear these here tight pants."

"You'll only have to wear them tonight," Jim said. "I'll wash your clothes in the morning. It should be hot tomorrow, and they'll dry fast." As Jim looked at the tight-fitting sweats on Jake's massive body, he hoped somehow the washing machine would break down overnight.

A loud popping and hissing noise startled them. The water, boiling in the second pot, spilled over the rim onto the hot cast iron stove top, turning instantly to steam.

"We can give Wiley a sponge bath now," Jim commented. "Jake, can you undress him? I think he'll feel better in the morning if he's clean."

Jake walked into the living room. He stood beside the daybed and looked down at Wiley for a few moments. When Dave came into the room, he turned toward him. "I sure hope Wiley's better in the mornin' an' can talk to me."

Dave slid his hand on Jake's shoulder. "He'll be fine. Let's get his clothes off."

They had just removed Wiley's long johns when Jim came in with the basin of hot water. He stared at Wiley's naked body for a moment, then knelt beside the bed, dipped a washcloth into the water and rubbed it on a bar of soap.

As Jim began sponging Wiley's chest, Jake grabbed the cloth out of his hand. "I'll do that. I gotta know Wiley's still with me, an' since he ain't been talkin' much, I gotta be touchin' him."

Reluctantly, Jim said, "That's an excellent idea. Don't forget to wash behind his ears, and the doctor said not to get his bandages wet." He got to his feet. "Dave, let's leave them alone and finish getting dinner."

A while later, Dave glanced into the living room and saw Jake draped over Wiley with his face buried in Wiley's hairy chest.

The three men sat down to a meal of hamburgers, boiled potatoes in brown gravy and spinach. Jake devoured four hamburgers and two huge helpings of potatoes and gravy. At first, he eyed the spinach with suspicion, then spooned a small dab into his plate.

"This here spinach ain't hard no more. How'd you do that?"

"I cooked it," Jim answered. "It was frozen when you felt it, but after it's cooked, it's just like fresh spinach."

"Not quite," Dave grumbled. "Jake, freezing helps to preserve food for about six months, but no matter what they say, it's never as good as fresh."

Jake poked his fork at the spinach. "This here spinach looks like that green stuff floatin' on the river back home." He tasted it, then spit it into his plate. "Kind'a tastes like it, too."

After the dishes were done, Dave pulled out the sofa bed in the living room and made it up for Jake.

Watching Dave tuck in the top sheet, Jake asked, "Is this here thing gonna fold me up while I'm sleepin'?"

Dave laughed. "There's no possible way it can fold up with you on it."

After downing a small glass of bourbon and making a fast trip to the outhouse, Jake stretched out on the bed and fell asleep within minutes.

Dave called Winnie inside, and they joined Jim in the loft.

CHAPTER 6

Wiley opened his eyes. He could tell the fever had broken, and the effects of the liquor had worn off. Why didn't his leg throb? He turned his head and saw the night sky through a window so large it allowed the faint starlight to soften the blackness of the room.

Wiley pulled the blanket to his chin, feeling colder than he usually did in their own cabin with its thick log walls and warm rock cliff.

Where was he?

Vague happenings of the day before began filtering into his mind. Suddenly, he was aware of the sound of someone rolling over in a bed close by and two persons lightly snoring above him.

Wiley raised his head and turned it toward the restless sleeper across the room. He could barely make out the end of the bed.

"Jake?" Wiley whispered.

No answer.

He whispered louder. "Jake?"

"Wiley?" Jake rasped. He threw back the blankets. "Is that you, Wiley?"

"It's me."

Jake rushed to the daybed and scooped Wiley into his arms. "I been terrible worried about you, Wiley."

With great effort, Wiley slung his right arm over Jake's back, then slid his hand to Jake's head and pulled him down until their lips met.

Jake melted onto Wiley's body.

After their lengthy and arousing embrace, Wiley asked, "Where are we? I seem to remember two men...and a strange wagon. Was I at a doctor's?"

Jake pulled back and whispered loudly, "You won't believe what's happened, Wiley. We're in another Time. Leastways, Dave

said it was nineteen ninety-three. I been scared, an' I missed you."
He kissed Wiley again.

"It's strange here, Wiley." Jake glanced at the window. "There's
fences an' roads all over Miss Castille's ranch an' cabins ever'where.
An' there's big things called semees 'er somethin' rushin' down
black roads, an' big red bugs with people in 'em." Jake slid his hand
over Wiley's chest. "I washed you all over so you wouldn't get
arrested, an' we went to Fairplay an' back in three hours."

"Jake, was I at a doctor's?"

"Sure was. An' the doc gave you booze in your butt. He used
long pointy things."

"I don't think it was booze," Wiley whispered. "I heard about
inoculations in school. It's a new practice from the war." He grabbed
Jake's arm. "Help me to your bed. I want to be next to you."

Wiley held his wounded leg and gently lowered his left foot to
the floor. After helping him sit up, Jake slid his arms around Wiley's
waist and hefted him to his feet. He ducked his head under Wiley's
left arm, and they slowly hobbled toward the bed. Halfway there,
Wiley became dizzy and nearly fainted. Jake quickly slid one arm
down, picked Wiley up, carried him the last few feet and placed him
in the warm spot where he'd been sleeping. He kissed Wiley's
forehead, then rushed to the daybed and grabbed the blankets and
pillow. After covering Wiley with two more blankets, Jake crawled
under the covers, nestled his naked body against Wiley and slid his
arm across his chest.

* * *

Long before Jake or Wiley woke up, Jim started a fire in the
cookstove to heat water to wash their clothes. When he picked up
Jake's pants, their weight surprised him, and he noticed both front
pockets bulged. Reaching into one, Jim felt a pile of small coins. He
grabbed a few and inspected them. Gold? He dumped the coins back
into the pocket, except for one, then quietly went outside to where
Dave stood tossing the tennis ball for Winnie.

"Dave, you know coins. Look at this."

After Dave carefully inspected the dime-size coin, he yelled, "A
gold dollar! Where'd you get this? This coin's worth a thousand

bucks! Maybe more since it was minted in eighteen eighty-six, and it's in perfect condition."

Jim looked closely at the coin. "Jake's pants pockets are filled with them."

Dave gasped. "There's a coin collector's convention in Denver this week. I wonder if they stole the coins and that's how Wiley got shot. Maybe that's why Jake made up the story about being from eighteen eighty-six?"

Jim frowned at him. "Why would they drive clear up here, then climb to the old cabin to find a doctor?" Jim shook his head. "Even if there was a doctor down there, Wiley couldn't have made it that far, and we would have heard them when we were sitting on the edge of the cliff."

Dave dropped the coin into Jim's hand. "I'm sure you're right, and it sounds like you're beginning to believe they are from eighteen eighty-six." He glanced at his watch. "It's two minutes to eight. I'm going to sit in the car and listen to the news on the radio. If there was a robbery at the convention and anyone got shot, it would make the news." He started toward the carport, then turned to Jim. "I just have to be sure."

After watching Dave walk to the carport, Jim briefly inspected the coin in the sunlight before returning to the cabin. Was he beginning to believe Jake's story? He wasn't sure, but nothing else could explain Jake's complete ignorance about modern things.

Twenty minutes later, Dave tiptoed into the kitchen and slid into a chair. "There was plenty about the convention, but nothing about a robbery." He sighed. "Thank God for that."

Jim put the lid on the washer and sat down at the table. In front of him were ten stacks of gold coins. "There's a hundred of them, and they all look new."

In a slow, serious tone, and staring at the coins, Dave said, "Jim, we are looking at a hundred...thousand...dollars." He picked up a coin and frowned as he turned it over and over. "They're uncirculated." He held it out to Jim. "There's not a scratch on any of them, and there weren't many minted that year."

Jim suddenly noticed Jake standing in the kitchen doorway tugging on the bottom part of his sweats. He'd gotten them up to his thighs but couldn't get them higher.

When Dave heard Jim snicker, he wheeled around and saw Jake's dick six inches from his face.

"Oh!" Dave stared at it for a moment, then gained control of himself, turned his head and sighed at Jim's knowing grin.

Still pulling at the sweats, Jake growled, "How the hell do I get these damn things on?"

Jim wiped away a smile with his hand. "You've got them on inside-out. You'll have to take them off and pull the legs through."

They watched Jake strip off the bulky blue pants, stand buck naked except for the rawhide bag nestled between his huge pecs and fumble with the sweats until they were a tight ball.

Dave chuckled and held out his hand. "Let me do it." As he worked at the knotted material, he said, "I'm glad you're up. Jim's washing your clothes. Those coins on the table were in your pockets. Where'd you get them?"

Jake grinned. "Them're the dollars I won in the wagon race at Ben Harrington's place. I had me a hunnert'n fifty of 'em, but we gave fifty of 'em to Thunder Joe." He yawned and stretched. "What time is it anyway?"

Jim forced his eyes away from Jake's body and glanced at the clock. "Eight-thirty."

"Damn!" Jake shouted. "I ain't never slept so late my whole life!" He grinned when Dave handed him the sweat pants.

"The string-tie goes to the front," Jim reminded him.

After Jake successfully put them on, he pointed to the coins. "Take somma them dollars fer payin' the doc. How much was it anyway?"

"It was fifty dollars," Jim answered. "But don't worry about it."

"Fifty dollars!" Jake yelled. "That's more'n a month's wages!" He slumped into a chair and shook his head. "But it was worth it. I think Wiley's gettin' better. He woke me up last night, an' I got him in bed with me." He slid several stacks of coins toward Jim. "These're yours. Don't know if it's enough."

"We can't take those," Jim said. "Dave said all these coins are worth a hundred-thousand dollars."

"That ain't no hunnert-thousand dollars. It's only a hunnert. Even I know that."

"This is nineteen ninety-three," Dave said. "Gold dollars in that condition are worth a thousand dollars apiece. We can't take even one of them."

Jake stared at the coins. "Why not?"

"What's all this talk of a hundred-thousand dollars?" Wiley rasped from the other room. "What's happening?"

Jake ran into the living room. "Wiley, you're awake! How do you feel, Wiley?"

"My leg aches, but I think my fever's broken."

The two men embraced.

Jim went into the room and sat on the end of the bed. Dave followed and stood beside him.

"Wiley, do you remember who we are or anything that happened yesterday?" Jim asked.

Wiley flickered a smile. "A little. I remember riding in a strange wagon, and getting yelled at about taking laudanum." Wiley pulled himself up, leaned on his elbow and singled Jim out. "You were with me in that wagon." He smiled and nodded at Dave standing behind Jim. "Who are you men?"

"I'm Jim, this is Dave. We live here. We found you and Jake down the hill yesterday and drove you to the doctor. He gave you penicillin and tetanus shots, also pain pills. Do you need one?"

"Yes. My leg aches quite a lot. But will it knock me out? I don't want to sleep all day. And what is penicillin and tetanus?" Wiley smiled weakly. "Sorry, my mind is filled with questions."

"Sleep is good for you," Jim said. "Especially since you've lost so much blood. To answer your question, penicillin is a drug that kills infection. It was called a miracle drug when it was discovered in the late twenties." He gave Wiley a once-over glance. "Glad to say, it looks like it's working. A tetanus shot keeps you from getting lockjaw."

"We bought you some grape juice," Dave chimed in. "Doctor's orders. It'll help your body build up blood. You can take your pain pill and penicillin with a glass of juice."

As Dave turned toward the kitchen, a sudden gust of wind outside caused him to rush to the window. After the breeze died down, he sighed and turned toward Jake. "Do you remember a strong wind yesterday just before you...uh, showed up here?"

"Sure. Wiley an' me was on Pinkel Rock an'...

"Pinnacle Rock," Wiley said.

"Uh...yeah. The wind was blowin' stronger'n a hog fart. That's when Winder shot Wiley in the leg."

Realizing Dave had forgotten about getting the grape juice and pills, Jim frowned at him and went into the kitchen.

"Yesterday, you said Chief Eagle Rising was in your cabin." Dave said. "What about the wind then?"

"No. Weren't no wind then. It'd stopped." Jake rubbed his eyes, then snapped his head up. "Wait! When I saw the feather on the floor an' tried gettin' it, stuff started blowin' around inside. I grabbed Wiley to pertect him, an' lights started flashin'. After that, there was nothin'...'til your dog was barkin' at us." Jake glanced at Wiley, then at the floor. He felt cold and scared. He hadn't had time to pick up the feather and, without it, they were trapped here. Forever!

Realizing Jake wasn't going to continue, Dave said, "Just before Winnie heard you down the hill, we had the strongest gust of wind we've ever experienced here. I thought the cabin would blow over."

Wiley didn't want to hear any more about it. The thought of traveling in time made his gut tighten. He waved his hand toward the kitchen. "What were you saying about Jake's gold dollars?"

"Wiley, that's a hundred-thousand dollars sitting in there," Dave said. "You and Jake are rich."

The news wasn't enough to shake the dread Jake felt about leaving the feather on the cabin floor. It was his fault they were trapped here. How would he ever explain to Wiley?

"Why did you tell us how much the coins are worth?" Wiley asked.

"Why wouldn't we?" Jim said as he walked into the living room holding a glass of grape juice and four pills. "Here's your pain pill, your penicillin pill and two aspirin."

Wiley peered into Jim's open hand, eyed the grape juice, and said, "You could have told us the coins were worth a dollar and kept the ones Jake offered."

"That wouldn't be right," Jim said. "We'd never do that. Especially not to you guys."

Jake helped Wiley sit up to take his pills.

Wiley popped the pills into his mouth and washed them down with grape juice. He handed the empty glass to Jim. "That's good juice. It tastes clean."

* * *

"Don't get nowheres near me with that thing!" Jake yelled as Jim started up the chain saw. "That thing's gotta be meaner'n them gators Ma said're livin' down south."

While Wiley slept, Jake helped Dave split wood as Jim sawed up logs. After they had cut and split a cord of wood, Dave and Jim rested on a log and watched Jake split another fifteen foot-long sections of dead trees they'd gathered earlier that summer.

After the wood-shack was filled to the roof and the pile outside it was half as big as the structure, Jake stopped and sat beside Jim. He extended his legs in front of him and pulled at the sweats, adjusting the crotch.

"When're my clothes gonna be dry?"

"I'll check." Jim got up and headed to the clothesline stretching between two trees. "They're dry." He took them down and returned to the log. He handed Jake his pants and held up the shirt. "Do you want me to iron your shirt?"

"Ain't no need," Jake said. "It fits so tight all them wrinkles get flattened out soon's I put it on." He pulled off the sweatshirt, handed it to Dave, then put on his stiff, wrinkled shirt. It stretched taut over his huge chest and arms. After he removed his boots, Jake peeled down the sweat pants, pulled on his Levis, then sat on the log to put his boots back on.

"Sure is good to be in real clothes," Jake said. He pointed at the sweats. "Them things're made all wrong. They're broken in the middle, an' they're too damn tight. They ain't got no piss'r shit holes in 'em, neither."

Jim laughed. "They aren't underwear. They're called sweat clothes. People use them when they're running or working out."

"Who's after 'em?" Jake asked.

Dave squinted. "Who's after who?"

"Them people Jim said was runnin'. Who they runnin' from? An' if somebody's after 'em, how do they have time to squeeze into them things before they get caught?"

Realizing Jake was dead serious, Dave squelched his laughter. "They're not running from anyone. People run for exercise and when they do, they usually wear shorts, or sweats when it's cold.

"We'll have to go to Fairplay and get Wiley some new clothes," Jim said. "I cut off the other leg of his pants, and he can use them as shorts until his leg is better, but he'll need other clothes later. Jake, do you know what size Wiley wears?"

"Same as me. I could go, too, an' try on clothes for him. I could get me some, too."

"Jim, I think we'd better go to Buena Vista. If the doctor told the sheriff about Wiley's leg, he may be looking for us in Fairplay. We'd have a hard time explaining any of this. Especially to him."

"That's a good idea. Let's go soon. Jake only has the clothes he's wearing." Jim smiled at Jake. "We'll pay for the clothes. You can't use those gold coins to buy anything. Personally, I think you should hide them."

Jake got to his feet. "I gotta use the shit house." He ambled down the hill to the small building that leaned slightly to the west and had a crescent moon on the door.

"I'll bring you some toilet paper," Dave said as he ran to the cabin.

Shortly, Dave knocked on the outhouse door. When it opened a crack, he held out a new roll of toilet tissue.

Jake opened the door a little wider, grabbed the roll, stared at it for a moment, then let the door slam.

After spending a few minutes helping Dave add to the kindling pile by picking up twigs and pieces of bark, Jim went inside to fix lunch. Dave was still on his hands and knees when Jake walked up to him.

"That thing you gived me to wipe my butt don't work," Jake said grumpily.

Dave looked up at him. "Why?"

"Hell, after I stuck two fingers in the hole so I could hang on to it, the damn thing was too big to wipe anythin' off. Then it started fallin' apart in a big pile on the floor. I watched 'til it got the size of a corn cob an' then it fit."

* * *

Wiley woke up in time for lunch, and Jim served everyone in the living room to keep the bed-ridden man company. After the dishes were washed, Jake and Wiley began telling accounts of the many things they'd encountered during their short time as partners. They talked all afternoon and well into the evening, stopping only when someone needed to use the outhouse. Jim had given Wiley a pee-bottle with a cranberry juice label.

Fascinated by the things he was hearing, Dave realized neither man could have made up these stories, especially since some of the people mentioned were named in the old newspaper article he'd read in the "Alma Gazette" office several months ago.

Dave broke into the conversation. "Wiley, what date was it when you were last in eighteen eighty-six?"

Wiley thought a minute. "It was Sunday, June sixth. Why?"

Dave ran to a bookshelf, grabbed the World Almanac and paged through it.

"What's wrong?" Jim asked.

Dave grinned. "I've got two ideas going on at the same time." He looked at Jim. "Remember that article I told you about from the 'Alma Gazette'? The one that mentioned the two missing men? Well, I think the date of the article was sometime in June of eighteen eighty-six." He looked at Jake and Wiley. "According to that article, Thunder Joe led a search party. I think that article was about you."

He looked at the Almanac, searched for a page, read for a moment, then his face brightened. "I don't believe it! The years eighteen eighty-six and nineteen ninety-three both use the same calendar. That means you didn't gain or lose any time when you came here. Yesterday was Sunday, June sixth, in this Time, too, and if you would have come any earlier, Jim and I wouldn't have been here to get Wiley to the doctor." Dave closed his eyes and shook his head. "I don't believe this is happening."

Jake jumped up and ran outside, letting the screen door slam.

Jim leaped to his feet and saw Jake disappear down the slope toward the cabin ruins.

"Jim, could you see what's wrong with Jake?" Wiley asked. "He looked upset."

"Sure." Jim left the cabin and headed down the hill. He found Jake sitting on one of the rotting logs with his face buried in his hands. He approached slowly and asked, "Jake, are you okay?"

"No, I ain't," Jake mumbled into his hands. "Wiley an' me can't never go home, an' it's all my fault." He snapped his head up and looked at Jim with teary eyes. "You can't never tell Wiley or he'll call me dummer'n hog shit."

Jim sat on the log beside Jake and put his arm across his shoulders. "I don't understand. Why can't you go home?"

"Cuz I ain't got the golden feather Chief Eagle Rising gived me to get here." Jake pulled out the rawhide bag and held it toward Jim. "I got the bag, but the feather fell on the floor somehow, an' I didn't have time to get it before the wind started blowin' in the cabin." Jake let the bag drop to his chest and hung his head. "Chief Eagle Rising said if I lose this here bag or the feather, we hafta stay in this here Time forever." He looked around at the spongy, moss-covered logs. "An' Wiley'n me's cabin ain't no more good, neither."

Jim patted Jake's shoulder. "It's not so bad in this Time." He groped for words. "You'll get used to it after awhile."

"Chief Eagle Rising said fer me to beware of this here place. That's why I put on Wiley an' me's guns."

"I'm sure you won't need them here." Jim tugged on Jake's sleeve. "Let's go back inside. Wiley's worried about you. If you don't want him to know you lost the feather, you'd better not let him see you upset."

"Guess yer right." Jake got to his feet, wiped his eyes and slowly followed Jim up the hill.

"What's wrong, Jake?" Wiley asked the moment Jake came through the door. "The way you ran out of here I thought someone had said something to offend you."

Jake sat down on the bed beside Wiley but couldn't look him in the eyes. "Got homesick," he said softly. "We only spent a few days in our new cabin, an' now it's already rotten."

* * *

After a huge dinner of fried chicken and mashed potatoes covered with Dave's milk gravy, and a rare steak for Wiley, they gathered around Wiley's bed and he continued talking. Jake hardly said a word.

It was fully dark when Jake suddenly stood up, stretched and went outside. He'd been outside only a short time when he yelled, "Fire! There's a damn fire comin'!"

Out of breath, Jake rushed in the door. "It's far away, now, but it'll be here soon! The whole range is on fire!"

"Oh, my God!" Jim yelled as he ran out the door at Jake's heels. "Where is it?"

Jake pointed east toward the distant Tarryall Mountains. "See! The whole sky's lit up orange!"

Jim saw the light to the northeast which silhouetted the Tarryalls. The glow got dimmer as his gaze swept south along the range of mountains, then it became somewhat brighter. It was a familiar sight at night.

"That's not a fire, Jake. And thank God it's not." Jim pointed to the northeast. "That's the lights of Denver." Then he pointed farther south. "Off there's the lights of Colorado Springs."

"Damn! What makes 'em so bright? Them're a hunnert miles away!"

"Denver's a big city...almost two million people. There's so many lights we can see them a hundred miles away. They're especially bright tonight because it's cloudy over the Tarryalls." Jim pondered what he'd just said, and it filled him with dread. Denver was encroaching on South Park.

As they entered the cabin, Jake shook his head. "Two million people? It must be the biggest city in the whole world!"

"Is it a fire?" Wiley asked.

"Damn, Wiley..."

"Don't cuss, *Jack*," Wiley said, smiling.

Jake snapped his mouth shut, then said, "Wiley, what I said was a fire is the lights'a Denver. Dave said there's two million people livin' there."

"Good God!" Wiley exclaimed.

"Don't you be cussin' neither, *Willy*," Jake razzed. He lightly punched Wiley on the shoulder.

"When you get better, Wiley," Dave said, "Jim and I'll take you both to Denver. We can stay in our house there for a week or so and show you around."

"I don't know if I'll ever be ready to meet head on with two million people," Wiley said. "Philadelphia only had five-hundred thousand when I left there, and it seemed huge."

To change the subject not wanting Jake to question him about Philadelphia, Wiley looked at Jim and Dave. "Jake and I have been doing all the talking. Where did you two meet?"

"We met in a bar also," Jim said. "Within a week, we'd rented an apartment together. Two months later, we bought this land.

"I'm from Milwaukee, and Dave was born in Denver," Jim continued. "We've been together for five years. Dave was in a monastery for three years after high school, and he just resigned from an accounting firm. I used to be a teacher. I taught Native Americans in southern Utah, and I'm trying to build my counseling practice."

"What's a Native American?" Wiley asked.

"That's what we call Indians now," Jim said.

Wiley pondered the idea. "Native American? I like that. Grandpa Grey Feather would like that, also." He rubbed his beard. "Native American. I like that."

"I like it too, Wiley," Dave said, "but the word Indian always makes me think of the freedom of the wind."

Dave and Jim talked about their life together until Wiley fell asleep and Jake's eyelids drooped. A half hour later, all the lights were out, and the only sound in the cabin was the rhythmic breathing of four men and a dog.

CHAPTER 7

Wiley became stronger during the week as his wounds began healing. With the help of Jim's old crutches, he learned to hobble around the cabin. On Thursday, despite Jake's constant hovering, he headed outside on his own.

"Jake, I want to do it by myself," Wiley said, chuckling under his breath. "If you keep holding my arm, I'll never learn how to use these crutches."

Jake snatched his hand back, but extended both arms around Wiley, never quite touching him, and shuffled his feet to keep pace behind his blood brother.

On purpose, Wiley stopped abruptly and braced himself. Just as he'd hoped, Jake plowed into his back.

"Damn," Jake said as he fell over Wiley's shoulders. "Wiley, why'd you stop like that?"

Wiley laughed. "I got scared and needed your arms around me."

"Hell, you ain't scared'a nothin', not even Bingsly."

Wiley turned his head and kissed Jake on the nose. "We don't have to be worried about Billingsly. He's been dead for years in the Time we're in now."

Wiley raised his head and sniffed the air. "I don't think I want to stay in this Time very long. The air's been fouled. But the scientific advancements are astounding." He pointed to the truck. "Dave said that runs on gasoline...made from oil. And now there are cabinets that make ice, lights in glass tubes and boxes that make music."

"Wiley, I gotta tell..."

Wiley turned and pointed to the rock pinnacle fifty feet away. "And it's amazing what a hundred years did to that rock. The huge wedge we used to climb to the top has now slid down the hill."

"Wiley?"

62

"Er...what, Jake?"

"Wiley...we can't go back."

"Go back where?"

"Where we come from. Our time." Jake shuddered and held Wiley tighter. "Before we come here, I saw the golden feather on the floor. I tried gettin' it, but the wind started blowin' somethin' terrible, an' I had to pertect you. Chief Eagle Rising said I gotta have the bag an' the feather to go back, an' all I got is the bag."

Wiley felt lightheaded. It was one thing to realize they were a hundred and seven years in the future, but the thought of having to stay here filled him with dread. He turned his head, saw Jake's teary eyes and knew he was blaming himself. Letting the crutches fall, Wiley balanced himself on his right foot, slid his arms around Jake and pulled him close.

As bravely as he could, Wiley whispered, "As long as we're together, I don't care where we are."

* * *

Wiley became more proficient on the crutches and found himself wanting Jake beside him all the time. They spent most of their time outside, either taking short walks or sitting in the plastic chairs on the cliff gazing at the vastness to the south. He didn't bring up the subject of being stranded in the twentieth century again, not wanting to see Jake's downcast expression.

On Friday, Jim and Dave decided to drive the forty miles to Buena Vista. Not only did Jake and Wiley need clothes, but food supplies were getting low. Jake had to go with them, but Wiley decided he didn't want to sit in the car the entire day with his leg aching and felt sure he could fend for himself.

Jake talked incessantly the entire trip to the town on the Arkansas river, exclaiming over everything he saw. As they entered a clothing store on Buena Vista's main street, he stopped in front of a mannequin dressed in a blue ski outfit, complete with boots and goggles.

"Who wears them things?"

"Skiers," Jim said.

"What does skiers do to be all dressed up funny like that?"

"They slide down the sides of mountains in the snow on skis." Jim pointed to a large poster of Breckenridge showing several skiers standing in front of a chair lift. "Those long things are skis. You put them on your feet and slide down the snow. I'm sure they had skis in the eighteen hundreds." He glanced at Dave. "Didn't they?"

Dave shrugged. "I don't know. You're asking the wrong person." He looked at Jake. "I don't mind skiing, it's all the stupid hype in the ski areas that I don't like."

"I ain't never seen them ski things before." Jake glanced at Jim. "What happens when you hit a tree with them things on?"

Jim laughed. "We try not to hit trees."

Frowning at the display, Dave growled, "Either they haven't taken this down from last winter or they're starting early. Pretty soon, Christmas lights and ski clothes will be out all year."

As they walked through the women's section of the store, Jake scanned the clothes. "What're we doin' in a women's store? I thought we was buyin' us clothes?"

Jim pointed to the far corner. "The men's department is over there."

"Women's stuff takes up most'a this here store. Do they wear all this stuff?" He grabbed at a bra. "What the hell's this thing for?"

"That's a bra," Jim said. "Women wear them on their breasts."

"Women wear eggs on their legs an' these here things on their tits?" Jake pulled the bra off the rack and held it up. "This looks like the slingshot Stinky an' me made when I was little. We used it to hit squirrels an' stuff." He stretched the bra and aimed it at a mannequin in a slip. "From here, I could knock the tits off'a that there statue."

In the men's department, Jake stroked the silk ties, peered into the sleeve of a short sleeve shirt and laughed, then grabbed a pair of sweats and held them toward Dave.

"These are them broken underwear with no piss'r shit holes."

"Remember, Jake? They're called sweat pants." Dave noticed two heads peek up from behind a rack of Hawaiian shirts. Both were women. They saw Jake and casually inched closer.

Jim eyed Jake's waist, grabbed a pair of wide-leg, pleated cotton pants and handed them to him. "Try these on. These are what most men are wearing now." He led Jake to the dressing room, told him what to do in the cubicle, then stood outside the door, just in case.

When Jake stepped out of the fitting room, Dave gasped. "Those make you look like you have child-bearing hips!"

Glaring at himself in the mirror, Jake growled, "These are like wearin' a split ridin' dress!" He turned to Jim. "Do men want to wear dresses now or do they only make women's clothes an' men hafta wear 'em?"

Jake finally settled on four pair of pre-shrunk Levis and six cotton shirts, after insisting he try on each one.

"Are you sure these clothes will fit Wiley?" Dave asked.

"Sure will. Wiley an' me trade clothes." Jake blushed, then flickered a smile. "Once Wiley an' me took all our clothes off while we was ridin'. After ridin' naked for a spell, I put on Wiley's clothes, an' he put on mine. We done that so we could smell each other without havin' to be on the same horse."

"Kinky!" Dave grinned at Jim. "We'll have to try that."

Jim sighed and raised one eyebrow. "First, we have to get some horses."

After picking out a dozen pairs of socks and the same number of briefs, Jake refused to buy the skimpy underwear until he tried one on. He stayed in the dressing room for ten minutes, then strode out wearing only a pair of tan briefs, stretched to the max. Spotting Jim and Dave standing at the cologne counter, he walked briskly toward them.

"How do these here things look?" Jake asked, standing straight and tightening his muscles.

Dave gasped when he saw him. "Jake, you can't walk around the store like that!" After prying his eyes away from the almost see-through briefs Jake had managed to get into, he spied the angry face of a man dog-paddling his portly body through racks of suits trying to get over to them. Several women customers gathered around. One covered her face with her hand, but made sure she could see between her fingers.

When Jim saw the angry-faced man approaching, he grabbed Jake's arm. "Come on, you've got to get back into the dressing room."

Jake pulled away. "What's the matter with ever'body? I ain't done nothin' but try these on. They got them pieces'a statues ever'where with these things on 'em."

Jim put his hand on Jake's arm. "The statues don't have a cock and balls. Look down at yourself."

Jake did, and gasped. "Hell, I didn't know I looked naked!"

"Let's go back to the dressing room." Jim pulled on Jake's arm, and he willingly went with him.

As they hurried through the men's department, they heard whistles and yells from a scattering of customers. Several women rushed over for a better view of Jake's front side, and squealed when they saw it. Jake glared at them.

"What's the meaning of that guy pulling a stunt like that?" the red-faced man yelled when he reached Dave. "I'm the owner of this store, and I might call the police. Is he a friend of yours?"

"Yes, he is," Dave said, trying to remain calm. "He was trying on the briefs and wanted us to see how they fit. He didn't hurt anyone."

"No one's going to walk around my store naked!"

"He wasn't naked," Dave said. "We picked out six shirts and four pairs of Levis. He wanted to try on the underwear. If you want us to leave, that's fine with me. We'll buy the clothes somewhere else. I apologize for my friend. He didn't realize what he was doing."

"I want you gentlemen to leave," the owner shouted. "You can take your business elsewhere. I don't want perverts in my store."

"Well, if they leave, so am I," snapped a shapely woman wearing a tight knit dress the exact color of her shoulder-length red hair. She shoved her shopping cart filled with expensive gowns down the nearest aisle. "That man's the best thing that's happened to this store since before I was born, Dale Rockford, so you be careful who you ask to leave. I think you should hire that gorgeous hunk of man and keep him in the front window all day." She flipped her wrist at the other women. "Don't you girls agree?"

Six women clapped and yelled, "Yes!"

Rockford smiled meekly at Cynthia Havertine. She'd always been the county's wealthiest woman and often spent a thousand dollars at a time in his store. He glanced at her buggy and realized the blue gown draped over the side cost seven hundred dollars.

He chuckled nervously. "Well, I guess there was no harm done." He glared at Dave. "Just make sure he doesn't do it again!"

Cynthia slinked to the portly owner's side, smiled and blinked her eyes. "Thank you, Dale." She spun around suddenly and craned her head toward the men's dressing room. "Now, where is he?"

As Dave watched Cynthia Havertine, he assumed she was wealthy judging from her jewelry. The large opal in her ring flashed sheets of red, green and brilliant purple, and the silver-dollar-size aquamarine cabochon that nestled in her bosom on a gold chain had a pattern of inner flaws resembling a sparkling mountain scene.

"Get ready, girls, here he comes," Cynthia announced.

Dave turned his head and saw Jim emerge from the dressing room with Jake at his heels. Jim's expression of checked laughter contrasted with Jake's frown.

Before they reached the counter, Jim led Jake to the briefs where they exchanged the ones he'd picked out for a much larger size.

When they approached the counter, Dale Rockford blustered to Jake's side, but drooped his shoulders when Cynthia grabbed his arm. Rockford looked at her, then at Jake and said timidly, "Did you decide to buy the briefs?"

Without saying a word, Jake dumped the dozen pair of underwear on the counter. As the woman behind the counter started ringing up the items, Jim plopped his credit card in front of her.

Jake silently glared at each person watching him. When his eyes rested on Cynthia, she immediately walked to him and extended her hand.

"I'm Cynthia Havertine. I'd like to offer you a job as my personal bodyguard." She looked Jake up and down. "I'll pay you twice what you're making now."

Dave spoke up. "He's just visiting. He lives a long way from here."

Ignoring Dave, Cynthia grabbed Jake's arm. "I'm offering you a good job, young man."

Jake jerked his arm away. "Get yer hands off'a me! Wiley's the only one that can touch me! An' I don't want no damn job workin' fer you!"

Recoiling, Cynthia said, "Don't tell me you're gay."

The customers standing around gasped.

"Not now, I ain't gay," Jake snapped. "Right now I'm pretty damn rankled." He glared at Dale Rockford. "Where I'm from nobody cares what you do unless you steal a horse or shoot somebody. You people ain't got no manners." Jake turned to Jim. "Can we go now? I don't like this here store an' these here people."

The onlookers, including Cynthia Havertine, stood in embarrassed silence as they watched Jim sign the credit slip.

"Do you want your carbons?" the clerk asked icily.

"Yes." Jim snatched the carbons from the clerk's hand, tore them into little pieces and dropped them on the counter. He frowned at Dale Rockford, grabbed the huge, candy-apple red plastic bag and headed toward the door. Jake and Dave followed him outside.

Cynthia stared at Jake as he walked to the door. Once the men left, she ran out the back into the parking lot and said a few words to her driver waiting in a maroon Jaguar.

As the three men stood on the sidewalk, Dave patted Jake on the back. "You handled that great. I like what you said to them."

Still frowning, Jake said, "Why'd she ask me if I was gay? She knowed damn well I was rankled."

"In this Time, Jake, the word gay usually refers to men like us...who have male partners. We're not liked by a lot of people, especially not by most Christians."

"But my friend Jesus likes us. If he didn't, I'd never a'met Wiley. Besides, Jesus likes ever'body."

"You know that, and I know that," Dave commented, "But they don't know that. And they don't want to, either. Many people nowadays try to get everyone else to hate anyone different, just like they do. The only way they can spread their hate is by saying God told them to."

"I don't like this here Time," Jake said. He scanned the area. Cars sped both ways in the street, and the curbs were lined with parked vehicles. Several people walking by gave them strange looks. They made Jake feel like he'd done something wrong. He shuddered.

"Now I know why Chief Eagle Rising said to beware of this here place. It makes me kinda sick what's been done." Jake pointed to the mountains towering above the valley. "You can't hardly see them mountains for all the stuff all over, an' there's a stink ever'where. Bein' in this here town with all this noise an' stuff is like livin' at a race track back home."

After they arrived at the car, Jim drove down the main business street. "Now we have to stop at the super market."

"What the hell's a super market?" Jake asked.

"A food store," Dave said. "You'll be amazed at all the different kinds of food there are now."

"After seein' all them clothes in that other store, I don't know what's gonna happen next."

When Jake saw the door swing open as they entered the grocery store, he stopped abruptly and stared at it, blocking the way for a couple behind him.

"Damn! That there door opened by its ownself!"

The couple behind him, steamed at being blocked, shoved Jake aside. He looked startled at them, then hurried to catch up to Dave and Jim. He turned back a few times to watch the door open and close as other people entered the store.

Jake grabbed the edge of the grocery cart. "We gonna fill this up with hay?"

Jim smiled. "No, food."

Jake held onto the cart as Jim pushed it to the produce department. When they reached it, Jake opened his eyes wide. "This is like them summer markets we'd have in Wilmore, only they was outside." He picked up an avocado. "This here's one'a them rotten ol' pears with the big seed like you was fixin' the other day when you showed me them people in the sky."

Dave let Jim do the shopping and followed Jake, answering his constant barrage of questions. Once he looked up and saw Jim heading toward the meat department. He coaxed Jake in that direction.

When they caught up, Jim asked, "What kind of meat do you want this week?"

Jake gasped and picked up a package of t-bone steaks. "Damn. These here pieces'a meat all got that rubbery-glass stuff stuck to 'em." He turned it over. "An' it comes on a plate, too."

Jake bent the corner of the foam tray, and it snapped off inside the plastic. Shocked, he dropped the package and glanced at Jim. "I broke that there plate. They gonna toss me outta here?"

Jim smiled. "Don't worry about it, Jake. We just throw those trays away." He inspected a three-pound rump roast before placing it in the buggy. "We'll have this tomorrow."

Jake scowled at it. "Wiley an' me'd have that piece'a meat gone in five minutes."

Jim stared at the roast, then chose another one the same size and placed it beside the first one.

While Jim answered Jake's questions about the throw-away plates, Dave put two family packs of thick pork chops into the buggy. He also selected four pork roasts, four chickens and five packages of thick, porterhouse steaks for Wiley. He and Jim winked at each other through the crowd of shoppers. They enjoyed having Jake and Wiley around, even though feeding them might cost a fortune.

In the aisles, Dave tried to keep a straight face while answering Jake's questions.

"What's this say?" Jake asked as he pointed to a white plastic bottle.

"All Outdoors."

"Outdoors?" Jake hefted the container. "A bottle of outdoors?" He sloshed the liquid inside. "Hell, it must'a been rainin' when they got it."

Dave laughed. "It's soap. For washing your clothes. They probably named it that because of its smell."

Jake opened the bottle, sniffed it, then screwed his face into a frown. "This don't smell like no outdoors I ever been in. It smells like Madame Bowfrey's place in Wilmore."

When they caught up to Jim, Jake pointed to two items in the buggy. "What's in these here boxes?"

"Scalloped potatoes."

"Taters in boxes? It don't hardly seem possible." He glanced at other things in the buggy. "You *eat* all this stuff?"

Jim laughed. "We must be used to it. I haven't thought about that for years."

They had no wait for a checkout stand.

In line, Dave suddenly turned to Jim. "I'll be right back. I forgot to get napkins. Jake asked me what the word napkin was at a display and I almost grabbed some then, but they were the wrong kind."

"I'll get 'em," Jake volunteered.

Dave pointed to the back of the store. "They're in aisle...ten, I think."

"I saw that napkin word again closer to here," Jake said as he headed toward aisle four. Shortly he came back with box and tossed it into the buggy.

Jim gasped. "Jake, those aren't napkins."

"Sure they are!" He pointed to the box. "Says napkin right there. But I don't know what that, uh...fem-nine word means."

Dave chuckled. "Jake, those are for women." He grabbed the box. "Come on. Let's both get the napkins."

"Women have their own napkins, too?" Jake asked as he tried to keep up with Dave.

"Is that guy a comedian or just plain nuts?" the male checker asked as he watched Jake dodge customers.

Jim smiled. "He's from a real small town."

"Where, on Mars?"

* * *

By himself at the cabin, Wiley felt like a lost soul. Having been a lone wolf most of his life, the feeling of loss with Jake gone was a new experience for him. He didn't like it one bit and hated the thought of Jake being so far away.

He bided his time by looking through the National Geographic and Life magazines on the coffee table. Leafing through them made him acutely aware of the different Time he and Jake were in now. He marveled at the colored photographs from all parts of the world and was startled by pictures of punk rockers. He read some of the article, first thinking it was about wild natives in Africa, and gasped when he found out these people with colored hair and bizarre clothes actually lived in the United States.

Dave had shown him how to use the stereo, and he leaned over and switched it on. He listened to the noon news and was stunned by the reports of flooding in the central United States and an earthquake that had rocked Japan. These disasters happened yesterday! But when he began hearing about gang murders, drive-by shootings, the rise in suicides, and parents maiming or killing their children by shaking or beating them to death, Wiley shuddered and turned the dial. The speakers suddenly blasted loud music and singing. At least, Wiley thought it was singing but wasn't sure it was music.

He turned the dial, heard more talking, and listened to a man yelling that homosexuals should be killed in the Lord's name. Were homosexuals Indians?

Wiley turned off the stereo.

He lifted himself up by the crutches, struggled outside to the edge of the cliff and sat in a plastic chair. As he gazed toward the south, he couldn't get the news reports out of his mind. So many in this Time seemed vicious and hateful. He worried about Jake and hoped Dave and Jim would protect him from people so eager to hate and kill. He cringed when he remembered that, because of Jake, he hadn't carried out the job he'd been paid to do...in eighteen eighty-six.

Wiley sighed and shook his head. Dave had said it was now illegal to carry a gun. At least that was some comfort. He didn't feel anyone in this Time could be trusted with a gun.

* * *

Several hours later, Winnie's barking woke Wiley. He carefully slid his legs over the daybed, and with the help of the crutches, struggled to his feet. He sighed and slid his fingers through the hair on his bare chest when he saw the Honda pull into the carport.

Once inside, Jake dropped his bundles on the kitchen table, rushed into the living room and pulled Wiley into his arms.

Dave and Jim quickly stashed the perishables in the frig, called Winnie and the three started walking to Brandon Lake, a four-mile round trip.

After they had walked a quarter mile, Dave broke the silence. "I've never seen two people as much in love with each other as Jake and Wiley are. Until now, I've been fantasizing having sex with them, especially Jake. But now, I couldn't do it or even try. They're so much in love and so perfectly matched, I'd rather never see them again than do anything to come between them."

Jim stopped and touched Dave's arm. "I'm glad you said that. I know what you mean about fantasizing. Wiley would be my first choice. But like you said, after what we saw back at the cabin, I think it would be wrong to interfere in their relationship." He grabbed Dave's shoulders. "Who knows, maybe they'll help put a little spark back into our lives."

"You mean we ain't got no spark no more?" Dave joked.

They laughed and hugged each other. Winnie began barking and jumped high enough a few times to nip the top of their shirt sleeves.

* * *

The moment they were alone in the cabin, Wiley dropped his crutches. He balanced on his right leg and pulled Jake closer. The eternity of waiting for Jake to return had ended, and he wanted Jake naked. The thickness of their Levis did nothing to lessen the spark he felt when their crotches pushed together.

A sharp pain in Wiley's shot-up leg suddenly ravaged his entire body. Instantly light-headed, he sagged into Jake's arms.

Sensing Wiley's pain, Jake gently cradled him to the daybed, then knelt beside him and caressed his face.

"Want me to get you one'a them pills for your leg, Wiley?"

Wiley opened his eyes and looked at Jake. "No. I don't want to fall asleep now."

Jake grinned and spread his fingers into the black hair on Wiley's chest, then bent down and blew on it to watch the hairs tremble. He was glad Wiley wasn't wearing a shirt. He loved looking at Wiley naked. Jake wanted to become real little and hide in the deep, hairy valleys of Wiley's chest. He'd be safe there. Wiley's iron-like muscles would protect him from the strange things happening to them.

"I missed you, Wiley," Jake said as he slid his hands up and down Wiley's chest, into his armpits, and down across the fly of his Levi shorts. "All them things I seen in that there town made me wish you was with me. An' I missed bein' here, knowin' your leg was hurtin'."

Wiley raised up a little. "While you were gone, I discovered I don't like being away from you." He shoved Jake's half-open shirt back over his shoulders.

Jake ran his hands up and down Wiley's muscular arms. "I love lookin' at you an' touchin' you, Wiley." He leaned forward and licked Wiley's right pec, softly bit his nipple, then slid his tongue up to his armpit.

Wiley groaned, leaned over and stuck his tongue into Jake's ear. Jake shuddered in pleasure. He slid his arm behind Wiley's head and kissed him.

After a moment, Wiley pushed Jake back and looked into his eyes. "Jake, can you help me get these...short pants off. They're getting too tight."

Jake reached down, ripped open the buttons of Wiley's cut-offs and started to yank them down to his boots.

"*Slowly,*" Wiley yelled.

Being as careful as he knew how, Jake maneuvered the cut-offs over the bandages. Wiley stifled a few groans until Jake got the shorts past the wounds.

After removing Wiley's boots and socks, Jake slid his hands up Wiley's massive, hairy legs to his crotch. He cupped Wiley's cock and balls with both hands.

Wiley raised up, grabbed Jake's shirt and shoved it farther down his back and arms. Another sharp pain made him groan.

Jake pushed Wiley back to the daybed. "You just lay there, Wiley, so your leg don't keep hurtin'. I wanna feel you all over while you're awake." Jake slid his hands over Wiley's body. "Like I done when I was washin' you."

Wiley closed his eyes and relaxed. "I can't think of anything I would like better."

With strong hands, Jake kneaded Wiley's muscles starting from his toes, his feet, then up both legs. He tried to avoid Wiley's wounds, but realized he'd gotten too close when Wiley jerked in pain. Jake slid his hands over Wiley's rock-hard stomach, bent down and licked his navel, then flung himself across Wiley's chest and shoved his hands down Wiley's arms and grasped his hands. With his fingers entwined with Wiley's, Jake lowered his head, rested his face on Wiley's crotch and slipped his mouth over Wiley's hard cock.

Wiley arched his back, squeezed Jake's hands and groaned.

Relaxing back to the bed, Wiley gasped, "Jake, that feels wonderful. Don't ever stop."

Jake let go of Wiley's hands, cupped one around his balls and slid his other hand up Wiley's chest. He slid his mouth up and down Wiley's cock.

Wiley's body jerked in ecstasy, then exhausted, he collapsed back to the bed.

After his breathing slowed, Wiley reached down, pulled Jake's head toward him and kissed him on the lips. "Jake, that was wonderful. When my leg heals, I want to return the favor."

Jake sat back on his feet. "Weren't no favor, Wiley. I love touchin' you an' makin' you feel good." He lowered his eyes briefly, then looked straight at Wiley. "I don't never want to do this with nobody but you. I was thinkin' it'd be fun rollin' around with Dave, but not now. I been thinkin' that Jesus gave us to each other for the time we're here." He paused. "An' after, too."

Wiley smiled and ran his hand over Jake's bare chest. "All my life I've wanted a partner like you, and never really believed I'd have one at all." He shook his head and smiled. "But I was wrong, and I don't want to share you with anyone, either."

When Dave and Jim cautiously entered the cabin, they found Jake and Wiley sitting on the daybed holding up the shirts Jake had bought in Buena Vista. Both men were clothed, but they knew Wiley had just gotten dressed, and in a hurry. His shorts were on inside out, and the fly was open.

"I hope we're not barging in on anything," Jim said.

Wiley smiled. "I think we all timed it just right. Thank you for letting us be alone."

"No problem," Dave said. "Just let us know when you want some time by yourselves. We'll do the same." He made a sweeping gesture with his hand. "This is a small cabin, not really built for four big guys. It's more of an eating and sleeping area than anything else right now. We all need time to be alone." He pointed at Wiley's open fly. "You can put your shorts on the right way if you want. I think you'll have a hard time trying to button them inside out."

They all looked at Wiley's crotch.

Jake laughed. "Ever'body's lookin' at your pants this time, Wiley." He shoved his hand inside Wiley's open fly.

Wiley grabbed Jake's wrist and pulled his hand out of his shorts. "Jake, you're embarrassing our hosts."

"Hell, they both got one, too."

"Yes, but remember what we talked about. Let's not make it harder for us than it will be."

Jake looked at Jim and Dave. "We talked about not havin' any rolls in the hay with you."

"It's not that we don't want to," Wiley added. "We don't want to share each other with anyone."

"That's funny," Jim said. "Dave and I talked about the same thing on our walk. Somehow, it doesn't seem right for all of us to play around with each other, even though it would be wonderful. But we don't want to come between you two...for any reason."

Dave slid into a chair. "Jim and I talked about never knowing anyone as much in love as you two guys are. We don't want anything to spoil it for you. If all of us have sex together, somebody would get hurt feelings, and I don't want any part of that. We all love each other too much."

Jake looked at Wiley and said, "Now I know Dave an' Jim're the pertecters Chief Eagle Rising told me about. After all them things that happened today, there ain't nobody else I'd want as our pertecters in this here Time, neither."

CHAPTER 8

Cynthia Havertine smiled at the sound of a car door slamming in the driveway. She headed toward a window of her palatial home that nestled high above the Arkansas River and overlooked the northern edge of Buena Vista. Across the valley soared the gigantic snowcapped wall of the Collegiate Range, a seemingly unscalable barrier to the west.

Parting the sheer curtains, Cynthia saw her driver walking toward the house. She noticed the black smudge on Brad's white shirt and his dusty shoes. Again, she thought of his resemblance to Tom Sellick. The sausage bulge in Brad's crotch moved with each step.

Seeing Brad's cock stuffed into his pants like that normally turned her on. But after seeing that muscular, blond hunk in Rockford's this morning, wearing only stretched, see-through briefs that made him look naked, the only thing she'd been able to think of since was making love to him until he passed out.

The slam of the massive front door, followed by Brad's echoing footsteps as he entered the polished-wood study, diverted Cynthia's thoughts. She turned and watched him approach.

Brad stopped a few feet from Cynthia, dropped his eyes to her slim waist and flat stomach, then slowly raised them to her breasts that bulged out the top of her purple, silk dress.

"I found out where he's staying," Brad said. He grabbed at his dick, expecting to entice her. When it didn't, he stated bluntly, "He's gay."

Cynthia glared at him. "I don't believe you. That man *couldn't* be gay. Gay men are all so...well, you know...skinny and limp-wristed. There's nothing skinny or limp-wristed about him."

"That may be, but he's still gay. I saw him sucking another guy's dick. He was really going at it."

"You're lying!" Cynthia shouted. "You know I'm after him, and you don't want me to get him. Do you! Can't you get it through your thick head our fling is over? I want that man, and you are going to get him for me." She pointed at Brad. "And in case you haven't forgotten, you are still working for me." She turned abruptly and headed for the antique, walnut back-bar that had decorated the Golden Horseshoe Saloon in Cripple Creek a hundred years ago.

"How can I forget I work for you?" Brad snapped as he watched Cynthia pick out a long-stemmed goblet. "But I'm telling you, I saw him giving another guy a blow job in the cabin where he's staying." He waved his hand. "It's up north by Bristlecone Peak."

Cynthia spun around to face him. "Bristlecone Peak! That's forty miles from here! You weren't gone long enough to drive clear up there and back."

"The hell I wasn't! I've been gone five hours, and you know it." Brad threaded his way through the large grouping of leather chairs, love seats and polished wooden tables all placed with their back legs on the edge of a rectangular, oriental rug in the center of the room. When he reached the bar, he grabbed a highball glass and a bottle of Jack Daniels. "After I left Rockford's, I had to sit in the damn parking lot of Grant's Grocery for an hour while they farted around in there." He poured the bourbon almost to the rim of the glass, then looked at Cynthia. "How'd you get home from Rockford's?"

Cynthia smiled snottily. "Mrs. Gunder gave me a ride home. She asked if you were off somewhere drinking, and I said you were."

As Brad watched Cynthia prepare her martini, he figured she hadn't really said that to Mrs. Gunder. He swilled half his drink in two swallows.

"It wasn't easy keeping my distance from them," Brad added as he stared at himself in the mirror of the back-bar. "Antelope Road's not too well traveled, and I didn't want them to know I was following them. I even had to hike to the cabin." Brad downed the rest of his drink and clunked his glass on the bar. "Fortunately, the other two guys living there went for a walk and took the dog."

Brad turned his head and watched Cynthia stare at herself in the mirror and sip her martini. He scowled and poured himself another glass of Jack Daniels. It pissed him off she didn't believe him about the blond being gay, but he had to admit he'd never seen gay men as big and muscular as the four living in that cabin. With his own eyes, he'd watched the blond guy suck the other one off. He'd never admit to anyone that it had turned him on to see the big man go at it so passionately. He had a stirring in his crotch just thinking about what it must have felt like.

After the second sip of her martini, Cynthia frowned at it. Brad had to be lying. But the blond hunk's own words that he would only let a man named Wiley touch him rang in her ears. With her drink in hand, she walked to a window, held open the sheers and stared at the snowcapped range in the distance.

"I want you to drive me to Bristlecone Peak on Sunday."

Looking at Cynthia in the mirror, Brad raised his lip at her. He'd found out the hard way that she was a selfish bitch and couldn't see anything beyond a male body and a hard dick. "What good would it do?" he snapped. "He'd just tell you to get lost. The way he was going at it, you wouldn't get anywhere. Even if you were the most beautiful woman on earth."

"You once said I was," Cynthia cooed sarcastically.

Brad closed his eyes and shook his head. "Yeah, well, I was probably drunk at the time." Cynthia was irritating him. Since her late father had owned most of Buena Vista, Cynthia believed she could have any man she wanted. He figured she'd try for the blond guy, or even the black-haired one when she saw him, and end up ruining both their lives...just like she'd ruined his. Before he'd met her, he'd worked construction and had loved it. Now, he was just her cast-off sex fling, too deeply involved with her money and no longer feeling good about himself.

Brad swallowed more bourbon. "As for driving you to Bristlecone Peak on Sunday, forget it! I'm through with your schemes!"

Cynthia turned to him. "You didn't understand me, Brad. I *demand* you take me there. Neither of us have plans on Sunday, and what better day is there for taking a ride to Bristlecone Peak?" She looked out the window and smiled. "I'll wear my pink silk dress. That ought to melt his stony heart, just like it did yours." She laughed and sipped her drink.

Angered by that remark, Brad drained his glass, slammed it on the bar and headed toward the door.

79

"Wait, Brad!" Cynthia said coldly, not even looking at him. "If I don't see you before then, have the car ready at eight o'clock sharp on Sunday morning. You *will* drive me to Bristlecone Peak." Brad stopped. Without turning, he yelled, "Yes ma'am!" He clicked his heels and stormed out of the room.

Cynthia smiled. She knew her new-found love would put up a fuss, just like Brad. "No man can resist me for very long," she said out loud, then laughed.

Returning to the bar, Cynthia downed the last of her martini and began making another one. It was going to be a long wait until Sunday. She just might get drunk...and stay that way until then.

CHAPTER 9

On Saturday, six days after the first trip to the doctor, the four men piled into the Honda and headed to Fairplay for Wiley's check-up visit.

In the back seat next to Jake, Wiley could see everything he'd missed while lying in the bed of the truck and felt more dismayed at the landscape than he'd ever imagined. He couldn't find words to comment on anything.

"Lookit all them roads, Wiley," Jake yelled. "We could round up cows usin' buggies in this here Time."

Dave and Jim snickered, but Wiley scowled.

"An' see all them cabins," Jake continued, pointing to the forested hills across the valley. He leaned toward Jim in the front seat. "Why do all them cabins got fences around 'em? They ain't got no cows."

"Some people like to be fenced in," Jim said. "I think they're trying to keep nature out."

Wiley's gut tightened as the car sped along the paved highway into Fairplay. He imagined they were flying down a corridor with walls of fence posts and power poles and was horrified that cars traveled so fast. From his knowledge of physics, he shuddered at what would happen if two cars hit head on.

Wiley gazed across the gently rolling landscape, dotted with houses, rusting hulks of old cars and mountains of junk that littered yards. Scattered businesses, all with gaudy signs, overflowing trash dumpsters and areas filled with parked cars lined several sections of the road.

Searching the hills beyond, Wiley wondered if there were any more antelope but was afraid to ask, assuming they'd been slaughtered like the buffalo. He remembered two weeks ago, he and Jake had ridden with a herd of antelope for a half mile until the graceful animals had darted in unison to the right and disappeared over the crest of a hill.

Wiley looked at Jake. He loved riding the horses with him, but in their time they rarely saw another person, and nothing marred the landscape. He took in Jake's handsome face and big frame and smiled. When they rode, he'd always watch Jake closely, thinking he looked so masculine with his hat pulled down in front and his massive body moving with the same rhythm as Mac's powerful gallop. Jake always rode with his shirt half unbuttoned, allowing glimpses of his smooth, muscular chest.

Wiley thought about the time they had ridden naked down Horseshoe Canyon, then had switched clothes, and he began getting an erection. He grabbed Jake's arm, pulled him close and whispered, "Somehow we have to find that feather. I want to ride naked with you again."

Jake looked into Wiley's eyes and slid his hand to Wiley's crotch. Feeling his semi-hard cock, he squeezed it and said, "I just had me an' idea to look for the feather under our cabin when we get back." He squeezed Wiley's cock again and grinned when Wiley trembled.

* * *

Doctor Blakely gave Wiley a good report, saying the wounds were healing nicely and for him to continue using the crutches for another two weeks. To Jim and Dave's relief, the doctor didn't mention Sheriff Daly.

* * *

That afternoon, Jim and Dave donned their painting clothes and quickly became engrossed in staining the north side of the cabin.

Jake sat next to Wiley in the plastic chairs at the edge of the cliff and smiled at the view to the south. He leaped to his feet and climbed down the cliff to the remains of their cabin. He grabbed one of the rotting logs from the collapsed north wall, ripped it away from the others and tossed it down the hill.

"What are you doing?" Wiley asked.

"Lookin' to see if the golden feather's hidin' under these here logs."

"After a hundred years, it's unlikely, but I'm curious myself." Wiley propped his left leg on a rock, adjusted the bill of his borrowed Rockies baseball cap and settled back to watch Jake. He wished he could help, but decided to remain calm about his injury. Grandpa Gray Feather always said, "Rest your body. Think of birds and flowers, streams and wind. Soul must be lightened when body heals."

* * *

Both standing on ladders, Jim glanced over at Dave. "I shouldn't say this, but I'm glad Jake didn't ask to help this time. We used up most of the paint thinner getting the stain off his boot and pant leg."

"I think Wiley had something to do with him not asking." Dave stopped his roller. "I love watching those two interact. Did you see what Wiley did when Jake saw we were going to paint?"

"No." Jim placed his roller in the tray.

Dave snickered and shook his head. "When Jake turned toward me to ask if he could help, Wiley lifted one of his crutches and grabbed it by the rubber bottom. Then he slipped the top of the crutch between Jake's legs, slid it up to his crotch, twisted it width-wise and pulled him back. I'll never forget the look on Jake's face."

Jim laughed. "I wish I'd seen that. Every time I think of last night when Wiley accidentally squirted Jake in the face with whipped cream, I start laughing." He steadied himself by grabbing the edge of the roof, then laughed out loud.

"And Jake sat in his chair like he'd been goosed," Dave added.

* * *

Down the hill, after searching the ruins for twenty minutes, Jake suddenly yelled. Chunks of rotted wood flew into the air. Jake laughed and scrambled up the cliff. "Wiley, I found it! I found the golden feather! It was layin' by the water pit under the floor!"

When Jake reached the top, he held the feather toward Wiley. "This here's the feather Chief Eagle Rising gived me!" He laughed and waved it at the sky.

A blast of wind nearly knocked Jake off the edge of the cliff. The two men covered their eyes as dust and sand tore at them.

The instant Jake lowered the feather, the wind stopped.

"Damn!" Jake yelled. "This here must be magic if it makes wind do that!"

Wiley gasped as he stared at the golden feather, still supple and unsoiled. He glanced up at Jake. "When I was little, Grandpa Gray Feather told me a story about golden feathers."

Wide-eyed, Jake asked, "What was the story, Wiley?"

"Grandpa said that before all the tribes went their own way, the Great One appeared in the sky as a golden eagle. The wicked assembled and shot an arrow at the eagle, wounding it in the right wing and sending a shower of golden feathers to the ground. The feathers scattered across the entire land, losing themselves in the rocks and crannies of the earth. Whoever finds or is given one of the feathers is granted special powers."

"I got special powers?"

"You got us away from Winder and brought us here."

"Hell, Wiley. I didn't do nothin' to get us here." Jake pulled out the rawhide bag from his shirt. "All I done was put the feather in this here bag like Chief Eagle Rising said to."

"I don't know what the powers are. Grandpa never told me. But he said if the feather is lost or stolen, great hardship and sorrow will follow the owner until it's recovered. Keep that feather in a safe place, and don't ever lose it."

"I sure won't, Wiley." Jake smiled and held the bag up in front of his face. "I'm gonna put the feather in here like Chief Eagle Rising said to."

Jake opened the rawhide pouch and stuffed the feather inside. A small burst of white smoke puffed out. Startled, Jake dropped the bag to his chest.

"What happened?" Wiley asked.

"Hell, Wiley, I think it burnt up in there." Jake grabbed the bag, opened it and brought it close to his face. "It ain't in there." He looked at Wiley. "Ain't nothin' in there, not even ashes." Leaning over, he let Wiley look inside.

Wiley smiled. "I think you have the perfect place to hide it. Grandpa told me a golden feather can't be destroyed, which is probably why it still looks like it does after all these years. It's in there, we just can't see it."

Jake peered into the bag again. "Damn. Sure is spooky."

"Did you guys feel that wind?" Dave asked as he walked up behind them. "It was like the one we had just before you got here." He looked back at the cabin and sighed. "It covered the new stain with a thick layer of grit. Jim's trying to scrape it off, but I think it's hopeless until it dries and we can use the sander. Fortunately, some of the stain dried before the wind came."

Jake held the bag toward Dave. "Do you see anythin' in this here bag?"

"Take it off so I can see inside better."

Jake jerked the bag back to his chest. "No! I can't never take it off'a me! I gotta have it touchin' me 'cause it's our only way home."

Dave shrugged, glanced at Wiley who was smiling at Jake, then leaned over and peered into the bag. "I don't see anything in there. What am I suppose to see?"

"I found the golden feather under Wiley an' me's cabin. It's the one Chief Eagle Rising gived me to get here. I held it up, an' that's what made the wind." He grinned. "Now we can go back home when Wiley's leg's better."

Jake shoved the bag inside his shirt. "Chief Eagle Rising said to put the feather in this here bag. When I did, we saw smoke come out an' now the feather's gone." He cut his eyes to Wiley. "You think it's still in there?"

"It's in there, Jake. When it's time to return, we'll see it again."

"I think this whole thing is freaky," Dave said as he looked over the cliff at the scattered ruins. Many of the logs had been rolled down the hill. "Boy, you did a number on your cabin. I always wanted to look around under those logs, but felt it would be sacrilegious to trash the remains of someone else's cabin. Besides, it's not on our property. Did you find anything else?"

Jake stared at Dave. "Our cabin ain't on your prop'ity?" He looked at Wiley. "Wiley, that ain't right! It's gotta be on Dave an'

Jim's prop'ity. I don't want nobody else ownin' where our cabin is. We gotta buy it." Jake's face lit up. "We can use somma them gold dollars!"

"I suppose we could," Wiley said. "Dave, do you know who owns it?"

"No, but I can make a telephone call to get the owner's name. We can't paint anymore today since everything's coated with sand." Dave spun around and headed toward the cabin. "I'll call now."

"Wait," Wiley said. He grabbed his crutches and struggled out of the chair. "I want to watch you use the telephone. Five years ago, when I was still in school, we had a lecture in science by Mr. Alexander Bell. He demonstrated the telephone, his newest invention, and said it might revolutionize communication. There were a few telephones in Boston and Philadelphia before I came out here."

Dave stopped and spun around. "Alexander Graham Bell? You actually attended a lecture by Alexander Graham Bell?"

"Yes." Wiley smiled. "I liked him. I take it the telephone caught on?"

"Caught on? Wiley, almost everyone in the world has a telephone. We can call France, Africa, Australia, anywhere from here." He glanced at the cabin. "It's funny, the phone hasn't rung once since you've been here. You'll know if it does, it sounds like a smoke alarm. The first time it rang, I ran around the cabin looking for the fire before I realized it was the telephone." He asked Wiley, "Do you want to make the call to the property owner's association?"

Wiley's face brightened. "Yes. Yes, I do."

"Can I use the telephone, too?" Jake asked in a little-boy voice, suddenly feeling left out. He knew about the telegraph, but there wasn't any talking on it, just a lot of clicking that made no sense at all.

As soon as they were inside, Dave turned to Jake. "How would you like to call Don, a friend of ours in Denver? Or Nick in New York?"

"Can I? Hear that, Wiley? Me, talk to somebody in New York?" His face turned serious. "Can I talk to Mr. Pritcher an' see how my farm's doin'?"

Wiley chuckled. "Jake, I'm sure Mr. Pritcher is dead."

"He ain't *dead*, Wiley." Jake stopped, thought about it and said, "Hell, I forgot. We ain't there no more."

As Wiley rehearsed out loud what he was going to say, Jim came inside and Dave mentioned Jake's desire to buy the adjoining parcel of land.

Dave handed Wiley the phone in the middle of a practiced sentence. Wiley stopped abruptly and asked, "Is that the telephone?"

"Sure is," Dave said, scowling at it. "We don't like it very much. It's hard to hold when you talk a long time, but it's cordless and we can sit outside."

Wiley turned the phone over and over in his hands. "This is amazing." He knocked the casing with his knuckles. "What's it made of?"

Dave raised his eyebrows. "It's just plastic. Oops! See, Jake, you're not the only one that forgets where you are. I forgot you've never seen plastic. Plastic is made from oil, but don't ask me how. Just about everything on earth is made from plastic nowadays."

Wiley gasped with surprise at hearing the clear, male voice on the other end of the line. The man told him a woman named Edna Scott, who lived in Alma, owned the two acres of land. Dave prompted Wiley to ask for her address and phone number. Wiley wrote down the information, smiled broadly as he said good-bye, then held the phone to his ear and listened to the dial tone long after the man hung up.

After reading the name Wiley had written down, Jim said, "I'll call Edna Scott and see if she'd be interested in selling."

Dave patted him on the shoulder. "That's a great idea. You're good at getting people to cough up information they wouldn't tell anybody else." He glanced at Jake. "Can you wait a few minutes before talking to Nick so Jim can call Mrs. Scott?"

The disappointment on Jake's face changed into a smile. "Sure. Reckon I'm just hankerin' too much to talk to somebody in New York."

Wiley finally took the phone away from his ear and examined it intently, turned it upside down and pushed the buttons to hear the tones.

Dave snatched the phone out of Wiley's hand, pushed the off button and said, "Pushing those buttons is calling someone." He handed it back to Wiley.

"Oh, I'm sorry," Wiley said. He again looked the phone over and ran his fingers along the antenna. He poked Jake in the ribs.

"Touché, Jake!"

Jake grabbed his body where the antenna poked him, faked death and fell on top of Wiley sitting alone on the couch. Even though it was a controlled fall, Jake bashed Wiley's wounds with his knee, causing Wiley to drop the phone and groan in pain. In Jake's efforts to quickly get off his partner, he banged Wiley's shot-up leg a second time and got the full force of Wiley's yell in his ear.

Dave smiled at the tussling men. Their interactions were so genuine and refreshing, and they always allowed their love for each other to show.

Jim sighed as he picked up the phone from the floor. He grabbed the piece of paper with Edna Scott's phone number written on it.

"Well, here goes nothing." Jim poked in the seven digits.

After talking only five minutes, Jim said good-bye and pushed the button to disconnect the call. He tilted his head and raised an eyebrow at Dave.

"She wants to meet us in the dining room of the Fairplay Hotel tomorrow morning at eight."

"We'll all go," Wiley said. He smiled at Jake. "We'll pay her in gold."

Jake wasn't paying any attention. He grabbed Dave's arm. "Can I talk to somebody in New York now?"

"You bet. Let Jim talk first so Nick knows who it is."

Jim dialed the long distance number and waited. Soon his face brightened.

"Nick? This is Jim." He paused. "We're fine, how are you?" A long pause. "That's wonderful!" He turned to Dave, covered the phone with his hand and whispered, "He's buying an apartment house." Jim remained silent for several minutes.

"What's a 'partment house?" Jake asked Dave.

"It's a big building where lots of people live."

"A boardin' house?"

"Sort of. But everyone has their own kitchen and bathroom."

"Dave and I are living at the cabin now," Jim said into the phone. "We have two guys living with us." Jim laughed. "No, not house boys. Friends. One of them is from a small town, and he wants to talk to someone in New York. His name is Jake." He handed the phone to Jake.

Jake grabbed it, grinned and put it to his ear, but didn't say anything.

"Hello?" Nick said on the other end.

Jake yelled and dropped the phone. It bounced on the rug. "Damn, Wiley! That thing cussed at me!"

Jim picked the phone up and checked it over before putting it to his ear. "Nick? Are you still there?"

"Yes, I'm still here. What's going on out there? Are you all smoking pot?"

"No, but after this week, I feel like we've been using mushrooms. Jake accidentally dropped the phone. He said you cussed at him."

"I just said, 'hello.' Who is this guy, anyway? Am I going to have to fly out there and get you two out of a jam?"

"It's nothing like that. I'm going to give the phone back to Jake." Jim handed it to Jake. "Just tell Nick who you are and where you're from."

Jake lifted the phone to his ear, smiled and said timidly, "I'm Jake an' I'm from Wilmore, Kentucky, but ever'body there's dead now."

Wiley shook his head and covered his face with his hand.

"Are you all drunk out there?" Nick demanded.

Jake yelled again, held the phone out in front of him stared at it. "Wiley, this thing asked me if we're drunk."

"That's Nick talking to you," Dave said, trying to keep a straight face.

Jake pointed at the phone. "I thought Nick was in New York? How'd he get in there?"

* * *

During dinner, Jake jabbed his fork into a chunk of fried potato. "Wiley, we could split our gold dollars four ways. Then we'd all be rich."

With his mouth full, Wiley grinned crookedly. He was glad Jake had found the feather, especially since it had greatly improved his mood.

"There's one problem with that, Jake," Dave said. "If you're going back to eighteen eighty-six, those gold dollars will only be worth a dollar again. You need to trade them here for something you can use there." He looked around the cabin and shrugged. "If there is anything in this age of plastic you could possibly use."

"We could bring us back one'a them trucks."

"That won't work. Once it ran out of gas, it wouldn't run anymore. Cars weren't used in America until the eighteen nineties and then there were only a few of them in the East."

"Dave, what about some of your gemstones?" Jim asked. "You could sell them to Jake and Wiley, and they could take them back with them. If the coins made the trip in Jake's pocket, the gems should also. Besides, the way you cut stones, I'm sure no one back then will have ever seen anything like them."

Wiley's eyes lit up. "You're a lapidary, Dave?"

"Not professionally yet, but one stone dealer in Denver called me a master gem cutter. Best compliment I've ever received in my life since I basically taught myself how. But just one of those coins would probably buy every stone I've ever cut."

"David, don't sell yourself short," Jim scolded. "You know you have plenty of valuable gemstones they could buy. And if you don't have them, you can get them."

Wiley smiled. "Jake, we could use the stones to get Billingsly's attention. It's too bad we can't find some unknown person who knows about gems to make him drool, then trick him into talking about himself."

Jake shook his head. "We don't know nobody like that." His face brightened. "Why can't Dave do it? Chief Eagle Rising said the pertecters can come back with us if they want to."

Dave gasped. "Us go back with you? God, I'd love to! Jim, would you want to go?"

Jim squint-eyed Dave. "Not unless we could take Winnie. How would we do that?"

Jake frowned for a minute, then brightened. "We all gotta hold each other when we go back. Winnie could be in the middle. Maybe that'd work."

They talked of nothing else for the remainder of the evening, and after lights out, Dave stayed awake for hours wondering what it would be like to actually live in eighteen eighty-six.

CHAPTER 10

Amid the squalor in a house on a hill above Alma, Edna Scott hung up the phone and turned her eyes to her husband passed out on the newspaper-littered couch. The bottle of scotch in Burt's hand had tipped just enough so the two remaining swallows dribbled out, making a dark spot on the filthy gray cushion.

Not bothering to retrieve the bottle, Edna looked slowly around the room. The turn-of-the-century mountain cottage with a peaked gingerbread roof, far from the traffic and pollution of Denver, had been their dream home six years ago. Now, it was her worst nightmare.

Edna thought back to the year after they'd moved here when Burt had tried to help his younger brother straighten out from drinking, drugs and gambling. Burt had held up through three years of violent arguments with Louis, but had become so frustrated at the failure of his preaching, he'd started drinking even more than Louis. Edna sighed. Things had gone downhill for all of them after that. Over a year ago, Burt had lost his county job and hadn't been sober a single day since. Louis was living with them again, and Edna knew he was up to his neck with gambling debts. She'd discovered money missing from her purse and various hiding places in the kitchen.

After five years of turmoil, she no longer cared about either of them or the house.

Edna stared at the phone. That man wanted to buy her two acres of land. Her heart pounded. Louis would be furious if she sold it, even though he'd conned her into buying it in the first place.

She frowned and bit her lower lip, remembering how Louis had hounded her for over a month to buy the land he'd won in a poker game. Despite what he'd said about needing the money to set himself up in business, she'd known it was to pay off gambling debts and buy cocaine.

Louis had even driven her to Bristlecone Peak, and for the entire trip he'd raved about the fortune in gold he knew was buried beneath the old cabin ruins he'd found on the land. Old timers, Louis had insisted, always buried their gold under the floor of their cabin just before they were attacked by Indians.

Even Edna had realized the land was worthless. All but a small section sloped steeply to the south and was covered with stubby clumps of razor-sharp grass that had torn at her ankles. The only redeeming quality, if one could call it that, had been a giant rock that soared twenty feet in the air.

Louis had expounded on what a nice cabin she and Burt could build, but the only level spot she'd seen hugged the north side of the rock and was uncomfortably close to the cabin on the adjoining lot.

She'd asked Louis why he hadn't contacted those people about buying his two acres, feeling they'd have jumped at the chance. Louis' plot would have given them the entire end of the ridge.

His answer had been a flat no, saying that one day he planned to dig up the treasure under the cabin ruins and wanted the land to remain in the family.

Edna shuddered when she recalled handing Louis four thousand dollars for the two acres, every cent it had taken her years to save. Her dreams of opening a dress shop in the up-and-coming Old Main Street area of Fairplay had been snatched out of her hand at the same moment. Two weeks after that, Burt had been fired.

Edna bent down and straightened the stack of magazines piled by the couch. She knew she should put them on the coffee table, but first she'd have to clear a place among the empty beer cans. Why bother? The magazines would end up back on the floor, anyway. She noticed one of her pay stubs stuck to the table in a dried pool of beer.

If it hadn't been for Smitty, they would be destitute. Through the kindness of his heart, he'd hired her as a cocktail waitress in the Dusty Miner Bar. The job had kept food on the table until Louis had moved back in. Now, most of her money went for booze for Burt and Louis.

Edna scanned the living room. She was glad she'd told the man on the phone to meet her at the Fairplay Hotel tomorrow morning.

She didn't want Burt to find out, and especially not Louis, who scared her. The wall clock with the missing minute hand, broken during one of Burt and Louis' fights, told Edna it was almost five. Louis had said he'd be back at seven. Then again, he might show up at any time. She hated his unexpected arrivals.

Edna hurried into the front bedroom and tried to close the door, but a pile of laundry blocked it. She shoved the clothes aside, gently shut the door and propped a chair under the knob.

On her hands and knees, Edna felt under the bed for a cardboard box and panicked when she couldn't find it. She yanked up the ragged spread, looked under the bed and saw the box had been shoved toward the middle. Straining, she reached for it and pulled it toward her through rolls of dust.

Frantically, Edna searched through the contents of the box until she found the warranty deed and title search documents for the land. Tears came to her eyes as she clutched the papers to her breast. They might be her ticket out of this filthy rat-hole, forever.

CHAPTER 11

"I hate using your gold coins to buy that land," Jim said as he took his eyes off the road and glanced back at Wiley. "Dave and I were planning to buy it sometime, but we just never got around to it."

Dave grabbed the steering wheel and swerved the car back onto the pavement. "Jim, you were on the shoulder. Would you like me to drive?"

"Sorry! No, I can drive. I'm just worried about what I'm suppose to ask in buying that land. Shouldn't we have a lawyer present?"

"A lawyer!" Jake yelled. "A damn lawyer'll end up gettin' that prop'ity an' yours too!"

Wiley chuckled. "Not all lawyers are like Billingsly, Jake."

Dave turned to the two men in the back seat. "From what you've told us about Billingsly, I wouldn't be too sure."

"Most of the unimproved lots in our area have been selling for five or six thousand," Jim broke in. "If Mrs. Scott wants more money, it means you'll have to use more of your coins."

"That ain't nothin'," Jake said. "Nobody back home'll believe us buyin' land for six dollars."

As the Honda pulled up in front of the Fairplay Hotel, the clock on the dashboard read five past eight. The street seemed deserted.

"We're late." Jim looked around. "Where is everyone?"

"Most of the tourists are probably still looking at themselves in a steamy mirror," Dave quipped.

The four men walked the length of the Fairplay Hotel lobby and crowded around the door to the dining room. They saw several older couples sitting at the smaller tables. A family of six, all with blond hair and wearing matching T-shirts and shorts, sat around the large table in the center of the room.

Wiley noticed a woman in her fifties with fuzzy brown hair, wearing a plain, navy-blue suit, sitting by herself at a table in the corner. She glanced up from her plate at them. When Wiley saw a quick glimmer of fear on the woman's face that quickly changed to expectation, he nudged Jim in the back. "She's in the corner."

Jim split off from the group and walked over to the woman's table.

"Mrs. Scott?"

"Yes." She smiled and extended her hand. "Are you Mr. Parnell?"

"Yes, I am." Jim took her hand and shook it lightly. "Not to alarm you, I came with my partner...and two friends who are staying with us. They can sit at another table if so many of us might intimidate you."

Mrs. Scott smiled weakly at Jim. "I'd very much like them to join us. I'd feel safer sitting with all of you."

Jim felt a chill at her comment but shrugged it off and motioned to the others.

On crutches, Wiley drew looks from everyone in the room.

Jake propped the crutches against the wall as the four men sat down. They remained silent while the waitress placed water glasses and menus on the table for each and refilled Mrs. Scott's coffee cup. As soon as the waitress left, introductions were made around the table. Wiley wondered at the woman's apparent relief after she knew all their names.

Frowning at the plastic-coated menu, Jake said, "Wiley, I don't know what this here thing says."

"I'll read it to you." Wiley glanced at his own menu. "Good God, look at these prices!"

"Don't you be cussin', *Willy*."

Wiley chuckled, and Mrs. Scott laughed.

"Don't worry about the prices," Jim said, not wanting an added issue. "Dave and I are paying."

While he read the menu to Jake, Wiley noticed Mrs. Scott smiling at Jake in a motherly way. Halfway through his reading the description of eggs benedict, their waitress walked up to the table.

Jake craned his head past her to the other waitress, just then serving a plate with a thick slice of ham, two over-easy eggs and generous pile of hash browns to a man sitting by himself against the adjoining wall.

"Is that all you get?" Jake asked their waitress, pointing to the plate of food. "I want two'a them like what he's gettin'." He glanced sheepishly at the others, wondering if he might have just committed a no-no.

The waitress smiled at him. "Would you like the two orders on one plate?"

Jake's face brightened when he realized his crude manner didn't fluster the woman at all. "Sure would!"

"I'd like the same as Jake, if it won't be too costly for you, Jim," Wiley said.

"Fine with me." Jim turned to the waitress. "I'll have the same thing. But only one order and eggs sunny-side up."

After Dave asked for the same as Jim with eggs over-easy, the waitress walked toward the kitchen.

Jake suddenly said, "Can somebody show me where the outhouse is? I gotta pee bad."

Dave snickered and scooted back his chair. "Come on, Jake. I'll show you to the rest room."

"But I ain't tired. I gotta pee."

Everyone in the room laughed, except Jake and Wiley. The two men looked at each other. Wiley shrugged, which made Jake grin.

Mrs. Scott watched Jake follow Dave to the hotel lobby, then turned to Wiley. "Where is Jake from? He's a delightful man."

"He's from Kentucky, ma'am. And I think so too."

Nervous about the land purchase, Jim said, "Mrs. Scott, how much do you want for the land by Bristlecone Peak?"

Surprised the subject came up so suddenly, she paused for a moment. "I...I paid four thousand for it. I'd like to get at least five."

"How about six?" Wiley cut in, strengthening the deal.

Mrs. Scott's face brightened. "Six? Oh my, yes, I'd take six. Right now, if you want. I have the warranty deed and the title search papers with me."

"This is Sunday," Jim said. "We'll have to wait until tomorrow to get the signatures notarized and the sale recorded at the courthouse."

Mrs. Scott took a sip of her coffee. "The owner of the hotel is a notary, and I don't have to be present at the courthouse. We can finalize it as soon as we're finished eating."

Wiley felt Mrs. Scott seemed too eager to sell the land. He glanced at Jim and could tell he was thinking the same thing.

They heard Jake's loud voice in the lobby. As he and Dave returned from the rest room, everyone in the dining room turned to watch, wanting to hear what he had to say.

"I ain't never seen nothin' like that my whole life," Jake was saying to Dave. As Jake slid into his chair, he added, "Wiley, there's a white thing hangin' on the wall that you pee in. Don't know where the pee goes, 'cause I looked on the floor but it weren't there. An' I don't know why it's called a restin' room, 'cause there ain't no place to lay down."

Amid snickers in the room, Mrs. Scott said, "I always wondered about that too."

"You knew what the toilet was, though," Dave said to Jake.

"Sure did. Seen one'a them things in Denver when I was there. It had a chain you pulled instead'a that silver thing. That toilet got me throwed outta the hotel I was gonna stay at."

"Why?" Jim asked. Even the waitresses stopped to listen.

"'Cause I tossed a rag in that thing to watch it go down, but after it did, it started making noise and then started throwin' up. I pulled the chain some more times, but it just kept throwin' up all over. Got my boots wet too, an' I hate wet boots. Then some man looked in the room, an' after that's when I got throwed out."

An older man, sitting with his wife at a table close by and laughing, wiped his eyes and said, "Son, you should go on Saturday Night Live."

"What's a saturday night alive?" Jake asked him.

"Ha, ha, ha! Oh, that's rich!" the man yelled. He clapped. Everyone in the room clapped.

Jake leaned close to Wiley and whispered, "Wiley, are they laughin' at me for not knowin' what a saturday night alive is?"

"I don't know." Wiley looked at Dave. "What is a saturday night alive?"

"It's a TV show. But neither of you have seen TV yet." Dave cringed at what he'd just said and glanced at Mrs. Scott. The woman had a puzzled expression, but didn't comment.

"We were talking about the sale of the land while you were gone," Jim broke in, trying to change the subject. "Wiley offered Mrs. Scott six thousand dollars, and she accepted it. We can get the transaction notarized here in the hotel."

Jake dug into his pocket and pulled out several gold coins. He counted out six and plopped them down on the table in front of Mrs. Scott. "Here's your money, ma'am."

"What's this?" she asked, staring the coins.

"Them're gold dollars," Jake said, grinning. "Dave said them coins're worth a thousand dollars for each one."

Visibly shocked, Mrs. Scott said, "You're paying me with these? What can I do with them? I'm afraid I need cash. These coins won't do me any good."

Dave spoke up. "There's a coin dealer in Breckenridge who specializes in old coins. We could take you there so you can sell them...today, if you like. I'm sure he's never seen such perfect gold dollars from eighteen eighty-six before."

"Where did you gentlemen get them?"

"Er...Jake and Wiley found them," Dave added quickly.

"Well, I suppose it wouldn't hurt to at least see how much they're worth. Could we leave as soon as you finish eating? I can't be gone too long from home today."

Wiley placed his hand on the woman's arm and smiled. "You won't be disappointed, Mrs. Scott. If we can't get a thousand dollars apiece for them, we'll add another coin or two to make the sale come to six thousand."

She looked at Wiley's hand for a moment, then looked him in the eye and smiled. "That seems fair."

"That's cuz this here's Fairplay," Jake said.

They all laughed.

* * *

As they followed Edna Scott's car through Alma on their way to Breckenridge, Jake and Wiley gasped at the change in the small town.

"What happened to all the buildings?" Wiley asked.

"Much of the town burned in nineteen thirty-seven," Dave said. "And a few buildings were moved to South Park City Museum in Fairplay. We should take a tour of that museum. I think you'd enjoy it."

"Wiley! The Silver Heels Bar's still there!" Jake yelled. "That's where we become blood brothers!" He stuck his head out the window. "Look how sad it is, bein' closed." He pulled his head in and looked at Wiley. "It misses us, Wiley."

"Jim and I used to go there," Dave said. "It was a great place. They made pizza in the front window and served good food." He sighed. "Then a couple from Denver bought it. The locals and skiers were angry when the new owners didn't bother to get a liquor license for Sunday night. It closed for good in the eighties. Er, the nineteen eighties."

* * *

Used to dealing with gemstone merchants, Dave held the six gold dollars in his hand as the group walked into the coin shop in Breckenridge. As the others began looking around, he walked to the older of the two men behind the counter and asked, "Can you tell me how much this coin is worth?" He placed a single coin on the counter.

The store owner picked up the dime-size gold coin and lowered the small magnifier on his glasses. He turned the coin over and over in his fingers for a long time. The other clerk walked over and peered at it.

"Where did you get this?" the older man asked.

"Found it," Dave answered.

"There's a few scratches on it." He glanced at the other clerk, raised one eyebrow, then looked back at Dave. "I'd say it's worth a couple hundred."

"Interesting," Dave said. He held out his hand until the clerk dropped the coin into it. "At the coin show in Denver, I was offered fifteen hundred for it. Guess I should have sold them there, but I'd settle for a thousand."

The owner's eyes opened wide. "Them? You have more than one?"

"I have six."

"Six?" The clerk straightened his tie. "I can't pay that kind of money for these. Why, coins like this are a dime a dozen."

"Not uncirculated." Dave squinted at him. "And I'm certain you know that."

The shop's only other customer, a tall, distinguished man in his fifties walked over to Dave. "My name is Linus Avery. May I see that coin?"

"Certainly." Dave dropped it into the man's hand.

Mr. Avery pulled out his pocket magnifier and studied the coin carefully. He peered at Dave over his half glasses and stated, "I'll give you a thousand dollars for this. It's the finest specimen I've ever seen. How many did you say you have?"

"Six," Dave said, then smiled.

"I'll buy all of them at that price."

"Sold. But I'm leaving Breckenridge today. I'd prefer cash since this is Sunday, and no banks are open."

Mr. Avery's face showed his disappointment. "Unfortunately, all I have is a thousand in cash." He handed the coin back to Dave.

Mrs. Scott walked up to him. "You can buy the rest of them from me, Mr. Avery. I live in Alma, and I just sold a parcel of land to these gentlemen." She smiled at Dave and held out her hand. Dave gave her the six gold coins. Mrs. Scott put five of them in her purse and held out the last one to Linus Avery. "You can pay me a thousand dollars for this one, and I'll give you the name and address of my place of employment in Alma. You can pick up the others whenever you wish."

"Now just one minute!" the older clerk yelled. "You can't make coin deals in this shop unless they're our coins!"

Linus Avery frowned at him. "We just did. If you weren't such a crook, you could have made five hundred dollars on each of these coins." He gently took Mrs. Scott's arm. "Shall we step outside and finish our transaction?"

CHAPTER 12

As the dust-covered, maroon Jaguar wound its way up the twisty dirt road, Cynthia Havertine glanced at her watch. "It's already nine-thirty. How much farther is it?"

"The driveway's just ahead," Brad snarled, shifting into low gear.

Shortly, Brad pulled to the side of the road and jerked the car to a sudden stop. "From here, we walk."

"Walk!" Cynthia shouted. "Are you out of your mind? I have on my new Italian heels, not to mention my silk dress. I won't walk *anywhere* in this wilderness."

"Well, I guess this trip was for nothing." Brad jabbed his finger in the direction of the steep, rocky driveway. "I'm not driving *this* car up *that* road."

"Try it!" Cynthia demanded. "Better yet, I'll do it!"

She opened the door, slid out of the car, then slammed it. Cynthia's pointed heels sunk into the sandy roadbed as she held onto the hood and struggled to the driver's side. She stuck her head through the open window and snapped, "Get out!"

Brad sighed and shook his head. "It's your damn car. If you wreck it, don't ask me to carry you home on my back."

As Brad stood on the side of the road and watched, Cynthia slid behind the wheel, slammed the door, jammed the car into low and gunned the engine. The wheels flung gravel five yards behind the sleek car, then it shot up the driveway. The Jaguar bounced and crunched as it hit large rocks and deep ruts. The car suddenly stopped dead, and the tires spun uselessly as they tried to grab loose stones. The right rear wheel finally caught, the car lurched forward, then slid sideways and high-centered on a rock.

Cynthia glanced around, forced the car into reverse and stomped on the gas pedal. The tires smoked as they spun in the opposite direction. One of the drive wheels suddenly caught hold, and the car lurched backward. Brad heard a grating noise as it scraped across the rock. Once free, the car careened backward and buried itself deep into the soft bank next to the culvert. The left rear wheel spun in mid-air.

"Now you've done it!" Brad yelled. "You're hopelessly stuck!"

Cynthia killed the engine, slid out of the car and held onto it as she struggled through the deep sand. She grabbed Brad's arm to steady herself, then frowned. "*Do* something! We can't stay here all day!"

Brad pulled his arm out of her grasp. "What I ought to do is start walking home and let you fend for yourself!"

Cynthia struggled to the car and held onto the trunk. "Maybe the men at the cabin will help us. Go up there and find out."

Brad shrugged. "And if they won't?"

"I'll *pay* them, for God's sake!"

Brad started walking up the driveway. "They're probably not even there," he muttered.

"So what! I'm sure they have a phone. You could break in and use it to call a tow truck to get us out of here."

Brad stopped and spun around to face her. "Break in? Oh that's real cute, Cyn! And while I'm sitting in jail, you'll be trying to put the make on that blond queer!"

Lying in the shade of a pine tree near the cabin, Winnie growled when he heard the whine of the tires down at the main road. When he heard yelling, he leaped to his feet and bounded down the slope.

Hearing Winnie's deep growls, Brad and Cynthia looked up the slope and saw a big dog with a long, gray coat charging toward them. Terrified, they scrambled over each other to get into the stuck car.

As Cynthia reached the passenger-side door, her foot slipped off a rock. She staggered and fell against the car. Her left spike heel caught in the hem of her long dress and pulled her backward. She clawed at the car as she slid to the ground.

"Goddam it!" she screamed.

Winnie stopped ten feet from her, crouched low and curled his upper lip, then advanced slowly.

Cynthia screamed and groped for a rock. Finding one the size of a lemon, she flung her hand back to throw it at the dog and bashed her knuckles against the car. She yelled in pain and let the rock fall.

With panic-stricken effort, Cynthia grabbed the edge of the wheel well and yanked herself to her feet. She felt her pointed heel rip a large piece out of the back of her dress. Somehow she managed to get inside the car and slam the door seconds before the dog charged.

Winnie pounded his paws on the car and barked through the half-open window, then dropped to the ground and growled as he pulled at the dress sticking out the closed door. With a piece of pink silk hanging from his mouth, Winnie leaped at the window again and barked.

"Close that window!" Brad yelled from the driver's side.

In the tightly closed car, Brad glared at Cynthia. "We're fucking trapped! I hope you're satisfied!"

* * *

At two that afternoon, a car with four laughing and singing men sped up the dirt road.

Jim slowed the Honda and pointed. "Look, that car's in our driveway!"

They all sat forward.

Tilted at a precarious angle, a dusty, paw-print covered, maroon Jaguar sat crosswise at the bottom of the steep incline. "How'd it get like that?" Jim asked.

As the Honda pulled to a stop, Dave jumped out and yelled, "Winnie!"

The dog yelped, bounded over the top of the Jaguar and leaped onto the road. He jumped at Dave's side.

Jim got out of the car and frowned. "Dave, isn't that the same car we saw parked down the road when we took our walk after we got back from Buena Vista?"

"It sure looks like it. I wonder who those people are?"

As they approached the passenger side, they saw a woman's face pressed against the slobber-streaked window, open only a crack at the top. Ragged pieces of bright pink material were strewn over the driveway.

Dave recognized the woman from Rockford's clothing store. "What happened?" he yelled. "What are you doing here?"

Cynthia lowered the window a few inches, eyed Winnie, then lowered it all the way. "We're stuck! And your damn dog has kept us in this hot car for hours!"

"That's one reason we have him, to keep people like you away." Dave looked past Cynthia to Brad. "Who are you?"

Brad grinned sheepishly and nodded. "I'm Brad Cummings, Cynthia's driver."

"Driver!" Dave shouted. "Don't you know you can't take a car like this up that driveway?"

Brad frowned and pointed to Cynthia. "Tell her that! She was driving!" He opened the door to get out but slammed it again when Winnie ran to that side of the car.

Ignoring everyone, Jim crouched next to the Jaguar and peered underneath to see if they could get them back on the road. He didn't want these people hanging around while they waited for a tow truck from Fairplay. Seeing a puddle of oil, a large area of gravel soaked with yellowish water and a strip of wires hanging down, he sighed and raised up to Brad's window.

"Winnie, stop barking and lie down!" Jim demanded.

Winnie dropped to the ground and panted.

Jim motioned for Brad to lower his window. Before it was all the way down, he said, "I think you have oil pan and radiator damage. And several wires are hanging down. Two of them have been snapped. You're going to have to be towed out of here."

"You!" Jake yelled when he saw Cynthia. "What the hell're you doin' here?" He waited until Wiley hobbled to his side. "Wiley, that's the woman that had her hands on me when we was buyin' them clothes." He balled his fists and glared at Cynthia. "I told you, I don't want no damn job!"

Seeing Jake again, and looking past him to Wiley, Cynthia swallowed her anger at being imprisoned in the sweltering car for five hours. She smiled and batted her eyes at them. "I said I'd double any wages you're making now." Cynthia gestured toward

Wiley. "That goes for you, too. There are many side benefits with the job." She felt she was gaining ground when Wiley smiled.

"Jake, we could bury her up to her neck in the road like the woman at the wagon race."

Jake's eyes brightened, and he snickered. "Sure can." He frowned at Cynthia, extended his hands like claws and started walking toward the car. "I'll get her this time, Wiley."

Cynthia screamed. "Keep away from me!" She raised the window and locked the door, then turned toward Brad and yelled, "*Do* something!"

Jim shook his head, sighed and started walking up the driveway. "Dave, I'm going to call a tow truck."

Brad decided he'd rather get bitten by the dog than stay inside the hot car with Cynthia screaming. He opened the door and yelled, "Call off your dog! I need to get out of here!"

"Winnie!" Dave yelled. "It's okay. No biting." He whispered to Wiley, "He wouldn't have bitten them anyway."

When Jake returned to Wiley's side, Dave leaned toward the blood brothers and asked, "Did you really bury a woman up to her neck in a road?"

Wiley flickered a smile. "No. She got away."

Jake snickered.

Edgy about Winnie sniffing his butt, Brad approached the men. He glanced back at the car, down at the dog and then at Jake. "She's after you. She had me follow you after you left Rockford's the other day. I didn't want to, and I wish now I'd told her I'd lost you. Even though you guys are gay, I'm sorry for bringing her here."

"How do you know we're gay?" Dave asked.

Brad blushed. "Well, I..."

"You were spying on our cabin, that's how you know." Dave snapped. "Jim and I saw your car parked here on the road." He turned to Jake and Wiley. "This guy must have been spying on you after we got home from Buena Vista."

Jake reached out, grabbed Brad by the shirt with both hands and yanked him closer. "What'd you see!"

Brad swallowed hard and said timidly, "Everything."

Jake mule-kicked his fist into Brad's jaw. The man dropped to the road like a sack of cement and didn't move.

In the closed car, Cynthia screamed, "You've killed my driver! I'll sue you! Help! Police! Someone help me!"

"Well done, Jake." Dave patted Jake's shoulder. "Should we go up to the cabin?"

"Excellent idea," Wiley said. "They need time to be alone."

After the three men and a dog piled into the Honda, Dave steered around the unconscious man, maneuvered the car past the Jaguar and up the steep road, following the curvy tracks through the rocks. Even at the cabin they could hear Cynthia screaming for the police.

An hour later, perched on top of the rock pinnacle, Dave and Jake watched the billowy dust of an approaching tow truck. At the foot of the driveway, they could see Brad sitting on a rock beside the road with his head propped in his hands. He slowly looked up as the truck backed up behind the Jaguar. The moment the driver got out to survey the situation, Cynthia slid out of the car, hobbled through the gravel to the rugged man's side and grabbed his arm for support.

For twenty minutes, Dave and Jake watched the driver work attaching the car. Finally, he raised the Jaguar, climbed into the truck and inched it forward onto the road. After he fastened the portable lights on the hood of the Jaguar, he helped Cynthia, then Brad, into the truck.

Dave sighed when the only sight of the tow truck and maroon Jaguar was a snaky cloud of dust drifting into the early evening haze.

CHAPTER 13

For over a week, while Jim and Dave sanded and re-stained the outside of the cabin, Jake and Wiley puttered around their newly acquired parcel of land, the same one they'd lived on a hundred and seven years earlier. They pondered the full-grown trees, trying to remember if they'd noticed them in their own time when they would have been only saplings. They discovered that the ancient bristlecone pine, named Old One by the Utes, had a few more dead branches, and its top was now jagged and scorched from being struck by lightning many years back. Both agreed the four-foot thick trunk had changed little in size.

One morning, Jake helped Wiley down the steep hill to the ruins of their cabin. They stood in silence for a long time staring at the rotting moss-covered logs lying in a jumble in front of the cliff. Even the rock that once had been the back wall of their cabin seemed more eroded, and large cracks ran through it where none had shown before. The huge spruce that had soared a hundred feet above their cabin and had masked the smoke from their fires lay dead and rotting beside the cabin ruins.

Wiley dropped his right crutch and slid his arm around Jake. "It seems impossible our cabin looks like this." He nodded toward the rock wall. "The spring isn't even flowing anymore."

Jake looked into Wiley's eyes. "It won't be like this when we go back. Will it?"

"I hope not."

* * *

The following Wednesday, Jim suggested going to Denver. He wanted to check the mail at their city house, assuming some hadn't been forwarded, and see if the neighbor boy had cut the grass and watered like he'd been paid to do. Jake and Wiley jumped at the chance to see a city of two million people, but both admitted it scared them to think of one that size.

Not knowing how long they'd be in Denver, they decided to take both vehicles. Dave and Jim packed the perishable food, clothes and anything else they might need in the back of the truck, leaving plenty of room for Winnie in the Honda. Growing fond of Winnie, Jake opted to ride in the car with Jim so he could be near the dog during the trip.

Remembering Chief Eagle Rising's warning about this Time, Jake wanted to be prepared for anything. While the others were outside, he retrieved his and Wiley's pistols from behind the couch. Like Wiley had told him to do, he removed one bullet from each one and placed the hammer on the empty chamber, then carefully wrapped each gun and holster in a plastic trash bag. When no one was looking, he stuffed the bundle behind the seat of the truck.

While they sat at the kitchen table eating a light lunch before leaving, Dave asked, "Jake, are you going to bring your gold coins?"

Jake looked at Wiley. "We gotta bring 'em, Wiley. Dave said his jewels're sittin' in a bank in Denver."

Wiley frowned. "I hate to take them all. Let's only take ten and hide the rest here."

"I'll hide 'em, Wiley," Jake said. "I'm good at hidin' stuff. I used to hide stuff from Zeke an' Sara Jean, an' they never found none of it."

"I'll go with you, Jake," Dave said. "It'll be better if two of us know where they are in case we all get separated."

Wiley cleared his throat. "Dave, if I didn't trust you like I do, I'd never agree to that."

Dave blushed. "I...I really didn't mean that the way it sounded."

"Sure you did," Jim razzed. "You were hoping to sneak up here, get the coins and take off somewhere by yourself."

After the laughter died down, Wiley said, "I hope we can sell the coins in Denver and buy some of your gems, Dave. I'm convinced Billingsly will tell all if we wave them in front of his face." He shrugged. "If we can get back." Wiley smiled at Jim and Dave. "I also need money to pay you two back for everything you've bought for us."

"Wait until you see Dave's gemstones," Jim said. "He has an opal that would literally choke a horse."

"Dave, where did you get your training?" Wiley asked. "And your stones?"

"My grandfather gave me equipment he'd made from scrap metal from the Denver Tramway trolly cars and taught me what he knew. He bought most of his stones during the war when prices were cheap."

"Your grampa fought in the Civil War?" Jake asked.

Dave laughed. "No, he fought in the First World War, but not in the Second."

Wiley gasped. "There have been two world wars?"

"I'm afraid so," Jim said. "And countless smaller wars since eighteen eighty-six." While he and Dave cleared the table, they told them what they knew about the past and present wars.

Jake suddenly put his hands over his ears and shouted, "I don't want to hear no more about them wars! It makes me think'a my pa. He'd always be yellin' at me an' tellin' me I'm dummer'n hog shit!"

Later, while Dave looked on, Jake walked four paces due west from the outhouse, dug a spade-deep hole and buried the plastic bag containing the remaining coins. He filled in the hole and packed it down firmly with his hand. After brushing the site with a pine branch, he placed a nickel-sized, white rock resembling an arrowhead on the spot and sprinkled it with dry dirt. Jake tossed a few pine needles and sticks around and blew gentle puffs from the southwest over the entire area.

Dave clapped, then laughed when Jake turned crimson.

They started toward Denver at five-thirty that evening. Dave, with Wiley, took the lead in the truck. He used county roads through several new developments rather than the highway to Fairplay. The route snaked along the Horseshoe River for three miles, crossed over a range of forested hills, then straightened out across a treeless expanse.

Amazed and somewhat sickened at the number of cabins in the hills, Wiley shook his head. "These cabins all look newly constructed, and they're so close together. It's almost like a town, but there are no stores."

"Most of these people use their cabins only on weekends to get away from the city. They usually bring all their food and booze with them."

"They come all the way from Denver for two days?"

"It only takes couple hours to drive up here. An hour and a half if there's no traffic. But now that they're working on the road, it can take up to three hours when they're blasting."

"Is the railroad still running?" Wiley asked. "I didn't see tracks when we went to Fairplay."

"No. It stopped running in nineteen thirty-seven, and the tracks were pulled up shortly after. The road from Denver to Fairplay follows the train route through South Park, but you can still see the old railroad bed on the east side of Kenosha Pass. I'll point it out when we get there."

"I just rode that train a few months ago. It seems strange that it's no longer there." Wiley shook his head again. "This jolt in time is almost more than I can handle."

"I know what you mean," Dave said. "It's still hard for me to believe you're from the last century." He peered into the rear view mirror at the Honda and saw Jake waving his arms. Jim was laughing. "It looks like Jake is entertaining Jim back there."

Wiley turned around and looked through the back window. He broke into a grin as he watched Jake hang out the car window and point at a cabin. After he'd faced the front again, Wiley said, "I love that man. He's so innocent and full of kindness. And Jake is the funniest person I've ever known." He shook his head. "Jake's father tortured him the whole time he was growing up because Jake didn't want to have anything to do with women. It's a good thing his father is dead." Wiley shook his head. "I don't mean that. I'm sure Jake's father had his reasons for treating Jake that way, but it certainly damaged him. He's always thinking people are laughing at him because he can't read and write."

Dave sighed. "It sounds like Jake's father was like many parents of gays nowadays. Many people who say they're Christians hate gays and call us abominations in the sight of God. But I learned a lot about Jesus while I was in the monastery. Jesus does not hate us." Dave glanced at the big man sitting next to him. "Many people in this Time are absurd in the things they do and believe as far as religion is concerned. The Religious Right, which is an oxymoron, misquotes Paul and the Old Testament to spread their hate for gays and those who don't fit into their belief agenda. They never quote Jesus. It's like they're ignoring Jesus because He didn't condemn gays like they think He should have. And they have the audacity to call themselves Christians. I think they should call themselves Paulists or Levitikites or Genesides." Dave shook his head. "They seem to practice a religion of self-salvation by condemnation. I hope they won't shock you too much, especially Jake."

Wiley looked straight ahead. "So do I, Dave. So do I"

They drove in silence for several minutes, then Dave asked, "What religion are you, Wiley?"

Wiley smiled at Dave. "I have no white man's religion. I believe as Grandpa Gray Feather did, that the Great Spirit is our Father and the earth is our Mother. He is life and the air we breath, and She feeds us from herself. White man's religion, with the exception of Jake's friend Jesus, seems to want to destroy, hate and dominate. My belief lifts me to the heavens and allows me to love Jake, the most beautiful man I have ever known."

Dave fought to keep the truck on the dirt road. Being gay had caused him many horrors. He remembered one time during Mass a priest had yelled at him in the confessional that since he was gay, he surely had to be unrepentant. The priest had loudly refused him absolution, and he'd escaped the confessional and glares of the parishioners. Years had passed before he'd gone to church again, and then it was only to receive Jesus' body and blood for sustenance.

"Why did you ask what religion I am?" Wiley asked.

"I don't know. Maybe I hoped you would say what you just did. I was brought up Catholic and I've struggled with being gay all my life. The passage from Luke seventeen thirty-four, when Jesus said, 'Two men were in one bed, one was taken, the other was left' has kept me going." Dave glanced at Wiley. "Two men in one bed was taboo in Jesus' time, but he mentioned it. The Conservative Christians would never admit Jesus said that. And they would probably rant to the media...er, the press that I'm damned for saying any of this."

Wiley sighed. "It sounds like those people are trying to save their own necks by turning us in."

"That's what it seems like to me, too."

After a mile of silence, Dave said, "I've often wondered what the first thing Jesus will say to me when I see Him face-to-face. I think it will be, 'Tell me about the downtrodden you have loved.'"

Wiley thought of Jake and his eyes teared.

Leaning halfway out the open window, Jake yelled, "Damn! Lookit all them cabins!" He pulled his head in and looked at Jim. "What town is this, anyway?"

"It's not a town. All these people bought two or three acres like we did and built a cabin. Most of them live in Denver and come up only on weekends."

"These here people live in Denver?"

Out the side window, Jake watched a fenced plot go by. The cabin sat a hundred yards from the road and just inside the forest wall. Much of the two acres was a treeless mosaic of bunch grass and silver sage.

"Hell, two acres ain't nothin'. Can't even graze an old cow on two acres for more'n a week in these here parts."

Jim chuckled. "None of these people own cows."

"Why're they buildin' cabins if they ain't got no cows?"

"People want to get away from the city, so they come up here to relax in the mountains."

"This here's like a town. What do you mean relax? Do they sit around all day drinkin' an' playin' poker?"

"I'm sure some do. But most of these people putter around fixing up their cabins or go for walks...things like that. I suppose some even have TVs to watch the games."

"You keep talkin' about that TV. Is it somethin' like a spyglass so you can watch 'em playin' poker?"

Jim laughed. "No, it's nothing like that. And I didn't mean poker games. The TV is a box that has pictures of things in it. I can't explain it. We have one at the house in Denver. You'll see it when we get there. We decided we didn't want one at the cabin."

As they approached the town of Jefferson from the back way, Wiley sat forward in the seat and looked at the buildings. "I remember this town. Isn't this Jefferson? On my way to Alma, the train stopped here and took on water and a few passengers. I got out and walked around."

"It sure is Jefferson. Were any of these houses here then?"

Wiley pointed out the few houses and the church he remembered. They lined the street one block south of the highway. Wiley let out an excited yell when the old train station came into view. He chuckled. "I'm beginning to sound like Jake."

Dave drove slowly through the tiny town. "I'm going to stop at the store on the highway and get a can of juice. Do you want to go in?"

"Yes, I'd like to see what it looks like inside. This building didn't look like that when I came through."

Dave parked the truck as close to the door as possible, and Jim pulled in next to it. While Dave helped Wiley with his crutches, the other two approached.

Jake grabbed Wiley's arm. "Wiley, it sure is somethin' how them people built them cabins back there an' live in Denver. An' they ain't got no cows, neither. Jim said they got them TVs to watch instead'a cows."

Wiley frowned at Jim as he hobbled toward the store. "What is a TV?"

"You'll just have to see it to get the full impact."

As they jostled through the door trying to keep out of Wiley's way, Jake asked, "What're we doin' here?"

"I want some juice," Dave said. "You can get whatever you want."

The store was empty of people except for the owner, and he was ready to close. The four men crowded around the cooler to pick out something to drink.

Jake grabbed a can from the cooler and asked, "What's this?"

"That's a Pepsi," Jim answered, not paying much attention since he couldn't decide on grapefruit juice or peach nectar.

"What's a Pepsi fruit look like? I ain't never heard'a that before."

Dave and Jim laughed.

After selecting the peach nectar, Jim said, "Pepsi isn't fruit juice, Jake. Try it, but it's pretty sweet."

Jake put the Pepsi back and grabbed a couple cans of beer. "I'll have me some beer even if it tastes like river water from back home."

When Dave finally chose grapefruit juice, Wiley grabbed a can of it also, then glanced around the store. "Jake, this reminds me of Mrs. Mercer's store, but it's not as large."

Jake only nodded as he grabbed a half dozen candy bars and a bag of potato chips.

All the items, including Dave's pack of cigarettes, came to twelve dollars and thirty-eight cents. Jake and Wiley's eyes both mirrored shock.

"That's over a week's wages!" Jake yelled.

The store owner raised an eyebrow at him. "Son, I think you'd better get yourself a different job."

As the truck led the way down the eastern side of Kenosha Pass, Dave pointed out the old railroad bed high up on the north side of the valley. Wiley followed it with his eyes until it veered northward up a draw and disappeared.

Dave looked over at him. "Wiley, if you don't mind me asking, what kind of...sex did men have together in eighteen eighty-six?"

Wiley laughed. "I'll tell you, but you'll also have to tell me what you and Jim do in bed."

"Boy, you saw through that one quick."

Wiley shifted his injured leg. "To be honest, I don't think of it as sex. The word sex makes me think of self-gratification. What Jake and I have is love. The mere touch of our naked bodies together is all we usually need. We often spunk at the same time just holding each other and kissing."

"Spunk? What does that mean?"

Wiley cut his eyes to Dave. "Squirt or shoot. What do you call it?"

"Come."

Wiley shook his head and chuckled, then stiffly turned around and looked out the back window at the Honda. He grinned when he saw Jake waving his arms as he talked. Sitting back in the seat, he stared out the front window. "Jake has brought life to my soul. When we're naked and holding each other...it's like we're one being."

Stunned, Dave fell silent. He thought of all the wild contortions he and Jim had gotten into over the past years while having sex. Was sex merely self-gratification? Not entirely, he didn't believe. There had been occasions when he and Jim had climaxed at the same time. It was always better that way, and it had usually happened when they were being slow and affectionate. But the times they'd had wild sex had been enjoyable, too. They never went in for dominance and submission and never did anything to hurt each other, but they were familiar with every square inch of each other's body. Once in a while they'd engaged in two-ways with someone else, three-ways, and several times even orgies, but were always cautious and both got AIDS tested every six months. Thank God their last test had come back negative. Dave shuddered. They'd been lucky. Why had they risked getting AIDS by playing around with others? Maybe they needed to concentrate more on their love for each other?

"It's your turn," Wiley said.

Dave glanced at Wiley. "What?"

"You have to tell me what you and Jim do." Wiley chuckled. "I guess Jake and I aren't very exciting."

"Exciting? Wiley I'd give anything to be able to come like that with Jim every time we have sex. But we also like to..." Dave paused. "Do you ever suck each other off at the same time?"

"That's what Jake was doing to me when that man spied on us." Wiley smiled and shook his head. "I love it. And I want to do it to Jake as soon as I can."

Dave sighed. "I love getting it or giving it."

After a long silence, Wiley asked, "Do you and Jim have sex with others?"

"Sure. We don't own each other. We were jealous at first, but now we both know we'll come home." Dave glanced over at Wiley. "Have you two screwed each other?"

"What?"

Dave squinted. "Have you ever...stuck your dick up Jake's butt?"

Wiley stiffened as thoughts of Abe raping him flooded his mind. "No! I never want to hurt Jake that way."

Grinning, Dave raised his eyebrows and side-glanced Wiley. "It doesn't hurt if you relax." He shook his head and sighed. "And nothing feels better or makes you more relaxed than a good reaming-out by a hard dick."

At Robert's Tunnel, Dave slowed the truck and pulled into the parking lot. Jim parked beside it.

Jake rushed to help Wiley, and they all walked the short distance to a fence. From there they looked down on frothy, green water cascading out the tunnel and boiling into the sluice under the highway that emptied into the north fork of the South Platte River.

"This water comes from the Blue River near Breckenridge," Dave yelled above the roar. "It flows down the Platte into Denver's water supply."

"Denver needs that much water?" Wiley asked.

"That, and much more," Jim said.

"How long is this here tunnel?" Jake asked.

Dave scratched his head. "If I remember right, it's over twenty-three miles long, and I think it was finished in nineteen sixty-three. I read it cost eighty million dollars to build the tunnel and Dillon dam. And that was thirty years ago."

"Eighty million dollars!" Jake and Wiley shouted in unison.

"Damn!" Jake added. "That must be all the money in the whole damn world!"

"Don't cuss, *Jack*."

CHAPTER 14

While the four men stared at the water cascading out of Robert's Tunnel, two motorcycles roared up the highway and pulled into the parking lot.

Dave turned his head and noticed the bikers were dressed in black leather pants and jackets. He cringed and nudged Jim as the pair of gut-swollen men got off their bikes and lowered the stands. One of them, sporting circular, black-mirror sun glasses, wore his blond hair in a high Mohawk and had several long, silver earrings dangling from his right ear. The man began adjusting the straps that lashed his pack to the motorcycle.

The other, much larger biker had a bald head and a thick black beard. His grimy T-shirt was torn in front from the neck to the top of his bulbous stomach. After searching through his pack, he lit up a joint and leaned against his bike to smoke.

Both men looked extremely dangerous to Jim, and he was glad neither biker gave them a glance.

Jake started walking toward the pair.

"Oh, my God!" Dave said under his breath. "Wiley, those two guys might be gang members. They really look mean."

When Jake reached the bikers, he pointed to the motorcycles. "What're them things?"

Mohawk didn't pay any attention.

Baldy held the smoke in his lungs for a moment, then blew it toward Jake. "Them're bikes, dude. You been living with yer head up yer ass?"

Jim glanced at Wiley. "Jake's going to get beaten to a pulp if he gets those two mad."

Wiley raised one eyebrow.

"How d'you keep from fallin' over on them things with only two wheels?" Jake asked.

118

Mohawk looked up. "You jivin' us or what, asshole?"
Baldy shook his fist at Jake and snarled, "Get lost, motherfucker, before I cut you to pieces."
"Jake, let's go!" Dave yelled.
"Yeah, Jake," Baldy said. "You'd better go. Your fucking mama's calling you."
"You ain't got no right talkin' about Ma like that!" Jake shouted. "She's dead. You ain't got no manners." He felt himself getting riled. Without thinking, he slid his hand into his shirt and touched the rawhide bag. He thought of his friend Jesus and Chief Eagle Rising. A feeling of knowing surged through him.
"Wiley, these here men're robbers," Jake said over his shoulder.
Baldy threw down the roach and pulled out a knife from the sheath hanging on his belt. The long skinny blade flashed in the sunlight as he tossed it back and forth in his hands. He started toward Jake. "You want manners, motherfucker? I'll give you manners. And I'll teach you to call us robbers."
"Jake, be careful," Wiley said.
"It don't matter, Wiley," Jake shouted, keeping his eyes on the approaching biker. "He don't know nothin' about no knife. He holds it like Sara Jean."
"You filthy, lyin' motherfucker!" Baldy yelled. He gripped the knife in his fist and lunged at Jake.
Jake reached out, grabbed Baldy's wrist and held it. Then he growled and shoved the biker's arm down, forcing Baldy to plunge the knife into his own leg.
Baldy screamed in pain. When he looked down at the knife sticking out the side of his leg, Jake bashed him in the jaw with his mule-kick punch. Baldy fell flat on his back and didn't move.
Dave and Jim ran to Jake's side. Wiley hobbled after them on his crutches.
Mohawk gasped when he saw his cohort lying unconscious in the middle of the parking lot. He stared at the blood oozing out Baldy's leather pants where the knife stuck out of his leg. Realizing he was outnumbered, Mohawk raised his hands and started backing away.
"Hey, I don't want any trouble from you dudes!"
Dave ran to the road. He waved and yelled.

A Highway Patrol car squealed to a stop, then backed into the parking lot. A patrolman leaped out of the car and ran to the group. "I'm officer McHenry. What's going on here?"

Dave pointed to Baldy, still out cold. "That biker pulled a knife on Jake."

The officer ran to Baldy and yelled, "Who stabbed him?"

"He was gonna stick that knife in me," Jake said. "I jerked his arm down, an' that knife got stuck in his own leg." Jake eyed the officer's gray uniform. "Are you a reb soldier?"

"What?" McHenry looked quizzically at Jake, then rushed to his car, opened the trunk, pulled out a first aid kit and ran back to Baldy. He pulled the knife out of the biker's leg and used it to slice his leather pants leg open in four directions well past the wound. He tossed the knife to the ground. After tucking the four leather flaps under, he wrapped a pressure bandage around the bloody puncture.

When he started back to the car, Officer McHenry kept everyone in full view. "I've got to call for an ambulance. Then, I want the whole story. All of you stay right where you are!"

The instant the patrolman got to his car, Mohawk leaped on his motorcycle and frantically tried to start it.

Jake yanked him off the bike and threw him to the ground. "That soldier told us to stay here. You ain't goin' no place."

Stunned by the whole ordeal, Dave and Jim silently watched as Jake used his boot to shove Mohawk back to the ground when he tried to get to his feet. They heard Wiley chuckle.

Baldy slowly regained consciousness. He shook his head, glanced around and spotted the knife on the ground a few feet from him. He gritted his teeth, rolled over, grabbed the knife by the blade and drew his hand back to throw it at Jake.

Watching everything intently, Wiley quickly balanced on his good leg, grabbed his right crutch like a spear and flung it at Baldy the second before he threw the knife. The rubber end of the crutch hit the biker in the right ear, knocking his head sideways. He let the knife fall to the ground.

"Dave, get that knife away from him!" Wiley yelled as he steadied himself against Jim's arm.

Dave ran over and kicked the knife away from Baldy and picked up Wiley's crutch. He looked at Jake, still using his boot to keep

Mohawk on the ground, then at Wiley. The two blood brothers had acted so quickly and were so calm about the whole thing, he felt like he'd been watching a Chuck Norris movie. He handed the crutch to Wiley just as the patrolman returned.

"Now what's going on?" Officer McHenry demanded as he saw Jake standing over Mohawk.

"You told us to stay here, an' he tried runnin', so I threw him on the ground." Jake stooped down, grabbed the biker by his jacket and yanked him to his feet.

"I want to know what happened here," McHenry demanded. "Who started this?"

Dave took a few steps closer to him. "Jake just asked them what kind of bikes they had, and they took offense." He knew he shouldn't lie, but didn't want the officer to know Jake had never seen a motorcycle.

The patrolman looked at Mohawk. "Is that right?"

"Hell, no! That dumb dude wanted to know what the bikes were." He turned his head and made a snotty face at Jake. "Then he wanted to know why we don't fall over since they only have two wheels. We don't have to answer stupid questions like that. We were minding our own business."

McHenry frowned at Jake. "That's a pretty dumb thing to ask anyone. Sounds like you were trying to pick a fight."

"No, he wasn't," Wiley broke in. He glanced at Jake's downcast face. "And Jake's not dumb. He's from a small town in Kentucky and has never had occasion to ride one of those...er, gadgets. Jake asked an innocent question but was met with foul language and ridicule from both of them."

Wiley pointed to Baldy, sitting on the ground and holding his leg. "When that one tried to stab Jake, he merely defended himself."

"Oh God, it hurts!" Baldy screamed.

"The ambulance is coming from Bailey," McHenry said. "You'll get help soon." He pulled out the clipboard from under his arm and wrote something on a form. "I want all your names."

Wiley frowned. "After you pulled the knife out of that man's leg, you left it in his reach. When he came around, he picked it up and was going to throw it at Jake. I had to throw my crutch at him." He pointed at Baldy. "He's still sitting there without his hands tied.

When the other one tried to get away, Jake grabbed him. Everything is now under control. What more do you need from us?"

The patrolman glared at Wiley. "Are you telling me how to do my job?"

"No!" Wiley snapped. "I'm telling you how we did it for you."

"They're robbers, too," Jake said.

"Pretty goddamn sure of yourselves, aren't you," McHenry growled. "I might run you all in for bad-mouthing an officer."

"Maybe you should check them out," Jim broke in. "The one did try to run when you went to call for the ambulance. Jake and Wiley were just trying to help you."

Officer McHenry snorted, looked at Mohawk and said, "You. Get in the car."

Jake shoved Mohawk toward the patrolman. "You can have 'im. He smells like Thunder Joe."

After McHenry ordered Mohawk into the back seat of his car, he stood outside while he called in the motorcycle licence plates.

They heard the siren blaring long before the ambulance skidded to a stop in the parking lot. Jake and Wiley uncovered their ears when the sirens stopped. Two men jumped out of the emergency vehicle and ran to Baldy.

During the questioning, McHenry's radio began blaring and he ran to his car. Shortly, he ordered Mohawk out of the car, handcuffed him, then shoved him into the back seat again. He walked back to the group and stood in front of Jake.

"I just got a call. Those two are wanted in California and Denver for armed robbery. I don't know how you knew, but I want to thank you for your help. You're all free to go." He nodded, turned his back on them and headed toward the ambulance.

Wiley noticed the officer handcuffed Baldy to the stretcher. He glanced at Jake. How did Jake know they were thieves?

Later, in the Honda, Jake sat in silence as they passed the town of Grant, then he turned to Jim. "What was them things those men was ridin'?"

"They're called motorcycles, and to answer your next question, if you don't know how to ride one, you will fall over."

Jake shook his head. "There sure is some funny things in this here Time." He leaned back against the headrest and glanced out the window. "Only time I feel safe is when Wiley an' me are naked an' huggin' each other."

"You love Wiley a lot, don't you?" Jim asked.

Jake turned his head toward Jim. "Yes. I ain't never loved nobody except Ma before I met Wiley. My friend Jesus gave Wiley an' me to each other, an' bein' blood brothers is forever."

Jim smiled. "How do you know Jesus brought you and Wiley together?"

"I asked Jesus for a friend like Wiley before I left home. Thought it might be Donny. He was a miner in Alma." Jake shrugged. "After Wiley saved me from them Harrises an' asked me to be his blood brother, I knowed he was the one Jesus picked for me. Wiley's the best partner there ever was."

Still in the lead, as the truck passed Santa Maria, Wiley said, "I remember this place. The train stopped here and several passengers got off. I heard someone say it was Cassel's Resort."

"Cassel's Resort?" Dave looked at the camp. "I never knew it was a resort. I thought it had always been a camp for kids."

Dave looked in the rearview mirror, realized Jim wasn't behind them and pulled to the side of the road. After they waited five minutes and the Honda didn't appear, he turned the truck around and started back the way they'd come. The curve just before the entrance to the camp was dangerously tight and many head-on collisions had happened at that spot.

Wiley sat forward in the seat when they approached the entrance of Camp Santa Maria. Dave saw the Honda parked in the half-circle driveway and pulled in facing it.

Dave spotted Jim standing by himself under the arched stone gate. He leaped out of the truck and ran to him. Jim looked close to tears. "What's the matter? Where's Jake?"

Jim smiled weakly. "Come see." He turned and walked a few yards inside the grounds.

"Where's Jake?" Wiley yelled as he struggled out of the truck. He stood on his good leg and grabbed the crutches propped against the seat. Had Jake run because of the altercation with the two men a few minutes ago? He nearly stumbled trying to walk too fast on the gravel road. When he caught up with Jim and Dave, he gasped, "Where's Jake?"

Jim pointed to a clump of bushes about twenty feet away and next to a building.

Wiley saw Jake on his knees. At first, he didn't know what Jake was doing but followed the line of sight where Jake was looking and spotted the huge, white statue of Jesus on the side of the mountain.

"Oh, my God," Wiley whispered. "That's beautiful." He stood next to Jim in silence for a moment, then said softly, "Jake's talking to his friend."

Wiley hobbled over to Jake, stood beside him and looked down at the man he loved.

When Wiley slowly raised his head and gazed at the statue, Jim saw the light of the setting sun flash from tears in his eyes.

* * *

It was almost dark when Dave pulled the truck into a parking area next to the highway. As the four men and a dog peed in the bushes, Jake asked, "Can Wiley an' me be together when we go into Denver? I'd like him near me so I can feel safer."

Wiley laughed. "Jake, you took the words out of my mouth."

"That's fine with us," Jim said. "Dave, why don't you take the Honda with Jake and Wiley, and I'll drive the truck. You know more about Denver since you grew up there. You can fill them in with more details."

After shifting things around in the back of the truck so Winnie would have room, Wiley climbed into the front seat of the Honda. Before Jake got in, he hugged Jim. "Wish we could all be in one truck. You'll be alone."

"I don't mind. But I'll miss your comments on your first sights of Denver."

"No, you won't!" Dave yelled. He opened the back of the Honda and began pitching stuff out to get to the small compartment under the back floor. He grabbed the walkie-talkies, handed one to Jim and said, "Keep yours on receive, and I'll keep mine on send and you can hear all Jake and Wiley's comments. Someday we should get cellular phones in the cars."

Jim held up his walkie-talkie. "I forgot about these. We could have been using them all evening."

"Are those telephones?" Wiley asked.

"Almost," Dave said. "Jim will be able to hear everything we say as long as we stay close together."

After they re-packed the car, Dave took the lead in the Honda. When they approached the road construction near the Tiny Town exit, Jake leaned forward and pointed at the earth movers and graders parked along the highway. "Wiley, look at them big things." He tapped Dave on the shoulder. "What're they for?"

"Those are the trucks and front loaders they use to widen the road. The ones with the big scoops in front pick up dirt and rock, dump it into the trucks, and they haul it away." Dave glanced in the rear mirror. No cars were behind Jim, and he slowed down to let Jake and Wiley get a longer look.

"They're taking away the entire side of that mountain," Wiley exclaimed. "In our time, men have to do it by blasting and pick and shovel. Those machines are amazing."

A few miles past the construction, the mountains ended and the lights of Denver came into view in a slot between the hills in front of them.

"Damn!" Jake yelled. "That's like seein' heaven!"

"Good God!" Wiley shouted. "Those lights are so bright."

As they approached the I470 interchange, Jake leaned forward and pointed. "Look at that bridge. There's more'a them trucks up on top." After they traveled around the cloverleaf and arrived on the top of the bridge, Jake's eyes became big. "Ain't that somethin' how we was down there an' now we're up here? Look at all them trucks ever'where. How do they keep from hittin' into each other?"

Dave chuckled. "Everyone who drives has to obey laws, but cars still crash into each other. Driving can be dangerous trying to watch out for the other guy, especially the drunks."

Wiley gasped. "People drive cars drunk? It's hard enough to stay on a horse when you're drunk, but to drive one of these cars while drunk...in this chaos...is madness!" He felt a cold chill wondering what they'd learn next about the people of this Time.

Jake leaned forward in his seat. "Wiley, Chief Eagle Rising told me to beware of this here Time. Seein' all these here trucks ever'where makes me kinda scared." He sniffed the air. "An' what's that stink? I smelled it when we was buyin' clothes, an' now it's gettin' stronger. Kind'a makes me sick all over."

"I've noticed that also," Wiley said. "I can't put my finger on what it smells like. The only thing that comes to mind is...a kerosene fire...in an outhouse."

None of them could hear Jim laughing in the truck behind them.

Dave chuckled at Wiley's comment, then shrugged. "It's called pollution. Cars burn gasoline or diesel fuel, and the result is a smelly gas that fills the air. Plus hundreds of factories and business, who could care less about anyone's health, burn all kinds of poisonous crap that spews smoke into the air. In the daytime, the horizon looks brown from here."

As they approached the I70 interchange, Jake yelled, "There's another big road, an' that one's bigger'n the one we're on. How many of them big roads are there?"

"Quite a few. They have to make them wide to carry all the traffic. None of the highways in most cities are big enough, but it costs a lot of money to build them."

"Look, Wiley," Jake said, pointing at the rapidly approaching highway in front of them. "All them white lights comin' an' them red lights goin' looks like red an' white rivers goin' different ways."

Following behind in the truck, Jim was looking at Denver with new eyes as he listened to the conversation on the walkie-talkie. Jake and Wiley's comments made him realize he never wanted to live in a big city again. The things they said were true. He'd gotten so used to everything, he'd rarely given them serious thought for years.

Jim chuckled when he saw Dave turn onto the Sixth Avenue Freeway. "He's going to take them through downtown," he said out loud.

CHAPTER 15

When they reached the crest of the first hill overlooking the city, Wiley gasped at the vast sea of colored lights. "Those lights must stretch for...fifty miles."

"North and south it's about fifty," Dave said, "but east and west it's more like thirty. But I haven't been to the far eastern part of the city for several years. It could be fifty."

Jake leaned forward. "It's like somebody spilled a box of them jewels Bingsly wears."

In the truck behind them, Jim laughed. If Jake and Wiley hadn't told them about Billingsly, he would have thought they had drag queens in eighteen eighty-six.

At Simms Street, they began the long descent into the heart of the city. Jake pointed from the back seat. "Wiley, when I was first goin' to Alma I camped up here. I remember lookin' back an' thinkin' I could most likely see clear to Kentucky. Weren't no lights nowhere when it got dark."

Jake and Wiley gawked in awe at the hills covered with street lights, row upon row of homes, and gaudily lit businesses. They both remained silent as they listened to Dave relate things he knew as they sped along the slot carved through the middle of the city.

When they reached Federal Boulevard, Jake slid to the left side of the car and yelled, "Wiley, lookit them buildin's stickin' up over there! I ain't never seen nothin' like 'em my whole life!"

"Neither have I. Dave, how tall are those buildings?"

"The tallest one is seven hundred and twenty feet. It's about fifty-three stories. There would be taller ones, but airport restrictions prevent it."

"What do you mean by that?" Wiley asked.

"The airport is too close to downtown. If the buildings were any taller, planes might crash into them when they land from the west.

Whenever they finish the new airport, they may cancel the height restrictions."

"Can we go an' watch them planes?" Jake asked. "Them things're so damn little, I want to watch people squeeze into 'em."

"We'll go sometime this week. But you'll be amazed at how big they really are. They only look little because they're so high up. It still amazes me how such huge things can get off the ground."

Dave took Sixth Avenue to Clarkson Street and turned north to Eighteenth Avenue.

As they approached downtown from the east, Jake pointed at a tall building with a double-curved top. "Wiley, that there pink buildin' looks like your stiff dick."

Dave snickered. Jim, in the truck behind them, laughed out loud.

"Jake!" Wiley scolded with a chuckle. He looked up at the building. "I have to admit, it does look like a dick. Why would anyone build one like that?"

"People call it the cash register building, but now that you mentioned it, it really does look like a hard dick. Just think, Denver's the home of the biggest phallic symbol in the world. The building is a bank, but it should be a monument to all the pricks who voted for Amendment Two."

Following in the truck, Jim shook his head and muttered, "Oh, no. There he goes again."

"What's Amendment Two?" Wiley asked.

"It's an amendment to change the state constitution to allow people to discriminate against gays."

"Wiley, what's he sayin'?" Jake asked.

"I'm not sure. What are you saying, Dave?"

"It's an amendment that a so-called family rights group wrote so people like us can be denied housing and jobs. Some even hope we'll be beaten and murdered. Over half the people in the state voted for it, saying it was their Christian duty."

"It doesn't surprise me," Wiley muttered. "They must have run out of Indians."

As Dave drove through downtown, Jake hung out the window and looked up at the tall buildings, occasionally yelling, "Damn!" Wiley stopped scolding him after he stuck his own head out and began whispering the same thing.

128

"What happened to all them houses?" Jake asked. "When I was livin' here people had yards an' chickens."

"Most of the houses downtown have been gone for a hundred years."

Dave took a side trip down Blake Street through lower downtown. As they approached Fourteenth Street, Jake pointed to a coffee house in an ornate aged, red sandstone building.

"Wiley, that's where I was gettin' my hair cut when I first seen them Harrises!" He put his hand on Dave's shoulder. "Why're somma the buildin's still here from when I was livin' in Denver, but most're gone?"

Dave squeezed the steering wheel. "Because greedy developers decided to tear down twenty blocks of beautiful old buildings and put up those tall monstrosities!" He squealed around the curve to Fourteenth Street. "It pisses me off how the city officials, wanting to change Denver's image of being a cow town, went along with the idea like dogs chasing a *weenie* tied to the bumper of a car." Dave made a sweeping gesture with his hand. "As you can see, most of Denver's beautiful historic buildings are now gone."

"What's a weenie?" Jake asked.

Still seething about the loss of most of Denver's past, without thinking, Dave said, "A weenie is meat in the shape of a dick. They're called hot dogs."

"Meat in the shape of a dick?" Jake raised his eyebrows. "What's it for?"

"What?" Dave asked, finally aware Jake said something.

"What's them hot dicks for?"

Dave laughed and relaxed his grip on the wheel. "It's hot dog, Jake. You eat them. We'll get some at the store tomorrow."

Jake stared at Dave and asked, "Do married men eat them hot dicks...uh, hot dogs, too?"

Dave snickered. "They probably eat more of them than gays do, especially when they're watching other men play with their balls." He laughed out loud. "And they accuse us of having an obsession with male genitals."

"What are you talking about?" Wiley asked.

"Base*ball*, foot*ball* and basket*ball*. They sell hot dogs, I mean, hot dicks at all the games." Dave laughed, again.

Wiley shrugged. Dave was getting flippant. Wanting to change the subject, he asked, "Why is Denver so deserted? When I came through here, this city was teeming with activity."

"Everyone asks that question," Dave said. "Downtown used to swarm with people, even at night, until twenty years ago when they tore down most of the old buildings forcing small shops to move away. Then they built those skyscrapers with huge, empty lobbies...like mausoleums. They also tore down all the beautiful theaters, and now they wonder where the people are? They're nuts!"

Jim honked the horn in the truck three times.

Dave sighed. "Sorry, guys. I get carried away at times." He stuck his arm out the window and waved at Jim.

After he turned left onto Fifteenth Street, Dave headed northwest. As they approached Wazee, Jake pointed up the side street and yelled, "Wiley, that's where I hid from Seth the mornin' I left for Alma."

Making a sharp left, Dave got honked at by an oncoming car. Jim veered to the left, but waited until the traffic cleared before turning.

Dave drove slowly down Wazee, heading toward Cherry Creek. When they reached the middle of the block, Jake scooted to the left side of the car and pointed. "That there's the Ellerfant Corral. When I was hidin' in there from Seth, a man wanted to buy Mac. Said he was good horse meat."

Wiley chuckled. "I'm sure he said horse flesh, Jake. I'll bet he wanted Mac in the worst way." He touched Dave's arm. "Mac is the most beautiful horse I've ever seen."

"Why'd they dig all the dirt outta that corral?" Jake asked.

Dave pulled close to the parked car on his right, stopped and glanced across the street. "I don't know. It was a corral for many years. Maybe it stunk?"

They looked at the sunken patio surrounded by hundred-year-old buildings with outside glass walls encasing staircases and walkways. An iron grillwork sign in front read Elephant Corral.

"I remember reading about that corral," Dave said. "There's controversy about how it got its name. Some say it was named after another corral in Iowa, and others swear it was named after the saying, 'Go west to see the elephant.'"

"I never seen no ellerfant when I was here," Jake said.

"Elephant supposedly meant the gold fields of California and Colorado," Dave said. "When the owners of the corral outgrew this location, they moved it where they now hold the National Western Stock Show." He looked over at Wiley. "That's a yearly rodeo held here in Denver."

Jim appeared on foot at the truck window. "David, what are you doing? You nearly got creamed back there."

"Sorry," Dave said. He pointed across the street. "Jake hid from..." He turned his head to Jake in the back seat. "Who did you hide from in there?"

"Seth. He was trackin' me. Them Harrises want me dead."

"They're the ones who accused Jake of being the father of Sara Jean's baby," Wiley said, dryly. "We told you that last week."

Dave looked apologetic. "Right. I remember now."

Wiley smiled. "I'm not surprised you forgot. With all the things you have to put up with in this Time...thousands of cars, drunks driving them, criminals on two-wheeled machines, two million people...and half the state wanting you dead. It's a miracle you can remember anything."

As they drove up a rise in the residential area called Highland, northwest of downtown, they passed a row of small, one-story brick houses. Only three were still standing since the rest of the block had been turned into a park.

"Damn!" Jake yelled as he pointed at the homes. "I worked over a month helpin' to build them houses there!"

"Really?" Dave asked. He stopped the car in the middle of the street. "What did you do?"

Behind them, Jim slammed on the truck breaks, put his forehead against the steering wheel and sighed.

"I carried bricks up ladders for the men makin' the walls, an' planted trees an' stuff. They weren't big trees like those there ones." Jake rubbed his jaw. "Hell, somma them trees *are* the same ones!" Jake leaned out the window and looked up at a blue spruce, forty feet tall. "Howdy, tree! I get to see you all growed up!"

After they unloaded the car and truck at the house, a few blocks from Federal Boulevard, Jim started fixing dinner while Dave showed Jake and Wiley the guest bedroom and bathroom on the main floor. He took them upstairs to the attic where the master bedroom, a bath and a small office had been recently added.

"We did all the remodeling in the entire house ourselves," Dave said as Jake and Wiley looked around. "I'll never do it again."

Wiley hobbled over to Dave and put his arm around him. "We don't have to stay in Denver very long. Ever since we got here, you've been annoyed with everything. I'm sorry you brought us here since it's made you so upset."

"I apologize," Dave said. "You're right, though. I hate living in the city. It's so confining with all the buildings, noise, traffic, people... Sometimes I want to scream. It's like living in an anthill. Just keep telling me to be more positive while we're here, okay?"

"Sure will," Jake said as he grabbed Dave's shoulder. "We gotta stick together since we're like a family." He looked at Wiley. "Ain't we, Wiley?"

Before Wiley could answer, Jim came into the room. "Did I hear you say we're a family?"

Wiley let his crutches fall, and he held out his arm to Jim. "Yes, and we always will be."

The four men hugged.

*　*　*

As they sat on the deck in the back yard eating the light meal Jim had fixed, Jake kept trying to look over the six-foot cedar fence that surrounded the small yard. He finally asked, "How come you got that there fence closin' in ever'thing? You can't see nothin'."

"It's for privacy," Jim answered. "Sometimes I like to sunbathe nude, and I don't want anyone to see me."

"Now you can bathe by the sun an' you don't need no water?" Jake glanced at Wiley. "Thunder Joe'd like that."

Dave and Jim laughed.

"Sunbathing is just a word we use for laying out in the sun to get a tan." Jim saw Jake's puzzled expression. "What I mean is, I lay in the sun to get my skin tan so it's not so white. It doesn't clean the skin, but it makes me look healthier."

"By the way," Dave interrupted, "You both can take a shower if you want to clean up before you go to bed."

"I would like to wash up, but what do you mean take a shower?" Wiley scanned the cloudless sky. Why were there so few stars?

Since they were finished eating, Dave took the two men into the bathroom on the first floor and pulled back the shower curtain.

"You take a shower in here. First, turn on the water with these knobs. This one's cold and the other is hot. Turn them together to control the temperature." Dave twisted the knobs and tested the water with his hand. "Then turn this center knob." As he did, water sprayed out the shower head.

Jake jumped back. "Damn, it's like a pourin' rain in there." He started unbuttoning his shirt. "I'm gonna have me one'a them showers."

"You can take one together if you want. Just remember to keep the curtain closed and in the tub so the bathroom doesn't get wet. You can use those towels, and soap is on that rack."

"It looks wonderful," Wiley said as he began taking off his shirt.

Dave watched them undress for a minute, sighed, then went out and shut the door. While he and Jim washed the dishes, they could hear laughing in the bathroom, followed by a long silence with the sound of water spraying against the shower curtain.

Fifteen minutes later, they heard Jake yell, "Help! How d'you get this here water from bein' only cold!"

Jim went to the door. "You used up all the hot water. You'll have to stop or take a cold shower from now on."

"Okay," Wiley replied.

Still puttering in the kitchen, Jim noticed the water ran for another ten minutes. A short time later, he heard the men walk down the hall, then the door to their bedroom slammed.

Jim suddenly realized Wiley shouldn't have taken a shower with his bandages. He rushed to their door and knocked. "Wiley, I'd better change your bandages. I'm sure they got wet."

"Come on in," Wiley said.

When Jim opened the door, he was secretly dismayed to see they had both donned the robes that had been hanging in the closet. He made Wiley sit on the bed while he removed the wet bandages. The wounds were healing nicely. Most of the red had disappeared, and the wet scabs looked healthy.

A half hour later and still in their robes, the two men came out of the bedroom.

Jake followed Wiley into the kitchen and said, "That there shower was like standin' under the waterfall me an' Wiley found in the Horseshoe River. 'Specially after the water got cold. Right, Wiley?" He grinned at Wiley, but his smile faded when he realized Wiley wasn't listening to him, being completely taken up by something in the other room.

Jake turned toward the living room and saw a man's moving face on the front of a black box. He reached for the sleeve of Wiley's robe.

"What is that?" Wiley asked.

"That's the TV," Jim answered. "Here's two mugs of hot chocolate. Take them in and watch it. I told you I couldn't describe it.

"Wiley, that man's in that box!" Jake turned and looked at Jim. "How'd he get in there?"

"He's not in the box. It's just a picture on the screen. That's the News Channel. Go on in and watch it."

The two men slowly walked into the living room. They held onto each other the entire way as they stared at the TV. Their forgotten hot chocolate still sat on the counter that divided the kitchen from the open dining and living room.

As the blood brothers slowly sat down on the couch, Jim brought in their mugs and set them on the coffee table. He smiled when he saw their faces, then crept upstairs to get Dave, not wanting him to miss this unusual event.

"So, what do you think of TV?" Dave asked as he reached the bottom step.

Wiley tore his eyes away from the screen and looked at Dave. "What?"

"What do you think of TV?"

"It...it's amazing." Wiley glanced back at the screen and asked, "How does it work?"

Before Dave could answer, Jake stood up, went over to the set and touched the screen. "Wiley, there's glass closin' in that little man."

The picture suddenly changed. A red truck spun its wheels as it roared up a mountainside.

Jake jumped back and yelled, "How'd that truck get in there? What happened to that man?" He touched the screen again, felt a static shock, gasped and rushed back to the couch.

"Wiley, that thing bit me," Jake whispered. He stuck his finger in his mouth.

Wiley slid his hand across Jake's shoulders and frowned at the screen.

"The truck's not really inside the box," Dave said. "But I don't know how it works well enough to explain it." He grabbed the remote. "There's quite a few channels to watch since we have cable." He pushed the "channel up" button and the scene changed to a black-and-white movie.

"Hey, there ain't no color now!" Jake yelled. "That looks like one'a them pitchers of people Ma used to have."

Dave flipped a couple more channels and stopped at professional wrestling. "I watch this a lot."

The two men in the ring bounced off the ropes and slammed into each other.

"Is that some kind of wrestling?" Wiley asked. "It looks phony to me. No real wrestler would do that."

Two more wrestlers leaped into the ring and it became a free-for-all. When one man bashed two others' heads together, Jake yelled, "Wiley, that's like the fight we had in the Silver Heels Bar!"

Later, as Dave and Jim cuddled in bed in the far corner of the attic, they faintly heard Jake and Wiley yelling as they watched late-night wrestling.

CHAPTER 16

In a dark corner of the Dusty Miner Bar in Alma, Carmen Jones sat on a stool with her hands folded over her apron and watched Edna Scott serve all six of the bar's customers. Wednesday's were usually slow, but tonight was no different than any other when it came to who got the tips. The locals yelled only for Edna when they wanted a drink, and it wasn't Edna's looks that made her so popular. It was pity. The townsfolk made it clear they felt sorry for Edna having to put up with her drunken husband. And now that Louis had moved back in, they had rallied behind Edna, even giving her decent tips. Carmen knew that was quite a statement in this community.

What made matters worse, she was dating Louis and often found herself embroiled in spats between him and Edna. Since she would always take Louis' side, Edna had little to do with her.

Carmen resented Edna for accusing Louis of being a worthless, gambling slob. Louis didn't gamble. He would have told her if he did, and she believed him when he'd said his debts came from a business deal that fell through. That kind of thing happens all the time.

Eager to help Louis pay off his debts, Carmen had followed his suggestion and had applied for the part-time job at the Dusty Miner. She knew Louis worked long hours, plus it was a sixty-mile drive to Cripple Creek where he'd said his office was located. She didn't believe Louis, however, when he'd accused Edna of having a boyfriend, but had agreed to watch her in the bar to find out who he was.

Still perched on the bar stool by the wall, Carmen smoothed back her long blond hair, then brushed away a strand that had fallen on her faded Levis. She watched Edna walk down the dimly-lit hallway to the women's rest room.

The front door opened and a tall, distinguished man walked in and looked around. A stranger, and he was fair game.

Carmen slid off the stool, waited until the man sat at a small table in the center of the room, then approached him.

"What can I get for you?" she asked, smiling. She tossed back her hair.

"Is Edna Scott here?" the man asked.

Carmen stuck her nose in the air and snapped, "Edna's indisposed at the moment. I'm sure she'll be out soon to take your order." She started to walk away.

"Wait," the man said. "Can't you take my order? I'd like a scotch and water."

Carmen spun around and smiled. "Coming right up."

After Carmen placed the man's drink on a napkin, she backed up a step and asked, "You're here to see Edna?" Thinking he might be Edna's mysterious lover, she decided to get the man to talk. She hoped Louis would treat her better if she gave him some concrete information.

The man shifted in his chair. "Yes. I have a little business to conduct with her."

"Business?" Now, wondering if the man might be a divorce lawyer, she added, "Personal business?"

"Why, yes. How did you know?"

Carmen smiled. She had him. "Why, Edna and I confide in each other about everything. I'm her…sister-in-law."

"Oh. Well then, you must know about the coins."

Trying not to look surprised, Carmen said. "Oh, yes, the coins. I almost forgot about them." She leaned toward him. "What about them?"

"Why, I'm here to buy the rest of them. Edna must have told you."

Carmen's mind raced. "Oh, yes, of course. So you're the man buying them." She extended her hand and said, "I'm Carmen."

"Linus Avery." He shook her hand.

Carmen slid into the chair opposite Linus and smiled. "Edna is such a case. She's talked about those coins and selling them and all, but the dear woman forgot to tell me where she got them. Did she tell you?"

"Why, of course. They were given to her by four men. As near as I could tell, it had something to do with the sale of some land. The men paid her with the coins. They said they'd found them, but I didn't catch where it actually was." He smiled. "I was glad to get them so cheap. At a thousand dollars apiece, they're a real find."

"Mr. Avery, how good to see you," Edna said as she walked up to the table. She glanced at Carmen. "You look a little ill, dear. I'll take over here. Why don't you lie down for a while."

Carmen looked up at Edna. "What?"

Edna forced a smile for Linus Avery's benefit. "I said you look ill. Why don't you go in the back and lie down on the couch. Anyway, Mr. Avery and I have a little business to conduct."

"Oh. Yes, I think I will." Carmen could barely stand.

Edna grabbed her arm. "I'll help you to the back."

Carmen pulled her arm out of Edna's grasp. "No! I'm fine. I just got a little dizzy all of a sudden." She nodded to Mr. Avery, snatched up her tip and hurried into the back room. Without turning on the light, Carmen stopped just inside the door. She had to know what kind of coins were worth a thousand dollars apiece.

Linus Avery saw Carmen's reaction to his statement about the value of the coins and realized instantly what was wrong with her. He hoped he hadn't said too much and felt embarrassed and ashamed for his big mouth.

Edna became alarmed when she saw the strange look on Mr. Avery's face. She sat down at the table and asked, "Have you changed your mind about buying the coins?"

"Er...no, I haven't." Avery couldn't bring himself to tell Edna what he'd told Carmen. "I have four thousands and ten hundreds, just like you asked." He handed Edna an envelope and said, "I'm sorry it's been so long since I last saw you, but I was called to Denver on business."

"Think nothing of it," Edna said. She smiled into the envelope. "Oh, this makes me so happy. Thank you so much." Edna reached into her apron pocket and pulled out a tissue-wrapped bundle. She unfolded it and handed the coins to Linus.

As Carmen looked on from the darkness of the back room, she knew the coins were gold. They seemed awfully small, only about dime size, and thought again about what Mr. Avery had told her. Edna had sold some land. She wondered if Louis knew.

* * *

The following morning, Louis Scott got up early and tiptoed through the small house. He could set off a bomb and it wouldn't wake Burt, but Edna was a light sleeper and he didn't want her to see him snooping around in the kitchen. Not that it mattered, but he didn't feel like an argument so early in the day. After he started the coffee-maker, he carefully searched in all the hiding places he knew Edna had stashed money in the past. First, he looked in the cookie jar, then the ceramic rose bowl on the top shelf beside the window, and finally behind the cookbooks in the cupboard above the stove. No money anywhere.

Irritated, Louis poured himself a cup of coffee and slid into a chair. Edna startled him when she came into the room. He noticed one of her pink curlers, loosely attached to a few strands of hair, hung over the collar of her faded, flower-print robe.

Edna looked harshly at Louis' skinny frame slouched in the chair. His elbows rested on the table and his dull, hazel eyes peered at her over the cup he held near his face.

"I don't have any money if that's what you've been looking for," Edna snapped. "The last of my paycheck went for Burt's bottle of scotch."

She shuffled to the sink, turned on the cold tap, then searched the cupboard and found a clean glass. She stood silently in front of the sink and watched the running water, occasionally testing its coldness with her finger.

"I need a hundred dollars by eight tonight," Louis said in his whiny, nasal voice. "I lost at poker again last night, and Al won't extend me any more credit." He wiped a few greasy strands of brown hair away from his eyes and took a sip of coffee.

Without turning around, Edna said, "Your gambling debts don't concern me at all. I'm not your mother. Even if I were, I wouldn't give you money for things like that."

She surprised herself that she could talk that way to Louis, but today she felt brave. Last night, after leaving work early, she'd called her friend Janice in Denver to ask advice about escaping somewhere, and Janice had insisted she come to live with her. After all, Janice had explained, her husband had recently died and she hated living alone.

Edna already had most of her things packed. Since she planned on taking the three-thirty bus to Denver this afternoon, the last thing she wanted to hear about was Louis' gambling debts. She drank her water slowly, staring out the window so she wouldn't have to look at Louis. He reminded her of a pock-faced weasel. She loathed him.

"I know you have money," Louis said. "Carmen told me some man gave you money for some gold coins last night. Where'd you get gold coins, Edna?" He decided not to mention the land...yet.

Edna nearly choked on her water. Her mind raced.

"Some friends of mine found them, and they gave me a few," she said without thinking.

"Found them where?" Louis asked. He knew she was lying and wanted to make her squirm."

Realizing she didn't know, Edna said, "They...they found them in an old shack somewhere. A man bought them from me and I...I put the money in a...money market. I won't get any pension, and I have to look out for the future."

"Who did you sell my land to, Edna? Carmen said the men who bought the land paid you with the gold coins. "

Edna set the glass in the sink and stared out the window. "I sold it to the men who own the land on the top of the cliff. You should have sold it to them in the first place." She turned suddenly and left the room.

Louis heard Edna slam her bedroom door. A shack? The gold coins were found in a shack? He slammed his fist on the table when he remembered the fallen-down cabin on the land he'd once owned. Gold coins? He panicked. If Edna had sold that land, this was his last chance to look in the ruins of that shack to find the gold he'd always known was there.

*　*　*

Louis chuckled to himself as he drove Burt's car down the dirt road toward Bristlecone Peak. He thought of all the things he would do with the money he'd get from the gold. First, he'd buy a Lincoln. Al would crap in his five-hundred-dollar suit seeing him drive up to the Gold Nugget Gambling Palace in a new Lincoln. Louis chuckled. He had no doubts there would be some kind of gold under the ruins of that old cabin. He should have looked for it sooner. He pushed his foot on the gas pedal and gripped the steering wheel tighter. What if there wasn't any gold? No matter. If he didn't find anything under the cabin, one way or another, he'd get Edna's money. He knew she'd lied about the money market.

Louis parked the car on the road and climbed the steep hill to the rock pinnacle that stood at the edge of the ridge. He snuck around the lower side of the rock, hoping no one would be in the cabin next door. Finally satisfied he was alone, he walked to the edge of the cliff and looked over.

Louis gasped when he saw the rotten logs of the old cabin scattered down the slope. "Somebody's been digging there already!" he yelled.

Cursing, Louis scrambled down the uneven face of the cliff. At the ruins, he saw some of the logs lying askew had clumps of dirt and grass clinging to them at odd angles. The grass was still green! Someone had done this only days before!

"Those assholes found those coins in my cabin!" Louis screamed. "They bought *my* land with *my* gold! I'll kill them!"

Louis angrily pulled at a log and tried tossing it aside, but he wasn't strong enough so he grabbed a rotted floor board. When he pulled up on it, the board crumbled. He cursed and threw the spongy wood at the rock wall. It shattered into hundreds of pieces.

Louis suddenly realized a car had climbed up the driveway and stopped at the cabin above. Thinking it must be the men that bought the land with his gold, he searched the area and spotted a three-foot section of weathered, but substantial board with two rusty nails sticking out the end. He pulled the board loose, felt the nails, then gritted his teeth and started up the slope toward the cabin.

CHAPTER 17

The morning sun filtered through billowy, sheer curtains and fell across Cynthia Havertine's arm as she lay sprawled across her bed. For days she'd thought of little except the two gorgeous men she'd seen at Bristlecone Peak. The other men with them weren't ugly, but the big ones were the most handsome and masculine men she'd ever seen. And she wanted them. Every inch of them.

"They can't be gay!" she yelled for the hundredth time, pounding her fist on the bed. "They're lying! Brad's lying! Two men that gorgeous *can't* be gay."

The phone rang.

"Dammit!" Cynthia rolled to the edge of the bed and grabbed the phone. "Who is it?" she snapped.

"Cyn? It's me, Donna."

"Oh. Hi, Donna." Cynthia relaxed, rolled on her back and raised her right foot into the air. A pink satin slipper hung over her big toe. "You're calling early."

"Yes, I know. I got to thinking about you and decided to see if you were over those two men you saw last Sunday. Is Brad talking to you yet?"

"No, and no! Brad's been acting like a baby, and I was thinking of those two gorgeous men when you called. Donna, I can't get them out of my mind. I don't believe they're gay."

"Did they come right out and say they were gay?"

"Not exactly." Cynthia tossed the slipper against the wall and lowered her leg. "Brad said they were." She sat up. "Come to think of it, the blond knocked Brad out after he'd said the word gay, but I couldn't quite hear what they were talking about. Donna, they're not gay! Why else would he have hit Brad?"

"It's sounding better all the time, Cyn. I think we should drive up there and check out the situation. We can take my Cherokee and leave Brad at home. I'd love to feast my eyes on a real man for a change. From what you've said, they sound like hunks."

"Oh, they are! Did I tell you the blond has a down-south way of talking that's wonderful? He's straight out of a western movie. Naked, he's breathtaking."

"What about the other one? You said he had black hair? Which one was on crutches?"

"The black-haired one was on crutches. He's just as gorgeous as the blond, but in a more reserved way. I can't imagine him marching through a department store wearing nothing but see-through briefs, but I'd love to see him do it!"

"When should we go?" Donna asked. "I can't wait!"

"What about today? Can you be here in an hour?"

"An hour! Are you kidding? I'm still in the tub, and I plan to be here for another half hour. You know Thursday's my milk-bath day. What if I pick you up at eleven?"

"It's Thursday already?" Cynthia glanced around the room. "Er...okay, eleven it is. See you then."

* * *

Reaching the driveway to Dave and Jim's cabin, the two women saw a pale blue car parked on the road.

Cynthia eyed it. "I don't remember them having an old car like that. Maybe they have visitors?"

"I hope the visitors are men." Donna put the jeep into four-wheel drive and started up the steep driveway. After a rocky hundred yards that severely tested the shocks of the Cherokee, they reached the top of the ridge. Donna drove around the circular driveway to the closest spot to the cabin and stopped. They both got out and walked toward the building.

Donna shook her head. "It looks deserted, Cyn."

They climbed the stairs to the porch and knocked on the door. No one came. Cynthia tried the door but found it locked. She peered through a window, then turned to Donna.

"It doesn't look like they're here. I think they've gone somewhere for a while. The place looks too tidy." She stepped aside. "What do you think?"

While Donna shaded the sun and looked inside, Cynthia turned toward a noise down the hill. She grabbed Donna's arm and whispered, "Someone's coming up that hill. Maybe it's them."

They ran down the steps, out onto the rocks, looked over the side of the cliff but couldn't see anyone through the trees.

Cynthia yelled, "Hello! Who's there?" She gasped when she saw a man approaching through dwarf aspens where the rocks of the cliff disappeared into the slope. He had a board in his hand with nails sticking out the end.

Donna finally saw him. She reached down and picked up a fist-sized rock, just in case.

When Louis saw the women his face contorted into rage. "Who the fuck are you? Get off my land!"

Cynthia glanced at Donna, saw the rock in her hand and picked one up also, then yelled, "Don't come any closer. I know you're lying. This land belongs to the two men who own this cabin. And you're not one of them."

"The property line is where you're standing, lady, so move it!" Louis waved them toward Jim and Dave's cabin.

Cynthia took two steps toward the structure and stopped. "There! Satisfied?" For some reason, she wasn't afraid of the skinny, greasy-looking man even though he held the board. She frowned, raised the rock as though she meant to throw it and asked Donna, "Shall we get him?"

"It's him or us," Donna said, tossing her rock into the air and catching it. It didn't feel as heavy as it did when she'd picked it up.

Louis' angry expression changed to uncertainty as he watched the women walk toward him. "Wait! I...I didn't mean to get so angry." He gestured toward Dave and Jim's cabin. "I'm pissed off at those two assholes. They found my gold, then bought my land with my gold!" He whacked a rock with the board and it splintered into hundreds of small pieces. "Damn them! I'll kill them if I ever see them again!" He sat on the same rock he'd smacked and covered his face with his hands. "They found my gold. Damn them!"

The women stared at Louis and both dropped their rocks.

Cynthia scanned the ground. "Gold?" Her eyes widened and she half smiled. "There's gold here?"

"Not any more," Louis whimpered. "Those assholes took it all." He pointed down the slope. "It was in that old cabin at the bottom of the cliff." Still sitting, he kicked a pine cone. "I knew I should have come here sooner."

"Who are you?" Donna asked.

"Louis. Louis Scott. I owned this land."

Donna put her hands on her hips. "What do you mean owned? Do you own it or don't you?"

"I did own it, then I sold it to my sister-in-law. But it was still in the family. Edna's the one that sold it to those assholes, and they paid her with my gold." He grabbed a rock and threw it at Dave and Jim's cabin. It hit the steps and bounced back at him.

Louis glared at the two women. "They paid Edna for the land with gold coins they found in that old cabin down there. And that cabin was on my land when they found them. I'm going to *sue* them!"

"That's a despicable thing to do," Cynthia said. "How could anyone do that?"

"Well, they did!" Louis wiped his nose with his sleeve. "The coins were worth a thousand dollars apiece."

"A thousand dollars!" Donna yelled. "How many were there?"

"I don't know. All I know is they gave Edna five of them for the land, and last night some man paid her a thousand dollars apiece for them."

Louis struggled to his feet and kicked one of the splintered pieces of board. He eyed the two women and demanded, "Who are you, anyway?"

"I'm Cynthia Havertine. This is my good friend, Donna Cornwall. We're from Buena Vista."

"What are you doing here?" Louis' eyes hardened. "Are you friends of those fucking crooks?"

"No," Cynthia said. "We just met them last week. At least I did. I wanted to ask the two men staying with them if they'd work for me." She glanced at the cabin. "But I guess they're not around."

Louis kicked a rock and sent it skittering across the top of the cliff. "They're probably living it up somewhere with my gold!"

Cynthia shook her head. "It really shocks me they could do something like that. Both times I saw them none of them looked like the type to do something like that." She shook her head. "I guess it's true that looks can be deceiving." She glanced at Louis. "Can we do anything for you?"

"Like what?"

"I don't know. Do you need any money? A ride somewhere? I don't know, really. I just asked because I feel bad for you."

Louis shook his head. "I have a car. It's parked down on the road."

"Oh, that's your car," Donna said. "Cyn and I thought the men had company."

Louis stared at Cynthia. "Sin? She calls you Sin?"

Cynthia laughed. "C-Y-N. It's short for Cynthia. It fits rather well, don't you think, Donna?" She smiled and flipped back her red hair.

"Oh, quite!" Donna laughed.

"I do need money," Louis broke in.

"Oh?" Cynthia's smile changed into a distrustful scowl. "I suppose I could give you a ten." She started toward the Jeep.

"Forget it!" Louis yelled. "I don't mean a few bucks. I need money to sue those guys for stealing my gold. I'd give you half whatever I recover if you help me sue them. They could have found a hundred of those coins. Two hundred, even. That would be two hundred thousand bucks!" He clenched his fists. "Dammit, I could *kill* them!"

Cynthia folded her arms. "You don't know they had more than five coins. In fact, you don't even know they found them down there. They could have found them anywhere."

Louis' eyes became slits, and he glared at Cynthia. "Oh, they found them down there, all right. When I got here, that old cabin down the hill had been torn apart. And it was done recently, too. I've been down there trying to see what they missed."

"Did you find anything?" Donna asked.

Louis glared at the ground. "No." He looked at the women. "So, you won't help me?"

Cynthia looked at Donna, then said to Louis, "Let me think about it." She walked to the jeep, rummaged through her bag, returned to the others and handed a pad and pen to Louis. "Write down your name and phone number. If I decide to help, I'll call."

Donna touched Cynthia's arm. "Why don't you give Louis your phone number? If he sees those men anywhere, maybe he can call you. The two we're after may not be involved in this."

"Good idea." Cynthia shook her head. "I hope they're not."

CHAPTER 18

The rising sun spilled parallel lines of golden-pink light into the living room through partly open blinds as Jim descended the stairs from the attic. He saw Jake and Wiley, in disarrayed robes, huddled together on the couch, sound asleep. The TV was still on.

Following behind, Dave laughed. "Worst case of couch potatoes I've ever seen."

When Jim reached the front window and raised the blinds, the flood of light caused Jake to pop awake.

"Damn, it's daylight." Jake rubbed his eyes. "How'd it get to be mornin' so fast?" He looked down at Wiley's head resting in his lap and stroked Wiley's black hair. "We must'a fallen asleep watchin' that there TV."

Wiley stirred, buried his face into Jake's crotch for a moment, then lifted his head and sat up straight. He grabbed his shoulders and planted a kiss on his lips. "Howdy, pardner." He glanced at Dave and Jim. "I heard that on a moving last night."

"A mo-vie," Jim corrected. "Probably a John Wayne movie."

"Oh, that's right...movie," Wiley said. "That TV is captivating. For a long time, Jake and I didn't say a word to each other. I hope you can explain to me how it works. It's the most amazing thing I've ever experienced. It seems to draw my mind into itself."

"It's scary as hell," Jake said. "Sometimes I didn't know where I was. But them things we saw sure was somethin'. 'Member Wiley, that man gettin' hisself banged on the head with a naked chicken?" Jake snickered and shook his head. "I ain't never seen nothin' like that."

Wiley grabbed Jake's leg. "And the cook that sat in his own pot of soup."

They held each other and laughed.

Jim raised an eyebrow at Dave. "We know where they'll be from now on."

"I didn't think the Three Stooges were on anymore." Dave rubbed his jaw. "I wish I'd seen it."

Jim grabbed the remote and started to switch off the television.

"Wait," Wiley said. "I have some questions about the things we saw last night. Why did something else always interrupt what we were watching? Like cars and food. Jake and I kept thinking they were part of the...movie. We'd get confused."

"Those are commercials," Jim said. "The company that pays for the program you're watching advertises their product every chance they get. Sometimes I think the commercials last longer than the actual program."

"I don't like them 'mercials," Jake said. "They make me feel like it's my pa talkin', an' if I didn't like what they was showin' I'd be dummer'n hog shit."

Wiley shot Jake a surprised glance. "I felt that way too." He looked at Jim. "After I'd watched several of them, I felt irritated. It was like they were shoving their food or gadgets out at me. Why would I even want any of those gadgets in the first place?" He slid his arm over Jake's shoulder. "Jake and I got especially tired of seeing the same car all the time, and all that yelling. But like Jake said, I felt insulted."

Dave chuckled. "That probably wasn't the same car. Cars all look exactly alike nowadays, so I can see why you'd say that." He raised his eyes to the ceiling and sighed. "I think they're all shaped like turds."

Wiley chuckled.

"Most commercials purposely try to make you feel guilty for not buying their product," Dave continued. "And if you think the commercials insult your intelligence, wait until you see some of the weekly sit-coms everyone thinks are so funny."

On the television screen, a man and a woman ran at each other through a field of yellow daises. Jake pointed and asked, "Why're they mashin' all them flowers?"

Dave picked up the remote and switched off the television. "Flowers don't matter, Jake, not when there's money to be made. Nowadays, nothing matters when money is to be made."

* * *

Dave let Wiley finish setting the table on the deck for breakfast and went inside to help Jim dish up the food.

Jake followed him into the kitchen, went to the sink and stood next to Jim. "I'd use that there basin outside to wash, but there ain't no dryin' rag, so I'll do it here."

Jim glanced at him. "What basin outside?"

"That round one sittin' in them flowers."

"The birdbath?"

Dave rushed outside with his hand over his mouth.

Jim smiled at Jake. "Did you wash up outside at home?"

"Mostly. If there weren't no water in the pitcher on the tree stump out back, I'd wash up in Mac's trough."

When Dave finally returned to the kitchen to help carry out the food, he didn't dare look at Jake.

The last one to sit at the table, Jake grabbed the pole of the umbrella and turned it. "This here thing's like bein' at a race track back home in Kentucky."

Wiley looked up at the umbrella. "Why is that, Jake?"

"Cuz all them gussied-up women sit under these here things tryin' to make like the horse-shit stink don't bother 'em."

Dave burst out laughing.

Jake grinned as he slid three fried eggs and a pile of bacon into his plate with his fingers.

Wiley frowned at Jake until he saw Dave serve himself the same way.

Jim picked up the thermos coffee server. "Would anyone like coffee?"

Wiley and Dave held out their cups.

Jake hesitated, but finally picked up his cup and stretched his arm toward Jim. "I only want a little. I had me some already, and it don't got much taste. Wiley an' me boil our coffee 'til it's strong, an' then toss in cold water so the grounds go to the bottom."

After Jim poured everyone's coffee, Jake took a sip. "I hope where were goin' today has restin' rooms. Coffee makes me hafta pee."

Jim laughed. "It does the same thing for me. Don't worry, I know where most of the rest rooms are in the entire city."

Jake served himself four more eggs, and Wiley took three more plus a half dozen strips of bacon.

"You guys had better watch your cholesterol eating all those eggs," Jim said.

"What the hell's colster-all?" Jake asked.

"Cholesterol is fat that gets into your blood and causes blocked arteries. Eggs are high in it."

"Hell, back home I was eatin' eggs before I even started peein' in the river, an' I ain't got fat blood." Jake looked at Wiley. "Do you?"

"How can we tell?" Wiley asked.

"A doctor can do a test on your blood," Dave said. "But I don't think either of you have to worry about cholesterol. I'm sure you both get plenty of exercise. I should be so lucky."

* * *

As they drove through Cheesman Park two hours later, Dave pointed to a gathering of men standing around several parked cars. "This park is where a lot of gay people hang out. When we lived in this area, we came here quite a bit. But now that we live across town, we don't get here as often."

"Don't believe him," Jim said as he looked back at Jake and Wiley. "We come here just as much now, even though we live across town." He laughed. "No matter where you need to go in Denver, going through Cheesman Park is always the best way."

Jake pointed to several young, thin men in bikinis. "Wiley, lookit them boys. They're wearin' them little pants I tried on in that store when I got yelled at. This here Time's crazy. You can go pretty well naked outside, but not inside. I should'a tried them things on in the street."

Wiley leaned across Jake and looked out the window of the Honda. "Why are those gay men parading around in the open if half the state wants them dead?"

"It's still against the law to kill anyone," Jim said. "Dave sometimes gets carried away. But if Amendment 2 is ever enforced, I'm sure many gays will be beaten and killed in the name of Jesus."

"That ain't right!" Jake yelled. "My friend Jesus wouldn't never tell nobody to do that!"

Jim smiled. "Most people don't know Jesus the way you do, Jake. They think Jesus is pleased with them for ridding the world of men that sleep with other men."

"Ain't they never read nothin' about Jesus? Ma read to me about two men in the same bed. My friend Jesus took one of 'em an' left the other one layin' there. I asked Ma if them two men was foolin' around. She said she didn't know."

Dave chuckled. "Jake, it doesn't say they were fooling around with each other."

"Hell, I know that! But if they *was* foolin' around, Jesus still *took* one of 'em!"

Wiley placed his hand on Jake's shoulder.

Calmed by Wiley's touch, Jake said, "Ma told me Jesus took the one with love in his heart even if he was foolin' around."

Dave peered through the rearview mirror. "Jake, you should have become a preacher."

"Hell, no! I don't wanna be no preacher an' start judgin' on ever'body. Ma said it don't matter what we are cuz we're all the same sinner." Jake looked at Wiley. "Hell, if we asked Jesus to our cabin for dinner, he'd most likely come. An' after we ate, we could all go ridin'."

Wiley smiled. "And Jesus would probably remind you to stop cussing."

As Dave drove through Capitol Hill, he pointed out various mansions built by the silver and gold barons of the last century.

"Some of these homes remind me of Philadelphia," Wiley said.

When Dave drove the circular drive around the state capitol building, Jake sat forward in the seat. "I know were we are now! When I was livin' here, this hill was mostly fields an' had a few houses scattered 'round. Most ever'body had some cows an' chickens." He pointed about midway between Fourteenth Avenue and Colfax along Grant Street. "That there's where Mrs. Higgins lived. She had lots a' chickens an' two milk cows."

Dave stopped the car, and they all looked where Jake pointed. Jake shifted his outstretched finger a little to the south. "That's where her garden was. I dug trenches for her corn an' beans an' helped her plant stuff."

"How did you get to know Mrs. Higgins?" Wiley asked.

"Hell..." Jake looked at Wiley and grinned. "I'd ride Mac up here ever' day after helpin' build them houses. Mrs. Higgins would wave at Mac an' me. I'd been missin' my farm some an' stopped once to see how her cows were doin'. The next week, she fixed me a big plate'a eggs after I helped her plant her garden."

Jake lowered his arm. "It don't seem possible all these buildin's are here now. I'd ride up here an' look at the mountains, but now I can't even see 'em from here."

Jim turned around and looked at Jake. "I'm sure Denver has changed a lot in a hundred years. It's changed even since I came here in nineteen eighty-seven." He put his hand on Dave's shoulder. "Why don't we go to the airport now and be at the Sixteenth Street Mall at noon?"

* * *

Jake laughed as he held onto the rubber handrail of the moving sidewalk in Concourse D at Stapleton International Airport. He looked back at Wiley. "Ain't it somethin' how this thing makes them other people walk slow?" Since no one was in front of him, he started walking faster.

Wiley turned to look at Jim and Dave. "This moving sidewalk is just as amazing as the moving stairs we were on a few minutes ago." He pointed to the huge windows lining much of the concourse. "And those panes of glass are so clear. They don't have any ripples or bubbles."

A loud noise in front of them and a woman's scream caused them all to turn forward. They saw Jake sprawled on the floor at the end of the moving walkway amid a pile of red luggage. An older woman shook her folded umbrella at him.

Wiley started to hobble down the walkway, but Jim grabbed his arm. "Wait, Wiley. Brace yourself when you get to the end or you'll fall like Jake did. We should have warned him." Jim steadied Wiley when they stepped off the moving walkway.

"Look what you've done to my luggage!" the woman screeched at Jake. "If anything is broken, you'll pay for it!"

Dave ran to Jake and helped him to his feet. A small crowd gathered, and the group snickered when a woman told them what had happened.

"Damn!" Jake said as he rubbed his left elbow. "Sorry, Ma'am." He pointed to the moving walkway. "That thing tossed me off the end. I didn't mean to fall over your cases." He bent down and picked up two of the bags.

"Don't touch that small one!" the woman snapped. "There's a cut-glass bowl in there I bought in London!" She snatched the bag out of Jake's hand, set it on the floor and opened it. After pulling out wadded sweatshirts, she sighed when the sparkling bowl appeared undamaged. The woman looked up at Jake and glared. "It's a good thing it's not broken!"

Dave and Jim helped the woman strap the four pieces of luggage to her dolly, and she stomped away in a huff.

Farther down the concourse, as the men looked at a 727 parked outside, Wiley asked, "Is that an airplane?"

"It sure is," Dave said. "I think that one can carry about three hundred people, but don't quote me on it."

Jake stared at the plane, then shrugged. "That ain't one'a them things we saw in the sky. That's too damn big. Them things we saw were little, like so." He held up his thumb and forefinger and measured a half inch.

Dave chuckled. "They only look that small because they're so high up in the sky. Jim, let's take them to where they can see the planes take off. They need to see the planes go into the air."

"You mean them big things go up in the air? I ain't never gonna believe that. Wiley, I think they're joshin' me."

"No, we aren't," Jim said. "Come on." He headed for the end of the concourse.

When they arrived at a window facing the north-south runway, a plane had just gained takeoff speed. As it lifted into the air, Jake and Wiley gasped and pressed their hands on the glass. They watched the plane disappear beyond their line of sight.

"Wiley, did you see that? That thing went right up in the air. An' it didn't even flap them wings."

"I saw it, but I still don't believe it."

Several people in the immediate area heard their remarks. One woman looked at the ceiling and drew imaginary circles with her finger beside her head.

* * *

At noon, the men sat under an umbrella at an outside table on the Sixteenth Street Mall in downtown Denver. They silently watched the hundreds of people taking advantage of their lunch hours and the warm, cloudless day by walking the mall. Dave noticed Jake putting his hand over his eyes.

"Jake, why do you keep covering your eyes?"

"Ma told me to never look at a woman in her underthings, an' there's women ever'where that're pretty well naked. Don't their ma's tell 'em to put clothes on?" He suddenly grinned at Dave. "Oh, I remember. In this here Time, you can walk outside that way, but not inside."

"That's not quite right," Jim commented. "But I'm sure the way people dress now is different than the late eighteen hundreds."

"I'll have to agree with that and with Jake." Wiley said. "I've never seen so many different types of clothes in my life, and many women do seem to be showing off their breasts."

Jim laughed. "I didn't think you noticed things like that."

Wiley shrugged. "It's hard not to. Another thing I've noticed is most men cover up their bodies with baggy clothes. And many of them look at me with longing. I don't understand it. If over half the people in the state voted for that Amendment 2, I think a lot of the men are lying."

"I don't think they're gay, Wiley," Jim said. He pointed at Wiley's hairy chest pushing out the front of his open shirt. "I think they're taken by your muscles. How many men do you see that look like you and Jake?"

Jim scooted his metal chair closer, leaned across the table and looked at Wiley. "I'm convinced that many people voted for Amendment 2 because their only knowledge of gay people are the one's that dress in women's clothes. Since drag queens make themselves the most visible, many men, gay and straight, don't want the association."

"Hell, somma these here men look like they're warin' them split ridin' dresses like I tried on in that store," Jake said.

Jim smiled and sipped his soda. "Several years ago, there was a study called the Kinsey Report. It found that many men, especially in rural areas, have sex with other men. Quite often, too. Since it never interferes with their marriages to women, they don't consider themselves gay or even bi-sexual. I'll bet every one of them voted for Amendment 2 just to convince themselves, and everyone else, that they don't do anything a gay person would do." He shook his head. "It's the most cowardly thing in the world to condemn others for same things we want kept secret about ourselves."

Jake's eyes opened wide, and he grabbed Wiley's arm. "Damn! That boy has purple hair! What happened to him?"

"He's a punk rocker, Jake," Wiley said, proudly.

Dave punched Wiley on the arm. "How do you know that?"

"I read about them in one of your magazines when you went to Buena Vista." Wiley raised his eyebrows when he saw three other young people walk by. The girl had fire-engine red hair, tipped in green, and the two boys had their heads shaved except for a tuft on top.

Jake laughed. "Them two boys look like they got bird nests sittin' on their heads." He felt his own hair. "Maybe I'll do that to my hair, Wiley."

"You do, and I'll set fire to it."

CHAPTER 19

Jake and Wiley wanted to ride the mall shuttle since it was so different from the horse-drawn trollies of their era, and the group rode it to the end of the line on Market Street. When they arrived in lower downtown, Dave headed toward Union Station.

"Where are you going?" Jim asked.

"Jeffrey Brothers Coins. I thought Wiley could see how much he can get for some of the gold dollars."

"Good idea," Wiley said. "I have all ten with me." He hastened his gait on the crutches.

Jake rushed to his side. "Don't you be goin' too fast, Wiley. You'll be endin' up on your face like me in that airplane station."

When they reached a refurbished turn-of-the-century building, Dave led the way inside. At the end of a long hallway lined with office doors, they crowded into the small elevator.

"Wait until you see this place," Dave said. "I've never seen anything like it."

The elevator stopped at the second floor, and the doors opened into a large glass-enclosed entrance room. Potted ficus trees, some ten feet tall, and huge blooming azaleas nestled in groups around brass park benches on lush grass-green carpeting.

Jake gasped. "This here's like bein' in the woods!"

"Look at those doors," Jim said.

Fifteen feet across the room, polished brass doors framed two stained-glass panels. A tipped treasure chest in the left door spilled gold doubloons into the other.

"Them doors're like the gates'a heaven!" Jake shouted.

"I didn't know this place even existed," Jim said. "Dave, where did you ever hear of Jeffrey Brothers?"

"From a lady I worked with. Her husband is a coin collector. She said he comes here all the time. But I never expected this."

Dave glanced at Wiley who seemed lost in the surroundings. "Earth to Wiley."

Wiley looked at Dave and smiled. "This is amazing. Glass walls?" He pointed to the tips of his crutches sunk into the deep pile. "And this carpet is like green fur."

Jake grabbed Wiley's arm. "Wiley, they ain't gonna let us in. Not how we's dressed."

"Yes they will," Dave said. "Let's go."

The instant they entered the sale area that wrapped completely around the glass-enclosed room, an attractive blond woman with large breasts and a low-cut yellow dress walked up and stopped in front of them.

"Hello. I'm Sally. May I help you find something?"

Dave smiled at the woman. "We have coins to sell. Who's the buyer here?"

"This way, please." Sally turned to Dave's right and gracefully zigzagged around a maze of brass-rimmed glass counters all brightly lit from inside and displaying hundreds of coins. The woman stopped beside a jungle of trees and plants that concealed a mahogany desk. In the shadows of the plants, a small gray-haired man sat in a soft leather armchair. Dave didn't see him until he was next to the desk.

"Mr. Jeffrey," Sally said, "these gentlemen would like to sell some coins."

The elderly man leaned forward and switched on his high-intensity desk lamp. He eyed Sally up and down and smiled, but when he saw the four men his face changed to a cool, business-like expression. He waved Sally away.

"I'm Ralph Jeffrey, gentlemen. Sit down and let me see what you have for sale. I'm a busy man, so make it snappy."

The four men sat in chairs nestled among the plants. Dave shuddered when he looked at Ralph Jeffrey and thought of a thin Peter Lorrie with thick glasses accentuating bug-like eyes.

Wiley picked the chair closest to Jeffrey. He felt an immediate distrust for the man and wanted to be near enough to pick up any indications that would validate it. After getting his crutches situated, Wiley pulled out one of the gold coins and handed it to Jeffrey.

Ralph Jeffrey lowered the magnifier on his glasses and carefully examined the coin under the light. Wiley caught the flicker of surprise on his face.

"Where did you get this?" Jeffrey asked.

"Found it," Wiley said.

Jeffrey peered at Wiley over the tops of his glasses. "You found it, you say? Where?"

"I'd rather not say. There are more like this one."

Having dealt with many men like Jeffrey in the gemstone trade, Dave was impressed at Wiley's calmness. The tone of his voice, while not unfriendly, was dead flat. He glanced at Jim and Jake and realized they were also watching Wiley.

"I can understand why you don't want to divulge that information," Jeffrey said with a forced chuckle. "How many do you have? To sell, that is."

"That depends on the price." Wiley stared at the man with cold brown eyes. "What is the price? The coin is uncirculated."

Jeffrey cleared his throat. "Yes, I can see that."

Wiley detected reluctance in that statement, but remained silent as the man examined the coin again.

"Eight-fifty is the going rate for these," Jeffrey said.

Wiley snorted. "I sold six exactly like that one for fifteen hundred apiece a few days ago in Breckenridge. If you're not interested in talking business, Mr. Jeffrey, we both have better things to do with our time."

"Fifteen hundred? Well, you won't get that kind of money from me. I'm not in this business for my health. I have to make money on any purchase. The best I could do would be a grand."

"A grand!" Wiley forced a sharpness in his voice. He knew he had control of the situation but didn't want to go overboard and ruin the chance for a sale.

"Ok, ok, twelve hundred. That's my top offer."

"Sold," Wiley said at once.

"How many are we talking about?"

"Ten."

"Ten? All uncirculated?" Jeffrey had a look of disbelief.

Wiley stretched out his right leg and plunged his hand into his pocket. After he pulled it out, he opened it on the top of the desk. Nine gold coins spilled into a ragged pile.

Dave noticed a gold reflection in Jeffrey's glasses as he leaned closer and carefully inspected each coin.

"Will you take a check?" Jeffrey finally asked Wiley.

"Yes, provided it's drawn on a Denver bank so I can cash it as soon as I leave here."

"It will be." Ralph Jeffrey picked up the telephone and punched in four numbers. "Carl, write a check for twelve thousand." He took the phone away and looked at Wiley. "What name should be on the check."

"David Younger," Dave said at once. He nodded at Wiley. "He's from out of town. I live here, and I'll have an easier time cashing it. We're all partners in this sale."

Jeffrey looked sharply at Dave, then put the receiver back to his mouth. "Make the check out to a David Younger. Have it at my desk at once." He hung up the phone and smiled at the coins in front of him. "You gentlemen can look at your coins one last time if you want to."

"Hell, we got lots more," Jake said. "We had us almost a hunnert of 'em before we sold these here ones."

Ralph Jeffrey's eyes grew wide with surprise. "You found a *hundred* of these coins? All in this condition? Good God, where?"

Wiley hard-stared Jake, who quickly lowered his eyes and looked at his hands in his lap.

"We have an agreement not to divulge that information." Wiley frowned at his companions. "Don't we!"

The other three timidly nodded.

With the check safely in his pocket, Wiley slowly led the way through the store. When he realized Dave had stopped at a glass counter to look at the merchandise, he sidled up to Jake. "Jake, I'm sorry I snapped at you back there. I was being tough so we wouldn't get skunked, and I went too far." Wiley held both crutches with one hand and grabbed Jake's arm. "Forgive me?"

"Hell, Wiley, I had it comin', flappin' my mouth like I done. I got excited about all that money, an' it just come out."

"Well, no harm done. Let's forget it."

They wandered around the store for twenty minutes, then slowly ambled toward the glassed-in room and the elevator.

As soon as the four men left his desk, Ralph Jeffrey turned off his lamp and sat in the shadows of his plants. He picked up the phone, smiled, and pressed four different numbers. After a brief wait, he whispered, "Badger, I have a job for you. Tail those four men that are here together. One of them is on crutches. I want to know everything about them, where they live, what they eat, who they screw. Get on it."

Jeffrey hung up the phone and watched the group through the carefully positioned foliage surrounding his desk. After they left, he looked down at the pile of gold dollars, tipped his chair back, put his hands behind his head and smiled at his plants.

"Yes, indeedy. This is proving to be a very fine day."

* * *

With twelve thousand in cash in a large brown envelope, the four men returned to the house. They arrived shortly after five and quickly gathered around the dining room table where Wiley dumped out the stacks of hundreds.

"I ain't never seen so much money!" Jake shouted. He touched a bundle of bills. "Wiley, we could buy us a ranch back home an' some cows."

Looking at Jake, Dave said, "You'll have to buy something here and take it back with you, then sell it, because this money won't be any good in eighteen eighty-six."

Wiley picked up a stack of bills, counted out a thousand dollars and handed it to Dave and Jim. "This is yours. I'm paying you back for all you've spent on us."

"That's too much!" Jim said. "We haven't spent that much on you guys." He counted out two hundred and placed the rest in front of Wiley.

Wiley shoved it back to him. "Please, keep it. You took us into your home and into your lives, not knowing who we were. You willingly brought me to the doctor, bought us food and clothes, and now you've helped us transform ten dollars into twelve thousand. Except for Jake, I've never known anyone as honest and loving as you and Dave." He smiled at Jake. "We should all become blood brothers."

"Hell, Wiley!" Jake shouted. "Then we'd all be brothers forever!"

Dave and Jim glanced at each other with solemn faces.

"Did Jake or I say something wrong?" Wiley asked.

Jim shook his head. "No. We automatically flinch when anyone mentions blood or body fluid exchanges. There's a disease nowadays called AIDS that has no cure, and it's contracted by the exchange of blood." He looked at Dave. "We haven't had sex with anyone else this past year, have we?"

Dave shrugged. "I haven't. I don't know about you. And our last AIDS test a few months ago came back negative."

"Wait a minute," Wiley said. "If you said this disease is spread by mixing blood, what does sex have to do with it?"

Jim pressed his lips together briefly, then said, "It's also spread by screwing in the ass."

Jake grabbed Wiley's hand. "I knowed there weren't no love in doin' that to another man. Abe choked the men he done that to in our time, and men're still killin' by doin' it now." He lowered his head. "I thought men like us was supposed to know more about love than other folks."

"Some men like having sex that way," Jim said. He winked at Dave. "We have to use condoms to be safe."

"They must like pain," Wiley muttered. He shuddered when he thought of Abe raping him and still remembered the pain deep inside long after that night. "Jake and I love each other too much to treat each other that way. Besides, we like being face-to-face when we make love."

"Since you had that AIDS test, can we all become blood brothers?" Jake asked.

Dave said, "I can't think of anything I'd like better than to be a blood brother to you three men. It would be like being married to all of you at once." His eyes brightened. "Can we become blood brothers while we're naked?" Seeing everyone's shocked expression, he shrugged. "Well, it was just a thought."

"David, you're always thinking of sex," Jim scolded. He scooted back his chair. "Is fried chicken for dinner okay with everyone?"

The others agreed, and Jake jumped up to help.

"I'm not going to cook it this time," Jim said. "I'm going to Colonel Sanders and buy it. Jake, do you want to come?"

"Hell, yes!"

Wiley struggled to his feet. "I'd like to go. Buying already-fried chicken intrigues me."

CHAPTER 20

Jake sat back and patted his gut. "That there Colonel Sanders must'a been a Confederate cook. Wish I'd seen him in that store we was in. I'da asked him where he was from."

Wiley smiled. "Jake, we're not in our time. If he was a Confederate cook, he'd be long dead by now."

"Hell, Wiley..." Jake dropped his eyes to his plate. "I keep forgettin' that. An' forgettin' not t'cuss, too." He pulled out his rawhide bag and looked inside. "Guess it ain't time to go back home yet. I don't see no feather in there."

Jim stood up and started gathering the empty plates. "Wiley's leg isn't healed enough yet. I'd say he has a few more weeks before he can walk without the crutches."

Wiley shook his head. "Less than a week. Each day, I can put more weight on it and for a longer time."

"How would everyone like to go to a gay bar later tonight?" Dave asked as he started picking up the empty chicken boxes. "We could go to the Pit Stop. The guys there are more masculine than in most of the other bars, but things don't start happening until about eleven."

"Gay men have their own bars?" Wiley asked. "In our time, everyone congregates in the one or two saloons in town. At least, in Alma."

"Denver, too," Jake added.

Jim touched the edge of Jake's plate. "Are you through with this?" When Jake nodded, Jim stacked it on the top of the others he held. "It's different now. If a gay man was discovered in a straight bar, he'd probably be dragged outside and beaten to a pulp.

Jake jumped to his feet and began helping clear the table. "We better not go in them kind'a bars, Wiley. We might end up hurtin' somebody."

164

"You'd probably get shot," Dave muttered.

* * *

While Dave and Jim took showers and got dressed for the Pit
Stop, Jake and Wiley sat on the front porch and watched the goings
on in the neighborhood. In the twilight, they could see several men
lounging on the front steps of a house on the corner. The man across
the street was fiddling under the hood of his car, and a couple
walked their dog along the sidewalk in front of them.

"I feel all closed in here, Wiley," Jake said as he looked around
at the houses, privacy fences and parked cars. "An' there's roarin'
noises far off ever'where. Back home at night, the only thing I'd
hear was the hoot owl sittin' on my ol' tree house."

"I agree, Jake. Even while I was at school in Boston, the middle
of town wasn't this noisy. All one heard was the occasional clop of
horses' hooves and laughter of children playing. If a horse galloped
by, everyone would get excited."

They both turned their heads as a purple, low-rider car, blaring
deep bass music that shook the ground, roared down the street in
front of them.

"Wiley!" Jake yelled as he held his ears. "Somethin' bad's
happenin' to that car!"

"That's music," Wiley said when Jake uncovered his ears. "At
least, I think it's music. I heard sounds like that on Dave and Jim's
stereo at the cabin when you went to Buena Vista." Wiley watched
the car screech to a half-stop at the intersection, then roar down the
next block. He shook his head. "Chief Eagle Rising was right. This
Time is dangerous...even scary. And the youth now seem rude and
self-centered." He gestured toward the distant car still blaring
bone-rattling bass. "If a child in Boston or Philadelphia made that
much noise in town, he would be whipped. People would talk about
it over back fences for weeks. But in this Time, no one noticed that
car but us."

Jake shuddered from the experience of the loud-speaker noise
and from Wiley's words about Chief Eagle Rising. He reached into
his shirt and touched the rawhide bag for reassurance that they could
get back home safely.

"I think the rudest young man I ever encountered in our time was on the train out here," Wiley said. "The train butch was a tough, nasty character."

"I know what a train butch is, Wiley. I come out here on a train, too." Jake scooted closer to Wiley...but not too close. He didn't know if any of the Christians that Dave had talked about were watching. They scared him. He figured all they did was walk around pointing their fingers at everybody and condemning them to hell. He wondered if Jesus would ever go to the houses of people like that for dinner. If he did, he'd tell those people about love. Jesus might even tell them how much he and Wiley loved each other.

"The train butch was so gruff," Wiley said, "I slammed my compartment door in his face." He slumped forward a bit. "I regret doing that now. He was gruff because he had to be...to survive. Selling magazines and cigars to the many travelers must not be easy." He watched another car, blasting a different kind of music and filled with teenagers, roar down the narrow street. Wiley shook his head again. "The youth of this Time seem to like being rude. They must have weak parents and too many gadgets." He noticed Jake smiling at him.

"What is it, Jake?"

"Wiley, my friend Jesus likes us bein' together. An' He likes us lovin' each other, too."

Uncomfortable dwelling on that subject, Wiley grabbed Jake's shoulder. "Tell me about your experience with the train butch."

Jake dropped his head. "He made me feel dummer'n hog shit. He laughed at me cuz I can't read."

"How did he know that?"

"Cuz he come up to my seat and told me to buy his newspaper. I told him I didn't wanna buy it cuz I couldn't read it."

Wiley rubbed Jake's back with the palm of his hand. "When we get back to our own time, I'll teach you how to read."

* * *

Jake glanced around the dimly lit bar, unusually busy for a Thursday night. He turned to Dave and asked, "Are all these here men like us?"

"I hope so. I'd hate to think the Pit Stop turned into a straight bar after all these years."

After their drinks were ordered and paid for, they slowly walked through the front bar. Wiley was the object of many glances since his partly unbuttoned shirt gave glimpses of his rock-hard, hairy chest every time he took a step with his crutches. A man dressed as a police officer approached, slid his hand inside Wiley's shirt and squeezed one of his pecs, then walked to the bar. Wiley smiled and raised an eyebrow at Jim.

"What'd that soldier do to you, Wiley?" Jake asked.

"Just a friendly feel."

"He ain't better do nothin' like that to me. I'll punch 'im like I done Winder."

Wiley laughed. "Relax, Jake. I feel we're among friends in here. And they're all men, not like the ones we saw in that park acting like giggly girls."

When their eyes grew accustomed to the darkness, Jake grabbed Dave and asked, "Why're somma these here men in black?"

"They're in leather. It's how they want to dress. Many of these guys ride motorcycles. You know, those two-wheeled things we saw on our way into Denver."

Jake glanced around again. "Somma these here men look like Thunder Joe." He frowned. "But they smell like women."

As they entered the next room, even darker and with bellowing music, Jim and Dave walked in front of Wiley to keep him from tripping over anyone until their eyes adjusted to the gloom. Jake followed with one finger hooked in Wiley's back belt loop. Finally, in the dull glow of a tiny red bulb in the corner, the shapes of men became visible. Some sat on a shelf along one wall and others stood around singly or in groups.

Seeing someone he knew, Jim went over to him. Wiley saw Dave turn around, say something, then walk toward Jim, but the loud music drowned out what he'd said. Rather than follow, Wiley stood by a wall with Jake beside him.

Jake noticed some of the men were looking at him and Wiley, and he became jumpy. He pressed against Wiley and slid his arm around his waist.

"This here place gives me the willies," Jake yelled into Wiley's ear. "What're these here men doin' standin' in the dark?"

"I think they're looking for a partner," Wiley said loudly.

"How can they get 'em a partner when they can't even see 'em?" Jake yelled over the music. But the end of the CD had come seconds before, and Jake shouted his question into the stillness.

Several men laughed out loud, and the next song blasted an instant later. Three men approached Jake from behind. The biggest in the group, outweighing Jake by fifty pounds, pressed himself against Jake's back, slid his arms around him and pulled him away from Wiley. He shoved one hand inside Jake's unbuttoned shirt and grabbed Jake's crotch with the other.

"This is how we get a partner in here." the big man said into Jake's ear. "And you're mine, you gorgeous thing." He nuzzled his face into Jake's neck.

Jake knew the man was drunk by his fetid breath. He tensed his muscles and hollered, "Keep your damn hands off'a me!" He reached back, grabbed the man around the neck, crouched into a ball and flung him over his head to the floor. Jake's motion was so quick and fluid, the big man found himself on his back before he realized what was happening.

Wiley turned when he heard Jake yelling and saw the man on the floor with Jake standing over him.

"Jake, what happened?"

"He grabbed me like Winder done, an' I dumped him on his butt."

"I'm sure he was just having fun."

Jake glared at Wiley.

One of the downed man's companions stepped up to Jake. "What's the matter with you?"

Wiley grabbed his arm. "Jake was taken by surprise."

When the man Jake had thrown finally got to his feet, he grabbed one of his friends to steady himself, then turned to Jake and hollered, "This is a gay bar, buddy! If you don't like the company, why don't you leave?" He weaved again.

Dave and Jim heard the shouting and pushed their way through the growing crowd that surrounded Jake, Wiley and the three men in leather. At the same time, a tall wiry man shoved his way toward the scene from the front bar.

"What the hell's going on?" Ron yelled as he saw the circle of men. "Lance, what happened?"

"This guy...flipped me over his head," Lance slurred. He weaved slightly and grabbed the shelf along the wall to steady himself. "I landed on the floor. On my back!"

"Lance, you're drunk! I warned you last night!" Ron looked at Jake. "What did he do to you?"

"He come up behind me an' grabbed me. Said I was his partner." Jake glared at Lance. "I already got me a partner, an' I don't want you touchin' me!"

Ron looked Jake up and down. "You better check your wallet if that's what he did to you. I'm eighty-sixing both of you, guilty or not." He glared at both men, pointed to the front door and yelled, "Out!"

"What happened?" Jim asked Wiley as the men began walking toward the front of the bar.

"Jake is being eighty-sixed. Does that mean thrown out?"

"Yes. But what happened?"

"That heavy-set man put his hands on Jake, and Jake flipped him over his head."

Dave gasped. "Jake flipped *Lance* over his head? Shit, I wish I'd seen that."

Once outside, Lance and his friends disappeared up the alley, not looking back once. Jake stood by the building until the others caught up, and they silently began walking up the street to the car.

As Jim unlocked the car door, Jake gasped, "Damn, Wiley! The bag's gone!" He opened his shirt and showed his chest. The rawhide bag was missing.

"Oh, my God, Jake!" Wiley yelled. "We have to find it! The golden feather is in there. Without it, you're in danger."

"Maybe it's on the floor in that bar. I gotta get it." Jake hesitated a moment, scanned the Honda and said, "Damn, our guns're in the truck." He looked Wiley in the eyes, turned and ran back toward the bar.

Dave took off after him. "Jake, wait! Ron will call the cops if you go back in there!"

"Get in the car, Wiley," Jim said as Dave disappeared around the corner. "We'll drive to the front of the bar and wait for them."

Jake ran into the bar and shoved his way through the crowd toward the spot where the scuffle had taken place. He'd only gotten halfway before Ron grabbed his arm.

"I told you to get out!"

"I lost my rawhide bag!" Jake yelled. "I gotta find it or Wiley an' me're stuck here forever!"

"Lance probably has it," Ron said. "But I'll get a flashlight and help you look. Then you have to get out of here. Understand?"

"I'll do anythin' you want so long's I find that bag."

Dave caught up with Jake as Ron began searching the back room. They found nothing, and no one remembered seeing it. A check in the lost and found section behind the bar proved fruitless.

Jake buried his face in his hands and whimpered, "Jesus, I gotta find that bag." He pushed his way through the crowd and ran outside. He hesitated for a second, looked at Jim and Wiley sitting in the car at the curb, then ran down the alley in the direction Lance had gone.

When Dave came out of the bar, Wiley pointed. "Jake ran that way!"

At the entrance to the alley, Dave spotted Jake standing at the opposite end, looking up and down the street. As he ran toward him, a green van screeched to a stop directly in front of Jake. The side door of the van slid open, and two big men jumped out. They grabbed Jake and wrestled him into the back. The door slammed shut, the van sped down the street, squealed around the corner and disappeared.

"Oh, my God!" Dave yelled. He ran to the end of the alley to see which direction the van went, but the street was deserted.

"Oh, no!" Dave turned and ran back to the car.

Wiley buried his face in his hands when Dave told him what had happened. "It's starting already!" He turned toward Jim. "We've got to find Jake! And we have to find that rawhide bag!"

They drove a widening area for an hour but didn't see a green van anywhere. Wiley finally agreed to go back to the house.

As they neared home, Jim said, "Wiley, remember that piece of paper we gave both of you with our address and phone number on it? If someone kidnapped Jake, maybe they'll try to contact us. But why would anyone want to kidnap Jake?"

"The gold coins," Wiley said grimly. "I saw Mr. Jeffrey's eyes when Jake said we had a hundred of them."

"But he's a reputable business man," Dave said. "He wouldn't stoop to such measures." He glanced at Wiley. "Would he?"

"From the look in his eyes, it wouldn't surprise me."

"What do you mean?" Jim asked. "How could you tell?"

"One of my college professors had a theory that facial expressions tell what a person is thinking no matter how hard he tries to conceal it. He didn't talk much about it in class because it wasn't an approved theory, but I believed it. After spending many hours with him after class, I began to understand that he was right." Wiley paused. "Mr. Jeffrey has been eaten up with greed."

CHAPTER 21

When they arrived at the house, Wiley got out of the car and carried his crutches. His leg pained him, but he gritted his teeth against it. If he was going to find Jake, he'd need better mobility than the crutches allowed. After getting his balance, he felt more confident by the time he got to the porch. Not trusting his leg on the steps, he used the crutches to get into the house, then propped them by the front door.

"I know why you're doing that, Wiley," Jim said as he watched the big man limp across the living room. "I think we should let the police handle this. You can't go after Jake by yourself."

Wiley stiffened. "I have to! Jake's my blood brother. Even if he wasn't, I love him too much to let someone else try to find him." He sunk into the couch and groaned, clutching his throbbing leg.

"You're in no condition to be doing anything like that," Dave said. He punched 911 on the phone.

* * *

After the two officers left, Dave glanced at the rising sun, then at the clock on the mantle. Five-thirty. The patrolmen had taken down as much information as he could remember about the van and the circumstances.

Wiley steamed. Neither police officer had listened to his theory that Ralph Jeffrey was responsible for Jake's kidnapping, preferring to suspect gangs operating near the bar.

When Dave and Jim heard the word "gang," they realized Jake could be dead but didn't dare mention it to Wiley.

* * *

Jake's head pounded. Something smelled worse than hog shit. He slowly opened his eyes into blinding sunlight, then shut them again. When he tried moving his arms, he couldn't.

Jake opened his eyes again and saw his wrists and ankles had been tied spread-eagle to a bed frame. He tried to yell but realized he'd been gagged. Jake thrashed his body trying to get loose. A bell sounded each time he jerked his arms. Where was he? The last thing he remembered was being shoved into the side of a truck, then hit on the head.

A door opened near him. Jake cut his eyes to his right and squinted into the sunlight. A person wearing a dark gray robe with a hood pulled forward entered the room and yanked the door shut. The ghostly figure glided to the head of the bed and untied a string attached to one of Jake's hands. The bell stopped ringing.

"I'm glad you're awake," the hooded person said in a male voice. "I have some questions to ask you. I'm going to take the gag out of your mouth, but if you yell, I'll crush your skull." He reached into a pocket of his robe, pulled out a two-foot length of pipe and slapped his hand with it. "Understand?"

Jake looked at the pipe and nodded his head. The man's voice seemed vaguely familiar, but he wasn't sure.

"Before I untie the gag, I want to make myself crystal clear. You have something we want, and we'll stop at nothing to get it. Not even murder." He paused, walked to the window and looked out. "I've been doing some checking on you the past eight hours. It seems, from all I can gather, you have no fingerprints on file anywhere in the area. I haven't finished searching yet, but I find no record of anyone knowing anything about you. It's like you don't exist." The man spun around and faced Jake. "And that's good news, because if I have to kill you, no one will know or care."

The instant the man removed the gag, Jake said, "Wiley cares what happens to me! He'll come lookin' for me!"

"Looking where?" The robed man chuckled. "He'll never find you, even if he looked for the rest of his life." He pulled the only chair in the room next to the bed and sat down. "Now, where are those gold coins?"

"I ain't tellin' you nothin'. Them're my dollars. I won 'em in a wagon race."

"You won them, did you? Cute. I've been told you found them. I want to know where the rest of them are, and where you found them. I can, and will, make your life miserable until you tell me. Do you understand?"

Jake didn't answer. He squinted as he looked at the dark figure. The smell in the room almost made him gag. A burst of pain exploded in Jake's head as the man slugged him in the face. As the man hauled back a second time, Jake yelled, "Don't hit me no more! I'll tell you where them coins are. I buried 'em by the outhouse at the cabin. Dave's the only one besides me that knows where they are. Wiley don't even know." He turned his face away from the man. "I hid 'em so good Dave might not remember 'zackly where they are."

"You'd better hope he does, because you're not leaving here until I get them."

* * *

For the entire morning, Wiley paced the house holding the cordless phone in his hand. When his leg began to throb, he dropped to the couch and propped it on the coffee table. He refused to take a pain pill since it might make him fall asleep, and the aspirin Jim gave him didn't seem to ease the pain at all. At one point he lost patience, shook his fist at the phone and yelled, "Call, you bastards!"

But the phone didn't ring.

At the deck table, opening the mail that had not been transferred to Fairplay, Dave and Jim heard Wiley's outburst and glanced at each other.

"I wish there was something we could do for him," Dave said softly. "And for Jake."

Jim closed his eyes for a few seconds and shook his head. "I'm scared Jake may be dead. If gang members are responsible, they won't like the way Jake speaks his mind."

The phone rang. Both men dashed into the house and saw Wiley sitting on the couch holding it to his ear.

"No one's called," they heard Wiley grumble. "What have you found out?" He paused. "Well, don't bother! I'll find him myself!" He jabbed the hang-up button on the phone and glared at Jim and

Dave. "The police don't have any idea where he is!" He slammed his fist on his knee.

Wiley closed his eyes and took a deep breath. What was happening to him? He'd been in countless tight spots before and had never acted like this. But he hadn't known Jake then. He gently set the phone on the coffee table, rested his elbows on his knees and leaned his forehead against his clasped hands.

"Forgive me. I just feel so helpless."

Jim and Dave slid onto the couch on either side of him. Jim put his arm on Wiley's shoulder, and Dave rested his hand on the big man's thigh.

Wiley smiled and raised his head. "Thanks. I don't know what I'd do right now if it weren't for you two. It's bad enough being in this strange Time and barely able to walk. But, now, with Jake gone, I feel half my soul is missing."

"Half your soul is missing," Jim said. He pulled away and looked Wiley in the eyes. "Promise me something."

"What?"

"Promise me that you'll relax and put your leg up. Give it a rest. You may need it later. Why don't you lie on the couch and watch TV?"

Wiley shrugged. "I'll try. But I can't stand watching that thing for very long. It makes me forget who I am. Besides, those commercials make me want to throw something at the TV to shut them up."

After Dave showed Wiley how to use the "mute" button, he went outside with Jim. Wiley sprawled on the couch, grabbed the remote and began flipping channels. He finally settled on a re-run of The Virginian. When he saw a man pull his pistol, Wiley remembered Jake had said their guns were in the truck. He struggled to his feet and hobbled outside, but both truck doors were locked. He peered through the window, then limped back into the house and out the back door.

"I need to get into the truck."

Dave tossed Wiley his keys. "It's the big one on the end."

Wiley caught them. "How do I get something out from behind the back part of the seat?"

Dave looked up at him. "Push down on the black lever behind the seat near the floor. There's one on either side. Then pull the back forward."

Wiley groaned as he rushed to the truck. It would feel good to hold his gun again. After he got the seat forward, he grabbed a black plastic trash bag and opened it. Both his and Jake's guns and holsters were there, plus the rest of their shells. He yanked the bag out of the truck.

The phone rang.

Closest to the back door, Jim ran through the house and grabbed it. Dave sprinted to the attic to pick up the extension, just in case.

Jim waited until Dave yelled, "Got it!" and pushed the button.

"Hello?"

"Who is this?" a man's voice asked.

"This is Jim. Who am I speaking to?"

"Never mind who. I have your friend, and I want to make a trade. Your friend said you have some gold coins. I want them. All of them."

Jim hesitated. "I want to know if Jake is all right. Let me talk to him."

Jim heard shuffling and several loud bumps on the other end. Finally, Jake's shaky voice came over the phone.

"Wiley?"

"This is Jim. Wiley's outside. Jake, are you all right?"

"They grabbed me, an' I don't know where I am. I gotta talk to Wiley to know he's still here."

"Just a minute, I'll get him." Jim ran to the front door. "Wiley! Jake's on the phone!"

Just then reaching the porch, Wiley gritted his teeth as he climbed the steps. He got to the couch and slumped into it. The trash bag slid to the floor as he grabbed the phone.

"Jake? Are you there?"

"I'm here, Wiley, but I don't know where here is. This here man wants our coins. He'll let me go if you bring 'em."

"Jake, is it Mr. Jeffrey?"

"I don't know. I can't think good. He's been hittin' me in the face."

"I'll kill that bastard!" Wiley shouted. He forcibly calmed himself. "Jake, did you tell him we don't have the coins here?"

"Sure did, Wiley. He..."

On the other end, Wiley heard what he thought was a small bottle being set on a wooden table. Jake yelled, "No! Don't stick that thing in me! Wiley! Help, Wiley!" Then nothing.

"Jake!" Wiley shouted. "What's happening? Jake!"

"Your friend can't talk now," the man said on the other end. "He's taking a little rest. You get those coins buried by the outhouse. I'll call again tomorrow evening at five. We'll deal then."

Wiley heard a click, then the dial tone.

Jim watched Wiley lean forward, hang his head and close his eyes. The phone dropped to the floor.

Wiley sat up straight. "They're doing something terrible to Jake. We have to get the rest of the coins. The man said he'd call again tomorrow night at five."

"I know," Dave said as he reached the bottom step. "I was listening upstairs. I think he gave Jake a sedative to keep him quiet and wanted you to hear it. I'll leave for the cabin now. I can stay there tonight and be back in the morning."

"I'm going with you," Wiley said. "I'll go mad if I sit around here doing nothing until five tomorrow evening."

"I'll stay here," Jim said. "If they call back, at least I can tell them you're getting the coins. Should I tell the detectives they called?"

"No! I want to meet those men on my terms."

Jim frowned. "You can't do that. What if you get killed?"

"If they kill Jake, my life won't be worth anything. It won't matter."

Dave glanced at the clock. "If we leave now, we'll be at the cabin about five-thirty."

After they gathered a few things for their dinner, Dave and Wiley piled into the truck and headed toward the mountains.

Jim paced the floor after they left. Then, against Wiley's wishes, he called the detective and told him about the phone call and the demand for the coins as ransom. He didn't mention that Wiley wanted to make the drop himself, or that he had a gun.

CHAPTER 22

After Louis met Cynthia and Donna at Dave and Jim's cabin, he arrived home at nine that evening. Still angry about the two men buying his land with his own gold, he wanted to take out his frustrations on Edna and force her to give him the money she'd been paid, but she wasn't home. Rather than go to the Dusty Miner and cause a scene in front of witnesses, he decided to join his brother and get drunk.

* * *

The next afternoon, Louis stumbled down the hill to the Dusty Miner and found Carmen sitting on her usual stool by the back wall. He scanned the bar, and not seeing Edna, he walked over to Carmen and grabbed her wrist.

"Where's Edna?"

"Louis, you're hurting me!" Carmen pulled her arm away and rubbed her wrist. "I don't know where she is. She didn't show up for work yesterday or today. She didn't even call."

"When was the last time you saw her?"

"Two nights ago. She left the bar shortly after that man bought her coins. I haven't seen her since. What's wrong?"

"What's wrong?" Louis snapped. "She sold my land, that's what's wrong. And the assholes who bought it paid her with my gold!"

Louis had tried to keep his voice low, but failed. Everyone in the bar turned and stared at him when he mentioned the gold.

"What bank did you rob, Louis?" a heavyset rancher named Art Peterson yelled. Everyone in the place laughed.

Louis glared at the patrons. "Where's Edna?" he yelled. "She's got five thousand dollars of my money, and I want it back!"

Smitty, the bald-headed owner, placed both hands on the bar and leaned forward. His black bushy eyebrows slanted into a frown. "Edna isn't here and hasn't been for two days. If she has five thousand dollars of your money, I say more power to her."

The men in the room laughed.

"Maybe she got smart and left town," Peterson said. "By herself!"

Everyone laughed again.

Louis glared at them and stomped toward the door.

Carmen slid off her stool and ran after him. She caught up to him outside in the street. "Louis, why did you say those gold coins were yours? Where did you get them?"

Louis spun around. "I thought I told you to watch Edna!" He raised his hand to hit her.

Carmen jerked her arm in front of her face. "Don't hit me! You didn't tell me to watch her anywhere but in the bar. I've told you everything I know about where she is."

When Louis lowered his hand, she looked him in the eye. "I'm through with you, Louis. You were going to hit me." She glanced around. "And I'm through with this stupid town." Carmen spun on her heel and ran down the street toward the motel where she'd been staying.

Louis watched her go and shrugged. He didn't need her anymore if Edna had left. Slowly, he trudged up the hill to the house. He slammed the front door hoping to wake Burt. When it didn't, he flipped his brother the bird, kicked a pile of magazines and sent them sliding across the threadbare rug. He headed to the kitchen for a beer. Not finding any, he slammed the refrigerator door, paced the room for a few minutes, glanced at the clock, then went to the phone and dialed.

"Hello," a man said on the other end.

"Bennie? It's Louis."

"Yeah. What's up?"

"Get a shovel, and...let's see...a pick, an axe, and a rake. I'll pick you up in a few minutes. And grab one of those old screens on your back porch. A big one."

Bennie sighed. "Have you been mainlining?"

"Just do it!" Louis shouted. "And fill your cooler with beer and something to snack on." He slammed down the phone, grabbed the car keys and ran out the door. With Bennie's help, they could tear the side of that hill apart and find at least one of those gold coins. There was still five hours of daylight, and he was going to use it.

* * *

Unable to get Jake out of his mind, Wiley remained silent most of the way to the cabin. Following the route he'd taken when he'd first traveled by train to Alma, he commented a few times on how many people now lived in the mountains and that it had been wilderness in eighteen eighty-six. As they passed Santa Maria, Wiley looked up at the statue of Jesus on the side of the mountain. For the first time in his life, Wiley asked Jake's friend to help him get his blood brother back safely. He swiped at his misty eyes and realized the knot in his gut hurt more than the ache in his leg.

"We'll find him, Wiley," Dave said softly. He reached over and squeezed Wiley's shoulder. Not wanting his own concern for Jake to take control, partly for Wiley's sake, but also because he was driving, he gripped the wheel and focused on the road, thankful they were almost to South Park.

* * *

Louis looked at his watch. It was five o'clock. He and Bennie had been digging, raking and sifting for over an hour and they hadn't even reached the area where the center of the cabin had been. He sighed, let the shovel fall and walked to the ice chest.

"Bennie, you want a beer?"

On his knees in the dirt, Bennie wiped the sweat from his face with his T-shirt. "Yeah. Just toss me one." He caught the cold can, passed it over his forehead and cheeks before he opened it, then took several big swallows. "I'm glad you said to bring beer or we'd have nothing to drink. Doing this is the pits."

Louis slammed the cooler lid. "Quit bitching! All you've done since we left Alma is bitch about everything. You've been living with Angie too long. You're beginning to sound just like her."

"Hey, man! Don't start on Angie! I'm here doing you a favor, and you're fat-lipping Angie and me?" Bennie struggled to his feet. His bulging gut hung over his belt and showed skin below the bottom of his filthy T-shirt. "Watch your mouth, or I'll pound you flatter'n a tortilla!"

Louis smiled weakly, glanced at the rotund man who reminded him of a Mexican bandido. He forced a laugh. "Boy, I sure pushed your button. I was only joking. I'm still pissed off about those two assholes stealing my gold coins." Louis gritted his teeth. "I could kick myself for not coming out here sooner. Those assholes probably found everything all in one place and we're just wasting our time. God, I *hate* them!"

Bennie glared at Louis as he guzzled the rest of his beer. He crumpled the can, tossed it down the hill, then picked up his shovel and dug into the thick layer of rotted planks. He dumped two shovels of dirt and spongy wood onto the screen and began sifting the moldy-smelling pile. After several vigorous shakes, he bent down and tossed aside the rusted nails, rocks and larger pieces of wood.

A half hour later, they heard a car approaching. At first Louis thought it was going on up the road, but the car began the long climb up the steep driveway toward them.

"Who the fuck is that?" Louis snapped. He motioned to Bennie to move back into the aspens. "This place is busier than a damn shopping mall!"

Dave stopped the truck in the driveway as close to the cabin as he could. He sat behind the wheel and looked around. "Someone's been here recently. I can feel it. And I wonder whose car that is down on the road?" Dave slid out of the truck and peered into the surrounding woods.

Wiley struggled out of the truck and limped to his side. He studied the ground. "There have been two women or children here recently. These footprints are too small for a man." He pointed at two sets of tennis shoe impressions in the sandy soil. "The tracks head toward the cabin." He walked slowly in that direction and continued to examine the ground. Stopping midway, he said, "Here's prints of two different sized boots." He motioned toward the easiest way to the bottom of the cliff. "The smaller prints were made on two different occasions, but the large boot prints go down the slope." He looked over at Dave. "They don't come back."

Dave's eyes widened. "You think they're still here?"

"At least one is, unless he was just passing through, but I find that unlikely considering that blue car on the road." Wiley re-examined the prints, then noticed the splintered pieces of wood scattered near a rock. "I wonder what's been going on here?" He folded his arms. "There's one way to find out."

Wiley returned to the truck, grabbed his holster from behind the seat, slid out his Navy Colt and shoved the gun in his belt. When he reached the edge of the cliff, he yelled, "Who are you and what are you doing on my land!" He paused for any response. Not hearing any, he hollered, "I know you're down there! If you don't come up with your hands on your heads, I'll shoot at random where I think you're hiding!" He pulled his gun and cocked it. The click was loud enough to be heard for twenty yards.

"Don't shoot!" Louis yelled. "I'll come up." He motioned for Bennie to stay put, then started up the hill.

Wiley saw Louis before Dave did. "I *said*, get your hands on your head!" he ordered as Louis trudged up the steep slope.

Louis clapped his hands on his head. When he got to the top of the cliff, Wiley looked at his boots. "Tell the other man to come up too, or you get it between the eyes."

"But I'm alone," Louis whimpered.

Wiley pointed the gun well to the left of Louis and pulled the trigger. The deafening blast echoed back and forth down the valley, sending the raven screaming from his home in the rock cliff. Louis grabbed himself in panic.

Dave flinched at the gunshot and silently prayed Wiley wouldn't lose control. But when he looked at the man beside him, he saw Wiley's white teeth glistening through a threatening smile. He couldn't remember when he'd ever seen a more confident and powerful-looking man in his life. He knew then why he loved to read westerns.

Down the slope, the gunshot blast jolted Bennie's big frame. Convinced Louis was dead, he raised his hands and yelled, "Don't shoot me! Please! I was just helping Louis find the gold coins he's looking for. I didn't mean any harm." The others could hear his loud wheezing as he scrambled up the hill. When he got to the top, he gasped for breath and was greeted by Louis' hateful glare.

"You had to tell them, didn't you!" Louis snapped.

"Hey, man, I thought you were dead," Bennie gasped. "I didn't want to get shot too."

Wiley dropped his hand so the gun pointed at the ground. "What gold coins are you talking about?"

Louis shook his fist at him. "Those gold coins you paid Edna for my land!"

"Your land?" Dave said. "Edna Scott's name was on the deed. Who are you besides a liar?" He touched Wiley's arm and winked. "Maybe you should shoot him."

Wiley raised the gun and aimed at the skinny man with greasy brown hair. "My pleasure!"

Louis covered his face with the backs of his hands. "Don't shoot me! My name is Louis Scott. I'm Edna's brother-in-law. She bought the land from me a few years ago."

Wiley lowered the gun again. "It's Jake's land now. And what makes you think there's gold coins down there?"

Louis lowered his hands and frowned. "There probably isn't now! You found those gold coins in that cabin down there, then paid for the land with them. By rights, those coins belong to me. And I want them!" He squinted his eyes. "I'll *sue* you unless you give them all to me. And just so you know, I have plenty of money backing me." Louis smiled and put his hands on his hips. He lied and said, "A wealthy woman from Buena Vista met me here and said she'd help me sue you."

Wiley looked at Dave with half-closed eyes. "Not her again." He turned to Louis. "Those coins were not found in that old cabin. They belong to my partner."

"Yeah, right," Louis snapped. "Where'd your partner get them?" He pointed down the cliff. "When I got here yesterday, those old logs had been scattered down the hill like someone had been searching for something. You found those coins down there, on my land, and I'm going to sue you to get them back."

Wiley glowered at him. "Jake won them in a wagon race."

"You found them in the old cabin down there!" Louis yelled. "And you found them when it was still my land!"

Wiley glared at Louis. "There's no point in arguing this. Get out of here, or I'll shoot you full of holes."

"You're bluffing," Louis sneered with lawsuit-threatening confidence. "You'd never get away with it!"

Wiley casually raised his Colt and fired at Louis' right foot. The bullet made a furrow along the side of his boot, but didn't rip the leather clear through to injure him. They all heard the whine as the bullet ricocheted off the rocks.

Feeling the heat from the bullet on his foot, Louis screamed and jumped into the air. After inspecting his boot, he looked up at Wiley, screamed again and started running toward his car.

Bennie jogged his heavy body after Louis. Neither man gave the tools or the ice chest a second thought.

Within minutes, Dave and Wiley heard the sound of a car speeding down the road. They walked to the edge of the cliff and looked out in silence. A short time later, through a slot between two hills far below, Dave pointed to the pale blue car kicking up dust on the road as it sped toward Alma.

Later, while Dave fixed their dinner, Wiley slowly hobbled down the slope to the ruins of their cabin. Louis and his cohort had made more mess than Jake when he'd found the golden feather. Wiley picked up a crumpled beer can and shook his head. Seeing garden tools scattered around and how thoroughly the area had been ravaged, he closed his eyes and whispered, "Oh God, Jake. Where are you?" After a moment, he tossed the empty beer can into the cooler, slammed the lid and struggled back up to the cabin.

"Where did Jake hide the rest of the coins?" Wiley asked as he entered the kitchen. "If you show me, I'll dig them up while you're cooking."

Dave slid the skillet to the simmer area on the cookstove and followed Wiley outside. He reached under the cabin for a shovel and led the way to the outhouse. After Dave paced off four steps, he got down on his hands and knees and carefully searched the area. When he found the small white rock in the shape of an arrowhead, he drew an X in the dirt with is finger and looked up at Wiley.

"Are you sure that's the spot?" Wiley asked. "This ground doesn't look like it's been disturbed for years."

"Jake did a great job hiding the coins. If it hadn't been for this white rock, I never would have remembered where he dug the hole."

Fifteen minutes later, Wiley joined Dave in the kitchen. He dumped out the coins on the table and counted them, making sure the eighty-four remaining were all there. Satisfied, he scooped them back into the zipper plastic bag, sealed it and slipped it into his pocket.

"Shouldn't we telephone Jim to see if he's heard from Jake's kidnappers?"

"Good idea." Dave grabbed the remote phone from the kitchen table and pushed the buttons. After a long pause, he said, "Jim, call us at the cabin as soon as you can. Bye." He punched the off button and placed the phone back on the table.

"Isn't Jim there?" Wiley asked.

"No. He's either playing ball with Winnie or went to the store. I can't believe he would leave at all."

"I hope no one went to the house and made trouble." Wiley shook his head. "This is a nightmare. In our own time, we had Billingsly and the Harrises after us, but it was nothing compared to this. With Jake kidnapped, all the cars, people everywhere, greed, hatred..." Wiley combed his hair with his fingers. "I'm close to losing control." He looked over at Dave. "I know you told me not to shoot the gun around here, but I had to. I didn't want to hurt Louis, just scare him."

"He might report it," Dave said. "If he does, the sheriff will pay us a visit for an explanation. Louis knew he was trespassing, so he might not say anything, but I don't trust him."

Dave flipped the two steaks. "That was some shooting. I've never seen anything like it."

"My grandfather first taught me how to use a gun. I learned a few other things about shooting from my father, but mostly on my own. In Jake's and my time, many people carry guns but use them only when they have to. Now, it seems, only hot-headed thugs have guns, and they kill anyone in their way. In eighteen eighty-six, punks like that are hung the day after they're caught."

The phone rang. Wiley grabbed it.

"This is Wiley."

"Hi, Wiley," Jim said. "I was in the alley playing ball with Winnie and talking to a neighbor when Dave called."

"Have you heard anything about Jake?"

"Not a word," Jim said. "Dave's message was the only one when I came inside. I'll call you the minute I hear something. How are things up there?"

"When we arrived, two men were here looking for the coins."

"Looking for the coins? Who were they?"

Wiley briefly filled Jim in on the encounter with Louis and Bennie. He also warned Jim not to open the front door for any reason and to keep Winnie with him.

They wished each other well and punched the hang-up buttons.

CHAPTER 23

When Jake awakened, he could barely see out of his left eye. It was almost swollen shut from being hit in the face. Still tied securely to the bed, he slowly turned his head toward the only window in the room. Sunlight streamed into his eyes. That horrible smell turned his stomach, and he heard loud machine noises outside. Jake raised his head and looked around the small office. The only furniture was a battered rolltop desk, a sturdy wooden chair and the iron bed he was tied to.

Jake noticed papers and trash...everywhere. The entire room was littered with grimy rags, pieces of cardboard boxes and filthy papers, most in windblown piles that seemed to climb the walls. He shuddered. Where was he? Jake lowered his head to the bed and stared at the peaked roof of the small building. Directly above him, globs of brown stuff had leaked through the boards and hung down in long drips. He quickly turned his face away, hoping they were hardened.

What time was it? Jake noticed the edge of sunlight moving slowly toward the floor, so it had to be morning. But what day? How long had he been here? He hoped Wiley would come soon and save him.

Being held captive suddenly angered Jake, and he struggled with his bindings. A bell rang outside each time he moved.

A few minutes later, the door opened and the room was flooded with sunlight. As a man walked in, he pulled the door shut and slid a hood over his face.

"Well, look who's awake," the man said as he walked to the bed. He untied the cord around Jake's wrist, and the bell stopped ringing. When he yanked down Jake's gag, he snapped, "You won't get hurt again if you keep your mouth shut. If you start yelling again, I'll stick that needle in you."

Jake tried to see the man's face but the sunlight blinded him, and his hood was pulled too far forward.

"I'm hungry," Jake said, trying to shove back his terror and rage.

"So what? I'm not going to untie your hands, and I'm definitely not going to feed you. If all goes as planned, you'll be free tomorrow morning. If they don't bring the coins...well, food won't do you much good." He laughed.

"Wiley'll get you!" Jake shouted. "An' when he does, you'll wish you'd never done nonna this to me!"

The robed man slugged Jake in the face. "Shut up! I told you to quit yelling!" Seeing a trickle of blood oozing down the side of Jake's mouth, he laughed. "Slurp up that blood on your lip. That ought to keep you fed for awhile." Chuckling, the man left and slammed the door, causing the building to shudder. Loose papers swirled toward the growing pyramids of trash in the corners.

Jake's eyes teared. Why was this happening to him? What had he done? He remembered telling Mr. Jeffrey they had a lot more coins. And he'd lost the rawhide bag when he'd tossed Lance over his head.

"Jesus, this here's my own damn fault," Jake said out loud. "If it weren't for my big mouth an' dumpin' that man on the floor, nonna this here stuff would'a happened." He closed his eyes, squeezing out the tears. "Jesus, you gotta let Wiley save me. An' I gotta find that bag." He whimpered, "I'm sorry for not talkin' to you as much as I did before I met Wiley. You'd a told me not to do them things." He jerked his hands and feet at the tight bindings. "I'm sorry, Jesus, for bein' dummer'n hog shit."

* * *

When Dave and Wiley arrived back in Denver at eight that same morning, Jim was sitting on the front porch waiting for them. The three men glumly ate breakfast together on the deck. None of them had slept much from worrying about Jake, but at least they had the gold coins, and Dave and Wiley hadn't seen any sign of the sheriff at the cabin.

In the city again after the brief trip to the mountains, Wiley felt like a caged animal. Convinced the air in Denver was poisonous, at times he found himself gasping for breath. But he was thankful he could walk without the crutches. The pain in his leg had diminished to a dull ache except when he walked too fast or turned it the wrong way.

Wiley slowly paced the small house, the backyard and the alley. Jim finally convinced him to rest his leg, and he spent several hours sleeping on the couch. He'd placed the telephone near him on the coffee table.

Dave and Jim took turns running errands. They didn't want to leave Wiley alone in case the detective or the kidnappers called.

At five o'clock, Wiley sat rigid by the phone, ready to pick it up at the first ring. Jim fidgeted nervously beside him on the couch, and Dave waited upstairs with his hand on the extension.

Wiley jumped when the phone rang. He grabbed it and pushed the button. Dave carefully picked up the extension as Wiley answered downstairs.

"This is Wiley."

"Do you have the coins?" a man's voice asked harshly.

"Yes."

"Good!" The man laughed, then his voice turned hard. "Now, listen carefully. Tomorrow, at three in the morning, drive to Eightieth and Tower Road. Go north on Tower Road. A little past the intersection, there's a turnout next to a cottonwood tree. Pull in there and wait. Be there at three sharp." The man paused. "Come alone or you'll never see your friend alive again."

"Let me talk to Jake," Wiley demanded. He heard birds in the background. They sounded close.

"Wiley?" Jake's voice sounded distressed, but calmer than Wiley had expected.

"Jake, are you all right?"

"My eye all swelled up, Wiley. This here man keeps hittin' me in the face. Did you find them gold dollars?"

"Yes, we found them. I'll pick you up in the morning. Just stay calm until then. I miss you, Jake."

"Hurry, Wiley," Jake whimpered. "This here place smells somethin' terrible, an' I ain't eaten nothin' since I got here. Had to pee in my pants, Wiley, 'cause this here man won't untie me."

The other man's voice came on the other end. "You damn well better come alone. If I spot any cops, your friend gets it in the head."

Wiley forcibly calmed himself. "I need someone to get me there. I don't know how to use one of those cars, and I don't know where the place is. Jake and I only arrived in Denver this week."

"I don't buy that about you not knowing how to drive a car."

"He don't know how!" Jake hollered. "We ain't from here! We ain't never seen them cars before two weeks ago!"

"I told you to shut up!" the man yelled at Jake. Wiley heard a smack, and Jake groaned.

Wiley gritted his teeth and squeezed the phone. Jim grabbed his arm, trying to prevent him from crushing it.

The man finally said, "Have someone drive you to Eightieth and Tower. You can walk to the turnoff. If I see you're not alone, your friend will be dead when you get there. Be there at three."

The loud click shocked Wiley as he realized the connection had been broken. He slowly pushed the button to hang up the phone, then stared at it.

"What did he say?" Jim asked.

Dave ran down the stairs, flung himself into the chair by the front window and grabbed the yellow pages from the bottom shelf of the table beside the chair.

"Wiley, did you hear the gulls in the background?" Dave asked. "I think I know where Jake is." After careful scrutiny of one page, he yelled, "Here it is! There's a landfill at Eighty-Second and Tower Road. Jake said the smell was terrible, and I kept hearing gulls. Jim and I have been there." He frowned and shook his head. "I wonder why we didn't hear the gulls yesterday when the kidnapper called?"

"You're right, they were gulls," Wiley said, impressed at Dave's deductions. "Let's go there tonight. Maybe I can rescue Jake before tomorrow morning."

"Do you think you should?" Jim asked. "The landfill is a horrible place to be sneaking around at night. It's bad enough during the day."

"What is a landfill?" Wiley asked.

"It's where everyone in Denver throws their trash and garbage."

"You mean a dump?"

"Yes, why?"

"I never guessed it would be a dump. Now, the gulls make sense. I knew there was no ocean here." Wiley smiled. "It's easy to sneak around in a dump. I've done it a few times in Boston and Philadelphia."

Dave replaced the phone book and said, "If that's where Jake is, I doubt they're keeping him anywhere near the trash. I don't know what dumps were like in your time, Wiley, but they're horrible now, and immense." He looked at Jim. "Remember when we were there? Weren't two shacks sitting side-by-side just inside the gate?" Dave squinted, trying to remember. "They were on the right as we drove to where we dumped the stuff."

"Didn't we pay at the largest building?" Jim asked. "The one farthest from the gate?"

"You're right." Dave turned to Wiley. "They could be holding Jake in one of those buildings."

Wiley touched Jim's leg. "Where is this dump?"

"It's about twenty miles from here." Jim frowned. "I think we should call the detectives. We can't go in there at night. Besides, the gate's probably locked."

"I doubt it," Dave said. "The gate was half buried in trash when we were there. I wouldn't have noticed, but a rocking horse somehow had gotten jammed into the hinges. I thought about rescuing it, but it was too far gone."

Wiley struggled to his feet. "Jake is out there. He's part of my soul. I have to rescue him." He looked at Dave and Jim. "Please, take me there tonight."

CHAPTER 24

Baked from the heat of the day, the stench of the landfill fouled the air for miles around as the three men traveled north on Tower Road. Jim drove past the gate twice. Each time, Wiley memorized the location of the two buildings that faced the rutted road heading to the mountains of putrefaction a hundred yards farther.

Wiley was appalled at the smell and the steady stream of huge, trash-splattered trucks roaring in and out of the landfill. Nausea crept up, and he was forced to breathe through his mouth and concentrate on the hope that the two grimy buildings wouldn't collapse and crush Jake before he could rescue him.

Since the breeze was from the southwest, Wiley asked Jim to park the car a mile south of the landfill to wait for twilight to fade. As soon as it got fully dark, Jim drove the car close to the entrance and killed the lights.

Dave pointed into the gloom. "There's the gate, Wiley."

"Are you sure you should be doing this?" Jim asked. In the dim light of a half-moon, he was barely able to see Wiley strapping on his gun belt. "You should have let us call the detectives. If anything happens to the kidnappers, you'll be the one that's arrested."

"Me? They're the kidnappers."

"Nowadays criminals have more rights than the victims," Dave quipped.

"Don't worry, I won't shoot unless I'm shot at. And I won't miss."

Wiley slipped out of the car. Favoring his left leg, he slowly crossed the road. Dressed in dark clothing, he seemed to vanish in the tall weeds along the fence.

The rotten odor nearly overpowered Wiley by the time he got to the gate. He saw the gate had been closed as much as possible, but mounds of trash prevented it from being shut completely. He squeezed through the gap. A brisk wind masked any noise he made. Papers whipped across the littered ground and flew high into the air. Wiley wondered if all this blowing trash ended up back in the streets of Denver.

Both times they had driven by, Wiley had noticed a monstrous piece of machinery, its huge wheels taller than a man. A metal tread ran around the outside of the wheels, with four-inch spikes its entire length. The thing loomed in front of him, and the dried slop clinging to its hulk glistened like sweat in the moonlight. Its hideous, black shape made Wiley's skin crawl.

Wiley crept up to the monster and started around to the back side, knowing he was only thirty yards from the two buildings. He stopped next to the bulldozer and grabbed his left leg. It ached more than it had all day, and he knew he'd used it too much earlier.

A shaft of light lit the ground under the bulldozer as a door opened in one of the buildings. Wiley crouched down and saw the legs of two men leave the larger building, then the door slammed shut. The two men walked toward the monster-like machine. One of them held a flashlight.

Wiley saw the man in the lead stop, then he turned to face his companion.

"I don't like it, Max. You and your brother are too damn greedy. You've gone too far this time. That guy in there will know it was your brother that's responsible for this. He may act dumb, but I'll bet he's not."

"You worry too much, Reggie," Max said. He threw back his hood. "Ralph and I have thought this out. Those coins are worth over a hundred thousand bucks, and that guy in there has no fingerprints on file." He chuckled. "Being an ex-cop has its advantages." Max put his hand on Reggie's shoulder. "Relax. Once we get the coins, we can kill them both. No one's around here at three in the morning. We'll bury their bodies deep in the pit. Who's going to know the difference?"

"What about the one driving the car?" Reggie asked. "When neither of them come back, he'll probably start snooping around. Maybe even go to the cops. If he hasn't already."

"I told you to relax. I plan to have Badger in the weeds where I told them to park. He's going to sneak up behind the one driving

and shoot him in the back of the head. We can drag the car in here
and bury it in the pit."

"Well, I don't like it!" Reggie snapped. "That's three murders
for those damn coins. I don't want any part of it!"

"Reggie," Max cooed sarcastically. "You don't know what
you're saying. You back out on us now, and I'll tell the cops where
you buried that woman you raped and killed last year. Remember
her? Let's see, what was her name? Oh, yes, Linda Cornwall. I
might even say you buried her body by the cottonwood trees on the
north side of the landfill." Max laughed at Reggie's silence. "Didn't
think I knew, did you?"

Reggie turned and climbed up the side of the bulldozer. Once he
reached the cab, he started the engine. The ground shook as the
monster came to life. The entire area blazed with light as Reggie
turned on the spotlights mounted around the vehicle.

Wiley gasped in horror and crouched under the huge machine
amid shredded plastic and stinking pieces of cloth that had caught on
the bulldozer's underside and hung to the ground in rags. It would
be impossible to get away without being detected. He felt along the
underside of the tractor for something to hold on to if the bulldozer
started moving and found a large metal door latched only on one
corner. Wiley pried the door open and shoved his fingers inside. He
no sooner got a good grip when the huge machine leaped forward,
sweeping him off his feet and dragging him along backwards.

The bulldozer had traveled only twenty feet when the latch tore
loose and the door opened, spilling Wiley to the ground. In a panic,
he grabbed a heavy piece of cloth and yanked it down as the tractor
roared over the top of him. The edge of the spiked tread brushed his
shoulder.

Laying on his back, Wiley hoped he was completely covered by
the cloth. He didn't dare move. As a gust of wind buffeted the area,
Wiley peered out a slit in the material.

A man, standing a few feet away, faced him.

"Get up!" Max ordered. "I've got a gun on you, so don't try
anything!"

Stunned and angered he'd been caught, Wiley didn't move.

"I said, get up!" Max hollered. He kicked Wiley in the foot, then reached down and yanked the cloth away. "Get up and put your hands on your head!"

Slowly, Wiley sat up, then struggled to his feet. His leg pained him from the fall to the ground, and he hoped the scabs hadn't broken. Since his leg was in such bad shape, using any of the surprise maneuvers he'd learned from Grandpa Gray Feather was out of the question.

In the dim light from the tractor, Wiley realized the man in front of him, called Max, looked like a younger Ralph Jeffrey from the coin shop. He studied Max's gun. He'd never seen one like it before. It had a wider barrel on the end, as if a length of pipe had been added.

"What are you doing here?" Max demanded. He saw Wiley's gun belt. "Take off that gun and toss it to the ground."

Not saying a word, Wiley unbuckled the belt and let it fall. The floodlights on the bulldozer, now at the brink of the vast pit, grew dimmer on Max's face.

"Kick that gun over here to me," Max said. "Make any sudden moves and I'll shoot you. Nobody will ever hear it."

Wiley balanced on his injured leg and grimaced in pain as he shoved the holster with his right foot. Slowly, he put his hands on his head.

Max snatched the gun-belt off the ground, then shoved Wiley toward the smaller building. "Go in there and face the wall!"

The light inside seemed blinding as Wiley opened the door. He stepped into the building and immediately saw Jake tied spread-eagle on the bed. Jake's eyes were closed, and his face was bruised and swollen. He didn't move. Was Jake sedated again...or dead?

Max shoved Wiley farther into the room and pulled the door shut behind him. He jammed his gun into Wiley's back. "Welcome to our little party."

CHAPTER 25

Still parked across from the landfill and sitting in the dark, Dave touched Jim's arm. "I'm going to see what that light is. If it's the bulldozer, Wiley might be discovered. Or run over."

"David, be careful."

"I certainly intend to."

Dave slipped out of the car and rushed across the road. Standing in the weeds, he peered through the chain link fence and saw the enormous tractor start toward the open pit. A man ran toward a pile of cloth and pointed a gun at it. Then the man kicked the cloth and yanked it off the ground. Dave's gut tightened when he saw Wiley lying on his back. He'd been so sure Wiley wouldn't have any trouble. What would happen now? Should they call the cops? But what if there wasn't time? They were miles from any phone.

Dave knew he and Jim were going to have to rescue both Jake and Wiley. But how? As soon as he saw Wiley get to his feet, Dave ran back to the car.

"Jim, Wiley's been captured," Dave whispered. "We've got to help."

"How? We should get the police."

"There isn't time. Some man was pointing a gun at Wiley." Dave quietly opened the rear door, grabbed Jake's gun belt and strapped it on. "I've always wanted to wear one of these." After he buckled it, he thought he felt some of Jake's strength enter him. It felt wonderful. He tied the holster to his leg.

As Dave ran across the road, he was glad Wiley had insisted they bring Jake's gun and wear dark clothing. He stopped at the gate and took a deep breath through his mouth. The wind whipped up a small cyclone of paper and trash. Dave shielded his eyes when it skirted the gate.

A hand grabbed his arm. Dave gasped and grabbed at the gun.

"It's only me," Jim whispered.

Dave sighed. "God, you scared the shit out of me, but I'm glad you're here."

They slipped through the gate. In the distance, deep in the huge glowing pit, the bulldozer's engine roared as it dug a hole beneath the mountains of garbage. The floodlights dimly lit the trash-filled field in front of them. Dave thought of a bombed-out city from some sci-fi movie.

"Where are they?" Jim asked in a whisper.

"I don't know. I should have watched longer to see where they went." He pointed to the structures. "Let's get on both sides of those buildings. Why don't you go to the far side of the biggest shack. I'll sneak up on the small building. We can meet between them. And be careful!" He squeezed Jim on the arm and started running.

Jim ran down the rutted road toward the far side of the bigger structure. He stopped and crouched behind the remains of a large cardboard box that slid his way in the wind. He looked at both buildings. If anyone was in them, he wondered why he couldn't see light coming from the windows, but then noticed the closed wooden shutters. Jim continued on and waved at Dave when he reached his destination.

A door opened in the larger shack, lighting the area. Jim sprang behind an oil drum near the corner of the building. His heart pounded, and he remained motionless. The person slammed the door and headed toward the smaller building.

Seeing the light, Dave jumped out of sight behind the smaller structure and nearly panicked when he heard footsteps approaching. He quietly sprinted to the back of the building and sighed with relief when the door opened and the person went inside. He pressed his ear to the wall and heard muffled voices above the wind.

"Badger, tie this guy up!" Max yelled. He still pointed his gun at Wiley.

Badger laughed when he saw Wiley sitting in a chair next to the bed with his hands on his head. "Well, where'd you find him?"

"You know him?" Max asked.

"Sure!" The gorilla-like man with huge, stooped shoulders and a crooked nose protruding from a red puffy face pointed at Jake. "He's one of his friends. I followed them, remember?"

Dismayed that Badger knew who he was, Wiley said nothing. Until this moment, even though Max had been holding a gun on him, he'd felt in control, convinced the silent treatment would have eventually angered Max to the point of doing something rash. But he'd suddenly lost the advantage when Badger arrived. Never for one moment did he think Dave and Jim would be able to get him out of this spot. He felt they were too mesmerized by TV and all the gadgets they owned to have a firm grip on their real potential.

"Tie him to the chair, Badger. There might even be another one out there waiting in a car. You can take a look when you're done there."

Max watched Badger tie Wiley's hands to the back of the chair and his feet to its legs. He sneered at Wiley, then waved his hand toward Jake. "So you were trying to save this idiot? How sweet." His eyes turned cold. "Where's your driver?" He balled his fists. "And the coins?"

"I came alone." Wiley knew Max wouldn't believe that since he'd already told him he couldn't drive a car.

"You're real cute!" Max backhanded Wiley across the face. Irritated his perfect hideout had been so easily discovered, he hit Wiley across the face again and yelled, "How did you find this place? And where's the damn *coins*?"

Dave heard the outburst inside and panicked. He tried to get to the open area between the two buildings where he'd told Jim to meet him. As he inched along the back of the structure, the bottom of his pants hooked something. He yanked his leg, and the rusted bed spring that he'd snagged toppled over and slammed him against the back wall of the building. Dazed and seeing the instantaneous light as the door opened on the far side of the building, Dave scrambled out from under the mattress skeleton and crawled behind a long jumble of wooden crates piled three or four high. He pulled Jake's gun and wondered if he could really shoot someone. Where was Jim?

Heavy footsteps headed in his direction between the two buildings. As two men approached, Dave peered through gaps in the crates and saw the circle of light from a flashlight dart in zigzag patterns on the walls of the buildings, on the ground and over the wooden boxes.

A crash was heard inside the smaller building. Max and Badger stopped.

"That guy must have tipped over in the chair," Badger said. "He's not going anywhere. I tied him good."

Max flashed the light on the bed spring. "That's what hit the wall.

"Could have been blown over by the wind," Badger offered.

"Could be, but something solid hit the wall. There's nothing that big anywhere near it." Max shined the flashlight around the area, then continued toward the jumble of crates. He pointed his gun at it and yelled, "Put your hands up and come out!"

Dave crouched lower and pointed Jake's gun at the blinding light source. He heard someone running, then Badger grunted, lurched forward and slammed into Max. Both men fell face-down into the wooden boxes. Max dropped the flashlight. It bounced on a board and slid into a crate with the beam pointing at him.

Dave jumped back when crates splintered from the weight of the two men. Able to see clearly, he scrambled to his feet and ran toward them. He raised Jake's gun and clouted each one on the head with the barrel. Wondering if he'd hit them hard enough, Dave whacked the men again.

A noise by the bed springs startled Dave, and he peered over the undamaged crates. He saw Jim leaning against the building with his arms folded, grinning.

"Jim, what happened?" Dave asked.

"I didn't know what to do so I used my old kidney-buster tackle from college football and rammed them from behind."

"It sure worked." Dave reached into the splintered crates, pulled out the flashlight and shined it on the two unconscious men. "I didn't want to shoot them, but I almost did."

At Dave's insistence, they dragged Badger and Max out of the splintered wood and placed them side-by-side on the ground at one end of the crates. Dave covered the pair with the bed springs and stacked a few wooden boxes precariously on top.

Jim squinted at him. "What are you doing that for?"

"If they wake up before we get Jake and Wiley out of here, the falling crates will warn us."

When Jim and Dave entered the office, they found Wiley, still tied to the chair, lying on his side on the floor. He had almost twisted the heavy, oak chair into kindling.

Wiley's eyes lit up. "You did it! I never thought you could!"

Dave sighed. "Neither did we."

While Jim untied Wiley and helped him to his feet, Dave freed Jake's ankles and wrists from the bed.

Wiley limped to Jake's side, bent down, caressed his swollen face and kissed his forehead. He bit his lip when he saw the wet spot on Jake's pants around his crotch.

"Let's get him out of here," he said softly.

Within minutes, Dave and Jim laid Jake in the back seat of the Honda with his head in Wiley's lap, then sped toward home.

* * *

Reggie decided the hole in the trash was finally deep enough. It could completely bury a semi, but he didn't want the car or any of the bodies to ever be found. He turned the huge machine toward the buildings and approached from the rear. Not yet wanting to shut down his power source, when he saw the stack of wooden crates, he remembered he'd been saving them for kindling for his fireplace. Reggie steered the bulldozer toward the crates. They'd been sitting there long enough. He drove one spiked tread over the pile of wooden boxes several times, crushing them into hundreds of splintered pieces.

CHAPTER 26

Jake slowly awoke from the drug-induced sleep. Before he opened his eyes, he cautiously moved his arms and legs. They weren't tied to the bed! Jake moved his right hand and it brushed a naked body lying next to him. He snapped his eyes open and turned his head. It was Wiley! Jake looked around. He could see only with his right eye, but realized he was in Jim and Dave's house. How had he gotten here? Jake snuggled against Wiley's huge arm and slid his fingers through the thick, black hair on Wiley's chest. This big, strong man, his partner, had saved him just like he knew he would.

Wiley opened his eyes and rolled on his side. He pulled Jake to him and gently kissed his swollen face. "God Jake, I'm glad you're back with me. How do you feel?"

"I feel worser'n after the fight in the Silver Heels Bar."

Wiley slid his hands up and down Jake's smooth skin. "It's good to feel you again." He kissed Jake's forehead.

"How'd I get here, Wiley? I don't remember nothin'."

"We can thank Jim and Dave for rescuing us."

Jake pulled back. "Jim an' Dave? Where was you? I thought you saved me?"

"I tried, Jake. Because of my leg, I got captured also. Last night, Max, who is Mr. Jeffrey's brother, and another man named Badger, tied me to the chair next to your bed. Jim and Dave saved both of us."

"Mr. Jeffrey's brother? That must'a been why I thought I knowed him from somewhere. Where are they? What happened?"

"I'll let Jim and Dave tell you. It's their story. Right now, I just want to hold you."

Still groggy after being sedated so many times, Jake relaxed and let Wiley caress his entire body.

Though his leg still ached, Wiley felt a whole person again as he slid his hands over the smooth, muscular body of the man he loved. He vowed never to let anything happen to Jake again.

Soon, they smelled frying bacon.

Jake pulled away from Wiley's embrace. "I love you an' all that, Wiley, but I'm starvin'." He kissed Wiley and struggled out of bed.

Wiley sighed, then chuckled and followed him.

* * *

For the remainder of the day, Jake and Wiley stayed around the house and ventured only as far as the alley to play ball with Winnie. Dave showed Wiley how to work the VCR, and he and Jake spent time staring at the screen.

While watching a program, Wiley noticed Dave come in the front door. As he walked by the couch, Wiley grabbed his arm and asked, "Dave, who are those people laughing while the actors in this movie shout insults at each other? Is insulting others humorous in this Time?"

Dave watched the program for a moment, then grimaced. "That's one of the sitcoms I told you about. You're right, Wiley. Sitcoms are nothing but insults and idiotic comments, not to mention insults to our intelligence. The scary thing is, most people in this country think they're funny." He shook his head. "That laughing is canned laughter that's turned on when you're suppose to laugh."

Jake turned away from the TV. "Wiley, I been thinkin' I'd bring some cans'a corn back to our time, an' cans'a them halipony peppers, but I ain't bringin' nonna that canned laughin' back."

Dave snickered. "It's Hal-a-pino peppers. And they don't sell canned laughter in the store. It's just an expression."

When Dave started for the kitchen, Jake said, "Wait." He pointed at the screen. "Can people in that TV see us, too?"

"No. At least, I don't think so." Dave rubbed his jaw. "Come to think of it, a few years ago I read an article in the newspaper about some TVs made in Japan that had tiny cameras mounted inside." He stared at the screen. "Maybe someone can see us."

From that moment, whether the TV was turned on or off, Jake felt it was a huge eye watching his every move.

Disgusted with the sitcom, Wiley decided to put on a porn video called "Leathered." As the partners snuggled into each other's arms watching the tape, Jake suddenly sat up straight, grabbed the remote and fumbled with it.

"What are you doing?" Wiley asked.

"How do you turn that thing off? I don't want to watch them naked men doin' them things to each other. They're usin' each other only for their ownselves. They ain't got no love for each other."

Wiley smiled. "They don't seem to be in pain, and they're very handsome men."

Jake sighed and sat back.

As they watched, one of the men stuck a long black dildo into the other man's rectum causing him to scream.

"I take back what I just said," Wiley muttered. He grabbed the remote and turned off the VCR. "I'd never treat you that way."

"I wouldn't do nothin' like that to you, neither. I love you, an' don't want you hurtin'." He shook his head. "Seein' that makes me think of Abe, an' how he done that to us."

Wiley shuddered. He'd been close to death when Abe had raped and strangled him. "Thank God you were there to save me." He grabbed Jake and kissed him.

* * *

Giving in to Winnie's begging, Jake played ball with the dog in the alley. He'd become attached to Winnie, who minded him without his usual sassing. Jake loved to watch Winnie catch the ball, amazed he could leap and catch it mid-air while running at right angles to it.

During the day, Jim kept busy in the yard. Being able to help rescue Jake and Wiley in the landfill gave him a feeling of confidence he'd never experienced before. He hummed while he weeded around the roses.

"What're you plantin'?" Jake asked as he and Winnie came in from the alley.

Jim looked up at him. "I'm digging weeds."

Glancing around at the many flowers in the small inner-city yard, Jake asked, "Don't you plant no corn er nothin'?"

"We used to." Jim sat back on his feet. "We got sick of working out here all summer. Now we just have perennials that come up every year. Since we moved to the cabin, we don't have to worry about planting the yard every year."

"Before Ma got sick, her garden was littler'n this here yard. She'd feed us all year from it."

Jim smiled. "I'm sure she did. We did too for a couple years, but we had other things to do."

Jake did a complete turn-around, shrugged his shoulders. "Ma'd like these here flowers. She'd always say somebody was rich if they could spend time plantin' flowers."

Jim shaded his eyes with his hand, looked up at Jake and saw his handsome, innocent face marred only by his swollen eye. "I would have liked your mother. She taught you beautiful things."

"Ma'd like Wiley. She'd always tell me not to get hitched with a woman if it weren't right for me." Jake flickered a grin. "I'm glad Wiley never knowed Pa. Wiley'd most likely tie Pa upside-down from my tree house." Jake snickered, then tried to squelch it.

Smiling, Jim grabbed the branch clippers, sat back and examined the roses. He got to his feet and reached into the center of the circular rose bed, carefully selected a velvety-red rose that was just opening and cut it off far down the stem. He held the rose out to Jake. "Let's put this in a vase in honor of your mother."

* * *

Dave became so engrossed in inspecting the gems he'd retrieved from the safety deposit box, he barely noticed anyone. He sat at the dining room table and placed the stones in rows, then grouped them by color. He wiped each one with a soft, cotton cloth to remove finger-smudges, then held each gem at arm's length in the sunlight to watch them sparkle. He figured the chances were slim they'd be going to eighteen eighty-six, even if Jake did find the rawhide bag, but Wiley had talked him into checking out the stones.

Awed by the beautiful colors of the gemstones, Jake pulled up a chair and watched. "How'd you get them rocks to look like that?"

Dave smiled. "My machinery's in the basement. If we have time later, I'll show you."

"How come you ain't brought that 'chinery up to your cabin?"
"I want to, but right now there isn't any place to put it. I plan
to...build an extra room up there so I can spread out."
     Bored with TV, Wiley switched it off and sat in a chair next to
Jake. "Billingsly would kill for these." He pointed at a group of ten
stones. "How much are all these gems?"
     Dave raised his eyebrows. "How did you know those were the
ones I'd picked out for you?"
     Wiley laughed. "I didn't. They just look more valuable than the
others. What kind of gems are they?"
     Pointing at each one, Dave proudly said, "This is a five carat,
light green emerald, these two are matching dark blue aquamarines
at eight carats each, this is a ten carat amethyst, here's a four and a
half carat sapphire and two tourmalines. The green tourmaline is
eight carats, and the wine colored one is six." He grinned and held
up an oval stone. "And this is a ten carat red-orange topaz. I love it.
It reminds me of glowing coals. I'm keeping the other half of this
topaz. It's cut the same way."
     Dave carefully held the last two stones in the sunlight. "And
these are matching black opals from Lightning Ridge in Australia.
They're two carats each." Dave tilted the stones toward Jake and
Wiley so they could see the brilliant flashes of red, purple and green.
     Jake nudged Wiley's arm. "Wiley, I don't see no carrots."
     Wiley forced himself not to laugh. "Me either."
     Dave squelched a smile. "Jake, the carat I'm talking about means
how much the stones weigh. It's a Greek word meaning carob bean
or small weight. It just happens to sound like the carrot we eat."
     "How much are those ten gems worth?" Wiley asked.
     "By today's prices, about five thousand. But if you're going to
buy them to resell in eighteen eighty-six, I'll sell them all to you for
a fourth that, and I feel guilty even charging you that much."
     Wiley went to their bedroom. He returned and handed Dave five
thousand dollars. "Wrap those up for us."
     "Wiley, I can't take all that money!"
     "Yes, you can. They're costing us a little over four dollars of
our money. That's a bargain."
     Jake pointed his finger at the table and made a wide circle.
"How much is all these here stones?"

"Why do you want all of them?" Dave asked.

"Hell, you said them gold dollars'll be worth only a dollar when we get back to our time. Wiley an' me gotta have somethin' to make us rich there."

"Jake, there's a lot more than money to make us rich," Wiley scolded. "We have each other...and Jim and Dave."

"I know, but when we get back home, maybe we can get us a ranch somewhere an' some cows."

"We have to find the rawhide bag first. If we never find it, we'll need the coins and the money to get settled here."

"Here? Wiley, we can't stay *here*! This Time's bad. Chief Eagle Rising said it was. All kinds'a bad things been happenin' to us. You know that."

"Think, Jake! If we don't find the bag, we'll be forced to stay here." Wiley looked around the room. "There's a lot of things to learn in this Time. If we have to stay here, I want to find out how a lot of these gadgets work. Especially the TV."

Jake shuddered in horror. He'd lost the rawhide bag, but never once believed he wouldn't find it. The thought of staying in this Time for the rest of his life filled him with a dread like the thought of marrying Sara Jean. He rushed into the bathroom and slammed the door.

For the rest of the day, Jake barely spoke to anyone. He sat by himself in the back yard, and not even Winnie could console him.

* * *

While watching the early evening news, Dave suddenly yelled, "Oh, my God, no!"

The others hurried into the room. Jim slid beside Dave on the couch, and Jake and Wiley sat on the edges of the two recliners. They all looked at the TV screen and saw a reporter standing beside a grimy building. Everyone, except Jake, recognized it as the smaller building at the Tower Landfill.

"Police say it was murder," the reporter said. "The two bodies were found under a pile of crushed wooden crates. They apparently had been run over by the monstrous tractor you see behind me. So far, their identification is not known since the bodies were crushed beyond recognition."

The camera panned to the gargantuan machine parked behind the reporter. A runny smear on one of the spiked treads was a dark reddish-brown.

Wiley felt bulldozer glowering at him. He pointed to the screen. "That thing almost ran over me."

"Damn!" Jake shouted. "When were you there?"

"That's where you were being held prisoner."

Jim waved his hand at them. "Shhh."

When the camera focused on the reporter again, he said, "Two guns, both equipped with silencers, were found near the bodies. Police aren't sure how the men got under the crates, but they say there is evidence that someone had been tied to a bed in the smallest of the two buildings. Police found blood and urine stains on the mattress. Someone had also been tied to a chair."

A small box appeared at the bottom of the screen showing the anchorman at the station. He asked, "Neil, do they have any suspects?"

"Bob, they have one suspect in the murders, a man named Reggie Norris. He's admitted driving the tractor over the crates, but claims he didn't know the two men were under them. Police say he's been uncooperative."

"Are there any more suspects?" Bob asked.

"Police will only say they are looking for other suspects. There are signs of a struggle inside the smaller building, but they won't say how many people were involved. I'll give more details as they become available. For now, this is Neil Bendrich, reporting from the Tower Landfill. Back to you, Bob."

The screen changed to the anchorman at the station who went immediately into a different story.

Dave dropped his head to his knees. "Oh, my God! I killed those two men! I'm the reason they were under the crates." He covered the back of his head with his hands and sobbed.

Jim slid his arm across Dave's back. "You had no way of knowing that man would drive the tractor over the crates. You were just being careful so we wouldn't get caught." He gasped and shot

Wiley a fearful glance. "Our fingerprints are everywhere in that room."

"Wiley, why's Dave cryin'?" Jake asked. "What's ever'body talkin' about?"

Wiley looked from Jim to Jake, then to Dave sobbing. He could care less about the deaths of the two men who'd kidnapped and beaten Jake. They would have killed them all once they'd gotten the coins. They had it coming. It was only justice. But he could understand how Dave felt. He remembered being devastated after he'd killed the man who'd given him the scar on his cheek. Wiley shuddered. His first killing.

"Wiley, did Dave kill somebody?" Jake asked.

"No." Wiley smiled at Jake and put his finger to his lips, then bellowed, "Dave, they had it coming! You can cry and blame yourself if you want, but you are not responsible for those two deaths!" He softened his voice and his face. "You acted responsibly by setting up a warning in case they came to. I would have done the same thing."

"But our fingerprints are everywhere," Jim exclaimed. "Even though Dave didn't kill them, we're all suspects now. The police will be looking for us."

"Fingerprints?" Wiley asked. "What does that mean?"

Jim leaned over and kissed Dave on the back of his neck, then smiled weakly at Wiley. "Everyone's fingerprints are different, and police can trace people by matching fingerprints from a crime scene to the ones on file. Almost everyone in the world has been finger-printed. We have to do it when we get our driver's license." Jim shook his head. "Ralph Jeffrey will also be looking for us."

"I told you this here Time's bad," Jake said. "Now we *gotta* find that rawhide bag."

"What about the detectives?" Wiley asked. "I mentioned to them I suspected Ralph Jeffrey in Jake's kidnapping."

"I forgot to tell you Wiley," Jim said. "I called one of the detectives and told him that Jake had been found safe and that we had no idea who grabbed him. He seemed satisfied with my story. He may not remember what you said about Ralph Jeffrey."

The phone rang.

All four men froze. They looked at each other as they let the answering machine take over.

When Jim listened to the message, he was relieved to find it had been from their good friend, Don Lindsay. He'd called to remind them about the Gay Rodeo tomorrow and a party in the evening and ask if they wanted to go.

Only Jake wanted to.

Dave wiped his eyes and blew his nose. "Jake, I don't think Jim or I should be going out in public. We don't know how much the police know about us. And like Jim said, we left a ton of fingerprints in that office."

"But if Lance is at that rodeo, I can get my rawhide bag back an' we can all get outta here."

Wiley saw the logic. "It's worth a try. The bartender at the Pit Stop keeps telling us Lance hasn't shown up there since the night he and Jake were seventy-sixed."

"Eighty-sixed," Jim corrected. He thought about what Wiley said. "Maybe you're right about going. We can always try to get lost in the crowd. We've never been to the Gay Rodeo anyway."

Dave stood up and began pacing the floor. "I just can't get it out of my mind that I'm responsible for those two men's deaths. It'll haunt me until I die."

"Dave, listen to me!" Wiley's voice was full and commanding. "I heard them say they were planning to kill all of us once they got the coins. The man that ran over the crates was digging a hole to bury us. You protected us from being surprised if they woke up before we escaped. You can hold yourself responsible if you want to, but you're not to blame."

Wiley stood up, planted his fists on his hips and looked down at the others. "We need to concentrate our efforts in finding Jake's rawhide bag."

CHAPTER 27

On their way to the Gay Rodeo, the four men stopped to pick up Don Lindsay. Since Dave drove and Jim rode shotgun, Don folded his six-foot-five frame into the back seat of the Honda next to Jake. When he pulled the door shut, the three big men became crushed together. They shifted positions to accommodate each other.

After Jim introduced the tall, sandy-haired man wearing rimless glasses to Jake and Wiley, he began telling Don of the past few week's happenings. He didn't mention that Jake and Wiley were from the past and decided not to say anything about the rawhide bag.

Don listened wide-eyed and said nothing at first, but then let out a low whistle when Dave told of the TV news program about the dead bodies in the landfill.

"Lately, you guys seem to fall in and out of one crisis after another. Can I do anything to help?"

"We gotta find Lance!" Jake yelled.

Don looked at Jake. "Lance? Why do you want to find him? I thought everyone tried to stay as far away from him as possible."

"He stole my rawhide bag. Wiley an' me can't get back home 'til we find it."

"Did you have money in it?" Don asked. "Not to make you feel bad, but Lance probably spent it by now."

"There weren't no money in it," Jake grumbled. "I had the golden..."

Wiley elbowed Jake in the side. "Jake won't leave Denver without the bag. An Indian...er, Native American gave it to him."

Don didn't believe a word of it. Jammed next to Jake, he also felt Wiley's nudge. Realizing the bag was a sore subject, he didn't intrude on the sudden silence in the car, feeling the men needed it to sort things out.

To Dave and Jim's relief, the rodeo was more crowded than they'd anticipated, and hoped it would be easy to lose themselves among so many people. With Jake, Wiley and Don surrounding them, they felt more at ease, but realized being completely inconspicuous was hopeless. Jake and Wiley turned the heads of everyone in the building.

As they walked down the main entry hall of the smaller arena at the National Western Stock Show grounds, they found it lined on either side with booths selling T-shirts, jewelry and various rainbow items. Most of the booths were giving out condoms and literature on AIDS.

Jim wondered why he and Dave had played around with other men, and thanked God that neither of them had gotten AIDS.

Jake peered around suspiciously. "Wiley, why's ever'body lookin' at us like we was some kind'a lollypop?" He pointed across the display area. "See them men over there lickin' their lips at us."

"I don't know what it means, Jake, but I can guess." Wiley smiled and nodded at the men. They all smiled back.

"Lollypop is a good word, Jake," Don commented. "It means they want to lick your...er, lick you all over. In a manner of speaking."

"Well, they ain't lickin' me!"

"Jake, calm down," Wiley scolded. "You have to stop getting so riled about other people looking at you or touching you. Doesn't it make you feel good they like the way you look? You're an extremely handsome man."

"I am?" Jake knew Wiley had told him that before, but couldn't remember any one else ever saying he was handsome. "Guess I thought they was laughin' at how I look."

Dave tapped Jake's arm. "Those guys smiling at you wish they looked like you. When you smile back at them, they feel cozy inside." He winked at Wiley.

"I'm really handsome?" Jake asked.

Wiley slid his arm over Jake's shoulder. "Yes, you are. I told you when we first met in the Silver Heels Bar you're the most handsome man I've ever seen. And that's still true. But you have to stop punching everyone who touches you. Lord knows, even I have a hard time keeping my hands off you in public."

"Ain't they tryin' to get me away from you when they touch me? You an' me're partners."

"They don't know that." Wiley slid his hand off Jake's shoulder, grabbed his right arm and pulled him close. "Knocking them out doesn't tell them you and I are partners. It only tells them you're a sorehead."

The others laughed, which made Wiley smile.

An older man, dressed in red-sequined cowboy attire, his face painted with eye shadow, rouge and lipstick, sashayed up to Jake and grabbed his left arm. "Darlin', where've you been all my life?" He batted his long black eyelashes. "Let's ride off into the sunset together."

Jake tensed his body and started to punch the man in his red kisser. Still holding Jake's right arm, Wiley prevented him from doing it.

Wiley smiled at the man. "Sorry, we're together."

"Well, damn! Can't blame a old cowgirl for trying!" The man waltzed away into the crowd.

"See how easy that was, Jake?" Wiley winked at the others.

Jake's eyes followed the man who called himself an old cowgirl, then turned back to the group. "Why're so many men now wantin' to be like women? Don't they like bein' men?"

The others looked at each other and shrugged.

* * *

While sitting in the arena, Dave commented, "I overheard someone say this was the first time the Gay Rodeo was being held inside." He glanced over his shoulder at the hundreds of people sitting so close. He hated crowds and felt trapped.

Jake grabbed Dave's left arm and asked, "Can I look through them glasses'a yours?"

"Sure!" Dave slipped off his binoculars and handed them to Jake. He turned to Jim and said, "I'm going to wander for a few minutes. It's driving me crazy to sit in the middle of this crowd."

"We can't sit by ourselves," Jim said. "Jake's the one who wanted to sit in the middle. Take Wiley with you. Look at him. He looks frozen in his seat."

When the rodeo started, Wiley loosened up and forgot about the swarms of people surrounding him. Never having seen an actual rodeo before, he remembered that he and Jake had left the Harrington Ranch the day before the event took place. The day after that, he'd been shot. It seemed years ago since that had happened. Wiley shuddered to think it had been over a century ago in actual time.

Dave suddenly caught a whiff of Jake's sweaty odor, and he breathed deeply. Having lived for nearly a month with the two men who refused to use deodorant or cologne, he'd gotten used to their manly scent, and it was now a definite turn-on. On this day, it fit in well with the rodeo, and he had to fight hard to keep from wrapping his arms around Jake and burying his face in his shirt.

Sitting on the opposite end of the group from Wiley, Don leaned over to Jim and whispered, "Where did you say you met Jake and Wiley? I've never seen such gorgeous hunks in my life."

Jim thought for a moment. "We met them at the cabin. Wiley had been shot in the leg, and we took him to the doctor. We found out later they're gay." He sighed. "And lovers."

The gate opened, a horse leaped out of the stall, lowered his head and bucked in a counter clock-wise spin. Wiley watched the cowboy in a blue shirt masterfully hold on with one hand. He rode like he'd been welded to the wild-eyed horse that spun and leaped into the middle of the arena. A horn sounded, and the bronc rider slid to the horse of the cowboy that rode alongside.

Wiley jumped to his feet and yelled. While standing, he glanced around at the huge arena over half-filled with people, many of them on their feet, waving their arms and cheering. The sight took his breath away. There were so many gay people. His heart swelled and his eyes teared. They all seemed so beautiful with their clear, honest countenances. Not like the pinched, jaded faces he'd seen crowding the Sixteenth Street Mall. Wanting to share this with Jake, he glanced down and saw Jake slouched in his seat with his elbows propped on his legs. The binoculars were pressed against his eyes.

Wiley sighed. He slid his arm across Jake's shoulders and lowered himself into his seat. "Jake, you're missing everything using those glasses."

Jake lowered the binoculars. "Hell, Wiley, I gotta find Lance an' get my bag back. We gotta be gettin' outta this here Time."

"But, if Lance isn't here, you'll have missed the entire show."

Jake frowned. "But if he is here, Wiley, an' I miss seein' him, we'll have to stay here with all them men wantin' to be like women, an' all them others wantin' to kill 'em."

Overhearing, Dave leaned toward Jake. "Not all gay men dress up in dresses, Jake. Look around, there's only a few here. Most of us like being men. At least, we do."

"Hell, I weren't talkin' only about men like us," Jake said loudly. "When we was walkin' downtown, all them fat men in dark suits walkin' around had faces like somebody'd cut their nuts off. An' they smelled like women an' wore them pants lookin' like dresses. Most'a these here men look like men, but they smell like women too."

Two cowboys sitting in front of Jake laughed, then turned around. One of them grabbed Jake's knee and said, "You hit the nail on the head about corporate America. And they think we're weird."

Jake had no idea what the man had said.

Wiley sighed, thankful Jake hadn't slugged the cowboy for touching him.

The group sat on the south side of the arena for an hour, then, at Jake's request, moved to the other side so he could search the area where they'd been sitting. Jake missed the second half of the rodeo as well, glancing up from the binoculars only a couple of times while drag queens tried to ride a calf across a line. But after all his searching, he never saw Lance.

The last event, bull riding, and clearly the crowd favorite, captured the attention of the entire arena. Only one cowboy stayed on the bull until the horn. After each bull rider picked himself up from the dirt, he ran to the clown and hugged him.

Wiley laughed and clapped loudly. Rough, tough men and they openly displayed their love for each other.

As everyone filed out of the arena, Wiley noticed Jake silently lagged behind. When Jake caught up to him, Wiley realized he was deeply depressed. He slid his arm over Jake's shoulders and pulled him close.

"We'll find the rawhide bag, Jake. Maybe not here, today. But we'll find it."

Jake looked at Wiley, said nothing, then dropped his gaze to the floor.

Startled that Jake had nothing to say, Wiley hoped it was due to his sore face. The swelling around his left eye had diminished, but it was still red and puffy, tending toward black. He hoped no one would tease Jake about the red ring around his right eye from using the glasses so long.

Wiley squeezed Jake harder, and they followed the others in silence.

Hundreds of people milled around the booths in the display area. Many circled the dance floor and watched men dancing with men and also women dancing together. Some crowded outside in the sweltering heat and smoked. Jim slowly edged the group through the throngs. Don bought everyone a drink, and they stopped at each booth for a few moments.

Jim coaxed them across the hall to a display of paintings. He began talking to the artist, and soon Dave and Don were engaged in the conversation.

As Wiley went from painting to painting, he was amazed at the imagination and beauty of the pieces. He turned and stared at the artist. The man looked Native American. "No wonder these are so beautiful," he said softly to himself.

Uninterested in the art and having finished his beer, Jake wandered to a waste barrel to get rid of his empty cup. He tossed the cup at the barrel. It hit the back rim and flipped to the floor behind the receptacle. Frowning at his aim, Jake bent down to retrieve it. As he straightened up, he was jostled by someone tossing something into the barrel. When Jake glanced at the person, his face came within inches of his rawhide bag. It was tied to the man's belt!

Jake gasped. Without thinking, he grabbed the bag, then raised up and looked into the startled eyes of Lance.

"Hey, let go of my bag!" Lance yelled in a deep bass voice. The same two men that were with him in the Pit Stop crowded closer.

"This here's *my* bag!" Jake yelled. "You stole it from me in that there bar when I flipped you over my head. I'm takin' it back." Jake yanked at the bag. It untied itself and leaped to Jake's chest, taking his hand with it. Jake grabbed the rawhide cord, slipped it over his head and shoved the bag down his shirt.

"Thief!" Lance yelled as loud as he could. "He stole my pouch!" The three men grabbed Jake and forced him to the floor. The smaller two began punching Jake while Lance struggled to get the leather bag.

Wiley heard Jake yelling, then saw him on the floor with three men on top of him. A crowd gathered quickly, and someone yelled for the security guards.

Wiley shoved his way to the scene. He pulled the two smaller men off Jake, one at a time, and tossed them aside as if they weighed nothing. He grabbed Lance around the neck with his left arm and yanked the heavy-set man to his feet, ignoring the sharp pain in his wounded leg.

Lance struggled and yelled for help, but Wiley tightened his grip around the man's neck. He yanked Lance's right arm behind his back in an arm-lock.

Many spectators gasped at Wiley's strength.

As Wiley held Lance in an iron grip, Jake got to his feet. His lip was bleeding.

"Jake, are you okay?" Wiley asked. He forcibly stopped Lance from squirming.

Jake pulled the rawhide bag out of his shirt and held it up. "I got my bag back. Now we can go home."

Two security guards elbowed their way through the crowd. The fat one shouted, "Okay, break it up! I'm in charge here!"

Many of the men standing around booed him. The smaller guard reached out to Jake, but Jake shoved his hand away.

The heavy-set guard grabbed Wiley's arm and tried to loosen his grip around Lance's neck. He couldn't. Wiley shoved the man away with his hip.

Wiley let go of Lance, spun him around to face him and gripped his upper arms. "What's the *matter* with you?" Wiley yelled as he shook Lance once, making his head snap back and forth like a rag doll.

The crowd gasped.

"First, you steal Jake's rawhide bag!" Wiley shouted into Lance's face as he shook him once more. "And now, you want to

steal it *again*? I ought to break every bone in your body!" He shook
Lance hard.

Stunned, Jake stared at Wiley. He'd never seen his partner so
riled.

"Let go of me!" Lance screamed. He looked pleadingly at the
security guards. "Help me!"

"You deserve everything that man can do to you, Lance!"
someone yelled.

"Stop it!" the fat guard hollered at Wiley. He fumbled with his
holster, finally popped the rarely used snap, and grabbed at his gun.
After he pulled it out, he pointed it at Wiley. "Let go of him!"

Still holding Lance, Wiley looked down at the guard, then at the
pistol. "If you know how to use that thing..." He jerked Lance
toward him. "Arrest this man! He's nothing but a thief! Jake was
only taking back what this thief stole from him several days ago!"

"He's lying," Lance whimpered. "That's my pouch." He grimaced
at the guard. "Make him let go. He's hurting me!"

Wiley squeezed Lance's arms even tighter, causing him to
scream in pain. "*Tell* him!" Wiley shouted, shaking Lance every time
he said the word "tell." "*Tell* him you stole that rawhide bag in that
bar! *Tell* him!"

Unable to stand the pain of Wiley squeezing his arms any longer,
Lance screamed, "Yes, I did it! I did it!" He began sobbing. "I
slipped it off when he flipped me over his head. Now, please let go.
You're hurting me."

A gangly man pushed through the onlookers. "I'll vouch for that
story. It happened in the Pit Stop." Ron pointed to Jake. "He came
back after their struggle and asked if I'd found a leather bag. We
looked but didn't find it. I told him then that Lance probably took
it." Ron glared at Lance. "You'd steal bread from your starving
mother!"

Wiley let go of Lance, and the man rubbed his upper arms with
his hands. He had teary eyes, but said nothing.

The smaller guard asked Jake, "You want to press charges?"

"What?" Jake turned to Wiley. "Wiley, I don't rightly know
what that there soldier just said."

"He called the guard a soldier!" one man shouted. The group
with him laughed.

Jake cowered and looked at the floor.

Wiley shook his fist at the group. "Leave Jake alone!"

Everyone backed up a few steps.

Wiley slid his arm around Jake's waist. "Jake, the man wants to know if you want Lance arrested."

Jake's brilliant blue eyes looked deep into Wiley's. "I just want us to go home, Wiley." He spun around, grabbed Lance by the shirt and yanked him forward.

The crowd gasped.

"You quit your damn stealin'!" Jake shouted into Lance's face. "Stealin' ain't right!"

Jake shoved Lance backward, slamming him into a pillar, then pushed his way through the crowd.

Since Jake didn't press charges, the guards yelled for everyone to disperse. Lance and his buddies slipped into the crowd and disappeared.

Wiley bulldozed his way in the direction he'd last seen Jake. He wondered what had happened to Dave and Jim. He'd seen Don in the fringes earlier, but now he was nowhere around.

Wiley found Jake at the beer counter. As he got to Jake's side, a tall skinny drag queen in a chartreuse velvet gown handed two plastic glasses to Jake. Wiley stared at her green wig, her caked eye shadow and long black lashes that had pulled away at the sides. Her name tag read Miss Fish.

Miss Fish sloshed the beers as she set them on a folded towel. Foam spilled down the sides.

"Five dollars," she snapped.

"Five dollars!" Jake yelled.

Miss Fish snatched back the two beers and set them on the counter in front of her.

"Next?"

"I'll pay for them," Wiley said. He pulled out a five dollar bill and placed it on the counter.

Miss Fish snatched it, examined it, then stuffed the bill into an overflowing cash box. After smirking at Jake, she handed Wiley the beers.

"Next?"

As they turned away from the counter, Wiley handed one of the cups to Jake. "Why do you have to be so grouchy? It isn't that man's..." Wiley glanced back at Miss Fish. "It isn't her fault these drinks are so costly."

Jake stared at his beer. "I don't like this here Time, Wiley. We ain't had nothin' but trouble since we got here. I wanna go back to Chipmunk Rock when jest you an' me lived there."

Wiley touched Jake's nose with his finger. "We will, Jake. Soon. You found the bag and the golden feather. That's a start."

Jake's face brightened. "You're right." Silent for a moment, he added, "I ain't never seen you so riled. You was like a crazy man when you was shakin' Lance."

Wiley shrugged. "I got tired of people hurting you."

As the blood brothers walked through the milling people, they smiled, talked and laughed with other men. Wiley almost became teary-eyed that Jake had finally snapped out of his rotten mood. Together they searched for their companions and found them outside in the hot sun while Dave smoked a cigarette.

"There you are." Wiley greeted.

Dave immediately offered Wiley a cigarette, which he accepted, but tore off the filter before lighting it.

Jim searched the area, then looked at Wiley. "When you two started fighting with Lance, Dave and I decided not to get too close." His eyes searched the area again. "We're wanted by the cops, you know."

"You're making too much of that newscast," Don teased. "They probably just want to ask you some questions."

"They did use the word suspects," Wiley countered. "I think you're both wise not to overly expose yourselves, but your fear might be a little untimely."

As soon as Wiley finished his cigarette, which he stated was tasteless, they all went inside.

While they watched the men dance, Jake tapped Dave on the shoulder. "This here's like I saw in a bar in Denver when I was workin' on houses. All them men was dancin' with each other like they are here."

"In eighteen eighty-six?" Dave asked.

"Sure. Danced like that in Alma, too, in the Silver Heels Bar where Wiley an' me become blood brothers."

After Jake turned to say something to Wiley, Dave watched the dancers. He tried to envision Alma in eighteen eighty-six. "God, I can hardly wait to go there," he whispered.

Jim grabbed his arm. "Are you all right?"

Dave nodded. "Now that Jake found his bag, maybe we can go back with them to their time. Isn't it exciting?"

"It scares me," Jim said. "But living here scares me even more with the police looking for us. If they find us, we'll spend years in court...maybe even in prison."

"Come on you two," Don shouted at them. "We have a party to go to."

Dave and Jim gazed solemnly into each other's eyes, bravely smiled at each other, then walked arm-in-arm as they followed their friends to the exit.

CHAPTER 28

The ringing phone woke him. Louis's left arm, wedged between his body and the wooden arm of the chair, had fallen asleep and hung limp when he reached for the receiver. He cursed. Awkwardly, he grabbed the phone with his right hand, knowing he couldn't hear as well with that ear. His left arm began tingling.

"Hello?"

"Is this Louis?" a woman's voice asked.

Louis pushed the phone closer to his ear. "Yes. Who is this?"

"This is Cynthia Havertine. Remember me? I met you when you were looking for the gold coins."

"I remember. What do you want?" Louis shook his left arm.

"I've decided to help you sue those two men. I don't know why. I guess I'm good-hearted." She grinned at Donna sitting beside her on the leather love seat.

"One of them shot at me yesterday when I was there," Louis said. "I went to the sheriff about it." He lied about the sheriff, but hoped saying that would solidify the woman's resolve to help him.

Cynthia raised her eyebrows. "They shot at you? That's in your favor right off the bat. I've contacted my lawyer, and he wants to take the case. I'll set up an appointment for both of us to see him tomorrow. It will have to be here in Buena Vista." She paused at Louis' silence. "Is that all right with you?"

Louis switched the phone to his other ear now that his left arm was functioning again. Able to hear and think better, he relaxed a little. "I guess I can make it tomorrow. When will you know?"

"I'll call him right now, then call you back." She hung up the phone.

Bert got up from the couch. In his drunken stupor he knocked over a lamp trying to get to the bathroom. Louis's gut tensed. He rushed over and picked up the lamp, hoping his brother wouldn't fall into the bathtub again. The last time it happened, he'd pulled a muscle in his back trying to get Burt back to the couch. As Louis straightened the lamp shade, the phone rang. He lunged for it.

"Hello?"

"This is Cynthia. The appointment is set for tomorrow at seven-thirty in the evening. Can you make it?"

Louis heard a loud thud in the bathroom, then a groan.

"Uh...just a minute." Louis dropped the receiver in the chair and ran to the bathroom. Burt had fallen. He was draped over the toilet bowl, and his arms and head were hanging into the tub. Louis thought he looked stable enough for the moment so he rushed back to the phone.

"Uh...hello? I think I can make it."

"Well, can you or can't you? I have to know now."

"Yes! I'll be there. Where is it?" Louis heard Bert moan.

"Do you know where the Lone Tree Motel is...in Buena Vista?"

"No."

"Well, coming in from US 285, it's on your right one block past the only traffic light in town. I'll meet you in the parking lot of the motel at a quarter after seven. We can go to the lawyer's office in my car. Remember, it's the Lone Tree Motel. Be there at a quarter after seven tomorrow evening."

"I'll be there, and thanks."

"Just *be* there!" Cynthia hung up the phone, threw her head back and laughed. "Donna, I can see it now. Those two gorgeous men will be sitting in the courtroom watching their friends get sued while I seduce them wearing pink chiffon and Midnight Tramp perfume." She laughed again and sipped her martini.

Louis stared at the phone, then ran into the bathroom to somehow get Burt back to the couch. He finally realized why Edna had left and wished he could find some place else to live. But that meant finding a job. Now that Carmen was gone, he didn't even have half of her paycheck anymore. He wondered how long it would take to sue the two men and collect his gold coins.

* * *

Silver-haired Detective Burchard pointed across the room of the small shack at the Tower Landfill, then glanced at stout, balding Sergeant Hoffman. "We think someone was tied to that bed, and we found ropes lying where the Xs are marked on the floor. There's a little blood on the mattress, and that yellow spot smells like urine." Burchard waved his hand to the wall behind the bed. "The string over there is tied to a bell outside, but we haven't figured out what it was used for." He pointed to the battered chair lying on its side. "Someone was tied to this chair. It could have been the same person who was tied to the bed, but we don't know yet." He shook his head. "Whoever it was had the strength of two men. That's an oak chair and it's almost been twisted to pieces."

Sergeant Hoffman bent down and inspected the blood on the mattress, then glanced at Burchard. "Any fingerprints?"

Burchard nodded. "Jud said the place was loaded with them. The lab's checking them out now. Jud thinks there were about seven different sets, but he reserved judgement until they can verify it."

Hoffman went to the window and looked out at the bulldozer. "The driver who ran over the two men won't talk yet, but he will. We have him in the room with Curly." The sergeant glanced around the small room once more then headed for the door. "Let me know when the lab calls. We're pretty much in the dark until then."

* * *

A handsome, dark-haired man in his early twenties stood beside Ralph Jeffrey's plant-surrounded desk. He rested his left hand on the desk and slouched into it, then raked his short, wavy hair with his other hand.

"Just how am I suppose to find them, Ralph?" Hank Foxton asked. "Badger didn't tell anyone where they lived, and the police have sealed off both buildings at the landfill. If Badger wrote anything down, the cops have it by now. Oh, and I'm sorry about your brother."

After working for Ralph Jeffrey for six months, Hank hoped his boss realized Badger had been the wrong one to be in charge of that job. The man been stupid to go to his grave without telling Ralph what he'd found out about the men with the coins.

Ignoring Hank's reference to his brother, Ralph Jeffrey shrugged and peered over his glasses at the muscular man dressed in Levis and a red tank top.

"We know one thing," Jeffrey said. "They're gay." Ralph checked for any kind of reaction from Hank but got none. He'd been positive he'd get some kind of reaction. Hank reminded him of his nephew Butch. Butch was a lady-killer in the looks department...and gay. Ralph smiled slightly. He liked Butch. Kindest man he'd ever known.

"At least, Badger told me they were gay," Ralph added. He thought he saw a flicker of something in Hank's expression.

Ralph sat forward in his chair. "Hank, I want you to check out every gay bar in the city, every gay function, gay movie house, gay everything. They're bound to turn up somewhere." He shifted his gaze through the plants to the sales area, then back at Hank. "Max told me the man they kidnapped didn't have any fingerprints on file. Anywhere. I find that quite odd. How could a man escape being fingerprinted for over twenty years?"

Hank shrugged and pulled himself away from the desk. "Who cares? I just wish I'd been the one to...oh, never mind." He glanced at the floor, then at Ralph. "I'll get on it right away." Hank turned to leave but stopped in mid-stride and turned back to Ralph. "I just want you to know I don't like the idea of snooping around fags. They make me sick."

"Well, get over it," Ralph said. "It doesn't rub off." He removed his glasses and smiled at Hank. "Who knows, maybe you'd have better luck with a man. You don't seem to do too well with women."

Stunned, Hank turned on his heel and left. Had his secret desire been obvious? He resolved to push it down even farther and start openly condemning fags even more. Hank shuddered. His parents would kill him if they ever thought he was a....

CHAPTER 29

Jake gasped when the elevator door opened into the penthouse suite of a high-rise condo bordering Cheesman Park. Loud music assaulted him, and an obese drag queen draped in a black velvet gown studded with tear-drop pearls barred their entrance to the party beyond. Holding a goblet containing peach-colored liquid, she wavered, then focused on Jake with half-closed eyes. She extended her gaudily-ringed hand and rasped in a deep voice, "Dahling, would you be...be sho-kind and help me to...to the ladies room?"

Jake jumped back and shot a glance at Jim, who was smiling.

Jim stepped out of the elevator and grabbed the drag queen's arm. "I'll help you, Glorine. I've never been here before, but I'm sure we can find the rest room." Jim steadied Glorine as he led her down a side hallway.

Jake spun around to Don. "Damn! Was that a man or a woman?"

"She's a man, but don't worry about it. Let's get out of the elevator." Don gently ushered Jake into the foyer. Dave and Wiley quickly followed before the doors closed.

A tall, thin man with graying temples and dressed in a white dinner jacket walked over to them. "Don, Dave, I'm so glad you could make it." He grabbed each man's hand and patted it.

"It's good to see you, Al," Don said.

Al looked questioningly at Dave. "Where's Jim?"

"He's helping Glorine find the rest room."

Al raised his eyes to the ceiling. "The poor thing drinks too much. She's gone through almost an entire bottle of apricot schnapps since she's been here." Al's face suddenly lit up. He stepped past Dave and approached Jake and Wiley. "My goodness!" He cut his eyes to Don. "Did you tell these" — he scanned both men up and down — "these Michaelangelo *masterpieces* that this is a gay party?"

Dave laughed. "Al, this is Jake and his partner, Wiley. Jake and Wiley, meet Al. This is his home."

Wiley smiled and shook Al's hand. "Glad to meet you, Al. You have an impressive place here."

"Why, thank you. I'm rather fond of it."

As Jake shook the host's hand, he said, "How do," then he glanced out the west window. "This here place is like livin' in a tree house like I had back home."

Still holding Jake's hand, Al smiled vacantly, looked into Jake's face and tried to ignore his black eye. "Yes...I suppose it is. I love your accent, Jake. Where are you from?"

"Wilmore, Kentucky. 'Course that was over a hunnert..." Jake snapped his mouth shut when Wiley nudged him in the back. He glanced at Wiley, saw Wiley was grinning at him, then turned back to Al and said, "Wiley an' me're stayin' here now."

"Well, fine." Al patted Jake's hand, looked him up and down and sighed, then grabbed Jake's arm and pulled him toward the open french doors leading into the living room. "Come in and meet everyone else." As he led Jake away, he added, "I have plenty of food and whatever your heart desires to drink."

As they entered the main room, Jake looked back at Wiley.

Wiley smiled at him and quickly put his finger over his lips, hoping Jake would get the hint and not say anything about the time switch. He turned to Dave and whispered, "I hope Jake keeps his mouth shut about where we're really from."

"Just say you're both in a play, and Jake really gets into his part. Let it go at that. No one will care."

Later, after breaking away from the last group Dave and Don had introduced him to, Wiley stood by himself for a moment and looked around. He estimated seventy-five people had gathered in the spacious living quarters. People, mostly men in cowboy attire, sat or stood in groups in the living room. He noticed several women, also wearing western clothes, talking with animated gestures. Overhearing, Wiley realized they were discussing the rodeo.

The dining room held the most activity as people crowded around the food. Wiley watched a tall, gracefully attractive woman in a sparkling red gown glide through the crowd. Someone said something to her, and she answered in a deep male voice. Wiley chuckled. She...he certainly had fooled him. His heart swelled as he realized gay people accepted everyone as equals.

Suddenly aware of the furniture, Wiley thought of Philadelphia in eighteen eighty-six and wondered if the beautifully carved wooden sideboards, cabinets and dining room set, all from his own era, had been in Al's family for a hundred years.

Wiley turned and looked out the wall of windows that stretched the entire length of the suite and overlooked the park and the mountains beyond the city. He remembered reading about the ruins left by the cliff dwellers in southwestern Colorado.

Sensing someone behind him, Wiley spun around and stood face-to-face with two men, both shyly grinning at him.

Wiley smiled and extended his hand. "I'm Wiley Deluce. You gentlemen are?"

Both men started talking at once, then stopped and snickered. The tallest, a slender man in his early twenties with dark brown hair, a slight cleft in his chin and a wide smile, stuck out his hand. "I'm Walter Beeson. My lover's name is Ken Dancing Bear."

Wiley shook Walter's hand, then raised his eyebrows at Ken. He could see the handsome, stocky man had definite Indian features along with glistening short, black hair. Wiley felt an instant kinship to him.

Wiley closed his hand over Ken's and asked, "Dancing Bear? My grandfather named me Great Running Bear. What tribe are you?"

Ken grinned. "Cheyenne. My mother is white, though."

"You've got me beat," Wiley said. "My grandfather was Iroquois, and my father was French."

"Are you from Canada?" Ken asked.

"Northern Vermont."

Walter grabbed Wiley's arm. "We came over to you because we both agreed you're the most handsome man we've seen in a long time. Would you like to have a three-way with us after the party?"

Wiley hesitated. He noticed Ken frown at Walter. "What's a three-way?"

Ken nudged Walter. "Maybe he isn't gay." He looked Wiley in the eye. "A three-way is where all three of us have sex together."

Wiley smiled. "To answer your questions, yes, I am...er, gay. I'm flattered at your request. But Jake and I don't have three-ways with anyone." He pointed across the room. "That big blond-haired man over there with the black eye and surrounded by cowboys is my partner."

Walter let out a low whistle. "Man, you two're like guys in a fuck movie. How long you been together?"

"Er...three months," Wiley said. Insulted Walter had compared his and Jake's love to the self-centered videos he'd seen, he decided not to comment. His own answer of knowing Jake only three months surprised him. It seemed like he'd always known Jake.

Ken eyed Wiley. "Did you give him the black eye?"

"Absolutely not. Jake...got into a tussle with someone."

Missing Jake and not wanting to be rude, Wiley asked, "Would you like to meet Jake? I'm sure you'll like him. I warn you though, he says whatever's on his mind."

"I'd love to meet him," Ken said.

As Wiley started across the room, his left foot caught the edge of the oriental rug, and he twisted his injured leg. A sharp pain surged through his body. He gritted his teeth and limped slightly the remainder of the way.

When he reached Jake's side, Wiley placed a hand on his shoulder. "You sure have an audience, Jake." He smiled at the cowboys.

Jake eyed him. "Wiley, I seen you limpin'. Are them bullet holes painin' you?"

Everyone within earshot gasped. Wiley suddenly became the center of attention.

"What happened?" Ken Dancing Bear asked.

"Wiley was shot by Winder up at..."

"Jake, let's not go into that," Wiley interrupted.

Ken grabbed Wiley's arm. "Why did that man shoot you?"

Wiley forced a grin. "Just a misunderstanding. I'm fine, and Winder has been...apprehended by now."

"Wiley was shot by Dave's an' Jim's cabin," Jake said. "They took Wiley to the doc's to get patched up."

"You know Jim and Dave?" Ken asked. "I've been to their cabin. That place is unreal. Especially the ruins of that old cabin at the bottom of the cliff. I got goose bumps when I stood next to it."

"Hell, that's Wiley an' me's cabin. We buil..."

Pretending to steady himself, Wiley squeezed Jake's shoulder. "Jake and I just bought that piece of land."

"Are you two lovers?" one of the cowboys asked.

"Wiley an' me are partners an' blood brothers." Jake looked at Wiley. "I been tellin' 'em how I trained Mac to race."

Wiley introduced himself to the cowboys, then acquainted Jake with Ken and Walter. He discovered that Rick, Tim and Lenny were all from Pueblo.

Wiley could feel Lenny undressing him with his eyes and realized that if he'd never met Jake, he'd probably try his hand at the handsome, muscular man. But that was ridiculous. If it hadn't been for Jake and the golden feather, he wouldn't even be here.

"Do you race horses with Jake?" Lenny asked Wiley.

Sensing the man's genuine, and sensuous, come-on, Wiley grinned. "No. Jake and I just met in May. Before that, I...worked a farm in Vermont. Jake and I work on a ranch in South Park. Right now, we're...visiting Denver."

Ken Dancing Bear eyed Jake. "What did you mean when you said you two were blood brothers?"

Before Wiley could stop him, Jake said, "Wiley an' me cut each other an' become blood brothers the same night we met. See?" He held out his right hand and pointed to the small scar on his palm.

Wiley cringed as all the men carefully inspected Jake's hand.

"Let me see your hand, Wiley," Ken said.

Reluctantly, Wiley let him look at his right palm.

"Weren't you afraid of getting AIDS?"

"Hell, no," Jake said. "Weren't no AIDS where we come..." Jake felt a hand on his shoulder. He spun around. "Jim! Where'd you hafta take that big...uh, man to find a restin' room?"

Jim laughed. "Poor Glorine was so drunk, Al had to call a cab for her. I helped him get her down to the lobby." He grinned at Ken Dancing Bear still holding Wiley's hand. "Ken, it's good to see you. I'm glad you got to meet Jake and Wiley. They're staying with us for a while."

Wiley pulled his hand back and introduced Jim to Lenny and the other two cowboys from Pueblo.

Ken looked at Jim. "When you came up, I was asking why Jake and Wiley weren't afraid of getting AIDS when they became blood brothers." He eyed Wiley. "And why become blood brothers? I know you're part Iroquois, but why didn't you just get married?"

"Married!" Jake yelled. "Hell, I'd never marry nobody. Not even Wiley. I don't want to be nothin' like them married folk. Wiley an' me are blood brothers, an' that's forever. Besides, I ain't never heard of two men gettin' married."

"It's becoming more common in the gay world," Walter said, eyeing Jake with suspicion. "If the straights can do it, we should be able to get married too."

Wiley chuckled. "From what I've seen on TV and read in the newspaper, married people in this Time are the last persons I'd pattern my life after. They don't seem to stay married. Even if they do, they're never home. They both have to work to pay for all their gadgets. Many leave their children alone so much, they're breeding a generation of child gangsters."

Ken Dancing Bear stared at Wiley for a moment. "You really tell it like it is. But we gays need some type of legitimate binding of our relationships. That's why we're hoping gay marriages will be legalized...to protect each other."

"Can't you just be partners like Wiley'n me without that married stuff?" Jake asked.

"It seems unlikely here, Jake," Wiley said. "Especially since over half the state wants people like us dead."

Jim laughed. "Wiley, you've been around Dave too long. I don't think most people who voted for Amendment 2 want us dead. Dave goes overboard sometimes. But I believe a lot of homophobics are trying to suppress the fact they're gay themselves."

Wiley raised an eyebrow. "They probably are, considering what they're up against."

"Jim, I've been looking for you," Dave said as he and Don joined the group. After greeting Jake and Wiley, Ken, Walter and the others, he turned back to Jim. "Charlie Faulkner is here. I haven't seen him for months."

"Where is he?" Jim asked. "I'd like to see how he's doing."

Dave pointed toward the door. "He's on the couch in the living room talking to Jackie Sorenson. He told me he just got out of the hospital yesterday."

"What's wrong with him?" Jake asked.

Dave glanced at Jake, softly said, "He has AIDS, Jake," then turned back to Jim. "Charlie said the doctors gave him only about three more months to live."

Jake gasped, then shoved through the crowd in the direction Dave had pointed.

"Where's Jake going?" Jim asked Wiley.

"I don't know, but I'd better go after him before he says something he shouldn't." Wiley excused himself and gently pushed his way toward the living room.

Jake went to one couch and asked a man, "Are you Charlie?"

"Charlie's over there," the man said and pointed across the room.

Jake headed toward a love seat where a frail, extremely thin man sat talking to a woman. Both seemed near tears. He walked up to them and asked the man, "Are you Charlie?"

Surprised, Charlie looked up at him. "Yes. Who are you?"

Jake half-sat between the two. "I'm Jake Brady. Wiley'n me are stayin' with Dave an' Jim."

Jackie excused herself and joined a group of women in the center of the room. They all looked at Jake.

Charlie watched Jackie leave, then turned to Jake and eyed him up and down. "I'm glad to meet you, Jake. I guess."

Jake slid back on the couch, then scooted closer to Charlie. "Could you do somethin' for me?"

Charlie raised his eyebrows. "What could I possibly do for you?"

"I heard you was dyin' soon. When you get to heaven, could you tell Ma I'm okay? An' tell her I met Wiley. 'Course, she knows already, but it'll mean more comin' from you. An' could you tell my friend Jesus I'm much obliged for him givin' me Wiley?"

Everyone in the immediate area gasped. All conversation ceased.

Wiley reached the couch just as Charlie covered his face with his hands and burst into tears. He grabbed Jake by the shoulder. "Jake, what did you say to him?"

"I didn't mean to make him cry." Jake wrapped his arms around Charlie and drew him to his body. "I'm sorry. Guess it weren't right for me to ask you that."

The silent gathering in the living room grew. Some guests frowned at Jake. A few whispers could be heard.

Charlie slowly took his hands away from his face, looked up at Jake with teary eyes and smiled. He slid his arms around Jake, leaned his head against Jake's chest and chuckled. "I'd be happy to give your mother the message. And Jesus, too." He gazed into Jake's face. "Thank you for asking. You've given me something to look forward to on the other side. And for some reason, I'm not as afraid of dying as I've been." Charlie hugged Jake. "Is there anyone else you'd like me to look up?" He laughed.

One cowboy snickered nervously, then looked at the others to see if it was acceptable.

"Could you ask my friend Jesus how my brother Shed's doin'? I ain't seen him since he left for the war when I was little."

"Yes." Charlie laughed again. "His name is Shed? Why did your mother name him that?"

"Ma said she named him that cuz God made him in woodshed. Pa alla-time called him a damn bastard."

Snickering broke out among the people standing around. One woman asked, "Who is that talking to Charlie?"

Wiley turned to her. "That's Jake. He's my partner. I hope for eternity."

CHAPTER 30

The moment Wiley woke up the next morning, he rolled over in bed and slid his arms around Jake. Feeling Jake's muscles and smooth skin sent tingles over his entire body. He pressed himself against Jake's back.

Jake became rigid. "Is that you holdin' me, Wiley?"

"Who else would it be?" Wiley slid his hand to Jake's crotch and cupped his balls. "I love you, Jake."

Jake sighed, relaxed into Wiley, then yawned. Wiley could touch him forever, and he loved it when Wiley held his nuts.

Slowly, Wiley released Jake's balls and slid his hand through Jake's blond pubic hair, up his smooth body and over the rock-hard mounds of his chest.

"Wiley?"

Wiley's body jerked from a deep chuckle. "What, Jake?"

"D'you know why I like it when you hold my nuts?"

Another deep chuckle. "Why?"

"Cuz that's where I feel I'm most a man. When you hold my nuts, it makes me feel I'm even more a man. An' I can hold your nuts, too."

Squeezing Jake harder, Wiley said. "I like your logic."

"What?" Jake lifted his head and turned it. "Wiley, I don't know what you just said. I ain't ej-a-caded like you."

Wiley snuggled his face into Jake's neck. "Thank God for that."

* * *

In the attic bedroom, Jim and Dave held each other under a single sheet. They could hear someone taking a shower downstairs.

Jim pulled away and looked into Dave's eyes. "I'm scared. What's happening to us? As much as I love Jake and Wiley, since they've come into our lives, we keep getting into more and more trouble."

Dave sighed. "I know. But it isn't their fault. They just seem to precipitate trouble." He shuddered and lowered his face to Jim's chest. "What are we going to do about the cops?"

Squeezing Dave tighter, Jim said, "Maybe we should turn ourselves in. Otherwise, we're fugitives. I can't live my life like that. I won't!"

Dave raised his head. "Our only hope, if you can call it that, is to go back with Jake and Wiley to their time." He sighed. "But that sounds too good to be true."

Jim pulled away from Dave, threw back the sheet and sat on the edge of the bed. "Right now, I can't deal with that idea either." He stood up, grabbed his shorts and pulled them on. "After breakfast, I'm going to call the police and tell them the whole story. If they arrest me, they arrest me."

Before Dave could say anything, Jim went downstairs.

Still lying in bed, Dave felt cold inside. He knew the police would never believe what happened at the landfill, nor would a jury. How could they prove any of it? And what would happen when the media found out that Jake and Wiley were from eighteen eighty-six? Even if they didn't find out, no one would be ready for Jake. Somehow, he'd have to stop Jim from calling the police, at least until...

"Wiley!" Jake yelled from below. "Wiley, the bag's glowin'! It's time for us to be goin' home!"

Dave leapt out of bed, grabbed his shorts and pulled them on. He flew down the stairs two at a time.

Jake stood naked in the bathroom peering into the wet rawhide bag hanging around his neck. Wrapped in a blue bathrobe, Wiley tried to see into it, but Jake's head kept getting in the way.

"Jake, let me see," Wiley said. When he looked, he added, "I can't tell if it's glowing or not."

Dave switched off the bathroom light.

"There!" Wiley shouted. "It's glowing faintly. What does that mean?"

"Hell, Wiley, maybe it's a warnin' that we got time to get back to our cabin."

Dave inched his way closer and saw the faint light inside the bag. "Wow! That's amazing! It really *is* glowing!" He rushed out of the bathroom to search for Jim, finally finding him sitting at the table outside on the deck.

"Jim, the inside of Jake's rawhide bag is glowing. He said we have time to get back to the cabin before they...we all go back to Jake and Wiley's time."

Jim sipped his orange juice. "It all sounds too far fetched. I'm not sure I believe any of it anymore." He clunked the glass onto the table. "At this time tomorrow, we'll probably be in jail."

Still in his robe, Wiley stepped outside. "Get ready. We have to go shopping for things you'll need when we arrive in eighteen eighty-six." He saw Jim's skeptical look. "Jim, we don't have time for that. I don't know how long we have before the feather glows brightly, but we have to leave for the cabin as soon as possible." He turned and went back into the house.

Dave smiled at Jim. "You heard the man. Let's get going."

* * *

"Damn, this here's like a town in a cave!" Jake yelled as they entered the mall. "I ain't never seen nothin' like this my whole life!"

Walking slowly without crutches, Wiley glanced around the vast open space. They had entered the shopping center at the focal point of three separate block-long malls, two stretching out on either side and the third yawning directly in front of them. Each mall had two levels with skylights, enabling forests of plants to thrive.

Wiley looked up at the huge fountain and watched the water nearly reach the clear glass dome in the roof. "This looks like a temple."

"It is," Dave said. "A temple to the god of money and the god of gadgets."

Dodging hordes of people, the four men walked to the food court and found it nearly filled to capacity.

"I'll grab that empty table," Dave said. "You guys order, then I'll get my food." He shoved his way across the room.

Standing with Jim at one of the fast-food counters, Jake saw a metal box with long pieces of meat rolling in groves. He pointed at them and said to the clerk, "I'll have me three'a them hot dicks."

Jim stuck his head over Jake's shoulder. "They're called hot dogs, Jake."

Once the clerk got over his shock, he doubled over with laughter. Trying hard to control himself, he asked in a shaky voice, "Regular or...foot-long?" He snickered, then bit his lip.

"What?" Jake glanced at Jim for help.

Jim smiled and pointed to the hot dogs rolling in the warmer. "He wants to know if you want the regular ones or the real long ones."

"Gimme three'a them dick-size ones." Jake glanced at Jim. "Are them hot dicks...uh, hot dogs made outta dog meat?"

The clerk clapped his hand over his mouth. His face reddened and his eyes teared. He turned his back on the pair, laughingly asked a girl attendant to fill the order, and disappeared into the back room.

"Hot dogs are made out of beef and pork," Jim said as he watched the clerk. "I don't know why they call them hot dogs. Dave might know."

Jake craned his head to see behind the counter. "Was that there boy laughin' at me?"

"I think he's laughing because you called them hot dicks. He's probably never heard that before." Jim glanced around. "I wonder where Wiley went?"

Jake spun around and scanned the food court. A sudden dread gripped him that something horrible might happen to Wiley in this cave filled with stores and people.

A female clerk set three hot dogs on the counter and smiled at Jim. "Are these for you?"

"No." Jim tapped Jake on the arm. "Your hot dogs are ready."

When Jake turned around, the girl asked, "Would you like something to drink?"

"I want me a beer."

"I'm sorry, sir, we don't sell beer." She pointed across the room. "They sell beer over at Beer and Burger."

Jim leaned toward Jake. "When I get my order, I'll walk over there with you." He smiled at the girl. "I'll have a foot-long, a large order of fries and a medium diet Coke."

After paying for their meals and showing Jake how to put condiments on the hot dogs, Jim walked with him to get his beer. On the way, they saw Wiley standing at the Pizza Palace.

"What're you gettin', Wiley?" Jake asked.

"I decided to try pizza."

"Do you want a beer?" Jim asked. "We can get you one when Jake gets his."

"I'll go with you," Wiley said as he picked up his tray.

After getting two beers, they juggled the trays and drinks through the crowded room to the table Dave had saved. Once they sat down, Dave left to get his food.

Jake eyed Wiley's three pizza slices. "Kinda makes me sick lookin' at that, Wiley. What's all that bloody stuff?" He touched a slice of pepperoni. "An' what're these here things?"

"I don't know what any of this is, but it smells good."

Jim tried not to laugh. "The red stuff is tomato, and the round things are pepperoni."

"What's a pep-prony?" Jake asked as he touched the slice of pepperoni again.

Wiley slapped his hand.

"It's sausage," Jim said.

"Sausage? Mrs. Pritcher makes sausage fer winter, but it don't look like them round paper-lookin' things." Jake looked at Wiley. "Can I have that piece of pep-prony I been pokin'?"

Half grinning, Wiley closed his eyes and nodded.

As Jake picked up the slice of pepperoni, a string of cheese came with it. "Damn! What's that booger stuff holdin' on to it?"

"Jake, will you stop? I won't be able to eat this."

Dave slid into his chair and began unloading his tray. "You didn't have to wait for me."

"We weren't," Wiley said. "Jake is making us sick with his comments."

"Stop that man! He stole my purse!" a woman screamed.

Wiley spun in his chair and spotted a thin man with long stringy, brown hair shoving his way toward them. He automatically reached for his gun, but remembered he couldn't carry it. Quickly, he picked up a piece of pizza in his open palm. As the man rushed by, Wiley stood up, mushed the pizza into the thief's face, grabbed his arm, twisted it behind his back and shoved him to the floor. He did it so fast, only a few people close by saw what happened.

"Where'd he go?" a security officer shouted as he maneuvered through the jumble of people, chairs and shopping bags.

Jim waved and yelled, "He's right here!"

When the officer reached their table, he found the man face down on the floor. Wiley held the thief's arm in a twist hold and forced his boot against the back of the man's neck, pressing his cheek into the slice of pizza.

The security officer let out a short whistle. "Good work, son." He pulled out a set of handcuffs and snapped them on the arm Wiley held. After Wiley let go, the guard secured the thief's other arm behind his back and pulled the man to his feet. The slice of pizza slowly pulled away and dropped to the floor, leaving long streamers of cheese stuck to his face and the front of his clothes. As the officer shoved the man through the crowd, some people laughed. Others clapped and cheered Wiley.

When a slender gray-haired woman approached, Wiley picked up the purse and handed it to her. "I believe this is yours, ma'am."

The woman smiled and took it. "Let me pay you for what you did."

"No need, ma'am," Wiley said. "It was my pleasure." He nodded to the woman. As he sat down, he grimaced slightly and grabbed his left leg.

Jake stared at him. "Where'd you learn to do stuff like that?"

Wiley smiled. "Wrestlers and boxers have to be prepared for anything coming at them. I'm glad I'm not still on crutches. However, using the crutches on that thief might have been interesting."

"Well, I'm impressed." Jim said. "I haven't seen anything like that since the last time I watched a Claude Van Damme movie." He felt safe being with these two men, and a thrill shot through him as he thought of going back in time with them.

* * *

Later, in a sporting goods store, Jim and Dave bought hunting knives, heavy boots and socks, rain slickers, bright red long johns, different colored nylon packs and other things Wiley thought they would need in eighteen eighty-six. He told them not to buy a gun, saying it would be easier to get one where they were going.

When Dave mentioned what they would have to go through to buy a pistol, Wiley sighed with relief that the people of this Time weren't trusted to own guns.

Wiley purchased a pocket compass, liking how it snapped shut to resemble a pocket watch. Unlike similar ones in his own time, it weighed practically nothing. Jake bought a small gold flashlight and a pair of blue-mirror sun glasses.

Back out in the mall, Jake put on his sun glasses and grinned at the others.

Wiley shook his head. "Jake, why did you buy those?"

"Can you see my eyes, Wiley?"

"No. They're so big I can't even see your black eye."

"I bought these here glasses so I can look at people an' they don't know I'm lookin' at 'em."

Wiley screwed up his face. "You said people, but you meant men, didn't you?"

Jake's countenance fell. "What's wrong with lookin' at men? I ain't gonna do nothin' with 'em. They're just good to look at."

Dave touched Jim's arm. "Wait for me." He rushed back into the sporting goods store.

A few minutes later, Dave came through the door wearing a pair of green-mirror sun glasses. He did a complete turn to observe the milling people, then faced the trio again. "I think Jake has the right idea."

Shoppers stared as four strapping men clomped through the mall. Jake and Wiley's sun glasses were blue, and Dave wore green. Trying to keep straight faces, they snickered at Jim's purple sun glasses and the way he mimicked walking like a thug.

Jim turned, and with a Popeye jaw, said, "Well, if we're bein' hunted by the cops, we might as well look like it!"

As they passed a toy store displaying baby dolls in the window, Jake skidded to a stop. "Hell! I almost forgot. I promised little Jenny

I'd get her somethin' for her birthday. It's in September sometime."
He went into the store and the others followed.

"Who's Jenny?" Jim asked Wiley.

"A little girl who calls Jake her uncle. She's quite taken with him. Remember the wagon race we talked about? She's the daughter of Ben Harrington, the owner of the ranch where the race was held."

Jake picked out a baby doll with soft life-like skin. The doll wet and had closing eyelids. It came with a pink velvet blanket.

An elderly woman smiled as she rang up the sale. "Is this for your daughter?"

"No, ma'am," Jake said. "I ain't got me no daughter. This here's for little Jennie, back home."

"Well, I'm sure one of these days you'll have a daughter and you can buy her one, too."

Jake looked at Wiley and snickered. "Wiley an' me ain't never gonna have no daughters, er sons neither."

The woman raised her eyebrows. "Are you two together?"

Wiley stiffened. "Yes, ma'am, we are."

Jake grinned and looked at Wiley. "We're the best partners an' blood brothers there ever was."

The woman grasped Jake's hand, then reached for Wiley's. "I hope you stay together for many years." She sighed. "I wish my son could find a good man and finally settle down. He's had so many lovers I can't even remember all their names."

Dave stepped closer and asked, "Did I hear you right?"

The woman laughed again. "I'm Mary Anderson, a member of PFlag. My son is gay." She smiled. "I knew Tom was gay ever since he was about three years old. I didn't put a name to it and denied it for years. But after meeting many of his wonderful friends and lovers, I finally accepted it. In light of my daughter's unhappy marriages, I thank God that Tom is gay."

"What the hell's a pee flag?" Jake asked.

"Jake!" Wiley snapped.

Mary laughed and squeezed Jake's hand. "The name PFlag stands for an organization called Parents and Friends of Lesbians And Gays. We realize that our gay children have been created that way by God." She squeezed Jake's hand again, let go of it and looked all four men in the eyes. "And do you know what? Since I've met so many gay men, I've discovered much more about God. Diversity is exciting! My husband is even beginning to realize it. He seems to get along better with Johnny, Tom's second lover, than he does with Tom."

"Is there a problem, Mary?" asked a tall, thin man with poofed brown hair and wearing a teddy-bear print shirt. He stood behind Mary and peered at the four men over his half glasses. Jim thought of a young Richard Chamberlain.

Mary spun around. "No problems, Darin. I want you to meet two partners." She turned back to Jake and Wiley and winked at them. "Darin is the owner of this store."

Jake nodded to Wiley and extended his hand. "This here's Wiley, an' I'm Jake. We're partners an' blood brothers. Dave an' Jim're partners, too."

Darin smiled and gently shook Jake's hand. He nodded to the others. "Very nice to meet you. I see Mary's been talking your arm off, and I suppose she's told you I was once her son's lover."

"She didn't tell us that," Dave said. "Isn't it unusual for a gay man to own a toy store?"

Darin sighed. "I suppose it is, but I'm still a child at heart, and I love children." He shrugged. "Out here in the suburbs, if anyone found out I was"...he glanced around..."gay, they would probably accuse me of being a gay child molester." He flicked his right hand. "But we all know that's just *addictive ignorance*."

The telephone rang.

Darin smiled at the men. "Excuse me." He snatched up the receiver and said, "Toys and Teddies."

"Jake, we have to get home," Wiley said. "The rawhide bag."

"Hell, I forgot just now, meetin' these here nice people." He looked at Mary. "Tell your son to ask my friend Jesus to find him a partner. He found Wiley for me." Jake grinned at her. "You even kinda look like my ma."

Out in the mall, Wiley slid his arm around Jake's waist and pulled him close. "Jake, I'm proud of you. I think Mary's son will find a partner that he'll stay with. And Mary's teary eyes were not because you said anything wrong."

"Look at that, will you!" a man shouted. "Queers!"

"Disgusting!" a woman snapped.

Jake pulled away from Wiley, spun around and saw the taunting couple glaring haughtily at him. He yanked off his sun glasses and shouted, "You ain't got no call sayin' that to Wiley'n me!"

The man stuck his nose in the air. "I'm a Christian! I have a God-given *right* to condemn you in public if I want to." He pointed his finger at them and shouted, "Sinners!"

"Jake, let's go," Dave said. "We shouldn't be standing so close to two of Satan's Christians."

"How dare you call us that," the woman hissed. "You homosexuals are the one's following Satan, not us."

Jake took a step toward the couple. "You don't know nothin' about my friend Jesus."

"We read the Bible," the man countered. "It says homosexuals are worthy of death."

Balling his fists and leaning forward, Jake said, "If you was at the supper table the night Jesus was killed, you'd most likely be callin' Jesus a sinner cuz he let John snuggle up to him. It ain't *right* you callin' Jesus a sinner. My friend Jesus was murdered by hatin' people like you."

Wiley grabbed Jake's arm and yanked it. "Jake, let's go. You're wasting your breath."

Dave looked at the ceiling. "Pearls of wisdom tossed to the hogs."

"Don't you homosexuals *dare* quote Scripture!" the woman snapped. She haughtily tossed her head.

Jake felt the rawhide bag around his neck turn ice cold. When he reached in his shirt and touched it, he felt something rush into his entire body through his finger. Startled, he jerked his hand out of his shirt, then reached out and snatched a small plastic bag from the heckling man's hand.

"Hey!" the man shouted. "That's mine! What do you think you're doing?" He lunged at Jake, but Jake shoved him back.

Jake frowned at the man. "It ain't right you callin' me a sinner cuz you're one, too." He held up the bag. "This here's a ring with a green stone. You bought it for that woman you been sleepin' with on Thursdays when you say you're workin' late."

The man's wife gasped and looked at her husband.

Jake reached into the bag, pulled out a small box and opened it. The ring inside, with a large emerald, caused astonished comments from everyone standing around.

Jake snapped the box shut, dropped it into the sack and held it out to the man's wife. "This ought'a be yours, ma'am, after bein' lied to an' beaten up by him like you been."

The man cowered and coughed. He watched his wife snatch the bag from Jake's hand and shove her way through the crowd. He shook his fist at Jake, yelled an obscenity, then ran after her.

Jake watched the couple disappear into the crowd, then glared at the people still standing and gaping. "They think they're so damn holy, pretendin' they ain't got no sins! You people make me wanna throw up!"

Jake plowed through the crowd.

When Wiley caught up to him, he grabbed Jake's arm. "Jake, slow down. How did you know all that?"

Slowing his pace to a stop, Jake glanced at Wiley then lowered his head. "I felt the rawhide bag get cold, Wiley. I touched it, an' all that stuff just come out."

Wiley patted him on the shoulder. "That happened once before when you forced that biker to stab himself in the leg. You knew the men were robbers. You've discovered one of the powers of the golden feather."

As the other two reached their side, Dave said, "That was amazing, Jake. I don't know how you did that, but I learned one thing today. I ain't gonna call you no queer sinner!"

They laughed and headed toward the parking lot.

* * *

As they approached the house, Jim spotted two men at the front door and heard Winnie's loud barking inside. "Just keep driving! Those are cops at our door. Let's get gas. Maybe they'll be gone when we come back."

"Good idea," Wiley said. "The sooner we get back to the mountains, the safer we'll all be."

Jake yelled and grabbed his shirt. "Wiley! I felt the bag tug!" He pulled it out. The glow was brighter. "We ain't got much time. We'd better be goin' fast."

When they arrived at the house after filling the car with gas, no policemen were in sight. Dave had to park the Honda in the next block since there were no spaces closer. They piled out of the car and walked rapidly to the house.

Once inside, Dave closed the front blinds so they could see out, but no one could see in. He hoped the police wouldn't notice the difference if they came back.

They carefully packed everything they wanted to take with them and placed the items near the front door.

Dave started outside to load the truck, but first peeked through the blinds. He noticed a battered green car traveling slowly down the street. The car pulled into an empty space across the street and illegally parked in a driveway. The two men in the front seat seemed overly interested in every aspect of their house. As Dave watched, they sat back, in no hurry to leave.

"Oh, my God!" Dave shouted to the others. "It's a stake out! We're trapped!"

CHAPTER 31

At two minutes after seven that same evening, heavy-set Sergeant Bob Hoffman grumbled to himself as he walked away from the radio dispatcher. He spied John Burchard standing at the pop machine and walked over to the tall, silver-haired detective.

"John, we aren't having any luck finding those men who were at the landfill. The two officers we've staked out in front of their house just told me there's been no sign of anyone being there all afternoon. If they're in there, it'll take a search warrant get them out."

"They have to come home sometime," Burchard said. "Didn't you say there was a dog in the house?"

"Yeah. Vicious, too. Practically tore through the door when the officers rang the bell." Hoffman put money in the vending machine, stabbed a button, then kicked the bottom of the unit.

"Why kick it?" Burchard asked.

"Insurance," Hoffman said. The can dropped, and the officer grabbed it, popped the top, took a swig. "You know, the funny thing about this landfill case is the lab couldn't find any trace of ID on two different sets of prints. We have Interpol checking, but so far two of the men have no history, at least in this country. They were the ones held captive. From what we can piece together, the two being staked out in North Denver helped them escape. We have to find out who the mystery men are and why they were being held prisoner. Curly hasn't gotten the bulldozer driver to talk yet. He's a sullen bastard."

"Has anyone questioned Ralph Jeffrey?" Burchard asked.

"Yeah, but he wasn't very cooperative. Told us he wasn't his brother's keeper."

Burchard glanced at his watch. "What about getting a search warrant for the house in Highland? We could get Judge Montgomery to give us one. He's pretty liberal."

"Good idea, but I'm way ahead of you." Sergeant Hoffman glanced at the clock on the wall. "I'd say he's signing it right about now. Do you want to walk with me to the City and County building to see if it's ready?"

"After you."

* * *

"I'd like to see the land and the old cabin," John Morgan said as he peered at Cynthia and Louis over his half glasses. "The problem is, I'm booked solid for the next two weeks. The only time I have is tonight. I have one other appointment at eight-thirty." He glanced at his watch. "How about you two getting a bite to eat and meeting back here at nine-thirty? It should only take us an hour to get there."

"It'll be dark!" Louis shouted. "What can we see at night?" He realized his plans to go on to Cripple Creek and gamble were being shattered.

The heavy-set lawyer with a red, puffy face ran his hand through his thinning gray hair. "I just bought two flashlights to use when my son and I go camping. I'll bring them. I'll even drive." He'd do anything necessary. Cynthia's money made even his toenails tingle.

"I'm not busy tonight," Cynthia remarked. "I can go."

"I have plans," Louis whined.

Morgan scowled. "This is your case. I suggest canceling your plans. We're doing this for you."

"Okay, okay!" Louis said. "We'll go tonight!"

* * *

"Let's try this one," Ralph Jeffrey said. Sitting shotgun in his own Lincoln, he pointed at the open the phone book in his lap lit with a small flashlight, even though it wasn't fully dark. "Twenty-nine fifty-seven West Masonic Temple Avenue." He looked at Hank driving, then out the front window. "It only says D. Younger, but it's worth a try. The easiest way from here is Speer Boulevard to Zuni."

"I don't care where we go as long as it isn't a fucking gay bar," Hank said, too forcefully. Realizing it, he lowered his voice. "I'm sick of seeing all those perverts." At the turn arrow on Colorado

Boulevard, he gunned a left onto Cherry Creek South Drive and headed west toward downtown.

After a long silence, Ralph asked, "Hank, what have you got against gays? They're people just like you and me. Is your strong dislike for them a cover-up? Are you one of those unfortunate people who can't admit he's gay?"

Shocked, Hank stomped on the brake pedal. The car skidded to the side of the road. When it hit dirt, it spun around and came to rest a few feet from the steep bank of Cherry Creek.

Ralph shined the flashlight on Hank's face and saw his wild eyes. Beads of sweat covered his forehead, and his white knuckled hands gripped the steering wheel.

Hank turned and squinted at the light. "Sorry," he said with a choked voice.

Ralph touched Hank's arm. "I'm an old man. I've been around a long time. Are you gay? Is that what's been eating at you? To tell the truth, your nasty comments about gays are too forceful. I could understand you acting that way if a gay person killed your mother or something. And knowing you, I doubt it's from any religious conviction. But it seems like you're trying too hard to hate them…like you're hiding something from yourself."

Hank jerked the wheel, spun the tires, and roared back onto the pavement.

"This is a speed trap!" Ralph yelled.

Hank braked to thirty.

When they reached the lights of University Boulevard, Ralph's flashlight illuminated a glistening tear-streak on Hank's handsome face. He touched Hank's arm. "You'd knock 'em dead in any gay bar." Turning tough, he added, "Let's get those gold coins!"

* * *

Fading twilight filtered through the partly closed blinds allowing the four men inside the house to see clearly. Sitting on the floor, Dave smoothed Winnie's long gray coat. Wiley and Jake sat on the couch and watched Jim pace the floor. Every so often, Jim peeked out the front window.

Wiley had insisted they not do anything until it got totally dark, which was minutes away. He had a plan but decided not to say anything about it until the time was right.

"How's the bag, Jake?" Wiley asked.

Jake pulled it out and looked inside. "It's gettin' brighter in there, but I don't see no feather."

"When it's time to go, I'm sure you will."

Jim stopped mid-stride and turned to Wiley. "I'm still having a difficult time believing all this hocus-pocus stuff about that bag."

"Come an' look in it," Jake said. He held the bag toward Jim.

Jim briefly glanced inside, then continued pacing. "I don't know. I didn't really see any glow."

"That's because you're so nervous," Dave said.

Wiley stiffly got to his feet, then gently rubbed his left leg. He checked the sky through the small window beside the fireplace. Satisfied it was dark enough, he turned to the others.

"What we need is a little diversion so we can get out of here. Jake, you're going to have to cause a ruckus in the alley. I'd do it, but I can't run."

The others stared at Wiley.

"Jake, I want you to slip into the alley, shoot out the street lights back there, then scream. Shoot into the ground a couple times, then get back in here fast. Hopefully, the two officers across the street will investigate."

Wiley looked at Jim. "As soon as the police drive away, you and I will carry the bags to the truck." He nodded toward Dave. "You go with Jake and lock up after him. If there's anything left, grab it on your way out."

"Great plan," Dave said excitedly. "Wait! The car's parked in the next block."

"That's right." Wiley looked at Jim. "You and I are going to have to carry all these things to the truck and start driving. Dave, you and Jake will have to take the Honda. When you leave, slowly cross the street, and I stress slowly. Walk to the car and make sure you turn you heads in the direction of the shooting as though you're wondering what happened. Jim and I will be waiting for you somewhere close by."

"How about the gas station we just went to?" Jim asked.

"Good idea. Let's do it!"

* * *

Officer Delahunty shifted his body in the seat behind the wheel of the battered green Pontiac. "I hate stakeouts. My butt goes to sleep."

"Want a candy bar?" Officer Mullnix asked.

"No. I'll just get thirsty."

"I brought a thermos of coffee." Mullnix searched through the trash behind the seat and grabbed a silver container and a plastic bag of candy bars.

Delahunty patted his gut. "Well, in that case, I will have a candy bar. There's nothing better than hot coffee and milk chocolate. You're a man after my own heart."

"Don't let your wife hear you say that." Mullnix unscrewed the stopper and started pouring. Two gun blasts startled him. He dumped hot coffee in his lap. "Dammit! Where'd that come from?"

They heard yelling and two more gunshots.

"It came from the alley behind those two guys' house! Let's go!" Delahunty started the engine, squealed away from the curb and sped down the street. He narrowly missed a black Lincoln as he skidded around the corner. Coffee flew in all directions before Mullnix could get the stopper on the thermos.

The Pontiac roared up the dark alley.

"I don't like this," Mullnix said as the car slid to a stop.

While Delahunty called for backup, Mullnix grabbed his flashlight, leaped out of the car and shined the light into thick bushes growing wild in a vacant lot bordering the alley.

After Delahunty made the call, he slid out of the car and flashed his light around. He jumped on a trash can and peered into a yard. Nothing. He pointed the light at a power pole, then the next one. "Hey! These street lights have been shot out. That's why it's so dark back here."

"We've been had!" Mullnix shouted.

Delahunty leaped to the ground and dived behind the wheel. Once both doors slammed, he gunned the engine and fishtailed to the end of the alley, squealed around the corner and screeched to a stop across from Jim and Dave's house. Everything seemed the same. A few people stood on their porches and looked at them. A white patrol car raced from the opposite direction and stopped beside Delahunty's heap.

"See anybody?" the officer in the patrol car asked.

Delahunty shook his head. "No. At first I thought it was a ploy by the guys we've been staking out, but now I'm not so sure." He pointed. "We'll meet you in the alley where it happened."

The white patrol car sped toward the alley.

Mullnix looked toward the house. "Wait a minute! Their truck's gone!"

Delahunty hit the steering wheel. "Dammit!"

* * *

As he turned the black Lincoln onto Masonic Temple Avenue, Hank had to swerve to miss a speeding green junk-heap. He sighed, then drove slowly up the street to let Ralph search for the right address. Hank stopped the car when he saw two men, both loaded with bags and packs, run from a dark house and toss the bundles into the back of a truck. One of the men limped. A dog at their heels jumped into the truck and began barking.

"Look!" Hank nudged Ralph and pointed at the men.

"It's them!" Ralph screamed. "Pull over and park!"

Just as Hank parked the car and killed the lights, the truck pulled away from the curb and drove up the street. Ralph almost told Hank to follow when two more men came out of the house. One of them locked the door. They stiffly looked around, half-ran across the street and headed to the corner.

Halfway up the next block, Hank saw the men cross the street again and get into a car. He turned on the lights and pulled away from the curb. Just as he'd cleared the intersection, the same green car he'd almost collided with before squealed around the corner behind them and headed in the opposite direction.

CHAPTER 32

All was quiet as the Toyota truck and the Honda pulled into the carport at Dave and Jim's property in the mountains. In the dark, the four men unloaded the truck and felt their way to the cabin. Jim closed the curtains and lit the kerosene lamps, then he and Jake started fixing something to eat.

Wiley retrieved his and Jake's guns, sat on the couch and propped his leg on the coffee table. After he checked both pistols to make sure they were loaded, he held his Navy Colt toward Dave.

"Here, take my gun and check outside. I think we've been followed. Winnie should stay inside."

"Why?" Dave asked.

"If someone is stalking us, they might be armed. Winnie would make his and their presence known, and he could get shot."

Dave nervously pulled on his new moccasins and missed the armhole in his leather jacket twice before he got it on. He hesitated, hoping Wiley would change his mind about him going outside. When he didn't, Dave sighed and slipped out the door.

Heavy clouds obscured the partial moon and made the landscape barely visible. Dave crouched in the dark beside the cabin for a few minutes until he could see the vague outlines of rocks and trees. He heard Winnie whining at the door. The mere thought of someone following them filled him with dread.

Dave felt his way completely around the cabin. Every few steps, he'd stop and listen. He heard nothing except a gentle breeze through the pines. Hefting Wiley's gun for reassurance, he crept toward the rock pinnacle. When he reached it, he could see the terrain better since his eyes had finally gotten used to the darkness, but he was still scared to be outside alone. Glancing back at the cabin, Dave saw the faint light inside was barely visible through the curtains. He shrugged and carefully picked his way around the base of the rock to a place where he could see the road below in daylight. Scattered points of light in the distance marked the few permanent residents in the area.

Something scurried in the brush a short distance away. Dave gasped and grabbed the rock. He remained frozen for a few minutes, then scrambled back to the cabin.

"Did you see or hear anyone?" Wiley asked as Dave slipped inside and quickly closed the door.

"Nothing." Dave caught his breath. "I went to the big rock and looked down toward the road but didn't see or hear anything." He grinned sheepishly. "Except an animal that scared the shit out of me."

"The food's ready," Jim announced. "Help yourselves. We didn't set the table so sit wherever you want."

Each took a mound of goulash and sat in the living room to eat.

Before he took his first bite, Wiley asked, "Jake, what does the rawhide bag look like?"

Jake set his plate on the coffee table and hauled the bag out from under his shirt. They gasped as the golden light brightened his face.

"That's amazing," Dave said in a hushed voice.

"It ain't much longer. I'll sure be glad to get home."

"Eat up," Wiley said. "We should wear everything we're going to take with us from now on. And let's keep Winnie close."

After Jim stuffed the used paper plates into the stove, they put on their loaded packs and spread out the bags evenly among them. They sat on the living room floor in a circle. Dave checked the cloth bags of gemstones in his pants pocket. Jake checked his own pocket for the remaining gold coins. Wiley had hidden the gems he'd purchased in Jim's nylon pack.

The door burst open. Hank stepped into the cabin, leveling a revolver at them. "Hands on your heads!"

Winnie growled and lunged at him.

Hank hit Winnie with the barrel of the gun and yelled, "Keep him away from me!"

Winnie yelped and fell dazed. Dave grabbed the dog and pulled him close.

"What do you want?" Wiley asked as he struggled to his feet.

"The coins," said a familiar voice as Ralph Jeffrey entered. He waved his own gun at them. "I've gone to a lot of trouble to get them, and I want them, now."

Wiley sat in a chair and sighed. "They're in a bank vault in Denver." He hoped Jake would keep his mouth shut.

"I don't believe you," Jeffrey said, shaking his head. "Oh no, I don't believe you at all." He touched Hank's arm. "Put your gun away and tie them up. Then search them. I want to see everything they have on them, and once that's done, search their packs."

* * *

In his office in Fairplay, burly Sheriff Daly sat at his desk going over the reports of a recent string of break-ins at a new development near Buffalo Peaks. The desk lamp caused the blond hair on his huge forearms to take on a reddish tint. The sheriff shoved his slipped glasses against his face, peered at the clock and sighed. Only ten-thirty. Sometimes the night shift seemed so long. But he hadn't minded trading with Deputy Colby tonight. Since his wife was visiting her sister in Denver, he'd rather be here than at home by himself. Daly raked his mane of blond hair, frowned at the reports and muttered, "I wish all those damn city slickers would quit moving up here. They bring their TVs and rotten kids, then everybody gets ripped off."

The phone rang. He reached for it.

"Sheriff Daly here."

"Sheriff Daly, this is Detective Burchard with the Denver Police department. How are you tonight?"

"Why, I'm just fine, Detective. What can I do for you?"

"We're investigating a murder, and four suspects have given us the slip."

Daly sat up straight in his chair. "And you think they're on their way up here?"

"Yes." Burchard cleared his throat. "We searched a home here and discovered two of the men have a cabin in your area. According to an REA electric bill we found, the cabin is on lot fifty-eight in the Bristlecone development. Do you know where that is?"

"I sure do. Want me to check it out?" Sheriff Daly grabbed a pencil.

"If you can. We've alerted the highway patrol. The suspects are believed to be driving a silver Toyota truck with a matching shell and Colorado plates BFTA 116.

"Lot fifty-eight you said?"

"Yes. We believe they're armed, so be careful."

Daly cocked his head. "Do you have any description of the men?"

"Not much," Burchard said. "We have the actual killer in custody. All he would tell us is one of them is a muscular blond in his mid-twenties with a hillbilly accent. Oh, and get this. The fingerprints of two of the men aren't on file anywhere in the States or Interpol. We don't know where they came from or who they are, and we think they're the ones who are armed."

"I'll check it out in the morning, if that's okay with you. It's a long way from here, and I hate to leave this town unprotected at night. It's always crazy here when the bars close."

After he wrote down the number for Burchard's direct line, Sheriff Daly hung up the phone. Something about the description of the blond man jogged his memory. That's it! The hillbilly accent. Doctor Blakely had mentioned an accent like that when he'd told him about the four men who'd been to the clinic several weeks ago. One of them had been shot.

"So that's where they're from!" Sheriff Daly yelled. He grabbed the phone and punched in seven numbers.

"Uh...hello?" said a half-asleep man on the other end.

"Dan, call Wally, and both of you get your butts to the office, pronto!" He pushed down the receiver button, then dialed again.

"This is Mel."

"Mel, it's Daly. Glad you're home. Meet me in front of your house when I get there. As soon as Dan and Wally show up, Dan and I will be on our way. We might have some dangerous men holed up in the Bristlecone area. I'll fill you in when I get there."

"Right!"

* * *

While Ralph covered him, Hank ordered the men to stand with their hands on their heads, then stuffed his gun into his jacket pocket. He grabbed the roll of duct tape he saw on a windowsill and wrapped Dave and Jim's wrists first. Next, he went to Jake.

Jake still had his hands on top of his head. When Hank grabbed them, he got a whiff of the musky aroma of Jake's armpits. The odor and the closeness to Jake awakened the strong carnal desire for a man that he'd always tried to keep imprisoned. He balked.

"What's the matter with you?" Ralph yelled. "Get them tied up! I don't have more than twenty years left to live!"

"I..." Hank breathed deeply, then grabbed Jake's arms, pulled them behind his back and taped his wrists. Touching Jake made Hank feel a strong flutter in his gut. Trying to hide the bulge of his growing erection, he hurried to Wiley and pulled down the man's hands to tape them. Before he could, Wiley grabbed him in the crotch. Hank gasped as years of squelched desire exploded into raging lust. He pressed himself into Wiley's hands.

Wiley instantly released him.

"Get on with it!" Ralph screamed, shaking his gun from side to side. "You better not be getting cold feet or I'll kill you along with the rest of these idiots!"

Breathing heavily, Hank slowly taped Wiley's wrists. He'd never seen Ralph act so hysterical, and it scared him a bit. And after touching the blond man and now this one, his hands were shaking.

Wiley turned his head in Hank's direction and whispered, "Let us go, and I'll make it worth your while."

Hank hesitated, gave Wiley's body a once-over, then quickly looked at the floor.

"Now search them for the coins!" Ralph yelled. "We haven't got all night! What's the matter with you, kid?"

Hank searched Dave first. He found the bags of gems in his pocket and placed them on the coffee table.

"Well, what have we here?" Ralph said. He dropped to his knees, dumped out the individually wrapped stones and started inspecting each one.

Finding nothing of value on Jim except some loose change, Hank went over to Jake. He stood behind Jake for a moment, then reached around the big man's waist and plunged his hands into Jake's front pockets. When he felt the plastic bag of coins, he pulled it out and tossed it onto the table.

Ralph grabbed the bag and spread the coins out beside the gems. He sat back on his feet and cackled.

Knowing full well Jake's pockets were empty, Hank reached into both of them again. As though digging for more coins, Hank grabbed Jake in the crotch with both hands. Sweat broke out on his forehead as he pressed himself against Jake's back. Everyone noticed except Ralph.

Jake lurched when Hank grabbed him and started to protest, but saw Wiley frown and shake his head. He kept quiet.

Slowly, Hank pulled his hands out of Jake's pockets and started toward Wiley.

Ralph Jeffrey stood up and asked, "Where do you keep plastic bags?"

No one answered. Everyone's eyes were glued on Hank.

Ralph grunted, went into the kitchen and started opening cabinets and pulling out drawers. He didn't want to re-wrap each stone and searched frantically for something to put them in separately so they wouldn't scratch each other.

While Ralph was in the other room, Wiley quickly whispered to Hank, "Help us. He's going to kill us. We'll make it worth your while." He smiled at Hank.

"I...I can't," Hank whispered. He stood behind Wiley, then slid his hands into Wiley's pants pockets. After he discovered they were empty, he grabbed Wiley's crotch and pressed himself against Wiley's back. "He...he's my boss. He's only bluffing about killing you." Hank trembled as he held Wiley.

Undaunted while being groped, Wiley whispered, "You don't want to be a murderer. The authorities already know Ralph planned this whole thing. You'll be an accessory if you let him kill us. If you help us, you can come with us." Wiley knew if he hadn't been shot, he could topple Hank and pin him with one leg. Getting the gun away from Ralph would be a cinch.

Ralph returned to the living room with a handful of plastic bags. He glanced at Hank still with his hands in Wiley's pockets. "Well, does he have any jewels in his pants?"

Startled, Hank let go of Wiley and nervously snickered at Ralph's comment. He snuck a glance at Wiley's face and held the handsome man's gaze for a few seconds, then quickly looked away and knelt down to help Ralph put each stone in a separate bag.

When they finished, Ralph stood up, grabbed the gun and pointed it at each bound man in turn. "Which one of you wants to die first?"

Hank gasped. "We have the coins and those jewels. Why are you going to kill them?"

"They know us, idiot. We can't afford to let them tell the cops. Use your head, for God's sake."

CHAPTER 33

"We're almost there," Cynthia said. "John, keep right after this curve." Cynthia held onto the armrest as the car made a sharp turn and started up the hill. "I don't think we'd better go up the driveway. You'll get your car ruined like I did. It took them a week to fix everything underneath."

As the car approached the driveway, the headlights illuminated a dusty, black Lincoln parked on the side of the road.

"I wonder who's car that is?" Louis asked. "This fucking place has more people coming and going than I've ever seen." From the back seat, he pointed straight ahead. "Keep going past the driveway. Last time I was here, I turned around at a wide place in the road a little past that bend up ahead. The car can't be seen from there."

John drove around the bend, turned the car around, parked and killed the lights. The three sat in the dark.

John broke the silence. "If someone's at the cabin, we might not be able to look around. I don't want to be discovered. They might leave the area for good if they get wind of a lawsuit."

"Let's wait in the car for a few minutes," Cynthia said. "But I don't want to go back without looking around a little. What do you think, Louis?"

"My evening's ruined," Louis whined. "We might as well stay for a while."

"You talk as if this lawsuit is my idea," Cynthia snapped. "This is your baby, and all you do is gripe. You say one more whiny word, and I'll pull out of this."

"Okay, okay! I'm sorry!" Louis opened the car door. "I'm going to sneak up to the cabin and see if there's anyone around."

John handed him a battery powered lantern. "Here, take this with you, but don't use it unless you absolutely have to."

The faint droning of a car far down the road got louder as Louis stepped out onto the road. He ducked his head back into the car. "Fuck! I think a car is coming."

"Get back in here and shut the door!" John hissed. "If it goes by us, everyone duck down."

Louis got in, slammed the door and opened his window so he could hear better.

They heard the car racing up the road toward them and saw the lights shining in the trees. When the car rounded the last curve, they saw the headlights. Cynthia cursed when the car started climbing up the steep driveway to Jim and Dave's cabin.

"We'd better sit tight," John cautioned.

* * *

A white Jeep Cherokee threw up dust as it sped along the twisty dirt road toward the Bristlecone subdivision. The car, driven by Sheriff Daly, was navigated by Dan Colby as he held a flashlight over a map of the area. Mel sat in the back seat and leaned forward so he could see the map.

"Up ahead is a road called Donkey Jaw Lane," Dan said. "Turn left there."

"What a stupid name for a road," Sheriff Daly snorted. "Some developers are the lowest form of life on this planet."

"There it is!" Dan yelled. "Turn left!"

The Cherokee skidded sideways on the sandy roadbed as it rounded the turn, then flung gravel backwards as it raced up the steep hill.

"Lot fifty-eight is on our left just beyond a hair-pin curve," Dan said.

After skidding around a hair-pin curve and passing a black Lincoln parked on the side of the road, the sheriff slowed the vehicle.

Dan spotted a small diamond shaped sign on the left that displayed 58. He yelled, "There! Turn in there!"

Sheriff Daly started up the steep, rocky road, stopped, shifted into four-wheel drive, then continued on. The vehicle slowly bounced through a forest of gnarled and leaning trees, long dead from lightning strikes.

"God! This driveway is the pits!" Daly yelled as they lurched through an aspen grove. Entering a clearing, the cabin was strobed by the dancing headlights.

Sheriff Daly stopped the car in the circular driveway and sighed.

CHAPTER 34

Realizing he didn't want to be involved in murder, Hank balled his fist and smashed Ralph Jeffrey square in the nose, sending the older man crashing against the wall. Ralph's gun fell to the floor, and the man slid into a heap.

Jake suddenly hollered, "Wiley! The bag's glowin' bright! We gotta get loose!"

Everyone looked at Jake. A shaft of golden light streamed out of the top of his shirt, lit up his neck and chin and made a shadow of his head on the ceiling.

Wiley strained at his wrists and yelled at Hank, "Grab that knife on the kitchen table and free Jake first. Hurry! We don't have much time!"

Hank walked hesitantly into the kitchen and fumbled around at the table until he found the knife.

"Hurry!" Jake yelled.

Hank ran back into the living room. He cut the tape binding Jake's wrists, then rushed to Wiley and freed him.

Wiley pulled his own knife and sliced the tape binding Dave and Jim.

Jake ran outside, pulled the bag out of his shirt, slipped the cord over his head, opened the bag and looked inside. He gasped when he saw the golden feather. He pulled out the feather, and its brilliance lit the entire area. Jake set the bag on the ground, scooped up a handful of sand, dirt and small rocks and poured them into the bag. As he returned to the cabin, the bag grew so heavy the strap almost cut into his hand.

"Wow!" Dave shouted when he saw the glowing feather in Jake's hand.

Wiley glanced at it, then grabbed the plastic bag of coins and stuffed it into his pocket. He gathered up the stones and handed them to Dave. "You'd better take care of these."

Hank pointed at the feather in Jake's hand. "What's that? What's going on here?"

"We're goin' home," Jake said. His eyes teared as he gazed at the glowing feather. He knelt down, opened the rawhide bag and glanced inside, then looked up at the others. "We gotta all hold on to each other. An' Winnie, too."

"Will somebody tell me what the fuck is going on here?" Hank demanded. "I saved your lives. You owe me that."

Wiley put his hand on Hank's shoulder. "Just wait, you'll see. We're going on a little trip."

"A trip? Are you all druggies? I saved a bunch of druggies? What kind of drugs are in that bag?"

"It's not drugs," Jim said. "I'm just as scared as you are."

"Scared? Scared of what?" Hank bent down and picked up Ralph's gun.

Wiley grabbed Hank's arm, yanked the gun out of his hand and tossed it into a chair across the room.

Jake peered into the bag again, then looked up at each of them. "You gotta get on the floor like me, an' we gotta hold each other real tight. An' we gotta hold Winnie an' the bags too." He watched Dave and Jim drop to their knees. After Wiley shoved Hank to the floor, Jake asked, "Ready?"

"Let's do it!" Dave yelled. He slid his arms through the straps of his pack, then grabbed Hank and Jim's arms.

Jim shivered and tightened his grip on Dave and Jake.

Jake gritted his teeth and stuffed the feather into the bag.

A white, sweet-scented smoke curled up out of the bag, then the bulging rawhide pouch collapsed flat. Everyone gasped. Jake held it up and looked at it, then slipped the cord over his head and stuffed the bag down his shirt.

"Now we gotta hold each other real tight," Jake said.

They all heard a car straining up the driveway. The headlights intermittently lit up the closed curtains.

"Oh, my God!" Dave said, "Who's that? What's going to happen now?"

"Lean together an' hold on!" Jake yelled.

Ralph Jeffrey groaned and lifted his head. "Wha...what's going on?" he asked weakly. He saw the men crouched in a group in the center of the room and started crawling toward the chair where Wiley had tossed his gun.

The five men kneeling on the floor leaned forward so their heads touched. Everyone clung tightly to each other and to Winnie. They heard three car doors slam.

A violent wind suddenly shook the cabin. Terrified, Winnie wiggled and tried to get loose, but Jake held him down. Bright lights swirled around their heads. Hank screamed when he saw darkness and light strobe the room.

Then, everything went black.

* * *

Sheriff Daly and the two other men got out of the Cherokee at the same time and slammed the doors. As they started toward the cabin, a violent wind hit them. It seemed to come from every direction at once. Flying sand and sticks stung their faces. With their eyes shut tight against the blast, they scrambled to get back into the car. Sheriff Daly tripped over a rock and fell to the ground. His glasses flew off his face. The sheriff held his hand over his eyes and groped for them.

The wind stopped instantly to a dead calm.

Sheriff Daly spat dust and grit and wiped his mouth. Finding his glasses, he blew on them and shoved them on his face.

Bone-chilling screams from inside the cabin suddenly pierced the silence. Still stunned from the wind, the three men froze at the ghastly sound.

Gun drawn, Sheriff Daly ran to the cabin and burst inside.

Ralph Jeffrey sat on the floor and leaned against the wall. With wide-open eyes, he pointed at the center of the room, screaming at the top of his lungs.

Mel pushed his way in and rushed over to the man. He set his paramedic case down, opened it and prepared a needle to give the man a sedative. Only half a dose. He wanted the old man somewhat lucid so they could find out what happened. But looking at him, Mel wondered if he would ever be able to tell anyone anything.

* * *

The wind hit with unbelievable force and Louis couldn't get the window closed fast enough. The inside of the car instantly filled with choking dust. Cynthia screamed and covered her face with her hands. For several seconds, the car rocked back and forth from the force of the wind.

The wind stopped. The trees became still.

Unearthly screams made them cringe.

"Oh, my God!" Cynthia yelled. "What's happening?"

"Sounds like someone's getting tortured." John started the car. "I'm going back to the driveway. Maybe we can do something."

"Help those crooks?" Louis snarled. "Maybe they're being killed like they deserve."

Cynthia turned and glared at him. "John's right, maybe we can help. You're a sick man, Louis." She paused. "And I must be sick trying to help you."

Using the flashlights, they scrambled up the driveway. All three were out of breath when they reached the cabin.

After John got his wind, he flashed the light on the white Cherokee. "That's a Fairplay sheriff car!" He rushed to the cabin and charged inside.

"Who the hell are you?" Sheriff Daly yelled.

"I'm John Morgan. I'm an attorney from Buena Vista. I heard the screams."

"You heard them clear from Buena Vista? Give me a break, Charlie."

Cynthia and Louis entered the cabin.

"What is this, a convention?" the Sheriff asked. "You three just stay right there!" He turned and looked down at Mel. "How is he?"

"He's calmer, but look at his eyes. They're full of terror. It gives me the willies."

Cynthia gasped when she saw Ralph Jeffrey sitting on the floor. "What happened to him? He looks like he's seen something terrible."

"We don't know, lady," Sheriff Daly snapped. "Who are you, anyway? What are you all doing here?"

"I'm suing the owners of this cabin!" Louis yelled. "They stole my gold coins!"

Daly eyed him. "What gold coins? What are you talking about?"

"No, no!" Ralph Jeffrey screamed. He raised his head and pointed at the center of the room. "They're gone! Help! They're all gone!" He threw up his hands. "Poof! They're gone!" Ralph slumped over on his side and began sobbing, "I didn't mean to kidnap that man. All I wanted were the gold coins. It's my fault Max and Badger are dead." He sobbed uncontrollably for a few minutes, then blubbered, "All I wanted were the coins, and now poof, they're gone."

"Who's gone?" Cynthia asked. She felt a chill down her spine. For some reason, she knew she'd never see those two gorgeous men again. Ever.

A crash of glass startled them. One of the closed curtains flared out as a huge black bird burst through the window and fell in a heap in the center of the room. The raven fluttered its wings, opened its beak, then lay still.

SOON TO BE PUBLISHED

Dave Brown's third book of

LEGEND OF THE GOLDEN FEATHER SERIES

HOME TO KENTUCKY

ABOUT THE AUTHOR

Dave Brown is a native of Denver. For the last twenty years, he and his lifetime partner, Jim Bannerman, have split their time between Denver and South Park, Colorado, hoping to make South Park their permanent home.

ORDER FORM

Send to:

GOLDEN FEATHER PRESS
PO BOX 481374
DENVER, CO 80248

Name_____

Address_____ Apt_____

City_____ State_____ Zip_____

	QTY	PRICE	TAX*	TOTAL
Bristlecone Peak	_____	$14.95	$.52	_____
The Protectors	_____	$14.95	$.52	_____

Plus $3.00 shipping and handling per book _____

Total enclosed _____

Please make checks or money orders payable to:

Golden Feather Press

Please do not send cash. Sorry, no credit cards or CODs.

*Colorado residents only